DELIVER ME FROM TEMPTATION

TES HILAIRE

Published by Sourcebooks Casablanca, an imprint of Sourcebooks, Inc.
P.O. Box 4410, Naperville, Illinois 60567-4410
(630) 961-3900
Fax: (630) 961-2168
www.sourcebooks.com

Printed and bound in Canada.
WC 10 9 8 7 6 5 4 3 2 1

To Tim. This one's for you. Thanks for the inspiration.

Chapter 1

LOGAN CALHOUN III WAS GOING TO DIE. NOT AS A result of fighting evil, as was his mission and destiny. Nor was he dying of old age, though if he were merely human he'd be but dust in his grave. Nope, Logan was going to die from the most rudimentary form of torture in the world: boredom.

Ever since the skirmish at the end of the summer, where the Paladin order had kicked evil's ass, the normally dark-edged city that was the preferred hunting ground for the treacherous Ganelon's demonic army had been all but peaceful. Which was not normal or natural, and all that peacefulness was making Logan itch.

Something had to drop. But what, where, and when?

Five nights straight, Logan had stood in the maw of the Bronx's various "sin" clubs scoping the writhing bodies across the floor, and so far? Nothing. Nada. Zip. Zero. Human stuff. Normal stuff the world over—since Lucifer set his sights on mankind. But he detected no demonic powers at work. Nothing to suggest the presence of true evil.

Oh where, oh where have all the merker gone? he thought to himself, scanning the seething room yet again. Same as before. No demons. Nor their harder to spot half-blood, merker relatives. Not even a vampire or an imp to provide some entertainment for the night. He shook his head, fighting off a yawn. The death of him. Truly.

"Don't look so interested to be here, Cal."

Logan straightened, shifting enough to glance toward the bull of a man who'd been mirroring him on the other side of the arched opening. Legs crossed, shoulder butted against the rough plaster, eyes scanning, he was a bulk of shadow to the average observer, nothing more. Only something evil would know he was akin to death waiting in the wings.

Alexander's attention shifted from the floor of grinding bodies to Logan, one of his heavy eyebrows arching in challenge. "I'm just saying. Look much happier to be here and you're going to get us kicked out."

Logan grunted. "I wouldn't worry about it. We're pretty much hidden. Besides, you should talk. Your sorry mug does a fine job of keeping everyone away."

"Not for much longer. That one doesn't even notice me. She's been watching you all night." Alex jerked his chin toward one of the strategically placed shot bars.

Logan followed the motion, focusing on the corseted brunette who sat on the edge of her bar stool twirling an empty martini glass. He'd skimmed over her a dozen or more times without thought, but this time, as their gazes lined up, he realized it wasn't the first time they had and he knew he'd screwed up. Big time. The girl—yes, she was a girl, no way she was legal, not without a fake ID—flashed a row of straight white teeth that probably still became intimate with a retainer at night, shifted off the black faux leather and struck out uncertainly on her towering heels toward him.

"Aw, fuck." He whacked his head back against the wall a few times, the rub of the rough plaster seeming like insufficient punishment for his indiscretion.

"Don't be alarmed," the big warrior across from him murmured.

Easy for Alex to say. He wasn't being eyed down by a recently-out-of-braces, probably-still-slept-in-Hello-Kitty-flannels girl. It would be one thing if it were a first for Logan. But it wasn't. Something about him—his best friend Roland claimed it was the damn dimples—seemed to draw the young and innocent like moths to a flame. Or, in his case, a raging bonfire.

He was definitely too old for this crap. Too old and too cranky. Damn. He didn't have the patience or the desire to let this innocent wish-I-were-a-big-girl down gently.

Drawing in a deep breath and trying to muster up the patience of a saint, he fortified himself for the challenge ahead: how to get her out of here and on her way home.

The girl's smile burned into him, hopeful and anxious: The first strike, though with his hardened shell it didn't even draw blood. He started to push away from the wall—never good to be backed into a corner during a battle—but found his path of attack blocked by one of Alexander's tree-trunk arms, followed immediately by Alex's freight-train body.

Logan jerked back, his body smacking into the rough archway, peeling plaster sticking in his hair as he tried to inch away from the warrior. "What the hell are you doing?"

Alexander blinked down at him, his mouth drawing into a pout as he answered, his voice taking on a pathetic, whiny edge that was just not natural coming out of the rock-solid man.

"What are *you* doing, baby? I thought this was our night. I thought we were here to have fun." Alexander shifted in closer, his breath brushing Logan's temple as he dipped his head down toward Logan's ear. "You want that girl to run home crying to mom and dad? Then play along, Cal."

The voice may have been low and dangerous like the warrior he knew, but the shock of that breath froze Logan stiff. No way. Yeah, he liked the man, as a friend, a brother in the war they waged, but not *that* way. His hand fisted, ready to pull back and strike out in a not-at-all-amused gut punch, but then he caught sight of the girl over Alex's shoulder. She'd stopped a few feet away, her eyes round as she shifted from one foot to the other, her cheap stilettos poised to run toward him or the door depending on what he did next.

Suck it up. Deal. So what if Alex was turning out to be a star actor? Find him a square on Hollywood Boulevard and chisel his name in it. But first, get this girl out of here.

He forced himself to unfurl his hand and lay it on Alex's waist. Turning his full attention, and what he hoped looked like an engaging rather than an I'm-going-to-kill-you-later smile on his Paladin brother, he said loudly enough for the girl to overhear, "Of course this is our night, XE. I was just going to get us a drink."

"Ah baby, that's sweet. But I don't need a drink. You know all I thirst for is you."

And then Alex did something that really did ice Logan's blood. Alex shifted his hands from the wall beside Logan's head and slid them alongside Logan's jaw. Those hands, deceptively gentle to an observer, closed around Logan's face like a vise, his golden eyes blurred together they were so close.

"Relax, Cal," Alex hissed, his breath like a scalding furnace across Logan's face.

"Then back off!" Logan shot back in an undertone.

"Just a few more seconds," Alex replied calmly, not moving in any closer, but not budging either.

Logan counted them off, each second punctuated by a hissing breath through clenched teeth. It wasn't so much the playing along as the feeling of being trapped. And it took all his control not to break the lock Alex's body had against his.

"There." Alex shifted back, resuming his cross-legged stance across from him on the other side of the archway. "And look, gone."

Logan stifled the growl that wanted to escape. Alex was right. It was the results that counted, not the method, if the girl's perceived humiliation would be enough to deter her from doing something so stupid again—at least for a few more years. He should be pleased with the victory, and was halfway to convincing himself to forgive Alex for his extreme, albeit successful, methods of counterattack when he felt the brush of a chuckle in his head followed by, *«XE?»*

Valin. Of course the eavesdropper was present for that. Crap and hell. There would be no end to the bastard's ribbing now.

«You think that was funny?»

«Why yes, I do.» There was a pause, then, *«But, that's not why I've reached out to touch someone. Though you boys seem to be way ahead of me there.»*

«Valin…» Logan growled the name, at least as much as he could through projected thought.

Logan sensed Valin's thoughts shift from his natural

state of black-edged humor, his voice coming through crystal clear and all business like. «*I think I've got one. Lone bogey, coming your way.*»

Finally. It was about friggin' time. Logan pushed off the wall, jerking his head toward the back of the club. Alex tilted his head quizzically.

"Val's found one," Logan explained.

"What's the strategy?" Alex fell into step beside him, his face showing no evidence of residual awkwardness from the scene they'd played out a few minutes ago. Oscar worthy indeed. Well, if Alex could do it, so could he.

"Bait and trap."

"And then?" Alex reached out, pushing open the heavy metal door to the back alley.

"Then?" Logan smiled as he stood in the opening, breathing in the dark-edged night. Maybe tonight wouldn't turn out to be so bad. "Then we make it wish it were back in Hell."

Slouched down in the Chevy's cracked vinyl seat, Jessica stared through the fogged-up window as she absently brought her hands to her mouth for another poof of heat, then rubbed them together. It was a routine she'd perfected over the last half hour. One she vowed she'd quit if she had to sit here for another ten. She wanted to turn on the goddamn heater, but a running car would be suspicious, wouldn't it? Not that there was anyone here to be suspicious. Grim was late and so, obviously, was his buddy.

She pulled her cell from the seat beside her, glanced

at her notices. No texts. With a curse she tossed the phone back down and resumed her wait. In general, Grim was a reliable source; his take on the Bronx party circuit was normally spot on. So when he contacted her the other day, saying he had information on her unidentified suspect in a case that seemed to be heading toward sub-zero levels, her interest had been piqued.

According to Grim, their stiff, Thomas Rhodes, had croaked because he'd gotten messed up in some really freaky paranormal shit. Of the sharp and pointy fang variety to be precise. And the guy he was going to introduce her to could prove it.

Uh-huh. Thomas Rhodes's death might've been freaky—as in freakin' frustrating due to lack of concrete evidence—but there was nothing paranormal about it. The guy had tried to date-rape a coed, and some vigilante type had taken exception and pummeled the shit out of him in a back alley. Jessica's problem was that she couldn't prove the last part. All she knew for sure was that the coed and vigilante left together, and Thomas Rhodes's body had washed up along Hunts Points shore, unidentifiable, more than a week later.

The only thing she considered inexplicable in Tom's murder was that it hadn't happened earlier. No one liked him. Not his boss, not his drinking "buddies," not even his own mother. And after learning from those bar-hopping acquaintances that this wasn't the first time he'd drugged some coed's drink, well, Jessica didn't like him much either. Okay, "didn't like" might've been mild for what she thought of assholes like Thomas Rhodes. Very mild. Still, it was her job to find his killer and bring whoever it was to justice. And though she'd love to bury the file, she owed it to Lady Justice to at least follow up on this new lead.

Jessica blew on her hands again, this time tucking them between her thighs for extra warmth. What she wouldn't give for some coffee. Just to hold. She thought of the Dunkin's down the street but didn't dare leave her post. Though it was tempting. Sitting in her beat-up Chevy at two a.m. was not how Jessica wanted to spend her night, especially when she had to be up bright and early for her real shift the next day. Tired and exhausted didn't cut it. Her recent MO was as close to zombiehood as she could get and still have a heartbeat.

She blinked, rubbed her eyes with the heel of her hand. It felt so good she stayed there a moment: head tipped forward, palms cradling her forehead, elbows braced on her rib cage. Just a couple seconds, maybe a minute.

There was a loud bang, the sound of metal on metal. Jessica jerked, grabbing for her phone as she scanned the street both behind and in front of her. Nothing. In fact, there were very few cars other than her own, and they were all where they'd been when she arrived.

"What the hell?" She sat up straight and squinted down the one-way street diagonal from her car. No cars there. The only sign of life was the half-erected set of scaffolding that fronted a building partway down and that looked like it had been set up long ago.

She was studying the rickety lawsuit-in-waiting when something caught the edge of her vision. A flash of shadow on shadow, something that might or might not have been a human melting into the darkness behind the Dumpster that was left to collect the debris of the never-started renovations.

Her informant? Or someone else?

Hand shifting from phone to gun, she pulled the Sig from its holster, thumb flicking off the safety. With adrenaline coursing through her system, she eased from the Chevy.

The darkened street stretched before her. Curling shadows formed the hazy edges of doors and windows of the abandoned buildings. She shivered as she crossed the street, her gaze honing in on the Dumpster a few yards beyond the rusting scaffolding. She could've sworn that's where she saw…whatever it was she saw. But no matter how hard she peered into the dark shadows, nothing morphed into substance.

"Grim?" she ventured, but tensed when a flash of movement up in the scaffolding caught her eye. She spun, gun raised and ready and came up against…a discarded newspaper trapped in one of the x-joints and flapping in the breeze.

"Brilliant." She lowered her hands, removing her shaking finger from the trigger as she calmly counted to ten.

Damn it. Obviously her chronic case of exhaustion had frayed her nerves. Jumping at shadows and the wind? Staying up to listen to a wild story from a man two leaps ahead of crazy? She could imagine what the guys at the station would have to say about this.

Squaring her shoulders, she glanced down at her watch, then frowned at the digital readout. Almost three. Where in the hell was Grim? He'd said 2:30.

Five more minutes. Then, intel or not, she was out of here.

Chapter 2

LOGAN AND ALEXANDER THUNDERED DOWN THE littered sidewalk, striving to catch up with the figure stumbling along on four-inch heels a block ahead of them. She was good. Or rather it was good. Three times the succubus had slipped through their net, starting the chase all over again. Quite frankly, Logan was sick of playing.

Flashing his hand up in the universal symbol for stop, he eased into the shadows of a basement apartment stairwell. Alexander followed, his brow wrinkled.

"What's up?" Alex asked, voicing his confusion in a hushed whisper.

"Hold on. I'm going to try and contact Valin." Logan closed his eyes, centering himself and reaching out on the other plane. Calling Valin while the Paladin was ghosting was never easy, but if he did it just right, a light tap across the shaded plane…*«Valin?»*

«You guys all tuckered out?»

Valin's voice, clear as a bell, caused Logan to jerk his head back into the rusted iron railing that flanked the stairs leading up to the first level. He rubbed the already sore lump, silently cursing the other Paladin. That was the second time that night one of his Paladin brothers had caused him to rap his head against something. Embarrassing.

«What is the succubus doing?» he asked.

«Not sure. When you guys backed off, she ducked into an abandoned building. I'm on a roof down the street watching the exits.»

Logan figured it would be something like that. It also proved the demon was playing them. The question was why? And could they turn the tables?

«I think she's sensing you.»

«Really...»

Logan sensed Valin's doubt. Understandable. When doing his ghost thing, Valin was virtually undetectable, even by his Paladin brothers. Yet each time Logan had sent Valin in to cut her off, their quarry had bolted. One time, maybe twice, could be coincidence, but three times?

«I have a theory I want to test. Draw back a few blocks and wait for my signal to join in. Alexander and I are going to do a little bait and hook.»

He felt Valin's internal shrug, then he was gone, ghosting again.

Logan turned to Alex, who had an expectant look on his face. "Valin is going to drop back and then you and I are going to split up. Not far, just enough to give her a chance."

"A chance to what?"

"To come after one of us."

Alexander scoffed, shaking his head. "You think a succubus is that stupid?"

"Not really, no. But she's not acting normal. I think she has an ulterior motive here."

"Like?"

"I'm not sure, but she seems to be trying to lead us somewhere."

"And you want to try and lead her."

"Exactly." Logan jerked his head toward the top of the stairs. "Two blocks down parallel streets. Then we'll meet back up. Don't let her draw you off course. I want to be able to hear you if you need me and vice versa."

Alexander nodded and took off for the nearest cross street. It occurred to Logan that he should've asked Valin exactly which building the demon had ducked into, but then he shrugged, figuring it didn't matter. If he was right, the succubus would come to them.

Logan passed the first intersection and began stealthily creeping up on the next when he heard the sound of a scuffle. Automatically he reached for the knife along his thigh before remembering it wasn't there—damn council edicts. Swearing, he bolted toward the intersection, following the source of the disturbance. Muscles burning, he rounded the corner in time to see the spandex-clad backside of their succubus take off down another side street.

He started after her, but a moan of agony stopped him.

"Alex!" he yelled, running toward the groaning mass half hidden by a tilted over garbage can.

The big man lumbered up into a crouch. He jerked his head in the direction the succubus had fled. "Go. I'll be…right…behind you. Just need to…get my breath."

Alex's skin resembled the color of a freshly peeled cucumber, but there was no blood. Nope, the only thing that seemed to be wrong with the big guy—based on the awkward vertical fetal position and protective cup of his hands—was some injured pride.

Guess it was going around.

"Catch up when you can."

With a grunt from Alex, Logan took off after the bitch. He didn't have to go far; as soon as he rounded the next corner he saw her standing in the intersection, her head twisting right then left as if undecided as to which way to flee.

He drew up short. Whatever trap or ambush she had planned for them must be nearby.

«Valin?» No answer. Which annoyed him. Just because he'd told the warrior to hang back didn't mean he wanted him incommunicado while he did it.

"What was that about her leading us?"

Logan turned toward Alex's rumbling voice, noting the tight-lipped grimace.

"You up for this?"

The Paladin gave him a disparaging look.

Logan opened his mouth to tell Alex to wait when the succubus looked over her shoulder, squeaked, and took off again. Alex bolted after her. The succubus twisted to take another good look over her shoulder, and let out a full-fledged scream.

Logan faltered. When she'd twisted her head, however briefly, he sensed something familiar about her.

He reached out with his thoughts and was immediately rewarded with a blast of pain in his head, as someone—no, something—stabbed into his mind.

Logan slammed up another layer of mental shields, but it did nothing to counteract the effects of the attack. His ears rang. And when he blinked it was to the sight of his hands gripping the gritty pavement. Talk about bringing him low. The succubus was proficient with mind gifts.

Not cool.

When the pain finally subsided enough for him to lift
his head, he was alone on the street.

«Damn it, Valin. Where the hell are you?»

A muffled curse and the sound of some more scuffling
had Logan pushing to his feet and stumbling around the
corner. Ahead of him, illuminated by a lone streetlamp,
Alexander struggled with the succubus. Not even half
his size, the succubus was putting up an awesome fight.
Her small fists pummeled Alex faster than humanly possible, each connection eliciting a grunt from the warrior.
Then all of a sudden her attack turned from well-aimed
punches to floppy hand slaps; her silent concentration to
small whimpers of fear and pain.

WTF? It was as if she were acting, playing a sec-
ondary game besides the cat and mouse one she'd been
leading them on.

Alex doubled over again, his deep growl indicating
the injury, whatever it was, couldn't be that serious, just
frustrating. It was, however, enough to allow the succubus to bolt, again.

Shit shit shit. Too damn good.

With a push of speed, Logan roared, his sights zeroing in on their prey as she whimpered and scrambled on
one high heel up the street.

The next thing he knew he'd smashed into the unfor-
giving pavement. Again. What had he tripped on? His
own feet?

"Hey, asshole. Why don't you pick on someone your
own size?" a woman's voice lashed out.

Shit. Not his feet.

He rolled over, ready to make honey with his tongue,
and came face to muzzle with a gun.

Logan took a deep breath, and closed his eyes. Why oh why couldn't he catch a break?

———~~~———

Jessica stared down at the scumbag at her feet, her finger tight over the trigger, even as her arm shook with fury. Damn it. She had to chill out. The man in front of her may have been an asshole of the highest order, but he was probably packing too. And though she half hoped he'd pull a piece—the temptation to shoot him was strong—there were consequences to that, too. Like having to file a weapons-discharge form, or the potential of getting shot herself.

"And you think that someone would be you?" he asked, his eyes popping back open.

His voice, a rich, aristocratic baritone, did not match his seedy bar clothing or his actions of a short while before. Nor did the smart, unclouded glare he was giving her match the stumbling, druggy act he'd done a half block back. She was so puzzled by the juxtaposition, that her arms lowered a millimeter or two.

Taking that as some sort of invitation, the man rose, his movements slow in a see-I'm-not-that-alarming kind of way as he brushed his black leather pants off and then flicked his hair, combing it back out of his eyes. His eyes, clear and definitely not drugged or riding the high of one too many drinks, dragged over her. His perusal, executed with a disdainful twist of his lip, was probably meant to send her scurrying away. *Uh huh, think again.*

Jessica planted her feet, staring right back at him. "I'm feeling real twitchy tonight, so I highly recommend you keep your hands still and where I can see them."

He lifted a golden-brown eyebrow, but obliged by folding his arms across his broad chest. A very broad chest, with equally broad shoulders, that, holy crap, were right at her eye level. Jessica was pretty tall, standing at five-foot-ten-something but this man was still a head taller than her, and his red-haired buddy who had recovered and was stalking up behind him had to be close to the seven-foot mark. For the second time that night, adrenaline spiked through her system as she realized all the various ways this encounter could go south.

Wow, Jess, and you had to go after them on your own.

The problem was that as the woman had run by, two men in hot pursuit, she'd realized something. The prostitute was hardly more than a baby. Eighteen maybe, twenty at best? Just about Julia's age when she'd died. The thought of these two massive men preying on someone almost half their sizes flipped her trigger switch and she took off, unwilling to waste the time to get back to her car and call in.

Use your brains, Jess. You have a gun and a badge. Play this cool and you can probably get out of here without even having to file a report.

Yeah, easier said than done. The man standing before her was not exactly shaking in his boots as he looked down the muzzle of her issue. And her badge? She wasn't completely stupid. She'd spent enough time scouring the seedier parts of the city while on the job to know that often all a badge would gain you was a fight. Brandishing her shiny tin at these two men could be akin to waving the red flag in front of the bull. Bad enough she'd tripped one of them and issued such a lame-ass challenge.

She took a step back, lowering the Sig to her side, though she kept her finger tight over the trigger guard.

"Tell you what, you forget about going after that girl and I'll forget I saw anything." Not that she really would, but these men didn't need to know they'd been made by a cop. A cop who'd make sure everyone in the 41st knew what these two assholes looked like.

"I'm afraid I don't believe you," the man said as his buddy shifted out into the street.

Jessica followed the second man's movement, her mind rapidly running through different scenarios for getting out of here without this turning into a headline.

"You don't really want to do this, do you? I mean, I do have a gun," she reminded them as she firmly shifted her Sig into a one-handed grip, then reached with her left back for the pepper spray clipped on her belt. Rich-boy-gone-slumming took a step toward her, chipping away at the distance she'd opened up with her retreat. Jess's peripheral vision told her his buddy simultaneously took another stealthy step or two in her direction.

Okay then. Guess the time for talk was over. She brought up the spray in her left hand and plunged down on the trigger with her thumb, catching the red-haired giant as he made a lunge toward her. He dodged, but some of the spray must've hit home because he roared, his forearm rising in front of his face. A flash of movement warned Jessica and she swung the gun back up, aiming for the general region of her other assailant's chest.

"Don't fucking move."

He sighed, did something with his hand, a negligible wave, that coincided with a sharp wrenching of her wrist as she stubbornly fought to keep her gun from sailing through the air…and failed.

"Jesus! How…" She clutched her smarting wrist against her body. Thoughts like *what the hell* and *how the fuck* flashed through her head as she commanded her other arm to get with the program and spray this fucker too. Only, too late. The next moment his body was flush against hers, his arms encircling her like a wrestler.

She wasn't too proud to scream, and the ear-splitting sound reverberated off the buildings as she struggled to find a weakness in his hold.

"Hush. Hush."

No way. She was not going to go down like some meek lamb.

Only she did. His words, so soothing, not only slipped like a blanket of calm over her body, but crept into her very being, easing her panic. Silence descended as she melted into his hold.

What the hell is this? What is he doing to me?

Hypnosis. It was the only explanation for the lax, out-of-body feeling she was experiencing. Only, right, she didn't believe in that kind of crap.

"Look at me."

Obstinately, she tried to turn her face to the side. And found she couldn't. Her own body betrayed her, her head tipping back, her gaze lifting…

His eyes shone. Like silver. But not cold. Molten like a turbulent sky just before a summer storm.

She was slipping under his spell and knew it. Worse, she didn't care.

"That's it."

His voice lapped over her like a warm wave. Her

body shuddered, warmth seeping in wherever his hard body touched her. And his eyes. God, those eyes.

Her assailant's pupils expanded into his iris until they were simply great pools of shimmering silver.

And then, everything in Jessica's world went white.

Chapter 3

THE BUZZING WOKE HER. AN INSISTENT, HIGH WHINE that vibrated through her apartment and pierced her peaceful dreams. Not that she could remember them. But whatever they were she was reluctant to let them go. She didn't have much of a choice though. A second round of buzzing dragged her away from the blissful state of nothingness, inserting reality as effectively as a bucket of cold water.

She bolted upright.

Last night. The alley. The certainty that someone watched her even though no one was there. Not even her snitch. He'd never shown and she'd…she'd gotten tired of waiting…and then she'd…

Jessica rubbed her temples, trying to search back through her memories of the night before. After her decision to leave, it was all blank. Not even a fuzzy recollection of getting into her beater and driving home. Yet here she was. In bed. In her tank top and jeans?

Must have been too tired to change. Though at least she'd peeled off the Kevlar and kicked off her boots.

Buzzzzzzzzz.

And whoever was down at street level pressing the intercom wasn't going away.

Crud and crapola. Her breakfast date.

Scrambling out of bed and down the short hall, Jess ran her hands through her hair. Hopeless. It was the same tangled mass of corkscrew curls as always and it was doubtful she'd brushed it before falling into bed.

Jessica didn't bother answering the intercom, simply pressed the button to unlock the street door for Damon and then raced back into her bedroom.

"Brush. Brush. Brush." Not immediately seeing one her chant turned to, "Hair band. Hair band. Hair band."

None on the nightstand, none tossed on the pile of clothes cluttering her side chair. She knew from experience not to even try the bathroom.

She dove for the bed, pretty sure she'd kicked her workout clothes under there the other day. It was a pretty good bet a hair elastic had followed the toss of clothing as she'd dragged herself to her shower.

"Jess?" Damon's voice, followed by a slight screech of hinges had Jessica rapping her head on the metal frame of the bed.

"Fuck. Fuck." She rubbed the rising welt on her scalp, then cringed when a stab of pain ran up her arm, as if she'd twisted her wrist wrong.

Odd.

She'd barely scrambled up from the compromising position of ass in the air when Damon popped into her room, his dark eyes dancing at the sight of her disheveled state.

"Babe, you really shouldn't leave your door unlocked like that."

The nickname grated on her nerves and she vowed again to mention it to him sometime. Just not when she was standing here in her rumpled clothing, her hair flying every which way.

"I didn't leave it unlocked." She always threw the

deadbolt, along with flipping on the door guard. Maybe once upon a time she would've trusted enough to leave the door unlocked, but that girl had been left behind the moment the pair of state troopers had knocked on her dorm room door, their long faces announcing before they even spoke why they were there.

Shuddering off the heart-clenching memory, she stalked back into the hall. As if seeing the unlocked door would prove something. The proof of her forgetfulness was trailing a few steps behind her, his voice puzzled as he called her "babe" yet again, this time with a question at the end.

Jess hardly noticed. The door was unlocked—duh—but more importantly her keys were sitting in the bowl on the console table in the hall, which was beyond rare. Keys went on the inside wall of the hall closet, never someplace so visible, and the blue glass bowl, purchased to cover a coffee cup ring on the console, was most often empty of anything more important than clutter since she'd brought it home.

What the heck had happened last night?

"Jess?" No babe this time, there was too much concern for that.

She closed her eyes, taking three deep breaths before pasting on a smile and turning around. Three *short* dates. And though they rubbed elbows a lot at the station, she didn't know Damon well enough to go all panicky, crazy woman on him. Besides, there had to be an explanation for her missing memories. Like say exhaustion multiplied by a hypothermic chill?

"Sorry, it was a long night. Guess I was more tired than I thought when I got in."

He leaned against the wall, his jacket hiking up around his shoulders as he crossed his arms. The movement drew attention to the single bud he carried. A rose. Orange, licked with flames of fire at the tips.

Here he was, a guy most women would dream of. He was kind, considerate, *and* a fellow police officer, so he "got" the life.

He brought her roses.

And she couldn't muster one ounce of enthusiasm for their date.

She sighed, finally catching sight of a purple elastic band in the bowl of clutter. She grabbed it, twisting her hair into a ponytail as she attempted to look anywhere but at Damon and the perfectly formed rose he held across his arm. She hated this. What was wrong with her anyway? He hadn't pressured her. He didn't ogle her body—well, other than the first time they met. He didn't try to monopolize her time. He laughed at her stupid jokes. He held doors open for her. But when he kissed her, no matter how good those kisses were, she just couldn't convince herself to let go. Something was missing. At least on her end. Which meant she had to end this. Now. Maybe if she did there'd still be a chance of them growing a real friendship.

"Damon…" she started, but when she lifted her gaze, meeting his steady black one, her courage just seemed to peter out. Putt, putt, plop.

His lip turned up in a wry smile. "I take it that it was a rough night as well as a late one."

And did he have to be so considerate? She tried for a smile. "Yeah."

He tapped the rose on his bicep, pushed off the wall

and took the two steps toward her, offering her the rose. "Rain check?"

"I have two court dates this coming week, a shitload of paperwork, and starting Monday I'm supposed to take that damn legal development training practically every evening…I'm going to be all but sleeping at the station for a while." She stopped, unable to continue against the disappointment in his tightly pressed mouth.

She nervously licked her lips, falling back on a self-depreciating laugh. "Look, things are a bit crazy right now, but I'm sure we'll figure something out."

"All right." His voice said he didn't believe her. Smart man. She expected him to leave in a huff, or possibly argue his case, but all he did was gently set the rose down on the console table. She ducked her head, going with avoidance techniques 101. She'd have coffee with him soon. When she was rested and had some wits about her and could break things off in a more mature fashion. But then his hands were on her shoulders and he was pressing a kiss that burned for all its chasteness against her forehead. Her breath hitched as a singe of heat rippled across her skin and she jerked her head up, staring into his eyes. What was that? A good-bye?

She couldn't tell. His eyes had always been unreadable to her. She might've asked but he laid his finger over her lips, effectively hushing her.

"Take care, Jess." And then he took himself out of the apartment.

Jessica closed the door behind him, flicking the deadbolt and door guard. Afterward she stood, head pressed against the solid wood, berating herself.

Stupid, stupid, stupid. Nice guy, understood what it

meant to be a cop. And all she seemed determined to do was fuck it up.

———∞∾———

Logan unfolded his legs and slid out of the cramped cab. Tossing some bills at the twitchy driver, he didn't even complete his sentence to "keep the change" before the guy's foot slammed down on the accelerator and he sped off. Understandable. This wasn't the best part of town, and in his surly mood Logan hadn't been the most pleasant passenger.

Logan struck out down the street, his anger propelling him forward. Last night had been filled with fuck-ups and a good portion lay on the shoulders of his "buddy" who was probably already back at Haven, warming his feet before one of the many fires. To think Logan had been genuinely worried about Valin for a while there, but as Logan had walked down the streets, searching for the car that matched the keys in the woman's jeans pocket, the Black Knight had finally put in an appearance. Coalescing out of the shadows, and clothed in nothing but his birthday suit, Valin had curled his lip at the unconscious human in Logan's arms and then turned his attention to the injured Alex and whistled. As if the warrior's condition hadn't been more than half Valin's fault.

Alex, besides some injured pride, had a cracked rib. A friggin' cracked rib! No pint-sized succubus should've been able to do that. They might possess some enhanced speed and increased stamina on top of their ability to seduce even a cranky, seventy-year-old priest, but mountain-man strength was not one of their powers.

Logan found himself before the security gate to Haven, not having really registered the passage of time or distance. With a quick look over his shoulder, he typed the code into the panel by the gate. It swung open. He braced himself for the power of the invasive magic as he passed through; accepting the almost painful sting to his senses as the magical cross housed in Haven's sacred hall tested and registered him as being of Paladin blood before pulling him to its plane of existence. It was an effective system, one that allowed the Paladin to hide in plain sight. While anyone with a code could make it through the chain-link gate, they would not end up in the same place as Logan or his brothers. To anyone but one of His chosen, the place would merely appear to be a three-acre lot filled with graffiti-ridden storage containers and one abandoned warehouse. No one would ever realize that a slight shift in reality away stood the sanctuary for God's warriors.

Ignoring the shiver of awe that he felt each time he crossed, Logan marched through the meticulously kept grounds to the front doors of the cathedral-like structure. A simple press of his hand and the massive doors opened. He stepped inside, his boots ringing on the marbled floor of the anteroom. Ignoring the entrance to the grand hall before him, he turned to the left and the east wing. Here he hesitated, sending out a silent inquiry. The answer made him forgo the ornate stairs that led to the general study rooms, libraries, and living quarters above. He took the narrow hall around to the narrower stairs leading down. Valin was below in one of the archive rooms. Fine by him. He'd rather confront Valin without an audience.

Perhaps it was wrong to feel such ambivalence toward a fellow Paladin, but Logan couldn't help it. He'd never liked working with Valin. It wasn't that Valin was unorthodox—Logan's exiled brother and best friend, the vampire Roland, took the ribbon for that category—it was Valin's unpredictability that pissed Logan off. Unfortunately, he and Alex were saddled with the man. All three warriors were on his father's shit list after their insubordination last summer when they'd helped Roland save his bond mate, and Calhoun Senior's idea of punishment was to force the three warriors, who'd never had much more than *boo* to say to each other, to work together.

Surprisingly, Alex was turning out to be a great partner, but Valin? Well, Logan figured the only reason Valin had agreed to the grouping was it had momentarily amused him to be amiable. Just like it had probably been something else amusing that had kept the Black Knight ghosting in the shade and not in position to come and back Logan and Alex when needed.

Some definite facial rearrangement was in order.

Logan reached the bottom of the stairs. Much of the sanctuary lay underground. The subterranean halls and rooms were even more extensive, stretching beyond the foundations of the sanctuary above and far under the rest of the grounds. It was just another measure of defense. Even if Haven's location was discovered, even if somehow Lucifer's forces found a way to circumvent the powers of the holy cross and discovered a pathway into Haven, the Paladin could always retreat to the maze of tunnels underneath—and attack their enemies from within.

Following the general direction of Valin's earlier response, Logan made his way halfway down the hall, turned left down another, then right until eventually he caught the low hum of murmured conversation.

Not alone after all. No matter.

Following the sounds, he slammed through the next door he came to. His sights flickered briefly over Alexander resting stiffly on a pallet and settled on the black-clad Valin who somehow managed to lounge negligently in a hard-backed chair. Three steps later and Logan slammed his hands down on the arms of the chair.

"Where the hell where you, Valin?"

Nothing but a blink. Logan pounded the arms of the chair, taking his frustration out on the hard oak rather than the Paladin's hard head.

"I called for you," he said softly, gritting his teeth to hold on to his control. "Where were you?" God, if the succubus hadn't decided to run…Neither Ganelon nor Lucifer's minions gave a damn about collateral damage. In fact, they fed off it. It still amazed him the succubus hadn't seen the possibilities of the woman being there. It's why the Paladin tried to hunt away from humans: the potential for hostages and innocent deaths was too great.

"I didn't abandon you," Valin finally replied, sounding bored.

"No? What then?"

"I found your ambush. Only it wasn't for us."

"What are you talking about?"

"Two vamps. They were sneaking up on your half-witted cop with no sense to stay out of dark streets at night."

"My cop?" Logan asked uneasily, not sure how Valin

had managed to discern the woman was a cop from her looks alone.

"The woman you were carrying. Brown hair, about five foot ten, Kevlar and gun? Yeah, definitely cop."

Logan nodded, though his gut clenched. "You sure it was her they were after?"

He shrugged. "Or she was at the wrong place at the wrong time. Whatever, it was fate you guys ran by when you did, drawing her away. I was afraid I would have to reveal my naked self to scare her off." Valin scoffed, shaking his head. "The cop was completely oblivious to those vamps."

And vulnerable. What might've happened to her if they hadn't happened along? What was a woman like her doing there in the first place? Yeah, okay, the badge stuffed in her back pocket had been like a neon sign screaming "cop," and more than explained what she could have been doing in that part of town, but that wasn't what he meant. She was a puzzle. Her ID said her name was Jessica Waters. She was five-ten, wore size nine boots, and had the body of a swimsuit model, which she hid behind Kevlar and a bunch of dingy sweats and jeans that lay in piles on the floor of her walk-in closet. And that was another thing. Judging by the sheer size of her upper east side apartment—a good deal bigger than said closet—she obviously had money on top of her cop salary, yet didn't use it for things like a decent car or fancy furniture. There was only one thing in her apartment that did scream taste and money; an impressive display of artwork on her walls, the sale of which could've kept her in luxury until her lustrous hair went completely silver and her teeth fell out, yet she chose to be a cop instead. A warrior of her own people. And completely, utterly, human.

Damn.

He became aware of Valin eyeing him oddly. No wonder. He'd been off in la-la land. Forcing his grip from the chair arms, he straightened, turning his attention to the other Paladin in the room. Alexander sat up but remained hunched over, his hand splayed protectively over the white bandage binding his ribs. That bandage was just another reminder of what a fuck-up the night had been. They really needed to convince the council to allow them to carry their weapons out on the street. He understood their concerns over detection—knives and swords were not exactly commonplace anymore—but it was getting too damn dangerous to go without them. Between the war and their own diluted gene pool, the Paladins' numbers were dwindling, along with them the power of their various gifts. And no gift was without cost. Even Logan's ability to call His purging light was not a cure-all, the time and personal energy needed to pull from His realm not always possible during the heat of the battle—not to mention it was a one-shot deal until his personal reserves could be restored. But one scratch from a Paladin's empowered knife, and subduing the succubus wouldn't have been nearly so challenging. The weapons had been forged to consume all things evil. As it stood, the bitch not only got away, but she'd managed to injure two out of the three Paladins who hunted her.

"Are you okay?" Logan asked.

Alexander straightened, grimacing, but nodded. "Fine, just…" He fingered his sore ribs, grunting. "I can't believe she got the best of me. Twice."

"She kicked my ass too." And he still had the headache to prove it.

Alexander perked up a bit at this, then grunted, scowling. "I had her, dammit. But that redhead could sure pack a punch."

"Red? You sure?" Valin sat up straighter, his bourbon eyes narrowing. "I could've sworn she was a brunette."

"She wore a wig. It slipped a bit in our last scuffle."

Valin sat back in his chair, a pensive frown marring his finely sculpted features. Logan opened his mouth to ask what he was thinking when Alex spoke again. "You get the human taken care of?"

He turned back to the big man, trying to determine if there was anything more to the question than the obvious, but the Paladin didn't seem to be anything but mildly curious. "Yeah. Her address was on her registration, her key on her ring."

"Anyone see you?"

"No one that will remember."

"Good. That's one complication we don't need."

Logan turned back to find Valin staring at the far wall. Logan nudged the chair to get his attention. "While you were ghosting, did you notice anything strange about the succubus?"

Valin looked at him oddly. "What could I have noticed while I was in the shade that I couldn't otherwise?"

"I don't know. It just seems odd that she always seemed to sense when you neared. And for her to get through my defenses like that?"

Valin smiled, his eyes dancing as he watched Logan rub the back of his head where the headache was the worst. "What did she take you down with, a frying pan or something?"

"She got through my mental shields."

"She did what?" Alexander stood up quickly. Too quickly. He swore, grabbing at his side as he doubled over. Logan stepped toward him to offer his aid, but Alex waved him off, carefully settling back down again.

"Logan?" Valin prompted.

"I said she broke through my shields. Practically knocked me out for the count without even touching me."

"A succubus can't do that."

"Not if that was all she was."

Silence descended over the room, each keeping his own council as he mulled over possibilities. Logan found each thought more alarming than the last. He couldn't let go of the idea that the succubus had been leading them into a trap—the presence of those vampires seemed too much of a coincidence.

But how did Jessica Waters fit in? He sighed, running his hand through his hair. He would probably never know. Suspicious coincidences aside, he thought it probable that she'd merely stumbled into the situation. The vampires could've been in that alley already, part of the trap for them, and it was pure chance the cop had been there. Wrong place. Wrong time. Simple.

Logan frowned.

"Logan?"

Logan blinked at Alexander and saw the furrow in the man's brow. Belatedly he realized it wasn't the first time the Paladin had called his name, just the first time it penetrated his deep brain fog.

"Wow, you're really out of it."

He shook his head, rubbing at his eyes with the heels of his hands. "Just tired."

"It was a long night." Alexander cocked his head to the side. "What took you so long to get back, anyway?"

Logan glanced up to see Valin eyeing him also. Nope. No way was Logan going to admit he'd spent the last couple hours standing vigil over a sleeping Jessica. Simply staring at her as the moonlight drifted in through her blinds to catch the highlights in her hair. In the soft light, she looked so delicate. At the time, he told himself he hung around simply to ensure she was all right after his necessary meddling with her memories. But even after she slipped into true sleep he hadn't been able to tear himself away.

Because you want her. You could have her too. Just go back over there and use those dimples of yours and…

Shit. It was that kind of thinking that was going to get him in trouble. He was the future head of the council and couldn't afford the head-fuck that would come with getting involved with a human…especially a cop. And using her to scratch his itch would be just plain wrong. Neither Alexander nor Valin would understand that though. None of the Paladin would understand. So he stared into Alexander's probing gaze and deadpanned, "Traffic."

Chapter 4

LOGAN'S HEAD BARELY HIT THE PILLOW WHEN HIS CELL phone went skittering across the bedside table and plopped onto the floor. With a groan he leaned over the side of the bed and scooped up the phone, pressing "answer."

"'Ello?"

"It's Karissa."

"Problem?" he asked and rubbed the heel of his hand into his eyes, trying to vanquish the residual sleepiness. There'd been no "Hey, how are you?" Which set all his alarms ringing. Roland might converse in short, to-the-point sentences, but in the couple months he'd known his half-sister, he'd learned that she was, in general, more chatty.

"You could say that."

Logan rolled over, squinting at the digital readout on his bedside alarm/radio. Three—in the afternoon. "Isn't it a bit early to be getting into trouble?"

Just because Roland could now go out during the day didn't mean he did so often. And Karissa, being bonded to Roland, tended to follow his schedule. Their need to be close, the mutual feeding of mood and energy through the mate-bond, was almost frightening in its intensity. Which was something Logan kept reminding himself when he woke alone in his bed.

Two hundred and ninety-five years. Not quite eternity but, damn, it sometimes seemed like it.

He ran his hands over his face, wiping away both sleep and morose thoughts. His sister wasn't an alarmist. She wouldn't be calling for something petty. "So what happened?"

"There was a damn kitten on the ledge. All fluffy and cute and yowling up a storm." She made a sound kind of like a growl. "Bleeding heart had to rescue it."

Thoughts of Roland's current popularity with the media had Logan swearing. There had been an incident over the summer. A middle-aged banker preying on coeds and Roland, righteous fucker that he was, couldn't just stand by and watch a woman get raped. And though any Paladin worth his weight—even an exiled one like Roland—wouldn't have stood for that kind of shit, Roland seemed to attract bad luck. The rapist later turned up dead and the woman Roland saved gave Roland's description down to a T. So much for gratitude. Now a sketch was showing up on the evening news.

"In broad daylight?" he asked.

Karissa's silence was answer enough. Logan groaned, swinging his legs over the side of the bed. "I take it he stopped traffic and drew in the fire department."

"Nothing like that. But that nosey woman in Twelve D saw him."

"Crap."

"Yup. And guess what she does when she's not sticking her nose in other people's business?"

"Let me guess…"

"…she watches the news," they finished together.

"Fucking spectacular." He plopped back down on the bed, trying to hold his brain in with one hand against his temple. It had obviously swollen from trying to process the full extent of his friend's stupidity and was attempting to explode out of his skull.

He resisted the urge to say I told you so. After Roland's penthouse had been trashed over the summer, Logan tried to encourage Roland and Karissa to move out of the city. Fewer people to tempt Karissa's new vampire instincts and fewer enemies to upend the happy couple's world. But his concerns were overruled. He knew why, of course. The Paladin may have turned their back on Roland long ago, but Roland would not turn his back on them. He'd stay and fight to the end. And Karissa? Well, she wanted to remain close to the only family she had left—her newly discovered half-brother, Logan.

And you're not secretly glad to have them both here?

Logan sighed, letting his hand drop to the mattress. "Why didn't you just do what everyone else does?"

"What's that?"

"Open the window, crack a can of tuna fish, and set it on the sill."

"Tuna fish, huh?"

Logan mentally chastised himself. They were vampires. Their cupboards weren't exactly stocked with tuna. And his ill-spoken words had rubbed her nose in the fact that she would never be normal again. "I'm sorry, Karissa. I'm an idiot at times. Forgive me?"

"Of course," she replied easily, though he wasn't fool enough to ignore the tension in her voice. Come to think of it, there was a lot of background noise. More than what could be explained by the TV or an open window. "Karissa, where are you now?"

There was a shuffle, then Karissa's voice came across the line, kind of muffled and echoic all at the same time, as if she were cupping the mouthpiece. "Well, see, Roland didn't know the woman called the police. And when they showed up one of them was, well, different."

Different? He hoped to hell she meant another human with diluted Paladin blood and not a merker. Those half-demon bastards of Ganelon's would have no qualms about sticking a shank in a Paladin's heart if the chance arose—even a disgraced one like Roland.

"Roland knew he wouldn't respond to a thrall and he didn't want to hurt someone who was only doing his job so he uh…" she trailed off, the background commotion of phone, wailing and bellowed orders telling the rest of her story.

"You're at the police station, aren't you?"

The phone crackled, like she had shifted, and her voice lowered further. "Don't suppose you know a good lawyer."

Logan was already up, stuffing his legs into a pair of clean jeans. "Hang tight. I'll see what I can do."

———

Thirty minutes later Logan pushed through the front doors of the 41st precinct with Alex, the warrior's shoulder-length hair tamed in a queue, five o'clock shadow gone, and bulging muscles trimmed down by the professionally cut lines of his suit. As soon as they were inside, Alexander took over, his grim expression revealing only professionalism and showing no sign of the fact that he'd been in a fight which had cracked a rib just hours before. A quick flash of a business card and a low-toned conversation with the front desk clerk, and Logan was waved through the metal detectors and into the waiting room, while Alex was ushered through another set of doors.

As much as Logan would've liked to go with Alex to see how Roland was holding up, he didn't press the issue. Better to let Alex do his thing, and besides, one look at Karissa, hugging her body tight as she sat in the corner, told him he had more than just his friend to worry about.

Logan worked his way across the room, avoiding two bored kids who were making a game of scooting in between the various table and chairs and the numerous sets of legs that stretched out into the narrow pathways. Karissa didn't say anything as Logan slipped into the chair beside her, but when he wrapped his arm around her narrow shoulders and he drew her close, she sighed and dropped her head against his shoulder.

"Was that Alex I saw with you?" she asked.

Logan nodded, his chin brushing the top of her head.

"He's a lawyer?"

Logan felt his mouth drawing into a curve before he was able to straighten it. "A damn good one, too. But no one expects there to be a brain behind the big muscles and Irish smile. Yet you get him in the courtroom, and he's as much of a warrior as he is on the streets."

She nodded, but he could tell she wasn't really listening. She'd closed her eyes and was concentrating on breathing evenly through her slightly parted lips.

"What's wrong, Karissa?"

"Their pain and misery. I can feel it."

He looked sharply around the room, taking in the drawn faces, the others blank with hopeless despair. "Even though you aren't touching anyone?"

She shook her head. "Doesn't matter anymore. Just being near is enough."

He shifted, drawing her closer as if he could somehow shield her from the turbulent emotions of the room. Maybe if he *were* to shield her...but he didn't dare. Not if Karissa was right and one of the cops here was sensitive.

Of all the luck. Why did it seem like there were so many of them around recently? Pairing with humans for anything but a night or two of company had gone out of practice with the decline in the Paladin's gifted lines. Logan figured the resulting years would have diluted the resultant offspring's blood to the point that their Paladin heritage would be negligible. But lately the Paladin seemed to be running into sensitive humans everywhere.

Maybe dear dad wasn't the only one spreading his genes around.

He rubbed his face, pushing thoughts of his father and the friction between them aside.

"Tell me about the cop Roland thought was different." He'd pretty much concluded the man wasn't a merker—Roland wouldn't have allowed them to take him otherwise, not when it meant leaving his bond mate alone and unprotected—but he wanted to hear Karissa's take on the human. Besides, it kept Karissa occupied and not thinking about the other emotions in the room.

Karissa seemed to cling to the distraction, her breathing easing as she spoke. "Detective Ward. About Roland's height, brown hair, brown eyes, goatee. Pretty average looking, but in good shape. I couldn't tell much about him other than I wasn't getting a lot of feedback on the emotional scale but I could tell Roland's gift was telling him something."

"Roland didn't tell you what?"

She shook her head slightly. "You know he's not great with projective thought, and I don't think he dared communicate through our bond for fear of alerting the detective."

Logan mulled that over. If Roland wouldn't even use their bond mate link around the detective, then the man must be more than just a bit sensitive. Logan would love to get a good look at the guy, though he supposed the person best suited for measuring the man's abilities was already in there.

There really wasn't a good term for what Alex's gift did, but basically he was a power sink. When near, he could measure, utilize, and if he so wished, drain another's energy—handy if your enemy didn't have stellar shields, though evil energy did have the tendency to make the Paladin extremely sick. Regardless, if the cop had a measure of power, Alex would sense it, and furthermore, would be able to tell whether it was a lot or a little.

Logan was so busy thinking that he hardly noticed Karissa shift away from him, her little foot slamming down on the peeling linoleum tiles as she swiveled in her seat. He shifted around to see what she sensed just as the doors opened and Alexander stalked out, striding toward them.

Karissa leapt up, wringing her hands as she searched the warrior's stoic face. "You aren't happy."

Alexander grabbed her elbow, urging her back into her seat in the corner. "And you need to keep your abilities in check."

"So he does have power," Logan said.

Alexander looked around, then took two giant steps over the kids who'd taken to wrestling on the floor and grabbed another chair from between two sweatpant-clad men who looked and smelled like they hadn't showered in days. He came back over, the chair's metal legs grinding on the dirty tile as he set it down and then plopped into it.

"Damn cop. I couldn't get within ten feet of him without him eyeing me suspiciously."

"Could you tell what his gift was?" Karissa perched on the edge of her seat, her voice low enough to not carry past their small circle.

"No idea. I'm not sure he knows either. He was puzzled by me, but he never once said or did anything to indicate he even subconsciously acknowledged his own power."

"Are you going to be able to help Roland or should I start looking for another lawyer?"

"I think things should be okay. Right now we're in a holding pattern. The witness who placed him at the bar with Thomas Rhodes and provided them with the sketch isn't going to be here for another half hour, so they're going to keep him until she arrives in order to do a lineup."

"Can they make him?"

"Unfortunately, yes. Lineups, fingerprints, blood samples…none of these are considered a violation of rights as it is physical evidence and he has not been asked to provide testimonial or communicate self-incrimination."

"That's…that's…"

"How the system works." He shrugged. "Don't worry. It's been months since she was in that bar and she'd had enough to drink that any identification is going to be questionable."

"Still…"

Alex patted her shoulder. "We should have him out of here soon. Detective Ward isn't actually the lead detective on this case, but once both witness and lead are here and the lineup is done, we should be able to process Roland through and get him out with the standard don't-leave-town bullshit."

Logan leaned forward to ask another question when he caught sight of a head of flyaway brown curls through the dividing glass separating those who'd been screened for weapons from those coming in off the streets. He didn't even have to look at her face to place her. He knew. Jessica Waters. She didn't hesitate, striding toward the front desk clerk like she was more than familiar with the place like, shit, maybe she worked here.

"Logan?"

Karissa's voice, questioning, brought Logan's attention back around. He cleared his throat, carefully keeping his head turned away from the front foyer. "We may have a problem."

"Oh?" Alex twisted in his seat, then immediately snapped back around, leaning forward on his knees. "Crap. That can't be her, can it?"

Logan nodded.

"Just how good was that memory wipe you did on her?"

Karissa sat straighter, her brown eyes widening. "Memory wipe?"

Logan patted her knee. "Nothing big. Just one of

those wrong place/wrong time things." He turned toward Alexander. "And it's not a wipe. Just a shield."

"I don't care what you and your dad call it. I want to know if it worked. And if it will continue to work if she sees us."

"It did. It should." As long as he or Alexander didn't do anything to set off any internal bells. Like, say, have *prolonged* periods of interaction with her.

Shit. He should've looked closer at her ID, found out what precinct she worked at and what she did there.

Not homicide. She couldn't be homicide. That would be too …yeah. It would be how his luck was running.

Alexander grunted. "Stay here, keep your head down. I'm going to see how much longer this is going to take."

With a grimace Alexander lumbered out of the room and pushed through the double doors leading into the inner sanctum of the station.

Jessica had made it past the front desk and was breezing by the metal detector—no strip search or shakedowns for a fellow blue, and he was in prime real estate to catch her eye. Logan frantically scanned the small waiting area. No seats to give her the anonymous nape view of his neck other than the one next to the old homeless man picking his nose. Logan could move, but the man smelled bad enough from here. Then he spotted the sign. A man and a woman over an arrow that pointed down a short hall, and then in smaller letters under it, almost an afterthought, a lacquered sign that read Vending Machines. Eureka.

"I'll be back," he told Karissa, bolting for the hall while Jessica paused to chat it up with her blue buddy monitoring the X-ray machine.

The hall wasn't long, maybe ten feet with two doors on one side. Across the way sat two vending machines stuffed into an alcove. Not really interested in any of the above, he began to pace the small space. Step, step, turn. Step, step...

And about plowed right into her. His hands automatically reached out to steady her. The slight contact sent fire licking down his arm, begging him to move in closer.

WTF? he thought, jerking his hands back.

"Sorry. I was just..." she pointed behind him to the vending machines. Then smiled and stepped around him. That smile—wide and honest and remarkably unguarded—had almost the same effect on him as the unexpected contact had.

Arms folded across his chest to keep himself for giving into the urge to see if touching her again would result in the same lick of fire, he watched her peruse her choices. She'd made an attempt to tame her curls, catching a portion of them into a messy half twist at the back of her head. It kept the worst of her hair out of her eyes but did nothing to stave off the urge he felt to run his hands through the coffee-colored tresses and loosen the corkscrew curls that were just waiting for their chance to spring free. The no-nonsense attempts at containment extended to her face, with its porcelain-smooth skin untouched by anything but a dash of clear gloss on her Revlon-worthy lips, like she knew how beautiful she was, but thought not to draw attention to it.

Good luck with that, angel.

After a few seconds she nodded, then dug into her pocket and extracted two singles. One went into the machine. The lights flashed.

"Waiting can be nerve-racking, can't it?" she said, punching in a letter and number, then bent to grab her prize of Doritos out of the bottom, showing off her delectable, heart-shaped ass as she did. Damn. How could something so curvy and sweet look so firm and spankable at the same time?

And he'd probably just lost his spot in Heaven for thinking like that.

Belatedly, he realized she'd turned her head back over her shoulder and asked him a question. Jerking his gaze from said ass, he focused on her face, noting the amusement dancing in her blue eyes. "Huh?"

"I asked if you saw something you liked?"

And that was his tongue that hit the floor. Only, that was not an invitation but a challenge. He'd scoped and she'd caught him—and didn't appreciate it.

"I'm sorry. I didn't mean to..."

"Of *course* you didn't." She retrieved her change and put it back into the machine, along with the other dollar. Punched in a few more buttons.

He bent down before she could, grabbed the Snickers bar and offered it to her, firmly keeping his gaze on her face as he did. "No. It's not all right. And I am sorry. No woman should be made to feel like a piece of eye candy."

She absently pulled at her bottom lip, her eyes narrowing slightly as she measured him. But then she nodded, taking the candy bar.

"Tell you what. You're forgiven if you get off your knee. Someone comes around that corner, they'll get the wrong idea." She softened the implied rebuff with an upward quirk of her lip. Not even close to the full-on smile she'd offered before, but damn if it didn't make him feel like he was flying on cloud nine.

Yeah so what, Calhoun? She smiled at you. That's not a reason to pant like a puppy.

He stood quickly, brushing off the knee that had touched the dirty floor. When he raised his head it was to find her leaning back against the wall between the alcove and the waiting room, her gaze taking its own perusal of him as he fumbled like a schoolboy before her. There was no doubt she was checking him out.

He quirked a brow.

"Hey. Payback's fair."

"And do you see anything you want?" he teased, then silently cursed himself when he realized he was holding his breath in anticipation of her answer.

Damn, Logan, you've got it bad. Whatever *it* was.

"Yeah, but I got my chocolate. So I'm good to go." She bit off a hunk of the candy, making a low moan around mouthful that had his blood flowing south with a rather human case of lust—God, how long had it been?

"I'll never doubt the power of chocolate again," he murmured, half to himself. She laughed, the sound surprisingly husky, almost scratchy even, like an old record dragged out of storage. He was rather disappointed when the laughter ended; he suspected she didn't laugh often enough.

As if to prove his point, she checked her watch. A quick grunt told him she wasn't pleased with the time, but she took another bite anyway, her eyes closing in true bliss as her head tipped back against the wall. He may have been a Paladin, but he was also man enough to steal the opportunity to appreciate her figure. Obviously the calories she took in with the candy bars tended to stick to all the right places. And the training she went through trimmed everything else down to pure muscle.

"Mmmm. This is so good." She opened her eyes, a split second after he managed to jerk his gaze back up. At least he hoped it was after. Must have been, because her look was almost apologetic as she held up the mostly devoured candy bar. "It's been a long day. And a long night before that."

And that was his cue to leave. That long night was half his fault. Obviously the memory wipe was holding or she'd be pinning him against the wall and snapping on the cuffs that he suspected were hidden somewhere in that blocky jacket of hers. Each moment he lingered increased the chances of that exponentially. Yet he couldn't seem to move. It wasn't that his feet were rooted to the spot; they just didn't seem to want to go anywhere but toward her.

Angry at himself and what was turning out to be a shitload of undiscovered weaknesses, Logan dug into his pocket and pulled out three quarters. Maybe she had a good idea with the chocolate.

"We've all had nights like that," he said, punching in E-8. The machine whirred and the Snickers fell. "I remember when these were a quarter."

She quirked her head to the side, her brow furrowing.

Crap. A quarter? How long ago was that? Probably before she was born. Or at least when she was still in diapers.

And that's why he kept away from humans. They lived, they died. He just existed.

Shit. How do I cover that flub?

"Have we met?"

He stilled, all but his heart, which accelerated as fast as Bennett's pretty blue Lotus Exige from the starting line. Should have left. He was a fool not to. There had been ample opportunity, but he was greedy, feeding his enchantment with her with stolen looks and flirtatious banter.

And now it was too late to bolt. Anything sudden or suspicious and that shield on her memories might crumble.

And every moment he didn't answer was just as suspicious.

"I'm hurt you don't know one way or the other." He flashed what he hoped wasn't too strained a smile, cursing his lack of balls. A simple lie. *"Nope. Don't believe so."* That's all it would've taken. Of course he sucked at giving flat-out lies, another "gift" from his damn pure genealogy.

He tensed, ready for the shield to crumble, for recognition to crinkle her model-worthy features. But all she did was shake her head. "You're right. Man like you? I'd remember."

He inclined his head. "Thank you. I think."

She chuckled again, popping the bag of Doritos. He watched her dip two slender fingers into the bag and extract a chip. She popped it in her mouth and chewed with the same drawn-out enjoyment as Roland when he indulged. The thought of his friend reminded him why he was here, and it was not to flirt with a woman. Especially a cop. No matter how beautiful or intriguing she was. He opened his mouth to speak, ready to bow out as gracefully as a man could when he was alternately sweating bullets and drooling like Pavlov's dog.

"So what you in for?" she asked.

Too late.

"'Scuse me?" He settled back against the wall. Her question had put all his good intentions on hold. "Oh. You mean why am I here?"

"Yeah. You don't exactly look the type to normally grace these doors." Her eyes narrowed. "You're not a defense lawyer are you?"

Defense lawyer was said in the same way one spoke of slime. He stared at her for a moment, his internal alarm going off. There were dozens of cops in the precinct. Chances of her being at all involved in Roland's case were slim to none, right? But if she were then she would probably have been given a rundown on the deets of how his buddy had been found.

"No. Not a lawyer," he answered then continued with the same vein. "Friend. Idiot got brought in for something stupid."

She shook her head. "Don't they all?"

"Yeah," he replied, though his voice must have expressed some sort of doubt because her chewing slowed further as she thought it over.

"And you don't think he should be here."

"No," he said carefully, then decided to test the waters. "Not for saving a kitten."

"A kitten," she deadpanned back. The stiff set of her shoulders told him her break was over. She was all cop again. Her eyes calculating as she regarded him.

He stilled. A chill coursing through his veins as he thought, *no fucking way*. But then reality set in. Coincidences like this just didn't happen.

Goddammit. Why couldn't he catch a break? Just

one. One tiny get-out-of-jail-free card. But no. She *was* the detective on the case.

She laughed, this one a bit forced. "Hardly even seems like a misdemeanor."

"Yeah, well." He bit into the Snickers, surprised at the explosion of flavors. Sweet chocolate, salty nuts, smooth caramel. He twisted the bar in his hand. Looking at it with new eyes. "This is good."

"You've never had a Snickers?"

"I'm not one for indulgences." Except where she was concerned. Crap. This totally sucked. He knew what his next step had to be. The Paladin couldn't afford to have their secrets revealed. Which meant Roland had to get off her list of suspects ASAP. If something didn't happen to turn her attention away from Roland, then more drastic measures were needed. Things like altering memories. He could do it too. It would be child's play to dive in there and dissect every memory to do with Roland or Thomas Rhodes. And while he was at it, he could pull out the names of anyone else who might give a shit about the case and then track them down to squeegee their brains too. He should do it. If not for the Paladin, then for Roland and Karissa. The problem was that he didn't want to. It felt like raising his hand against an innocent. Like the action would be at the cost of his goodness. It felt like…Holy crap. He didn't know what it felt like; he just knew that he didn't want to.

His shoulders tensed and he fought the urge to fist his hands. *You'll do it, Calhoun. Your friend, your sister, every one of your brothers are counting on you.*

She wasn't looking at him suspiciously anymore, but with knowledge on her face. Nope, Jessica Waters was no rookie, and her detective instincts had kicked into full gear.

She crunched up the empty Doritos bag in her hand, tossing it into the nearby trash before flicking her wrist again to look at her watch. "Damn. No rest for the weary." She pasted on a smile as she brushed off her hand on her jeans and offered it to him. "It was nice to meet you, Mr..."

He hesitated, but he answered, knowing that when the time came, he was going to have to strip this memory from her too. "Calhoun. Logan Calhoun."

It took every bit of his willpower to take that hand and not drag her to him, yet he somehow managed.

He knew she was waiting for him to ask who she was, but he figured why bother? After a prolonged stare which ended in her nodding her head as she took away her hand, she turned to go. She was halfway to the waiting room, him still rubbing the residual tingles out of his fingers from their handshake, when she turned back. "Oh, Mr. Calhoun?"

"Yeah?"

"You aren't planning any trips, are you?"

He folded his arms across his chest, inclining his head slightly. "I'll be around."

"Good," she said, then strode through the waiting room to disappear through the double doors.

He wasn't sure he'd agree with her on that assessment, but he *would* be around—watching her closely. And when the time came, he would also do what was right.

Chapter 5

"So, what do you think?" Mike asked, pushing open the door from the observation room and waving his hand for Jessica to go through.

Jessica took the lead as they weaved through the crowded station, skirting around a misplaced chair and narrowly avoiding a street beat jogging toward the back door, Styrofoam cup in hand. It wasn't until they arrived at her desk and Jessica plopped down in her chair, the thick file thudding on the surface of her desk, that she replied. "I think we have jack shit."

"Why do you say that?" Mike eased his hip onto the edge of her desk. "Witness identified him."

"Yeah, and then went on to act as a glowing character reference. Can you imagine the field day his lawyer would have with her on the witness stand?"

Mike's face tightened into a scowl. The slightly crooked nose and his scruffy beard along with his torn jeans and hooded sweatshirt made him look like he belonged in the holding cells with the other street scum rather than perched on her desk. That misimpression was what made him so good at what he did. Normally, Mike worked undercover narcotics, but a volatile situation had put him under scrutiny and necessitated that he lay low. It just happened that the timing corresponded with his old friend's arrival at the station bearing tales of attempted date rape, roofies, and the darkly handsome

knight who rescued her, thus landing the intended victim a spot in Mike's recently emptied caseload. The
case was eventually connected with Jessica's East River
John Doe, giving her their current suspect and her newest partner.

"Sorry. I know you and the witness are friends."

He gave an indifferent shrug. "Not really. Rach grew
up down the street from me. That's all."

That wasn't all, but she didn't press. Instead, she
sighed as she reached for the file on her desk. The words
blurred in a jumble of letters. Jessica rubbed the heel of
her palm against her forehead, trying to ease the headache pounding her skull.

She was sleep deprived and cranky. Mike quietly
waited for her to gather her thoughts. That made him
not only the newest but the most patient partner she'd
ever had.

"Okay, let's review what we have." She skimmed
through the material in the report. "Witness statements
place Thomas Rhodes in the bar with Ms. Rachael
Harrison at approximately 11:45. She'd already had a
few with her friends, but they left to go to the next bar
on their crawl, leaving her with the gentleman who'd
offered to buy her a drink."

"Gentleman, my ass."

Jessica's mouth curled up in a sardonic grin. "Thomas
Rhodes was an exceptional player. A good one, too, if
what his buddies say is true."

"World is fucking full of them, ain't it?"

Hell yeah it was. And they came in all different flavors too. Middle-aged banker who liked to pretend he
was still the shit. Vigilantes who liked to act out white

knight fantasies. And bullies who liked to play at being Mr. Nice-and-Sensitive.

Jessica sucked in a breath, her brow furrowing against the pain that spiked deep into her skull. Where the hell had that thought come from? Or more to the point, who was it about? Mr. Logan Calhoun? But he was no bully. He'd flirted, she'd flirted back, but the moment they'd caught on to who the other person was, they'd both taken a giant step back. Professional. Respectful. Poor taste in friends aside, there wasn't much else she had on the guy. Other than a lingering desire to run her hands through the wealth of his thick chestnut waves. Yeah, real professional.

"Jess?"

She blinked, focusing her attention back on her partner's concerned face. "Sorry, long night."

Mike shook his head. "You're really going to have to look into getting some Lunesta. This zombie thing you have going on is getting out of hand. What the hell are you doing before bed that keeps you from sleeping?"

Jessica winced, guilt assailing her. Nothing, actually. She slept just fine once she finally hit her pillow, it's just she wasn't there very long before she had to get up again. Luckily she didn't have to come up with any sort of excuse as Mike just sighed, grabbing the file from her and taking over.

He cleared his throat. "Okay, so we have multiple witness reports that Thomas and Rachael sat at the bar for another twenty minutes or so. Bartender says it was busy, per usual, but he remembers serving them at least a couple drinks each. Rach leaves for the ladies' room…yada, yada, yada…guy shows up and takes her place. Tommy gets pissed. Rachael returns and our suspect tells her that her drink's been spiked. Thomas leaves with suspect for the alley."

"Never to be heard from again."

"Until weeks later when his body was finally ID'd," Mike pointed out.

Jessica grunted. Too bad they hadn't known in the beginning that it was a homicide. No, too bad no one ever reported Tom missing. Not even his employer. By the time Thomas was identified, everything was stone cold. No matter how much legwork they did. No matter how many pretty connections, Jess still had positively nothing she could bring before a jury. Everything was coincidence and conjecture. Nothing concrete.

And wasn't that the sticking point.

She cracked her knuckles as her gaze slid over toward the interrogation room that her suspect had no doubt been led back to after the lineup. She could prove without a doubt that he and Rhodes walked out of the bar together into that alley. And given the witness statements and the suspect's own tight-lipped, hard-assed personality, she bet she could even convince a jury that the beat down had indeed occurred there. But that was it. Water and wildlife had taken care of any evidence on the body, the elements removing any traces of blood from the alley. And although not a single person had come forward to say they'd seen Thomas after he'd left that bar, she didn't even have the goddamn car to connect any dots between one place and the other. Ergo, she had no proof.

"So…" Mike drawled, closing up the file and setting it back on her desk. "What are we going to do?"

"Damn it. I'm going to have to let him go."

———

Logan stared morosely at the door that swung shut behind the blonde "witness" exiting the station house, cutting off the outside traffic. Three hours of silence, sitting alongside his tense-as-rebar sister. Three hours of rolling his own tense shoulders and wondering how everything could have ended so completely screwed up.

"Do you think she…" Karissa trailed off, leaving the rest of the question unasked.

Didn't take a genius to figure out what Karissa wanted to know. Did Logan think the witness had identified Roland?

Hell yeah, he did. The young blond woman who'd been ushered into the back shortly after Detective Jessica Waters hadn't struck him to be as much of a flake as her misadventure in that bar would suggest. Her eyes were sharp, her determination palpable, and given how accurate the sketch of Roland had been, he doubted her memory was faulty either.

Which meant that what he had to do just got harder.

Should've cornered *her* in the vending area. Erased her memories.

No, what he should have done was found the witness right after that sketch came out and altered her memories then. But he'd been busy with other things. Like, say, twiddling his thumbs waiting for some real action, and playing power games with a father who didn't approve of Logan's association with "monsters" like his best friend, or said monster's bond mate, aka Logan's disowned sister.

Logan sighed. Too late to agonize now. There was no

going back. Not unless he wanted to wipe the memory of everyone here, which was completely impractical. Both in execution and in results. A couple of people missing a chunk of time could be explained away, but a whole station house?

Karissa shifted beside him, her hand tightening exponentially on his with each silent second that passed.

"It's going to work out." He'd make it work. Somehow.

He was still staring at the exit door when Karissa dropped his hand, bolting upright. Logan stood as well, then sucked in a breath as both Alex *and* Roland pushed through the doors that lead into the back. No paperwork? No bail? Roland briefly met Logan's gaze, then turned his attention to his mate, spreading his arms. With a half whimper, half squeal, Karissa leapt over the tangle of legs and chairs and scrambled into his embrace.

Knowing how tense Karissa was, Logan was content to let them have their moment, but it seemed Alex wasn't. He grasped Roland on the shoulder, his voice gruff as he spoke. "Come on. Let's get out of here."

His reason was made obvious when the door swung open again, and Jessica stepped through. She didn't actually enter the room, merely stopped on the threshold, arms folded as her gaze zeroed in and hardened on their little reunion. Alex's fingers tightened on Roland's black T-shirt. That slight signal got them all moving, Alex placing his large body between Detective Jessica Waters and his client as he ushered them out of the precinct.

"She didn't look too pleased to let Roland go," Logan said when they'd reached street-level.

"She's not," Alex replied, falling into step beside Logan and behind Roland and Karissa.

"What happened? Didn't the witness identify him?" Logan asked.

"Oh yeah. But then she started singing Roland's praises. How he saved her. How she was sure he wouldn't have killed Tom. Think our detective realized the field day I'd have with her in court, so unless they get something more concrete they're stuck playing the 'don't-leave-town' card."

"You're kidding me."

Alex gave a jerk of his shoulders. "Nope. And I'm not going to look too closely at it."

Logan grunted a muffled agreement, but if anything, his nerves jumped more not less. Even though Alex might have been willing to take this gift horse at face value, Logan was all for a proper vetting. Jessica Waters struck him as tough, smart, and tenacious. How long before the other shoe dropped?

"Hey! Wait up!" A feminine voice pierced the bustling traffic noises around them. Logan spun, saw the flash of Jessica's brunette head as she pushed her way through the other pedestrians toward them.

Not long. Crap. And that's what you got with gift horses.

"Why…?" Karissa's voice, sharp and worried made Logan turn back to his friends. If possible, Karissa was wound even tighter than she was in the waiting room. As if she, too, felt like they were barely slipping through the noose. In response to her tension, Roland's eyes had sparked, the crimson tinge marking the edge of violence that rose with the threat of danger to his mate.

Attempting to control the potential fallout, Logan laid a settling hand on his best friend's shoulder. "I'll take care of this."

"You think that's a good idea?" Alex asked.

"Better than the alternative." With a last squeeze and a reassuring smile for Karissa, Logan released Roland's shoulder. "See you guys around."

They hurried to the next cross street, rounding the corner, Alex continued to play guard dog. Not a moment too soon, either. A brush against Logan's arm announced that she'd entered his space and stopped. He twisted and received the same solar plexus punch he'd gotten earlier

Damn. Did she have to be so beautiful?

She stood beside him, hands on hips, a handful of errant curls billowing around her face as her eyes narrowed on his retreating friends.

He folded his arms across his chest, half to suppress the urge he had to caress the scowl off her face and half to put a cap on his own frustration. The entire situation was impossible. The coincidence that this woman, whose memories he'd had to wipe, was the lead detective on Roland's case seemed totally improbable. Someone upstairs had a warped sense of humor. Either that or there was something sinister going on. But figuring out which with her standing right beside him, her scent calling to him in a way that was brain numbing and adrenaline pumping? Yeah, not gonna happen.

He closed his eyes, took a deep breath before opening them again. Steel back in place. "What do you want?"

"You. Walk with me." She jerked her head back down the street, heading out at a clipped pace.

Logan turned and fell into step beside her, scanning the pedestrians around them, checking to see what might be hiding in their midst. Demons, merkers...at least there would be no vampires during the day.

"I'm not sure this is the best time," or place, he silently added, "to talk."

"Oh? And when would be a good time?"

Um, never, but he didn't think that answer would appease her. If there was one thing he'd figured out about this woman, it was that she was passionate about her job, and unpredictable. Which was probably why he couldn't seem to get enough of her.

He jerked his head as they passed by the station house. "You're not at all worried about what your buddies might say about you taking a walk with me?"

"Nope."

He swore silently. She wasn't going to be satisfied without some answers. But beyond reiterating what she expected, which was a whole lot of 'my best friend didn't do it,' there wasn't much he could tell her.

"So, Mr. Calhoun."

"Cal or Logan. Mr. Calhoun is my father."

She nodded, but didn't use either as she addressed him. "Where were you on the night in question?"

He slowed, staring at her with an acerbic lift to his brow. "Wow, that was direct. Should I be calling my lawyer?"

"Do you need him?"

"No. And neither does my brother. Given that he didn't kill Thomas Rhodes."

Her gaze landed on him, her eyes sharp. "Roland Moreau doesn't have any brothers. So unless he isn't who he says he is..."

"Brother-in-law. His ma—wife, Karissa, is my half-sister."

"Ah," she drawled. As the silence stretched for another half block, he began to wonder what her strategy was. She slowed her pace until more people passed them than the other way around, her body no longer stiff, hands planted in the back pocket of her jeans. Like they were two friends out for a stroll. Unlikely. Yet, it worked. Logan found himself relaxing too, his worries over being seen or even why they were having the conversation faded as he let himself enjoy being near her. Perhaps the simple brush of her shoulder against his arm as they walked should've made him tense more, not less, but he couldn't seem to help it. Human or not he *liked* being around her. And since the opportunity for these little interactions was going to end sooner rather than later—either by simple fate or because he was going to have to make it so—Logan decided to do a selfish thing: enjoy this time with her.

Too bad she had to ruin it by talking.

"Off the record?"

"Is there really such a thing around you?"

The corner of her lip twitched up. "Probably not. But as a woman, I can both understand and appreciate why your friend did what he did."

"You mean save a woman from being raped?" He purposefully used the word—a test to see if anything would unravel Jessica Water's single-minded focus—and yet he was surprised when her steps seemed to falter slightly.

"You can tell him that I commend him for that." She rolled her neck back and forth on her shoulders. "I just can't condone what he did after."

"Roland didn't kill Thomas Rhodes."

Her eyes narrowed on him, a silent fuck-you and don't-be-fucking-with-me all rolled into one. For some reason her look had him feeling the urge to explain. It was almost an unbearable urge. If he could make her understand then maybe she'd let this go, start looking for another suspect and leave Roland alone. He didn't want to have to take her memories. Not again. Doing so had always made him feel a bit dirty, but with her…

He ran his hand through his hair, tipping his head toward the sky as if somehow He might give him a clue of what to do. Something simple like a parting of clouds or better yet, a chorus of angels.

Yeah, and uh, nothing. Well, other than that stupid ache in his chest.

Logan stopped and turned to face her. She stopped too, her gaze expectant as she folded her arms and stared back at him. "Listen," he said, keeping his voice low. "I can't tell you everything that happened that night, but I can tell you one thing. Thomas Rhodes was alive when Roland left him. End of story."

"Alive and well?"

He shrugged, pausing long enough for the next pack of pedestrians to split around them and keep going. "I think that would depend on your personal definition of well. Any man willing to prey on a woman who'd…indulged…too much isn't exactly well, is he?"

"Let me rephrase. Alive and physically unharmed?"

"And now I think we're getting into lawyer territory again, don't you?"

She pursed her lips, a scowl forming along her brow. "I could bring you in, obstruction of justice."

"You could try. But I'd have to ask on what grounds? I wasn't there that night. And I'll swear under any oath that Roland didn't kill Rhodes, even if he did deserve it."

"I thought you said you weren't there?"

"Doesn't matter. I know Roland as well as I know myself. And before you ask, no, I don't think there is a place on this earth for miserable assholes like Thomas Rhodes, but I wouldn't have killed him either."

"What would you have done?" she asked, seemingly genuinely curious.

"Me? I would have turned him in so that justice could help show him the error of his ways. If he chose to repent before his day of judgment then I'd have had the satisfaction of saving one soul. And if not? Well then I think we both know where he was headed."

"I'm not sure I quite follow."

"What's not to follow? I think we both know that as it stood, Thomas Rhodes's soul was destined for Hell."

She rocked back on her heels, her blue eyes dimming. "That's some awfully strong faith you seem to have there. Repentant souls, divine judgment, Hell."

"Don't you believe in anything, detective?"

"Yeah, my badge."

He stared at her. Searching for something more. Searching for…what, exactly? He wasn't sure. He just knew her conviction in her badge, and that alone, made him overwhelmingly sad. Exhaustion settled heavy on his shoulders.

The world was full of nonbelievers and it had never bothered him before. His job as a Paladin warrior was to protect God's children from the sort of evil that they had no ability to fight, like the type that came with claws and hooves, or seductive voices that tempted those who wouldn't normally stray into the darkness of true evil. The Paladin had always upheld that as long as the human scumbags of the world didn't become tangled in their fight, then they should leave the human squabbles of right versus wrong to the religious leaders and the peacekeepers. Now Logan began to wonder whether that policy was a bit naïve.

He looked down the street, his eyes locking on the distant station house. It was more than just a place for the work of law to get done. It was the line between human goodness and evil deeds, a sanctuary to Justice's warriors. But without faith in…something? Could that line really be held? Could Justice survive?

"Mr. Calhoun?" A hand touched his arm.

He drew his thoughts and attention back to Jessica, realizing she'd probably said his name at least once before. She was staring at him with a mixture of suspicion and concern in her expressive blue eyes. Not that he could tell her any of his thoughts or what, exactly, his worries were.

And why did that about break his heart?

"Anything else, detective?" he asked, his voice sounding hollow to even his own ears.

She shook her head, dropping her hand. "No. Just stay—"

"—available." He finished for her, sighing. "Doesn't that ever get old?"

"No." She turned around so she too faced back toward the station, her voice barely more than a whisper as she spoke next. "But the death does."

And wasn't that God's honest truth?

Chapter 6

JESSICA SWERVED THE CAR TO THE LEFT, FRONT BUMPER barely missing an intimate moment with the banged-up yellow Ford in front of her. She yanked the wheel back to the right, popping them into a somewhat-short-of-Smart-Car slot. Brakes squealed, middle fingers extended, and the gap grew just in time to save the little amount of paint remaining on her Impala's bumper.

"Jesus Christ!" Mike shouted beside her, knees lifting, hands grabbing for a nonexistent oh-shit handle.

"Sorry," she replied automatically, even as she began to measure the next opening gap in the jostle-and-go Manhattan traffic.

"Goddamn." He craned his head to glance back at the irate cabby, then blew out a breath and faced forward again. "Ever hear of a little something called road rage?"

"I'm not angry." Annoyed, frustrated, edgy, but not *angry* per se.

"No? Well you're doing a fine job of pissing everyone else off!"

She chuckled, easing her foot a hair off the accelerator. Just a hair though—they had places to be, people to see…holes to shoot in her theories.

Damn Logan Calhoun. His conviction in his friend had made her doubt her own. And sure, uncertainty was often part of the job, but the distinct feeling of unease she had, this want to twist her head like there was something big, scary, and unexplainable just over her shoulder, was not a sensation she was used to.

Crap. She didn't even know why she'd chased after him, other than as she'd followed her suspect out of the station, something in the depths of her brain screamed at her to go after him, not to let him get away.

Whatever. She'd gotten both a lot more and a lot less than she wanted out of that little interaction. While she was all but convinced Logan Calhoun didn't have anything to do with what had happened to Thomas Rhodes, her instincts screamed that he knew a hell of a lot more than he was telling her. Problem was, she wasn't sure she wanted to know what that was. She had a gut-sinking suspicion that his answers, if she could convince him to give them up, might have a real ass-over-teakettle effect on her well-ordered case.

And her world.

The light turned yellow. "Come on. Come on!" she grumbled at the slow van in front of her. It slowed down, sped up, slowed down, then burst through the light…right as it turned red.

"Dammit!" Jessica slammed on her brakes, the nose of her Chevy well into the crosswalk. Not that the pedestrians cared; they just weaved around.

She stared at the light, foot itching on the brake.

"What's up with the wrist?" Mike asked.

She blinked down at the steering wheel and saw she was rotating her wrist back and forth back and forth. It still ached, and in the light of day she could just make out a fine line of discoloration, a rough, three-inch oval area of darker skin that suggested a deep bruise finally making an appearance.

"Nothing. Bumped it on my bed frame." *I think.*

She frowned at the mark that wrapped most of the way across the bones and to the soft underside below. Didn't exactly look like she whacked it. More like she'd been grabbed or gotten it caught in something.

She blew out a breath, turning her attention back to the light. An unexplainable bruise was not the only indication that she needed to screw her head back on. Besides the inability to remember driving home, she still had the damn headache she'd woken up with, only now it was accompanied by a tickling sensation that rode up the back of her skull. The tickling had started the moment she ran into Mr. Calhoun at the vending machines. There was something about him, a moment where she was convinced she'd met him before. Though for the life of her she couldn't remember where or when. She'd passed the moment off, blamed it on attraction—the hum in her lower body certainly gave credence to the theory—but when she spoke to him on the sidewalk, the sense of déjà vu grew, as if her mind was encased in a great fog, and that tickling sensation was her body's way of trying to break through it.

Weird? Definitely. A mystery? No. Jess shook her head. Over-exhaustion explained her gaps in memory. She obviously zoned out after a long night, found her way home on autopilot, then collapsed into bed the moment she wrangled off her boots. The sense that she'd met Mr. Calhoun before? Well, there was that sexual attraction thing again. Not that she'd act on it, given his involvement in the case. Still there was no denying that, unwanted or not, the man packed a powerful punch to her lagging libido.

And why couldn't she have that with Damon?

"Because you're messed in the head," she muttered.

"What's that?"

"Nothing, just thinking aloud."

Mike grunted, but his long look told her that he was as worried about her head as she was. Luckily she didn't have to expound. The light changed and, after waiting for a straggling pedestrian, Jess punched the gas, speeding ahead of the clog of cabs around her and bolting up on the backside of the slower-than-molasses traffic that had just made the light they'd been stuck at.

After a swallowed curse, Mike cleared his throat. "You want to tell me where we're going in such a hurry?"

"On a wild goose chase."

"I got that part. What are we looking for?"

"Thomas Rhodes's car. It never turned up."

"Sooo…"

"So, where is it?"

Mike's shoulders lifted and fell. "Chop shop. Bottom of some upstate lake. Who knows?"

Right. They'd been going on the assumption the killer used Tom's car to ditch the body and then disposed of the vehicle. Tracking stolen vehicles—especially those without GPS systems—wasn't as easy as people thought. And the moment a car left the city, their job became next to impossible. So it wasn't a shock they never found it.

"I want to know where the car was *before* Tom took it out that night."

"Before?" Mike's brow furrowed. "Why? Besides, we canvassed the garages within walking distance, and found nothing. No receipts in his personal effects either."

"All the *commercial* garages," she pointed out, as she swerved around an Escalade.

Mike didn't even swear; his focus was too intent on their conversation. "Well, we know he wasn't using any of the micro-sized spaces in his own building. And it's next to impossible to get a spot somewhere you don't live. You really think it's going to get us somewhere?"

"Now that's the million dollar question, isn't it?"

———

Logan eased his car into the micro-sized spot, cursing as he had to back up and realign, twice. He normally loved the city. Loved the bustle, the vibrant throb of humanity, the reminder of what he fought for day in and day out. But not when he was in such a hurry.

Probably already lost her, he thought, pushing open the door.

Why was she out last night? Was it simply coincidence she'd stumbled upon those vampires? That the succubus he and his brothers hunted led them there? And how crazy was it that Jessica was also tied up in Roland's troubles? Troubles that centered on Thomas Rhodes and whoever, or whatever, had dispatched him to Hell.

It was the last thought that had a shiver running down Logan's spine. A vampire had trashed Roland's penthouse over the summer. Not just any vampire either, but the former head vampire, Christos himself. Roland had moved out—anything to keep Karissa safe. But that break-in occurred the same night Roland's latest blood-donor redemption project—aka Thomas Rhodes—disappeared. Logan didn't know all that much about blood ties, but Roland said he could always find someone he drank from through that tie. What if it could be utilized both ways? What if that was how Christos found Roland's apartment that night? It would certainly explain a lot of unanswered questions, and also made Logan reevaluate the set of coincidences that led to him running into Detective Jessica Waters twice now in less than two days.

What were the chances Jessica was in that area of town last night for something to do with her Rhodes case? What if those vampires weren't there as a part of a trap for Logan and his brothers but because they were sent to keep a certain nosy detective from getting too close to any real answers?

Logan didn't buy into coincidences. At least not that many. The thought of Jessica being firmly lined up in the vampires' sights made him uneasy. Which was why he was taking a chunk of his skin off now, trying to squeeze himself through the six-inch gap between his car and the next in a pitiful attempt to catch up to her.

After mulling on those questions all day, he'd arrived back at the station just in time to see her head out after her shift. But she hadn't gone home. After a night-marish cat-and-mouse chase across town to Harlem, he'd followed her to one of the rarely found self-park garages, hanging back until she'd made it past the gate. Then he pulled in after her, taking a spot a level away from her own.

Now, afraid he might miss her again, he bolted across the cement and hit the nearby stairwell. The numbers were flashing on the elevator, so he went ahead and took the stairs. Easing out into the darkening evening, he caught sight of her all but running down the sidewalk, the streetlights picking up the highlights in her brunette curls as they bounced across her shoulder blades.

He hung back, his curiosity spiking as he watched her loiter near a parking garage for one of those posh high-rises that always got blamed for gentrification.

A couple minutes later, when a large SUV pulled up to the steel curtain and flashed his card at the sensor, Jessica dashed up beside it, running half crouched alongside the vehicle past the rising barrier and down into the dim recess of the underground garage.

Slick. And not exactly legal. And for some reason he wasn't at all surprised.

Torn between amusement and worry, Logan waited. Three buses from the nearby stop went by before Jessica emerged, looking frustrated.

Logan was about to step out to follow when two men beat him to it, folding out of the shadows of a narrow side street, their pace matching hers exactly.

Damn, the woman had no luck…but bad luck.

Chapter 7

JESSICA STRODE DOWN THE SIDEWALK, FRUSTRATION lengthening her stride. The car was there. Only she couldn't touch it without a warrant because it was a private garage. Otherwise, anything they collected would get discarded for illegal search and seizure. She needed some sort of evidence—besides her findings from her recent B and E—like, say, evidence of a concierge taking a bribe on the side and filling up unrented slots with a nontenant's car.

Many buildings with private garages needed a key card for access. Most of the attendants they'd asked earlier in the day had been more than willing to let her and Mike in for a quick look-see. Of the few who weren't, she got the impression they refused for job security concerns and nothing more. There was only one who set off her alarms. Something about the shifty-eyed concierge in the second-to-last building they visited and his assurances that he knew every car in every spot of his garage—of which Tom's Mustang was not one—had rubbed her nerves wrong. She'd taken Mike back to the station, the plan being to work on getting what they might need for their warrants in the morning, but something in her gut told her not to wait.

Jess didn't doubt the man knew every car in his garage. Which meant he knew Tom's was there and probably other cars that shouldn't be. Jess was willing to bet that after she and Mike left he was on the phone telling those pocket-lining customers they might want to find alternate housing for their vehicles, just in case. At least it wasn't like Tom could answer his phone if the guy called and told him to move his Mustang. Still, the sooner Jessica had that warrant the happier she'd be.

Jessica hurried down the block, fighting the urge to break into a run. She needed to make a connection between Thomas and that building or at least his car and that building. Which meant more canvassing. And since she'd left the photos in her car that was where she was going. It was only nine thirty. A little late but not so late that she couldn't start flashing both Tom's picture and the description of the Mustang in question to some of the apartment's inhabitants. Or maybe the concierge was gone for the night and she could convince whoever was managing the desk to tell her if anyone actually lived in the apartment that corresponded with parking slot C-15. If no one did, that might get her permission to "legally" check out the garage.

Jessica walked on, dodging other pedestrians. After a few blocks, she got the creepy suspicion someone was dogging her steps. It was hard to tell for sure when there were over a dozen candidates for her paranoia. Maybe it was the strangeness of the last twenty-four hours. Abandoned streets, missing memories, and then her little talk with her suspect's friend outside the station.

Something about her encounter with Logan had really rattled her and it wasn't just the sexual attraction. There was no denying she was drawn to him. No. Drawn wasn't the right word. All she knew was that her thoughts never completely focused on the task at hand. Instead, she found herself returning to Mr. Logan Calhoun and his steel gray eyes, the rolling timbre of his voice as he spoke with conviction about his faith in his friend and his belief in a higher power.

That was probably it. The whole faith thing. Mr. Calhoun might be willing to put his trust in a higher power, but Jessica had learned the hard way that if there were a higher being, He stopped looking out for the innocents like Julia long ago.

Argh. She swallowed down the hard knot in her throat. She had to get it together. Even with her shoulders itching, she had become unfocused when she should be alert for the source of her unease.

She stretched her stride, easing her hand onto the butt of her gun inside her jacket as she entered the garage where she'd left her Chevy. With a last quick glance behind her she stepped inside the elevator and pressed the button for her level. No one followed.

Taking a deep breath, she allowed herself to slump against the back of the car. It had been a long day, filled with breakthroughs and roadblocks, one right after the other. And as much as she'd love to go home and get some real sleep, the clock was ticking on getting that warrant.

As soon as she was out of the garage, she needed to call Mike. Unlike her last couple partners who could have cared less, she'd been working with Mike long enough to know he wasn't going to be happy that she went back without him, would probably even bark a bit over her little excursion, but she doubted he'd bite.

I'll buy him coffee and donuts or something. Food always tames the man-beast.

The doors swished open in front of her. She stepped out onto the pitted cement, squaring her shoulders. She took five steps when the first scuff of shoe announced she was not as alone as she'd thought. Trying not to look obvious, she twisted her head around.

Two men. Two sets of eyes. Watching her. Intently.

Crap.

She spun, planting her feet as she pulled her jacket back, making sure they got a good look at her Sig. "You gentlemen aren't following me, are you?"

Instead of answering, the men spread apart, one staying between her and the way out and one flanking her.

She took a step back, and the man in front of her took his own step to follow. Her scalp prickled. Something about this seemed damn familiar.

She shook off the feeling, flicking the strap off her gun. "Come on, boys. You don't really want to end tonight in lockup do you?"

The one in front of her smiled, his lips curling back slowly to expose a dentist's dream set of pearlies. Nice and even and...What the hell? Something was seriously fucked up with his canines.

Probably just caps. Some sort of cosmetic dentistry. Even so, those teeth, more than the flickering lights of the garage or the two bulky thugs made her palm sweat a bit against the butt of her gun. *Stop it, Jessica. You don't believe in this shit, remember?*

A shiver ran over her exposed skin, sweat chilling in the cool night, but she forced herself to move, popping the gun from its holster. She hadn't even gotten the gun level when the second thug lunged, coming in at her from the side. Still, she should've been able to spin into the attack. Even if she didn't get a chance at a clear shot, she should have been prepared for the impact, yet she barely blinked and he was on her, his hand slamming against her already abused wrist and sending her weapon sailing.

Fine. She could play, too.

She turned into the attack, knuckles skimming off an iron jaw. He laughed, a thick hand snaking into her hair and jerking her back against him. Jessica twisted, trying to get a good elbow into his ribs, but she lacked the leverage to cause any damage. She went for the instep, but he released his grip on her hair and pushed her away.

She stumbled, trying to spin. A booted foot slammed into her spine, sending her to the ground. Pavement smacked her hard in the jaw. Her assailant followed her down, his weight enough to knock the air out of her lungs and plant her face back into the pavement. Pain radiated across her cheekbone. Darkness tunneled in, contorting the edges of her vision.

"Aren't you going to be a nice treat?" Heat seared across the nape of her neck by her ear. His words were contorted and slow as she struggled against the dark, against the heavy weight smothering her.

The reality of what was happening spiraled Jessica further into panic. Not possible. His speed, his strength. The way he tossed her around like a rag doll? None of it made sense. She was a better fighter than this. This couldn't be happening.

And then it wasn't. Abruptly the weight lifted off her with a ground-shaking roar.

She sucked in deep breaths. Lights sparkled in front

of her eyes. Warm moisture ran down one side of her face and neck, the scent coppery and sweet.

Blood. Her blood.

She tried to push up, her arms shaking beneath her, pain radiating through her jaw and up her right cheekbone. What happened? Did they leave?

A grunt told her she'd had no such luck. She lifted her head to see why they gave her a break and felt her mouth go slack.

Her assailants weren't attacking her anymore because they had a bigger problem. Another man, a good head taller than the guy who smacked into her, and definitely more fit than both, had come to her rescue and was occupying all their attention. The fight was vicious and dirty, fists and feet flying so fast she could barely follow. It looked like something right out of an urban fighter video game. Their styles were a mix of martial arts and down and dirty street moves as they tussled, blocked, and slammed each other around, always moving, the action too quick to allow her to decide who was winning.

It was after one such slam that her rescuer's head lifted, his hair falling back from his eyes, his steely gaze meeting hers. "Jessica, run!"

She blinked again. A precious second lost as she watched her rescuer, in his moment of distraction, take one to the face, knocking his head back in neck snapping action.

"Logan!" she yelled, even as she watched him return the punch, sliding away from the second man's attack in an elegant twist that had them both swatting at air for a moment before they recovered, double-teaming him again.

Hell no.

Jessica scrambled to her feet, shaking off the last of
the fuzziness and spinning back toward the stairs and
elevator. She'd be damned if she'd run, but she also
wasn't an idiot. Her gun was the only thing that could
level the playing field. Only, crap, there was an added
complication. Halfway between her and the stairs was
another man dressed in a slick dark suit, his tie loosened
around his neck and a leather briefcase slung across
his shoulder. He was holding her gun, looking slightly
dazed as he watched the ongoing struggle behind her.

In shock? Or just scared into inaction?

"Police. Give me the gun," she said levelly, approach-
ing the man far slower than she actually wanted to for
fear of startling him into pulling the trigger. She must
have been weaving, or her vision wasn't clear yet,
because the next thing she knew the man was directly
in front of her, his arm stretching out to steady her. She
gasped as his hand closed around her forearm, her face
tipping up to his. Only something with his face was
wrong. Almost too perfect. Her second request for the
gun died on her lips just as his mouth pulled back into
a twisted smile.

"He is right. You are a treat."

A shiver ran down her spine, horror punching through denial and twisting into her belly. The
man's voice did not match his face. Not at all perfect.
Scratchy. And his eyes. They were absolutely black.
Empty. Void of anything.

Jess was so repulsed by his eyes that it took her a
moment to notice the sharp points of stinging pain in
her arm. She drew her gaze away from the horror of the

man's eyes, her nose crinkling against the smell of burnt eggs, and pulled back in shock at the sight of his hand. His fingers had elongated into four distinct joints, the tips like black crow claws, dark liquid seeping into the cotton fabric of her jacket. Blood. From her arm.

It was too much. It was positively too much. Jessica screamed.

Infused with urgency after hearing Jessica's scream, Logan smashed his hand up into the base of the man's nose in front of him, slamming the bone up into the skull. The man crumpled. The blow would've been mortal for a human, but merely temporarily immobilized this asshole while his skull and its sloshy fill regenerated. Because, fuck, this was no human, and neither was his buddy.

Vampires. Jess had been attacked by vampires. Whatever. Man. Vampire. Both these fuckers were going to die for daring to touch her.

With a snarl, Logan plowed his fist into the creature's chest, using a twist of power to transform his inner light into a pulsing stake. It flared with just enough energy to burn through the muscled organ. A split second later there was a pop and a roar, and a cloud of dust exploded around Logan.

Only the take down hadn't been nearly fast enough. Hands closed like vises around his biceps. Sharp pain sliced into the base of his neck as the second vampire's fangs latched on. Logan roared, grappling behind him until his fingers found the soft bulge of the creature's eye sockets. Ruthlessly he jabbed his fingers in. The vampire howled, stumbling back. Logan followed, grasping one of the creature's flailing hands and wrenching the vampire around. A good shove and yank and the vampire was on its knees, its arm up behind his back, the shoulder twisted into an unnatural state.

With another roar Logan called his light again, though this time his stake pierced up from under the creature's shoulder blade. Another pulse of power and another poof of ash.

Logan spun around, squinting to see through the curtain of dust settling around him. Jessica stopped screaming too long ago. It was almost a relief to see her standing near the elevators twenty yards away, until he focused in on the creature standing in front of her shredding its human skin for its true form. Joints popped, fabric ripped, exposing flesh that was darkening as it tightened like bat skin on the creature's protruding bones.

Claws, hooves, fangs. Oh yeah, a demon.

"Jessica!" He called her name, hoping to snap her out of her apparent shock, get her to move, get her to react enough so he'd have a better chance at a clear shot. But she was deaf to all but her terror—a roaring ocean that threatened to drown her as it surged over him.

And when the hell had he become so in tune to another's emotions?

His heart pounded, his gut clawing up his esophagus. His skin turned clammy as he grasped for the light. His weapon. The one thing sure to eradicate the creature threatening Jessica. If he could just calm himself enough to pull from it...

He flung out his left arm, icy panic forcing him to

resort to childish movements in order to channel the power. Even then, only a pitifully small ball of His light rocketed from his hands, barely fizzling as it smacked the demon in the temple. The demon jerked, but didn't dissolve. It merely lifted its head and snarled at Logan before turning back to its prey.

Logan watched in horror as the creature spread a hypnotized Jessica onto the floor. The contents of Logan's stomach curdled as the demon's clawed fingers cupped Jessica's face, its forked tongue darting out as if it could taste the soul of the woman recumbent before him.

No way. No fucking way.

Logan sought the light again, trying to breathe through his anger and fear. But the power of the Almighty's light, which normally lay but a twist of his senses away, seemed to recoil from him. The most Logan could grasp was a sliver. Insufficient, he knew, to do more than put a scratch in the demon's thick skin.

Fine. He'd do it the old-fashioned way.

Logan began chanting, his hands weaving in an intricate pattern of symbols in the air. That got the creature's attention. The demon growled, casting him a black-eyed glare, even as it continued to lower its face toward Jessica's.

Logan stumbled over the words as if someone had grabbed him by the throat and pressed him helplessly against the wall. The sight of the demon hovering over Jessica, a breath away from her lips? Logan wanted to scream his horror. He wanted to roar his defiance. Instead he locked down his emotions and forced the melodic chant through his restricted larynx, taking the last ten feet in two huge strides. The demon remained intent on its soul-sucking lip lock.

With panic clenching around his chest, Logan grabbed the back of the demon's torn suit jacket, yanking the creature away from Jessica's prone body. The demon growled, spinning at him, but Logan's anger, the same that had kept him from grasping heaven's light before, empowered him now. He bent, flipping the creature over his shoulder, where it smashed against a nearby pillar. Fist-sized chunks of concrete crumbled away and rained onto the floor with the demon. The demon bellowed, its inhuman voice slicing at Logan's concentration. For a moment he faltered, resisting the urge to cover his ears, to cringe. But then he straightened, standing over the crouched demon, his voice rising in speed and volume as he continued chanting the spell that would send this creature back to Hell's fires.

The demon hissed, its claws slashing as it lunged, but Logan easily evaded it, slamming his fists down into the creature's back as it stumbled past, sending it into the gritty asphalt. The banishing spell was taking its toll.

A simple twist of power and Logan bound the creature to the ground. The demon's cry became an inhuman, earsplitting, screech as it fought ineffectively against its new bindings. Logan stepped forward, the archaic language of the banishing spell rolling off his tongue like an endless crash of waves against a breaker. With the last words of the spell on his tongue, Logan paused, kneeling beside the creature that was Lucifer's chosen weapon of chaos.

The demon screeched, knowing that three more words would send it back to its master, trying to explain the extent of its failure. The thought of what Lucifer might do to this thing was almost enough to make Logan smile. He might've too, if not for the enormity of the demon's offense.

It tried to possess Jessica.

And for that, both it and its master were going to pay.

"Tell your master no one touches my woman." He laid his hand on the creature's chest. "Now, go rot in Hell."

Chapter 8

LOGAN DIDN'T BOTHER TO WATCH AS THE CREATURE beneath him melted into the oily tar substance of Hell's black lakes and began to seep into the cement floor. The center of his focus was the prone woman who lay five yards away. Her eyes were no longer open and she looked so…still.

He lurched up and then stumbled back to his knees beside her, his innate Paladin grace stolen with a mix of fear and fatigue.

"Jessica…Jessica!" He pressed his fingers against her throat, panicking a bit when, at first, he didn't feel the reedy pulse, but when he did he sagged with relief, rubbing his face with one hand. "Damn it, Jessica. You scared me."

She was alive, but unconscious. The question was what did that mean? What sort of damage had the demon managed?

He touched her cheek, wincing at the abraded skin beneath the layer of sticky blood. It was a nasty looking wound, but one that should heal fine with a bit of cleaning and ointment. No, it was her internal injuries he worried about. Most specifically what Lucifer's creature might've done to her soul.

"Goddamn it!" What should he do? Logan had no idea how to measure that sort of injury. The Paladin had no healers anymore and this was not something a human doctor could fix. The only person who he dared call who had the ability to see how extensive the taint of evil might be was…

"God save us both."

—∼∼∼—

Logan whipped into an open street spot near his brownstone in Greenpoint. The windows were lit, indicating his guest had already let himself in. The door opened, the spilling light outlining the one brother he never thought he'd willingly call upon: Valin. The Black Knight folded his arms, tilting his head as he watched Logan extract Jessica from the passenger's side seatbelt.

"My, my. Isn't this becoming a habit?" he said when Logan drew near with his burden.

Logan grunted.

"So what exactly happened?" Valin asked, moving back to let Logan into his own home. "You were a little vague on the details."

Logan had been too concerned with getting Jess away from the garage and into someplace warded to bother filling in Valin. The newest attack left his mind swirling. It wasn't often demons paired with vampires and set an ambush for a human. Not without the go-ahead from Ganelon or Lucifer himself. The thought sent Logan's protective instincts into overdrive.

"It involves a demon," he told Valin when the front door was closed.

"A demon this time?" Valin's brow rose. "What is it about your cop that would cause so much interest?" He reached out, running a caressing thumb from Jessica's temple down to her lips.

"Back off," Logan warned, his grip tightening on Jessica, drawing her closer to him.

Valin jerked his head up in surprise, his eyes narrowing. "Interesting indeed."

Logan's reacted with a growl that rumbled in his rib cage, his lips pulling back in a snarl.

Valin took a step back, smart man that he was, and folded his arms across his chest, his easy tone belying the tension in his body. "You sure you want me doing this, Lite-Brite? I am going to have to touch her, you know."

Lite-Brite? Logan glanced down at himself. Damn, he was glowing. He drew in a deep breath, centering himself as he carried Jess to the bedroom and put her into his bed.

Valin hovered in the doorway. "So, I gotta ask, why'd you come to me?"

Logan shrugged. "I needed someone who could read the darkness in a person's essence."

"And I was the top of your list?" Valin scoffed. "How flattering."

Well no, but everyone else was out for various reasons. "Valin. We don't have time for this."

"Right." Valin pushed off the door frame, stepping over to the bed. "And right now you need *my* help. Or rather, she does."

Logan nodded, then gritted his teeth as he watched Valin run his hand over Jessica's face and down her neck. Valin grunted, removing his hand and folding his arms across his chest. Long seconds dragged out while Logan anxiously waited for Valin's assessment, but all the Paladin did was spend those moments staring first fixedly down at the occupant of the bed, then up at Logan.

"Well? Do you sense any darkness in her?" Logan demanded after one such scrutinizing stare at Jessica ended with Valin pulling at his bottom lip thoughtfully as he glanced over at Logan.

"Well, she's not housing any demons." Valin dropped his hand, folding his arms again. "So I'm assuming they didn't have any sort of lengthy chat."

Logan sighed, his muscles tightening with his remembered failure. If only that were true. He dived into the story, filling Valin in on why he'd followed Jessica and then how he came to realize he wasn't the only one doing so. Logan glazed over his fight with the vampires, only filling in enough to tell Valin how he'd been busy with them when the demon appeared and sank its claws into Jessica…literally.

Valin sucked in a breath.

"What is it?" Logan asked anxiously.

Valin reached out again, his eyes narrowed as he pushed back the sleeve of Jessica's jacket to get a good look at the puckered wounds in her arm. They weren't deep, just angry looking. "How long *was* the demon attack then?"

"Too long. I couldn't focus to pull enough light and—"

Valin looked at him sharply. "Why not?"

"I don't know. I guess I panicked and then I was too angry."

Valin's brow winged up. Logan's gut churned. If she suffered any permanent damage because of his failure…

A hand closed on his arm; he blinked at Valin, surprised by the contact. "It's all right, Logan. She's going to be okay."

"How do you know?"

Valin dropped his hand, stepping back quickly as if he too had been shocked by his action. "Because there's nothing really wrong with her. Bumps and bruises, cuts and scrapes."

"Then why is she still unconscious?" Logan snapped, his voice, empowered by fear, lashed out like a whip through the room.

Valin stiffened, darkness fuzzing the edges of his figure. Almost as quickly, his edges solidified as a look, suspiciously like compassion, crossed his face.

"Don't look at me like that."

"Like what? This?" Valin opened his mouth, de-solidifying the soft tissue of his face so that, for a split second, he looked amazingly like an Etch-A-Sketch rendition of a screaming skull.

Logan took another handful of deep breaths. Trust Valin to be a dick. Normally Logan didn't stoop to his level, but obviously tonight he was giving Valin a run for his money as five-year-old of the year. "Sorry. I just don't understand this."

Valin shrugged, taking back up his cross-arm pose. "Not sure I do either. But I suspect she's unconscious because she's undergone a traumatizing ordeal. Her soul was attacked by a demon and the way she survived was to draw inward…as far as she could."

Logan looked down at Jessica. She was so still, so pale. If he didn't know better, if he hadn't felt the faint pulse for himself, he would think she was dead.

"So," he swallowed. "She just has to decide to peek back out?"

"Kind of." Valin frowned, working his upper lip with his teeth. "Think of it as a concussion," Valin went on.

"Her soul has been bruised. Not bad enough for permanent injury. It will heal naturally. However, it's going to take a little time."

"How much?"

Valin shook his head. "Hell if I know. I'm not exactly a doctor."

No, the Black Knight wasn't. Quite the opposite in fact. It was his pair mate who'd been the Paladin equivalent of one. And she'd died. She and Valin's unborn child slaughtered by vampires.

God. It could have been Jessica's fate too. If he hadn't been following her. If he hadn't snapped out of his panic.

He sat on the edge of the bed, carefully checking over Jessica's hands, checking the abraded palms, then gently touched her jaw and cheek. "Did you bring the stuff I asked you to?"

"Yup."

Valin turned and disappeared out the bedroom door. In less than a minute he returned, a plastic bag from the local drugstore dangling from his fingers. Logan took it from him and immediately starting digging stuff out. Hydrogen peroxide, iodine, ointment, bandages. Logan began cleaning the wounds, flinching each time new blood sprung up from her abrasions where they'd been hidden under the gravel and dirt.

"Are you going to let her wake up here?" Valin asked as Logan carefully set aside the jacket and gun holster he'd removed so he could better see the punctures on her arm.

Logan twisted to look at Valin, who'd moved back to one of his favorite spots—leaning in the doorframe.

Logan never figured out if Valin did this because he liked options of escape or if he simply didn't like being around other people that much and the doorway left him with the option of going or staying as he pleased.

"This is one of the safest places for her, barring Haven. And you know I can't bring a human there." Though, damn, he wished he could. But one had to have at least a drop of Paladin blood to reach Haven. Either that or Logan would have to remove the protective relic from its home in the sacred hall's altar, which was something he'd never do. Not when it would mean Haven would fall from its perch between realms and solidly into this one. Talk about serving up his brothers on a platter.

"How far back did you take your wipe last night?" Valin asked.

Logan frowned down at her, unsettled by how pale she looked against his navy blankets. "Back to the moment we came along."

"So she only knows you from the police station."

Logan nodded. "And now this."

Valin was silent, his gaze traveling from the patient in the bed back to Logan. "Maybe she shouldn't remember this."

Logan stilled, even his heart seemed to pause for a moment as the meaning of Valin's statement fully sunk in. "You mean I should block her memory again."

No, not block all her memory. There would be no explaining the cuts and bruising, so that meant Valin was suggesting Logan simply cut off her memories from the point where the vampire had first knocked her down, dazing her. It wouldn't be much of a stretch to convince her she'd fully blacked out. And then, something, or someone, came along, scaring off her attackers.

She just wouldn't remember the someone was him.

And why did that bother him so much? He wasn't a Paladin for the glory of it. Ego had no place in their order. In addition to being contrary to the character makeup of the angels they were descendant from, there were reasons why the Paladin did their best to remain low on the radar. Their fight against evil required a certain amount of secrecy to be effective. Humanity, as a whole, tended to cling to the logical and scientific. To swallow the whole concept of evil walking among them and the idea of heavenly warriors protecting them would be a stretch. There was a greater chance they'd be totally freaked out by their angelic saviors and would be as likely to persecute them as revere them.

Nope, being incognito was by far the best option, which meant the logical thing to do was to eliminate yet another portion of Jessica's memory.

But then what would you do? Dump her back in that garage? Take the chance Ganelon might've already sent another demon after her?

"I'll think on it," he mumbled, knowing he wouldn't. Knowing he'd already made up his mind. He was going to keep Jessica safe. No matter the cost.

Valin turned his gaze fully on Logan. "It's what the council would call for."

"You will not tell the council!" He didn't even realize he'd leapt up and crossed the room until he found himself, one hand bunched in Valin's shirt, the other arm pressed across his throat as he pinned the Black Knight to the doorframe.

"You're glowing again," Valin choked out, his gaze steady on Logan's as he made no move to fight.

Logan blinked down at himself, surprised to see that Valin was right. He dropped his arm, stepping back as he quickly pulled in the power that was slipping out of him, capping off the pathway to His light. "Shit. Sorry."

Valin shrugged, fixing the neckline of his shirt. "It's okay. Not like it would hurt me. It's just…"

Logan hung his head. Valin didn't need to finish the sentence. It was just odd. And as alarming as his actions of a moment ago. Logan prided himself on his control and twice that night he'd lost it. Once back in the garage when his emotions had spiked, preventing him from drawing from His light, and now here when his emotions caused him to attack a brother without even realizing what he was doing.

Logan was not used to losing control. As future leader of the Paladin, he could not allow volatile emotions to screw with him and what needed to be done.

Valin's softly spoken words interrupted his train of thought, drawing his attention back. "I'm just suggesting you think on it, Logan. Not telling you what you have to do."

"You just said I should."

"I said that the council would tell you to," Valin pointed out, then with one last glance at Jessica shook his head and took himself out of the room.

Logan waited for the outer door to the brownstone to close before he sat back down on the edge of the bed, his fingers twining in the tight locks of silken hair spread over his pillow. The chest-punch reaction that her silky hair had on him was not good. Not at all.

Why? Why her? What was happening to him that this simple human, though admittedly beautiful and intriguing, could cause him to fuck up so badly?

Valin was right. It was his duty as a Paladin to ensure that who and what he was stayed secret. To do that, the demon must also stay secret. And if he were honest with himself, erasing her memory wouldn't mean abandoning her to the wolves. He could easily drop her off at a hospital. Let her wake there thinking it was some anonymous Good Samaritan who'd brought her in. Really, did it matter who she believed saved her?

He fisted his hands. "Yes it does. Because it was me."

It took him a moment to realize he'd said the thought aloud. He forced his hands open, rubbing them down his stubbled face. By even considering leaving her memories intact he was behaving selfishly and, worse, not thinking at all as the future leader of the Paladin should.

It shouldn't matter what she thought of him. That it did meant one of two things. That he was either turning into an egotistical maniac who had no place leading his fellow Paladin or that… shit…*she* mattered too much.

Tell your master, no one touches my woman. It's what he'd told the demon before he banished it. At the time he hadn't thought much of what he'd meant by those words other than, of course, the implied stop fucking around with me and mine. But now?

His woman. As if there could be a bond. Which was not possible. She was human. With almost three hundred years under his belt, Logan had taken human lovers before. Some gifted, some not, but none recently. And none of them had drawn out these kinds of visceral and primitive reactions from him. He ached with the need to curl up with her in his arms, feel her warmth sink into him, the beat of her heart, and shift of her ribs assuring him of her health. And they hadn't done more than flirt over candy bars—and that had ended with an exchange of wary glares.

Logan had had pairings with humans—compatibility pairings, pairings from desire, some that were truly based on love if only in a very simple human form. But a full bond? A true mating where they shared every aspect of their body, heart, and soul?

Only one other Paladin had bonded fully to a human mate. And look what happened to him.

Insanity followed by a betrayal excused as revenge. That man sat by Lucifer's side now.

Ganelon's spiral into insanity had started before his mate's death, though. His unyielding drive to "save" her turned him again and again to the path of darkness. But nothing he did worked. She still died. And though Ganelon seemed to accept it on the surface, deep within laid a barren wasteland of anger, hatred, and greed, those emotions eventually leading to the moment he fully turned his back on both the order and his God.

Ganelon's betrayal became a lesson to all Paladin: Serve God's children, but don't become attached to the point where one could be compromised. And always, always, hold one's duty to the order first.

Logan sat back on the bed, forcing his hands away from Jessica as he looked up at the stucco ceiling.

"Why? Why would You ask this of me?"

Chapter 9

JESSICA'S DREAMS WERE FILLED WITH NIGHTMARES. Dark parking garages, men who turned into creatures right out of a horror flick, and a web of evil that smothered both light and reason. She couldn't fight that sort of thing. Didn't know how.

And it really pissed her off.

She thrashed out, striking at the dark web that encased her, determined to shred her way out of the paralyzing blanket of terror. Understanding didn't have to be part of survival.

Hands grabbed her shoulders, hot air branding her face. "—kay. I got you."

Not for long. She arched up, hands pushing against the massive chest above her, a war cry worthy of Xena erupting from her throat as she tried to get enough room between her and her captor to inflict real damage. The hands on her arms shifted, and like solid bands of iron they clamped around her wrists forcing her arms above her head. A man's body pressed down on her, entrapping, leaving no room to maneuver. Except for her head.

Unable to pinpoint more than a vague outline of the man in the dimness of the room, Jess went on instinct. She jerked her head forward as hard as she could, pain splitting through her skull and blurring her already compromised vision as her forehead connected with her attacker's face.

"Fucking hell!" The man swore, and counterattacked by closing that distance more. His mouth clamped down on hers in a punishing kiss, the taste of copper coating the line of her clamped lips.

Good. She hurt him. Split his lip.

She didn't know what possessed her to open her mouth, perhaps it was the shock of drawing first blood in this warped reality, perhaps it was simply the shock of warm lips against her own in the cold landscape of her nightmare, whatever. She did. And it took her assailant less than a split second to take advantage of her weakness.

The kiss deepened. Liquid heat stroked past her parted lips, branding a path of flame across her tongue that challenged her to deny him. The fact that Jessica found herself unsure she really wanted to was highly alarming, until she realized she could work this to her advantage. She kissed him back, her legs no longer trying to strike but opening to link around his own. Bodies arched, hips twisted as they played for supremacy of the kiss and volleyed for position on the bed. And then just like that, it changed, their battle for dominance turned to something else. Something more about desire than about gaining the advantage.

Of course, perhaps that was just because it was hard to fight someone who'd given over all control.

He rolled, pulling her over him, his hands stroking down over her body, the touch soft, though not tentative. "You're so fucking perfect," he whispered, his hands continuing on his trail of worship down her body.

He was worshipping her?

That truly clued her that she was not in a nightmare,

but for another glorious ten seconds she ignored that thought. Worse, she moaned as his hand passed over the side of her breast, her body all but crying with need to follow the retreating heat of his palm.

"Ah, fuck." His hands fisted around her hips. She sucked in a breath as he used his grip to move her to exactly where he wanted her…and exactly where she wanted to be. She arched her back, searching for the angle that would allow her to get the most sensation as she rubbed her aching center along the hard length pressing against her. Damn it had been a long time. And hell if she could remember ever aching like this.

"Jessica." Her name was accompanied by another caress, this one more firm, more solid as he slid a hand back up her tank top to cup one of her breasts that were all but begging for his attention. It felt good, too good. And okay, whoa, dream lover knew her name. How the hell did he know her name?

Jessica gasped, blinking as reality intruded. The change of position had also allowed for a change in illumination, her captor no longer a hovering shadow above her, but a very real man beneath her. A man she knew.

"Logan?" she gasped, staring back into his heated gaze. And wasn't this a total WTF moment rolled up into one hell of an *awwwkwaaard* as the reality of their position hit home. They both breathed heavily, his one hand cupping her breast, the other snugged against her buttocks, holding her tight against his pelvis. Her own hands held tight to his biceps as if she'd guided said hands there.

He didn't respond—though he did release her breast.

"Crap!" She thrust herself off him and landed with an inelegant plop on the mattress beside him. Trying to scramble farther away, she bumped her back into the headboard.

Whoa, they'd really traveled on that bed.

She pulled her legs back. "I'm not going to ask how…"

He stood abruptly, bouncing her a bit on the bed as his weight shifted and then left the mattress. She barely noticed as her eyes were stuck on his chest. Ripped. There was no other word. There was not an ounce of body fat on the man. And his abs? They rippled and dipped enticingly, drawing her attention to how his low-slung jeans seemed to hug not only the tight contours of his trim hips but, something else. Something that obviously had enjoyed their make-out session as much as—she closed her eyes, banging her head against the headboard a couple times. Yeah, no reason to complete that sentence. It was easy to see how this had happened. Deprived woman plus hot man equaled…

"Fuck." She banged her head one more time then took a deep breath and opened her eyes. It was time to face reality, whatever the hell it was.

"Sorry…I didn't mean." He fisted his hand, dropping it back to his side. "Are you all right?"

"I'm fine," she answered, unsure whether it was even true. She certainly wasn't thinking clearly, not if she was plastering herself against a near stranger. A nearly naked stranger. Who also happened to be tied to her case— however remote that tie might be.

Um, can you say compromised, Jess?

An awkward pall of silence descended upon the room as she tried really hard to keep her mind on why the best kiss she ever had was not something she dare repeat, but damn if he didn't keep distracting her.

He moved across the carpet, grabbing a T-shirt that had been folded in half and draped over the back of a desk chair. Even after he pulled it on she had a hard time dragging her thoughts back, the image of his muscular torso burned into the back of her retinas.

Did they really make men like him?

Guess so. If proof was seeing, that is. Of course maybe this was just a dream. Maybe she'd left reality when she lost that chunk of time after the alley. Maybe she was actually home in bed right now, her imagination taking things to places that only her well buried, and long deprived, sex-crazed subconscious wanted.

She pinched her arm, not exactly relieved by the sharp sting. Nope. Really here. And those *really* were some nice-fitting jeans.

He cleared his throat. The sound allowed her to finally drag her gaze up, looking where she should have been—at his face. His eyes were a cold, steely, gray now. Had she imagined the stormy look of heat?

"I um…" she took stock of the room. No doubt this was his place and his room. Not just because the navy and gray color palate screamed bachelor, but because it had neat and orderly stamped all over it, not a pile of clothes in sight. Which confirmed that her subconscious was a horny slut. Theirs was definitely not a match made in Heaven.

"How did I get here?" That's right. Concentrate on the important things and not what her body wanted to go back to doing with the really hot guy in the room.

"You don't remember what happened?" he asked, his gray eyes scrutinizing her uncomfortably.

She lifted her chin. Meeting those cold gray eyes

stare for stare even as she grasped for memories that
seemed just out of reach. "I remember talking with you
outside the station. I remember you going all Hamlet
with your Heaven and Hell crap."

He arched his brow, giving her a silent is-this-really-
what-you-want-to-talk-about look.

She closed her eyes, took a deep breath. She knew
why she was being snippy. She was scared. She hated
having holes in her memory. It made her feel helpless.
Out of control. She didn't deal well with being out of
control. It reminded her too much of that day when nothing she said or did could change the fact that her world
had fallen apart.

"Do you remember what you did after we talked,
Jessica?" Logan prompted, sitting back down on the
bed. He didn't touch her, but for some reason his
simple nearness calmed her frazzled nerves, allowing
her to think.

"Yeah. My partner and I went out, trying to track
down a lead."

"A new one?"

"No, an old dead one." She didn't share that she
thought it might be one with new life to it. She had no
idea how long she'd been unconscious, but for it to have
been long enough for her to have turned up here with
him, then she feared it was probably enough time for the
unhelpful concierge to have realized Tom wasn't going
to be coming to get his car out of that garage.

Evidence. Garage. She rubbed her head.

"Don't worry about whatever you're worrying about
now. Just tell me what you did after. Did you go back
to the station?"

"Yeah. To drop Mike off."

"And do you remember what you did after you dropped him off?" he asked carefully, his voice low, even soothing.

If he knew it was the same tone police officers had been trained to use with the victims of traumatizing events, and that, having once been on the receiving end of that training, it had a tendency to set her off rather than calm her, perhaps he wouldn't have tread so carefully. But he didn't know. And Jess could feel the clenching bands of pain in her chest.

"Jessica, it's okay." A hand touched her back, rubbing up and down soothingly. "I'm here. You're safe now."

And of course he'd misinterpret what was wrong. She took ten deep, even breaths, fighting back the urge to punch something. It was somewhat surprising to realize that Logan's steady presence, the rhythmic rub of his hand, the repetitive assurance that she was okay, actually fended off the shakes. No, more than that. His touch, simple, soothing, had her aching to turn into it, turn the tender comfort into something else, something she shouldn't want from a near stranger.

She cleared her throat, shifting away. His hand dropped to the bed giving her space.

"You okay now?" he asked.

She nodded, taking a deep calming breath. Safe from what? What was it that had happened after she'd dropped Mike off? She tried to remember but all she came up with was a jumble of nightmares. None of which could actually be true.

She rubbed her temples, aware of her pounding headache. Belatedly, she realized she'd had it since before she'd smashed her face into Logan's…though it had become more pronounced. The more she tried to remember what happened after she'd waved good-bye to Mike, the more it felt like her head was splitting in two.

What had happened? If she'd followed her typical pattern, she'd have either headed back to her place for a bite to eat as she pored over the case files, hoping that eventually sheer boredom would send her to bed, or perhaps, if she was feeling really antsy, or unsettled over their findings that day, she would grab something from the diner to take with her before she went out again.

She hadn't gone home. She'd felt a pressing need to get something done. To track down a lead. What was it?

"Tom's car," she murmured. Her rejuvenated lead. Of course. She'd gone back to check it out.

Logan ducked his head, watching her intently as he waited for her to go on, but he didn't press. All of a sudden, the rest of the memories flowed free. Sneaking into the garage. Finding the red Mustang in C-15. She didn't want to have any evidence she collected thrown out, and had been about to canvass the apartment building to see if she could get anyone to say they'd seen Tom on the premises or at least the car so as to get a warrant. But she'd left the pictures of Tom and the Mustang in her car and gone back to grab them. She hadn't been paying much attention to her surroundings. Her thoughts were on other things. Besides, there were plenty of other late commuters out on the streets but then…

She sat up straighter, meeting Logan's gaze. "Two men, they followed me. I remember thinking I was just tired and being paranoid, but when I stepped off the elevator they came up behind me and…"

She looked down at her hands. The palms were scraped up and stung when she opened and closed them, like she had really bad rug burn or, in this case, pavement burn.

"Jessica?"

She looked back to Logan, and was immediately sucked into his gaze. His eyes weren't gray anymore. More shimmery, like polished silver. How did he do that? She didn't think she'd ever met someone whose eyes were so changeable. Logically, she knew that different lights or colored shirts could change someone's eye color, but his seemed to do so without any external influences.

"Do you remember what happened after they followed you into the garage?" he asked.

She closed her hand into a fist, laying it on her leg as she gathered her scattered thoughts. "I tried to draw my gun but they were too close and disarmed me. Damn, the one guy was fast, hardly blinked and he was on me and I was...down."

She took a deep breath, blowing it out slowly. She didn't think she'd ever felt so helpless. At least not since her sister died. The impotent feeling she'd had after being told her sister had been murdered eclipsed even this. If Jessica had gone with Julia to that party like she had wanted. Or if she'd insisted that she pick Julia up. But Jessica hadn't and Julia had gotten drunk and had willingly gotten into that car.

After that, Jessica had decided she would never be helpless again. She'd learn to protect herself and others. She'd get her badge and use her skills to put assholes who preyed on the Julias of the world behind bars. She'd uphold justice and sleep at night knowing she'd helped make the world safer for others.

She'd done all that. But obviously not well enough.

In that garage she'd been helpless. She'd almost become another statistic. Would have, if not for Logan.

"Thank you for helping me." There was no hiding the choked quality of her voice, though she honestly didn't know if it was residual terror from the near miss or anger that she had to say the words at all. She was a cop, not a damsel in need of a white knight.

"No problem," he replied sincerely. The fact that he made no production about it, nor did he preen, helped and she found herself admitting, to herself at least, how spectacular he was back in the garage. Though not white knight material. Not with those moves.

"Where did you learn to fight like that?" she asked, trying to distract herself from her mind's running film-strip of alternative endings.

"I learned a bit here and there."

Which explained the lack of a distinct style, though, holy crap, it had worked. She found herself scanning him, partly because yeah, he was damn fine to look at, but more because she still couldn't figure out how any man could have pulled some of the moves he had, even in his admittedly stunning shape. Her gaze narrowed on an angry pair of scrapes that ran across the base of his collarbone. It looked like something had punctured deep into his skin and then been jerked out as he pulled away.

"You're hurt," she pointed out. And why did that piss her off so damn much?

Probably because he got those injuries protecting your stupid ass, Jess.

His mouth twisted up, his eyes crinkling slightly in the corners. "No worries. I'm okay. But thanks for the concern."

"Being injured in a fight is nothing to smile about," she snapped.

His smile faded. "I'm sorry. I wasn't smiling at being hurt. More that we're both okay. Well, basically okay," he conceded.

"What happened?" She shook her head, fighting against the foggy headache that seemed to obliterate her memories from that point on. "I can't seem to remember much after hitting the pavement. I thought there was another man, but I can't remember anything after that."

Logan folded his arms across his chest, a scowl turning down the corners of his mouth. "I don't recall seeing another man, but I was a bit preoccupied."

Jessica frowned, trying to remember that part of the incident. Couldn't. There was absolutely nothing beyond Logan telling her to run, going for her gun, and then a very fuzzy memory of the man in the rumpled business suit standing in front of her. "Did I pass out?"

He shifted on the bed, opening another inch between them. "You seemed to be in shock. You passed out for good right after I dispatched your attackers."

Dispatched her attackers. Okay, then. Forget the no-ego bit. She shook her head. "And the other man I saw?"

He shrugged again. "Like I said, I never saw anyone besides your attackers."

"He didn't stay to help?" She could have sworn he'd picked up her gun. She thought he was shocked by the violence, or perhaps unsure of how to use it, and she went over to him and...

She clamped her fingers over the bridge of her nose,

trying to pinch away the abrupt pain that slashed into her skull.

Logan rubbed a hand across his jaw, his gray eyes unfathomable as he looked at her. "I never saw the man you're talking about. Sorry."

She gnawed her lip, unwilling to believe she'd imagined the third man. But it didn't make sense that Logan hadn't seen him at all, unless the man bolted the moment he got a full bead on the situation. She could understand that a bystander might not want to get involved. But why hadn't he called the police?

"He didn't come back? No other police officers showed up?"

"I didn't exactly want to wait and see." He indicated the angry cut on his collarbone. "You don't mess around with those who can do that."

That might be a good point, but... "And you brought me here. Instead of taking me to a hospital...?" More important, how had he been there to do the bringing? But she'd get to that in a moment.

He shifted again, his gaze dropping slightly before leveling back out on hers. She waited him out, giving him a look that said she was still waiting for his answer.

"I've never been comfortable in hospitals." He flashed a chagrined look. "I'm sorry. I guess I tend to assume everyone holds my prejudices."

She merely hummed in response. The fact that she did, in fact, dislike hospitals was not something she was going to tell him. That would be like saying it was okay that he brought her to his home. Which it wasn't. And not just because she didn't know him from Adam—even if her body seemed to want to.

She folded her arms, hands tucked under her armpits. Better that than give in to the urge to touch his collarbone to check out his wound—and then check out the rest of him. Why her imagination kept skittering off into unwanted territory was beyond her.

"Okay. Assuming all that is true."

"It is."

She glared at him. "I said I was assuming it was. What I want to know now is how you were there to come to my rescue at all. And don't try and tell me that you just happened to be in that garage at that moment in time."

"Not that garage." He gave a wry twist of his mouth. "Just that part of town."

She narrowed her gaze on him.

He held up his hand. "Scout's honor. I had some business in that part of town and saw you walking. I didn't say hi because I figured you probably didn't want to see me again but then, when you ducked into the parking garage and I saw those two thugs break from the crowd and follow you in …"

"Uh-huh. And you just knew they were up to no good."

"No. I didn't. But I had one of those feelings, you know?"

"Hmm." She did know, because she'd had one herself. The problem was she didn't really buy his answer. It seemed too convenient. Too pat.

He tilted his head to the side. "Hey, let's not overanalyze things. Coincidence, fate, whatever. I'm just glad I was there to help and that you're basically all right." He ducked his head to look at her more closely. "You are all right, aren't you? And don't tell me you're fine. That's not a real answer, that's an avoidance technique."

She scoffed, though it was half chuckle. "You must know Mike."

"Who?"

"Nobody important." She twisted, flinging her legs off the bed to stand, and then groaned as she lowered herself the couple inches back onto the mattress.

"Jessica?" His concern was palpable in both his voice and the firm grip on her arm.

She breathed through her teeth, actually glad for his steadying touch. "You're right. Fine is not an answer. It certainly can't encompass this hit-by-a-semi feeling I'm having right now."

She lifted her left hand, bringing it to her temple where she encountered the gauze bandage. "Damn, no wonder it feels like my brain is trying to explode out of my head."

"Let me get you some aspirin."

Carefully, he let her arm go, making sure she was steady in her perched position on the edge of the bed before releasing her fully. As he padded into the adjoining bathroom and began rustling through a cabinet, she used her fingers to explore the extent of the damage, simultaneously checking her muscles and joints to make sure they all worked properly. Bumps, abrasions, sore, sore, sore—though nothing broken, she thought. By the time he came back, she decided she'd live, though until she got that aspirin she was going to reserve judgment on whether she actually wanted to.

"Two, three, or four?"

"Six," she replied, rubbing the bandage over her

aching forearm. Have to check that out later. After she checked her cabinet to see if it was stocked to replace the dressing if needed.

"Four then."

She growled at that but he just smiled, dumping out the pills and handing them to her along with a glass of water. She took the pills, then closed her eyes, rubbing the empty but still cool glass against her forehead.

"Better?"

She cracked an eye open. "Not yet. But hopefully soon."

"How about some food?"

She grunted. "Probably a good idea."

He offered her a hand, which she grudgingly took. Not because she didn't appreciate the chivalry, but because even feeling like she'd been dragged by that Mack truck through Hell and back, his touch set her imagination to removing that shirt he'd just put back on.

She was definitely one warped puppy.

He led her down a short hall to the stairs. She gripped the dark, ornately carved wood as she wobbled down them. The base opened up into a wide entryway, two closed French doors probably leading into some sort of living room or parlor. He turned back down the long hall, leading her into the back of the house. They entered a kitchen, dark granite countertops catching her eye. Not because they were sparkling but because they were crammed full of appliances. Keeping with the theme of crammed and functional, the island was canopied by racks of pots and pans, and a huge fridge lorded over them all.

The man was either a gourmet cook or liked to pretend so.

"Sit. I'll whip something up."

She carefully levered herself onto the bar-height chair, resting her bandaged forearm on the artfully weathered pub-height table. She watched, fascinated, as he pulled together an impromptu meal. Eggs were scrambled, fresh dill chopped, leftover ham was diced up along with mushrooms, onions, and green peppers. Some butter in a pan—real butter, her mother would have a fit—and they all went in together, sizzling and popping in time to his occasional flicks of the wrist that sent the ingredients in the pan flipping up in the air, then back down to sizzle some more. His movements were quick, efficient, but graceful, and she didn't dare blink for fear she'd miss something. The meal looked yummy. *He* looked yummy.

Whoa there, Jess. Let's analyze this.

She was getting in way over her head, way too quickly. This was not the morning after or a date. She was here because she'd fucked up. She went out again, without backup, searching in places she wasn't authorized to trespass in. Even this. Sitting here in Logan's kitchen watching him make her a meal that sent her glands to salivating. It wasn't right. She shouldn't be here. Seriously, the chances of him just happening to be in that part of town and just happening to see her go into the garage, and just happening to have a bad feeling about the two men following her in seemed like way more than a coincidence. The only way she could buy into that series of events was if he'd been following her too…which was downright disturbing.

This whole thing had stalker written all over it. And now she was in his house. Alone. Without a weapon.

"Hey, you okay?" Logan asked.

She blinked, noticing for the first time that a steaming omelet had been set down before her. The scents lifting off it did indeed cause her to salivate, but the possibility that she could be sitting in the kitchen of a stalker had her gut churning. She didn't want him to be a freak. She wanted to believe him, take him at face value. She wanted to dig into that pile of fluffy eggs and then after, with her belly fully sated, she wanted to take care of her other appetite and dig into him.

"Where is my gun?" she asked abruptly.

"In your harness, under your jacket which is in the closet." He jerked his head toward a smaller, six-panel door under the stairs.

Tossing her unused napkin beside her uneaten meal, she pushed back her chair and walked over, heart thumping as she'd opened the closet. And there it was.

Taking a deep breath, she retrieved the gun, checking her ammo before slipping into the harness and turning back around. She thought having the gun strapped on would lower her heart rate, but it didn't. It still beat like she was chasing a perp fleeing the scene. Damn it. She fidgeted with the safety strap that held her police issue in as she stared at the homey scene before her. This whole encounter was almost as warped as her nightmares, and the fact she was drawn to it? That she wanted to go back and settle into that chair?

"I have to go," she said, pulling on her jacket.

Logan momentarily stilled, then set down the plate he'd been holding, ready to scoop his own meal out.

"Okay…Where do you want to go?" he asked, moving the pan to a cool burner and covering it with a lid.

Next he washed his hands, drying them off with a handy dishtowel. Meticulous. Controlled. Everything she wasn't right now and needed to be.

Crap. Get it together, Jess. What's he going to do? Attack you with his spatula? She shook her head.

"Well, first back to my apartment to change, but then I have to get down to the station." She glanced at the clock over the stove. "Which, crap, I'm already late."

"Okay. I'll drive you home first and wait outside while you change." He brushed past her, grabbing his wallet and keys from a bowl that sat on a small side table by the front door. Something about the action made her frown, her mind churning to come up with a reason why it would bother her so.

"Jessica?" he asked, his face skewed into a puzzled expression.

"There's no need to do that. Just drop me off at the garage where my car is."

"That doesn't make much sense when that's all the way across town. Your apartment is closer. I can wait for you. Then we can pick up your car together later."

A vital organ plummeted from behind her ribs down into her gut, the slim hope that it had been all a quirky coincidence extinguished. His words proved just what she feared: He knew way more about her than he should.

She turned to face him, folding her arms across her breasts. A defensive position, sure, but one she needed at that moment, and not because she was scared, but for some damn odd reason, she was hurt. "How long have you been following me?"

He stilled with his hand on the door, tension riding

across his shoulders. "I told you I had business in that part of town."

"And I'm telling you I'm not buying it. If you haven't noticed, New York is a damn big city. The chances of you and me running into each other twice in one day?" *Or that he knows where I live?*

Research. Yeah, she was unlisted, but still. A good hacker could dive into enough records to find out, though why Logan would've felt the need to…

His other hand tightened around his keys. She waited him out, trying not to be impressed with the way he visibly forced himself to relax his grip. So strong, but so much control.

Like any other psychopath before he went over the edge.

She looked over his shoulder to the front door. Would it be unlocked? Could she make it by him without him trying to stop her? Without her having to draw her gun?

An image of him, legs twisted awkwardly, eyes staring as blood bloomed from his chest onto the polished hardwood floors sprang into her mind, causing her to shudder. She told herself she could do it if she had to, but the trembling in her limbs told her a different story.

"There's nothing I can say that would convince you I'm not that man, is there?" His voice seemed sad as he said this, but she refused to let that sway her.

"Probably not," she said, forcing the image out of her mind. Deal with the now. This instant. She'd cross that bridge only if she were forced to.

He sighed, jiggling his keys as he pushed open the door. "Come on. I'll drive you to your car. Unless you'd rather I call you a cab. Or maybe a friend?"

Okay, except maybe that. What stalker would tell her to call a friend? He could still be playing her, she supposed, but she didn't think so. Or at least she didn't want to think so.

She tapped her jacket pocket, comforted by the weight of her cell phone, but when she opened her mouth she said, "I'll take the ride."

He nodded, gesturing for her to go first. She walked down the steps, her brows rising as she took in the car and neighborhood. They screamed money. Both the understated yet classic lines of the Audi and the well-kept brownstones.

"What do you do?"

"I'm an antiquities consultant," he said as he opened the passenger door and held it open for her.

She nodded, sliding into the passenger seat. Though she didn't buy it at all. Not after seeing him fight, and not after being the recipient of that wow-fuck-me-now-please kiss.

And that was something she should not be thinking about. She looked straight ahead, ignoring everything other than the street signs as he drove them out of the neighborhood. Greenpoint. Brooklyn. One of those nice, quaint, Victorian streets with a pretty church at the end. And quite the jog back to the garage where her car had had its sleepover.

They did finally arrive, and she waited tensely as he got his ticket, then sucked in a breath as they drove forward, passing from the light of day into the artificial light of the garage, and then shivered as they took the ramp to the level where her car was parked. She made a point to stare directly at the spot where she was taken down, and then turned her gaze to the elevator where she imagined the third man. It made her tense, and a glaze of sweat slicked over her skin, but she had to do it.

Like getting back onto a bike.

Logan double-parked his car behind hers, the locks clicking to their unlocked position. She reached for the door handle but his hand on her arm stilled her.

She turned her head, then wished she hadn't when their gazes lined up. Her breath caught at the intensity in his eyes. He held out a business card, his voice earnest as he spoke. "Promise me you'll call if you need anything."

She stared at the card like it was a snake, and shook her head. To take it would be akin to inviting temptation. Her reasoning was so far from acceptable where he was concerned.

"Please. Just in case."

"Anything like what?"

He shrugged. "Help with anything. Or just to talk."

And that was exactly what she was afraid of. It would be so easy to give in to her desire to know this man.

She stared at the card. Block letter script on white. Simple. Harmless unless she allowed herself to make it otherwise. "Just because I take it doesn't mean I'll ever call."

"I know." His eyes saddened as he said this, his mouth turned down in a grim line as if the thought of never seeing or hearing from her again was truly painful for him.

Oh yeah. Definitely a stalker. Yet...

She reached out, snapping the card from between his fingers and stuffing it into the back pocket of her jeans.

His eyes flared, stormy gray before warming to a bluish-green slate color, but all he said was a simple, "Thank you."

"I've got to go," she said and pushed out of the car, then jogged across the garage to her own.

Chapter 10

JESSICA FELT ACID EATING THE LINING OF HER STOMACH as she approached the block of the crime scene. She'd barely stripped out of her ruined jacket when the call came from dispatch. She'd slapped on some new bandages on her arm and a healthy dose of concealer while dialing Mike's cell. He was already on his way.

It had taken almost thirty-five minutes to get through the midday traffic, and the body wasn't getting any fresher. Not that freshness would matter. If she were right, it had already been there for a while.

Pausing at a stoplight, Jessica checked her phone again. Its display confirmed what she already knew: no calls, no texts. Though what did she expect?

Heart thudding, she made the turn onto the street dispatch had indicated and cursed. Definitely the last one here. And didn't that piss her off all over again. It was Logan's fault. If he hadn't brought her to his place. If he hadn't seduced her with forest-fire kisses and mouthwatering omelets. If he hadn't…*saved you, Jessica? What then? Would you even be here to be late?*

"Crap." Striking Logan from her mind, she double-parked across the street from the crime scene and grabbed her phone. A couple buttons and she was redialing the same number she'd tried over a dozen times since she'd heard from dispatch. It rang. And rang.

"Come on. Come on!" Nothing. She cursed, ending the call. "This better not be you in there, Grim."

Shoving the phone in her belt clip she stepped out of her car, a shudder running over her.

"Damn it," she muttered under her breath and crossed the street to the dim alley she'd visited two nights before. Her boots rang on the hard pavement, drawing attention from the nearest officer. She was relieved to see it wasn't some green-faced newbie, but one of the older cops nearing retirement.

Good. He'd keep it together and hold the line against any gawkers. Not that there were any. Even in the middle of the day, this place seemed to be all but abandoned.

"Yo, Jessica! I think this is a first. Mike even beat you," Tony said.

Jessica tried to flash a rueful smile at him, but ended up grimacing instead as the movement pulled on the newly scabbed skin across her cheekbone. Tony's eyes widened and he whistled. "Wow. What the heck happened to you?"

"Just a little mishap on the way to my car."

"With what? Another car?"

"No, uh, just a couple of evening commuters."

He shook his head. "Bastards. Did they at least say sorry when they knocked you down?"

"Not exactly."

"Damn. What is the world coming to?" He sighed, holding up the yellow and black tape to let her through. "Go on back. Mike's talking to the ME while they wait for the photographer and crime scene unit to finish."

"Right."

She made her way down the side street, the sounds

of the investigative team playing like a homicide-cops urban symphony. The clicking of a camera was the erratic drummer, the scuff of boots on gritty pavement the counter beat, and the gruff voices lowered in funeral hall tones claimed the melody. It was punctuated by other sounds as well, the occasional static of the police scanner and the distant hum of midmorning traffic, but all in all the scene, right smack in the middle of the Bronx, was eerily subdued. The street clung to the isolation she'd felt the other night when she stood in its entrance at nearly three a.m.

Mike and the ME stood just on the outskirts of the CSU team, their arms folded in similar poses as they waited.

"So what do we have?" Jessica asked quietly, sidling up beside them.

"A dead body," the ME, Melissa, deadpanned, breaking the unusual silence with a large snap of her gum. Melissa always had a piece of gum in her mouth, said it helped distract her from the odors. And though the snap caused a few heads to turn, no one was going to ask her to spit it out or give them a piece. Smart, considering Melissa, with her tree-trunk arms and spiky gray hair, looked more like a tough-edged biker than the grandmother she actually was, and the gum was her replacement for the cigarettes she used to suck down.

Jessica sighed. "Homicide I presume?"

Melissa shrugged. "Can't tell for sure since the body is half buried in trash, but judging simply by the location?"

"Christ, Jessica, what happened to you?" Mike exclaimed, drawing another handful of stares. Even Melissa dragged her eagle-eyed focus away from the

Dumpster to look at her. The ME's eyes widened, and she whistled.

"Wow, purdy."

"It's noth—" Jessica flinched as Mike's hand closed around her chin, turning her face to the side to get a better look at the angry looking scratches on her cheek. At least she'd managed to cover the bruise to her temple.

"Jesus." He fingered her temple, sending off shots of pain beneath her skin across her forehead and scalp.

Okay, so the bruise might be hidden, but she guessed the lump wasn't. She reached up, slapping at his hand. "Stop prodding it, will you?"

He glared at her and crossed his arms across his chest. "Well?"

"Well what?"

Jessica's skin itched as her guilt levels spiked. Mike was concerned, and she was being a bitch. But she really didn't want to get into what happened. Especially with others around. Nope, her stupidity was something she'd like to keep private, thank you very much. She shrugged. "Just a little mishap. Nothing big."

"A mishap? What kind? Hit and run?"

"Yeah, you know those evening commuters."

The skin around his eyes crinkled, his gaze narrowing. She was beginning to think the impending shake down and lecture might be unavoidable when someone whistled, drawing their attention.

"We're going to have to remove the body to finish collecting evidence from the Dumpster. You want to get in here first?" one of the members of the CSU team asked them.

"Hell, yeah," Melissa said, boots clicking on the pavement. Mike gave Jessica a look that said, "We'll talk about this later," and fell in beside her. They moved forward as the rest of the team moved back to the edge of the scene, taking a breather. Not that there could really be one, the smell of death already clogged the alley, though it was definitely worse next to the Dumpster. Jessica was tall, but she still had to lift onto her tip toes to get a good view inside. She didn't even realize her gut had clenched up until the knots eased, allowing her to swallow. Not Grim. The body was beaten to a pulp, the limbs at odd angles, dried blood coating the fabric, but even though the face wasn't visible this man was Caucasian and Grim was not.

"Did you do a preliminary time of death yet?" she asked Melissa, hoping against hope the ME would say last night or early this morning.

"No. But judging by the bloating and the smell? I'd say more than a day."

Jessica swore. The coincidence that it was this alley, fewer than forty-eight hours after her botched meet and greet, was too much. Even with the garbage, she should have been able to smell a dead body rotting in the Dumpster—unless it was a fresh dead body. Which meant it was more than likely that this was the informant Grim had been trying to set her up with.

Damn, damn, damn. Of all the luck. Why her? And where the heck was Grim?

A hand touched her arm, drawing her back. Jessica turned to look into Mike's baby-blue eyes, his stare accusing. "What else aren't you telling me?"

Time to pay the piper.

She stretched her neck. One way, then the other. "I, uh, may have a lead on who our victim is."

Mike sucked in a breath, glancing briefly at the Dumpster before returning his gaze to her. "How?"

Jessica sighed, nodding to Mike to step further away. She'd seen enough and wanted Melissa to do her thing and get them the details they needed.

"It could be coincidence, but there's a good chance I was supposed to meet the man in there."

"When? Why?"

"Two nights ago. Well, a day and a half really. It was more of an early morning meeting."

Mike's lips thinned, but he didn't say anything, rolling his hand to indicate she should go on.

"One of my snitches who knew I was looking for leads on Thomas Rhodes claimed to know someone who knew something about Tom's death. He was really spooked, though. Insisted on just me and the super secret meeting spot."

Mike shook his head. "Who was it?"

"Not was. Is." She glanced at the Dumpster. "Anyway Grim—my snitch—set me up to meet the guy. Grim was just going to show long enough to make introductions."

"Not much blood other than on the body." He lifted and dropped his shoulders. "Probably dumped."

She nodded, but she'd wait for the ME's and CSU's report before she decided one way or the other and then take it from there. "Anyway, presuming our victim is the informant Grim was setting me up with, then he supposedly had some intel for me on Thomas Rhodes."

"What kind of intel?"

"What offed Tom kind of intel."

Mike folded his arms, looking back at the Dumpster. "Huh. You think he really had something?"

"Grim is usually reliable."

Melissa scrambled down from her precarious perch on the Dumpster. She waved at a couple of her techs and they ran over with a stretcher, body bag unzipped and on top. Mike and Jessica were silent as they watched Melissa's team pull the body and stuff it into the black bag and roll it out of the way for CSU to get to work on the contents of the Dumpster itself.

"Come on," Jessica jerked her head toward where Melissa was bending over the stretcher. Mike followed with a sigh. Jessica couldn't blame him. Smelling the body in the Dumpster would be bad enough. Seeing the full extent of the damage up close and personal? Not a job anyone enjoyed. But if doing so was a way to take the criminals off the streets, then she'd suck down as many breakfasts as she had to—not that she'd had one that morning. Damn, those omelets had smelled good.

Don't think about it, Jess. Or him. Definitely not him.

"Anything interesting?" she asked Melissa when they were close.

Melissa glanced at them absently, motioning them to get closer. Not a good idea. Jessica may not have had breakfast but the pulverized face that stared back at her was porcelain-goddess-worthy anyway.

"Nice," Mike said, his face as green as hers felt.

"And positively screaming his life story at me too," Melissa put in excitedly, obviously not at all phased by the sight.

"How so?" Jessica sucked back down the bile to ask.

"See these scars?" Melissa pointed to some scarring around the throat. Jessica and Mike bent closer as they tried to pick out the marks against the bloated and bruised skin. To Jessica it didn't look like anything but a mess of old scarring.

"What is that?"

"If I had to guess? Bite marks."

Her head jerked up. "Bite marks. Like a dog?"

"Not exactly."

"What then?"

"Not sure, but the other side is even better." Melissa pressed her latex gloved fingers against the side of the corpse's head, forcing it the other way so the left side of the neck was better exposed. "See this?" The ME pressed two fingers against the scarred flesh on that side, pointing out two spots where the scarring was thickest, then slid her fingers slightly lower and pointed out another couple of scabbed-over puncture wounds, two twin trails dried blood coming out from them. "And this?"

Jessica nodded, a tug of a memory drifting in and out of her mind before she could grasp it. Something about the partly scabbed wounds did look familiar. Like she'd seen a similar wound recently. Like maybe on...*Logan?*

She shook the thought off, forcing herself to concentrate on what the ME was saying.

"Both this newer one and the older ones were formed the same way." Melissa's fingers moved back to the older scarring. "If you can get past the layers of scarring and recent bruising you can see these pairings on both sides of the neck. This is where the canines sunk in; the rest of the scarring, which isn't as thick, is minor tear wounds."

A chill ran down Jessica's spine, making her shiver. Bite wounds. Punctures, scraped and torn flesh. What was it Grim had been spouting? Something about this guy knowing about shit that would make your hair stand on end. Paranormal crap like vampires. Creatures with sharp canines and superhuman strength. Maybe even claws? Claws that might match the strange puncture wounds she'd found under her bandages?

She rubbed her arm. *Has to be another explanation.* Those men last night had been strong and fast but then again, she'd been damn tired.

She shifted, indicating to Mike that he should take over. Hopefully, he thought she was letting him take the lead because she was mulling things over, not because she was mentally freaking out.

"So...punctures and tearing," Mike drawled. "Wouldn't that indicate some sort of animal? Like, you know, a dog?"

The ME shook her head. "I've seen scars from dog bites." She fingered the punctures again. "These don't strike me as that. Possibly another animal, but..."

"But what?" Mike pressed.

"Don't laugh, but I think they're fangs." Melissa made a hissing noise, her mouth open as she used her two fingers to curl down like canines before her mouth. Jessica sucked in a breath, remembering the flash of the thug's fucked-up teeth last night; her own momentary shock as Grim's babblings leapt to the front of her thoughts, serving up a totally unreasonable explanation: vampires.

Not possible.

"Oh, come on," Mike scoffed. "Fangs? As in vampires?"

"You seen some of the crap they're doing with cosmetic dentistry recently?" Melissa asked him.

"You think a human did this?"

Melissa shrugged. "I'm just saying. There are some real wackos out there. Some people into some really freaky Goth shit."

Jessica made some excuse and stepped away. For a few moments, she'd actually entertained the idea that the men she saw last night could have been vampires. But Melissa indicated their victim had been gnawed on not just once, but multiple times, to result in that sort of scarring. Which was asinine. No person, no matter what sort of freaky shit he was into, would lie there and willingly let someone gnaw on his neck—and come back for more. Obviously their ME had been watching way too much *True Blood* recently. And Jessica had been getting too little sleep. Oh, she didn't doubt that Melissa was partially right. Their victim had obviously been attacked at one point by something with enlarged canines, but even if it was human, the poor fool must have been restrained during the freaky Goth-vampire bloodletting session.

Frankly, she didn't know what was worse. To think there might be something to the paranormal crap Grim had been spouting, or to think that human beings would get so hooked on the idea that they'd alter themselves to live out some sick fantasy. And that somehow she had gotten dragged into the shit. Though fuck it, it might actually make finding their victim's killer or killers easier. Simply go around NYC asking everyone to say "Ah" and then drag in everyone sporting pretty, sharp pointy canines. No biggie.

Yeah, right.

Sighing, she made her way to her Chevy and leaned against the hood. She scrubbed a shaky hand over her face, blinking through her blurry vision at the street before her. On top of the aches and pains from her encounter last night, on top of the perpetual exhaustion, the damn headache had returned. She knew why, of course, and it had little to do with her momentary slip into fantasy land. It was because she was here, staring at the same street she must have driven back home on the other night, and couldn't remember a fucking thing. If this kept up she was going to have to get a damn MRI to find out what the hell was wrong with her fucking mind. Had she actually witnessed something and couldn't remember? Was the key to their victim's killer locked up in her foggy brain?

"I'm a mess," she grumbled.

"Yeah, you are."

She jumped, spun, and had to force her fisted hand back down to her side as she came face to face with her partner. "Damn it, Mike. Don't sneak up on me."

"I didn't. Stomped like a damn elephant all the way from the alley over here."

She made a noise along the lines of a grunt and leaned back against the dented hood of her Chevy. Mike took up position beside her, arms and ankles crossed in a deceptively relaxed pose, but she didn't miss the scowl as he scanned the vivid abrasions on her face.

And here it came. The lecture.

"How much sleep *did* you get last night?" he asked.

"Actually, a fair amount." Granted she'd been knocked unconscious, but that counted, right?

"Uh-huh. And did you see a doctor for that bump on your head?"

"It's noth—"

"Nothing. Right. You already said that." Mike fell silent as he began a series of long deep breaths. As if he were silently counting to ten—multiple times. However long it was, it was enough time to gnaw a huge chunk in her determination to stonewall. Mike didn't deserve it. He was a good cop. She liked him and she wasn't exactly a people person. But like him or not, she wasn't about to go all crybaby on his shoulder over a bump on the head and a small chunk of missing time. That kind of revelation would land her first in the doctor's office, which, okay, was maybe warranted, but then after, she'd be deposited in the department shrink's office where she'd come away with nothing to show for it other than a shiny certificate of her mental incapacity and a leave of absence. Nope, not going to happen. Best answer to her personal problems? Get her shit together. Focus on her job.

She cleared her throat, forcing the strain out of her voice as she took on a professional tone. "I may have another lead. One that we can follow up on while waiting for Melissa's report."

Mike turned his head slightly toward her, his expression held in reserve. "Oh?"

"I think we should canvass the tenants in the apartment building with the jumpy concierge. See if anyone recognizes Thomas Rhodes and or his car."

He shifted on the hood, turning his body toward her more. "Why? We were already there. They wouldn't let us in."

"Because I saw Tom's Mustang parked in slot C-15 of the underground parking garage. Along with what appears to be a nice, crusty blood stain on the driver's headrest."

Mike's eyebrows flew up. "How?"

"I just slipped in and saw the vehicle and peered through the windows." She kept going before he could protest. "I didn't touch it. But if we flash Tom's picture and ask enough tenants about a certain red Mustang they'll say *they've* seen it."

Mike shook his head, letting out a string curses.

She talked over him. "We could have our warrant before lunchtime…" She glanced at her watch. "Well, a late lunch that is." A really late lunch. Damn.

"Jesus."

She narrowed her eyes, folding her arms. "Why are you so mad? We might have a lead."

"I don't care about the damn lead. Why didn't you call me? When you dropped me off, you didn't make one mention that you planned to go back out. Even if it was an impulsive kind of thing then, damn it, you could have at least called me after you saw the damn car." His eyes widened, understanding dawning. "Wait. That's when you got hurt, isn't it? You didn't call me because you were lying on the floor of the garage passed out with a fucking concussion?"

She shifted uncomfortably from one foot to the other. Definitely dangerous ground. "Not exactly." She hedged.

"Not exactly?"

"It wasn't that garage, and someone came along and helped out."

"And you didn't call me then?"

She opened her mouth, then clamped it shut. Angry with herself or not, she really didn't want to go into the details of what happened. First of all, she still wasn't one hundred percent clear on all of them, and second, she had a feeling that telling Mike that Mr. Logan Calhoun, their suspect's best friend, was also her knight in shining armor last night would not go over well. Hell, it didn't go over well with her, and she kissed the jerk. Talk about suspicious. Not to mention a major conflict of interest on her part.

Mike pushed off the car, pacing. "Christ, Jessica. I thought we were partners. You know, I've got your back you have mine? And now I find out you've been out two nights in a row without me? Without any sort of backup? And that you were fucking injured while doing it?"

Jessica rubbed her arm, the sharp ache of the multiple puncture wounds a pointed reminder of her fuck-up. "I admit, last night I could have used the backup."

He ground to a halt, spinning on her. "But not the night before? Did you look in that fucking Dumpster? Did you not see the same body I did? What the hell do you think might've happened if you'd been there when they were stuffing that man in it?"

She remained silent. Really, what could she say to that? *Um, actually, Mike, I'm not even sure if I was or wasn't there. There was this really loud bang and then—without calling for backup—I got out of my car to investigate and I swear it felt like I was being watched. But I really don't know since I don't fucking remember much of anything after that.*

Oh yeah. Not.

Mike took a deep breath, closing his eyes as he cracked his knuckles. When he opened them again he'd regained his cool, putting on the face she imagined he'd honed for working the streets. Cold, indifferent. It chilled her more than all the swearing, and her gut, which had still been churning after the alley, turned into a hard, frozen lump.

"I like you, Jessica. I really do. You've got heart, you're a good cop, and you don't take shit. But here's the thing. I don't take shit either. And I'm sick of yours." He paused, letting that sink in. "Shape up. Work with me. Or find a new partner."

He turned and stalked off toward his car. Jessica wavered for a few seconds, anger making her want to flip him off and get into her own car, but shame, that he was right, making her want to run after him and apologize.

"Mike!" she called, refusing to chase after him, but willing to meet him halfway and offer some sort of olive branch at least.

He spun around, his brow raised in question. She opened her mouth but he must have seen something he didn't want to see in her face because he held up his hand, fending her words off. "Nope. Don't say anything now. I'll call you in a couple hours with whatever I've found at the apartment building."

She ground her teeth, but tried to keep the hostility out of her voice. "And what am I supposed to do in the meantime?"

He shook his head. "I don't know. Maybe see a doctor. Get that damn stubborn head of yours examined," he added as he spun around and stalked off.

Chapter 11

LOGAN FIDDLED WITH HIS CELL PHONE WHILE THE REST of the council milled about, slowly filing out of the room. The stubborn piece of electronics remained frustratingly inert in his hand. No vibration meant no calls. Not that he'd necessarily get them. Even if there wasn't the little problem of not being entirely in one realm or the other, Haven, though only a couple centuries old, was a maze of elaborate stonework, hand-smeared stucco, carved timber beams, and thick iron bracings. Logan wasn't sure how much of the archaic design had been done as a hats off to the true origins of the Paladin order and how much of it was because its builders were simply old sticks-in-the-mud, but the result was something right out of the medieval era, and played just about as well with technology.

Normally Logan kind of liked the cut-off feeling he got when he was inside Haven. But there was nothing relaxing about being here today, at least not for Logan.

Jessica was out there. Unprotected and at the mercy of his enemies. Logan worried he'd made a fatal error—fatal for her that is. Trying to find a compromise between what the council would want and what he could stomach, he blocked her memories of the demon and made it virtually impossible to keep her safe. She had no idea the extent of the danger she was in. And she certainly wasn't going to let him help her, not when her opinion of him had plummeted from an already dubious person of interest to stalker. It didn't matter that he saved her from her two other attackers. In her mind, what obviously mattered was that he'd been following her.

He should have erased all her memories. Then at least he could have continued to discreetly follow her. As it was, however, she'd be watching for him and be just as apt to drag him in and stick him in a cell then to let him protect her.

"It was nice of you to show up, even if you were late."

Logan lifted his head. The room was empty, the others having finally left after the long meeting. Logan would have gone too, anxious to get out and see if he'd missed any messages, but one look at his father's face as he started to stand had been enough to make him sit back down.

Better to just get the verbal whipping over with. Logan had been late for the weekly council meeting after having missed the last one. Such infractions by the future leader of the council did not set a very good example, and were, therefore, completely unacceptable to his father. As the last pure-blooded Paladin, Logan would follow in his father's footsteps, whether he wanted to or not.

Funny, he'd never minded the responsibilities of that fate before.

"I was unavoidably detained," he said, slipping the cell phone back into his jeans pocket.

His father's brow winged up. "By something more important than your duties? My, you shall have to tell me about it."

Yeah, as if that would happen. His father would definitely not want to know about the human who occupied all of Logan's waking hours—as well as most of his non-waking ones—for the last couple days. Not that dallying with a human would set his old man off—his father knew better than to play pot and kettle—but the fact that he allowed this particular one to become such a distraction?

Logan was still trying to rack his brain for a reasonable and acceptable excuse that could be twisted to fit within the confines of the truth when his father spoke again, startling him.

"Alex tells me you had to put a block on a human's memories the other night."

Logan blinked, barely managing to snuff the rest of his reaction. "We ran into her on the streets while chasing a succubus."

"So Alex said." His father leaned back in his seat, his eyes earnest as he looked at his son. "What Alex also said was that you ran into her again the next day."

"We did," he answered after a moment of hesitation. Damn, couldn't Alex have given him a heads up on what exactly had been told to his father? Yeah, it would've been nice if the warrior could have not said anything at all, but truthfully, Logan didn't expect that. His father was a tenacious bastard when it came to extracting information, and lately Logan and his activities were of primary interest. Especially since learning that Logan had associated with a vampire for the last ninety-four years...even if that vampire was once one of their own.

His father waited a couple beats, swirling the brandy in his glass. "I understand also that you recently saw your sister?"

"And if I did?" Logan asked.

"Nothing." His father looked down at the amber

liquid, as if it held all the answers to his questions. "I just wondered how she is."

Logan folded his hands in front of him on the table. This was new. His father never asked about Karissa. Never. The fact that he did was a major breakthrough. One that sparked hope in Logan that the messed up family unit they had could someday be salvaged.

"You could ask her yourself," he suggested carefully.

His father waved his hand, his tone suggesting he was sorry he'd said anything. "It doesn't matter. Not after what that thing did to her."

Logan's fingers curled against the hardwood. He had to breathe deeply and force them back open. Calm and logical won with his father, not emotion. "It's Roland. And he is one of us."

His father slammed the glass down on the table, liquid sloshing onto the dark wood. "He is a vampire!"

"Not quite. Not any longer. Nor is your daughter."

"Close enough," he growled, picking up the glass, his hand rolling it on its edge against the table.

Logan clamped his mouth shut, a headache almost immediately brewing from how tightly he clenched his teeth. Nothing he said was going to change his father's opinion. He waited as his father continued to play with his glass, then frowned as he realized he'd never actually seen his father sip from the glass. Not once. Not today. Not last week, month, or year…not in ninety-four years.

Mother. He hasn't had a drink since Mother died. Logan wasn't quite sure of the importance of that other than it seemed ass backwards. Shouldn't his father be trying to drown his sorrows in liquor not sobriety?

Ahhh. Control. His father prided himself on his control. The liquor was a test to see if he still possessed it. A proof that he still had it and would not succumb to his emotions. Logan wasn't sure whether to be proud of his father's control or be concerned by it. It was that sort of control, after all, that had allowed the senior Calhoun to take a mixed-blood human lover, impregnate her for the sole purpose of producing offspring capable of becoming a Paladin warrior, then subsequently turn his back on both child and mother when they became unacceptable in his eyes.

"She is good then?" Calhoun Senior asked.

Logan cleared his throat, pressing this discovery and the grief that gripped him at the thought of his deceased parent to the back of his mind. "Karissa is doing exceptionally well. Her bond with Roland has curbed any unwanted cravings she suffers."

His father's lip curled back in disgust at the mention of cravings. Logan ignored it, continuing, "Her powers are also becoming stronger. Her empathy has increased in range and sensitivity and she can teleport with a lot less effort now."

His father's only answer was a back of the throat hum and a rhythmic tap on the table.

"She could use some training."

His father looked at him sharply. "You just said she was doing well. Increasing in power even."

"Yes, but her sensitivity to others' emotions is taking its toll." He waited a beat for his father to mull that over before offering his suggestion. "Bennett is an empath. He could teach her to shield properly."

Logan's father laughed at that. "Bennett, like most

of your brothers, thrives on spilling vampire blood. He would as soon kill her as train her."

"Bennett has already agreed to teach her if the council will approve."

His father's lips thinned at this little surprise. He became quiet for a long while. Long enough that Logan nearly stood up to leave him to his thoughts, but then his father said sharply, "Tell me about this human woman. Did there seem to be any slippage in your memory block when she saw you again?"

Logan tried to hide his flinch of surprise, but must have failed as his father sat up straighter, his jaw tensing as he stared down the table at his son.

"Well?"

"It didn't slip," he replied, shifting minutely in his seat.

"Then why do you seem so concerned?"

"I'm not, it's just…" He leaned forward, hesitating for a second as he was torn between the need to know and the need to keep his interactions with Jessica private. "I've been, uh, monitoring her. To make sure I didn't have to take further steps." He didn't offer what sort of steps those were—let his father figure it had to do with keeping the Paladin's existence secret. "Anyway, last night she had another encounter. This time with a couple vampires *and* a demon."

His father set his cup down with a snap. "A demon? You're telling me a demon paired up with a couple vampires and went after a human?"

Logan nodded.

His father pulled at his bottom lip. "And you're sure she has no Paladin blood?"

"Positive. Which is why I don't understand why the demon and vampires would be working together. The vampires, yes, because the case she's working on might have some tie-in, but I highly doubt Ganelon would have interest enough in that to send in his demons. Especially without a strong vampire leader anymore to request such a favor."

His father's eyes narrowed. "To clarify, you were following her when this attack occurred."

"Well, yes. Like I said, I wanted to—"

"And did the demon attack with the vampires or after?"

Logan sucked in a breath as a horrible churning started in his gut. "It, uh, went after her as I was dispatching the vampires."

"Have you lost your mind, Logan? Of course the demon attacked her. That demon probably followed you *to* her. You know they'll use humans as collateral damage if it means gaining advantage in a fight." His father shook his head in disgust. "I assume you dispatched the demon."

Logan inclined his head, unable to pass enough air through his tightening esophagus to form words.

"Good. Then she should be safe. Ganelon can't exactly question the thing if you purged it with His light."

And all that tightness and churning froze over into icy shards in his stomach. The entire room spun to the point where he had to place both hands on the table, lowering his head.

Oh God, what had he done? He *hadn't* used His light. He'd panicked and relied on a traditional banishment spell instead. That demon was currently boiling down in Hell's tar pit of souls, and though it would take a sacrifice to resurrect the creature into form and substance, it could be done, especially if Ganelon wanted his demonic soldier back badly enough and was willing to pay the price. And given who the creature had been assigned to trail—Logan, one of the hated Calhouns— then there was a damn good chance Ganelon would be willing to do whatever sort of groveling it took to get the creature into his torture chamber.

Oh fuck. Fuck! If Jessica wasn't already in danger, Logan had certainly put her there. Ganelon was going to get ahold of that demon, and it was going to tell Lucifer's General about Logan's unhealthy obsession with a certain NYC cop. At that point, whether the vampire attacks were coincidence or not wouldn't matter anymore because Ganelon would not pass up the chance for revenge. Not when he could fuck over the grandson of one his most hated rivals by going after Logan's mate. Logan's *human* mate.

"Logan!"

Logan sat up, realizing his father had said his name a couple times now. "What?"

His father was looking at him with narrowed eyes and a suspicious pinch around his nose. "The human? She won't remember this either, will she?"

A muscle in Logan's jaw spasmed. Of all the things for his father to worry over, he would worry about that? But of course, it made sense. His father didn't know what she meant to him. Not yet. "No. I blocked the encounter with the demon from her memories."

"Well then I wouldn't worry about it. As long as your memory wipe holds, we won't have to do anything more."

Logan tensed, his eyes narrowing on his father. "What do you mean anything more?"

"What do you think I mean, Logan? You know we cannot allow a mere human to know of our existence."

Yeah, he did. But duty be damned, he was coming to the realization that he might have no choice but to break that most honored rule. He'd fallen for a human. A full human. And one in danger from an evil she couldn't comprehend, didn't believe in, and, warrior that she was, wouldn't allow him to protect her from. And now he endangered her from another front too, because the thought of what his father might do if he had an inkling of his son's growing emotional attachment to "a mere human" came to mind—none of them good.

He can't find out. Ever. Nor would Logan allow her to die. Not when he had the means to protect her.

"This woman, is there anything else you need to tell me about her?"

"No." Logan shook his head as he stood, pushing his chair back from the council table for perhaps the last time. "Nothing at all."

—⁂—

Valin stared down at the cross in his hand, the citrine gem embedded in its center catching and reflecting the flames of the hearth's fire. He was alone in the rarely used room—a catchall for all kinds of interesting things. Most Paladin were either too young, not powerful enough, or not smart enough to inquire about the sorts of treasures buried amongst the junk. Valin figured Calhoun senior didn't realize he knew about the room either—most likely because the elder lumped Valin in with the later group—and doubt-lessly would have a shit fit if he knew the Black Knight had been in here uncountable times to handle the holy objects hidden within. As if he might taint them with his darkness. Whatever.

Valin still remembered the shock Calhoun Senior got when Valin had been presented this very cross as part of the ceremony into joining the Paladin ranks. The stuck-up prick had probably assumed Valin was going to stand there, hopelessly clenching the inert relic for a time, before eventually tucking tail and tak-ing himself forevermore from Haven's sacred halls. What fun it had been to see the old man's jaw drop open when the relic came alive at his request, bathing him with His holy light. And yeah, Valin probably didn't need to rub his acceptance into the Paladin ranks with that over-the-top speech about how much he looked forward to serving Him and His chosen council with the use of his "unconventional" gifts, but he had, and been on the head councilmember's shit list ever since.

Yeah, he'd definitely made his bed that day. The only thing that had made lying in it palatable was the presence of Angeline. With his acceptance as a Paladin had also come the ability to court her properly. Less than a month later he and Angeline were joined in the ceremony that proclaimed them pair bonded. And everything was golden and perfect for a good hundred years.

Until she died.

Valin ran his thumb over the carved etchings on the arms of the cross. Theoretically, if he held nothing but hope in his heart and a willingness to serve, speaking the ancient tongue aloud would open a gateway into His realm. Though, if he were discovered using it for anything other than ceremony he'd probably be kicked out of Haven—if not the brotherhood itself. Hell, there was a good chance it wouldn't work anyway. He may be a Paladin, but there had always been a blight on his soul. A darkness that, even the first time, during his triumphant moment of acceptance, kept him from ever being comfortable in His light. And since the loss of Angeline?

Fuck. He wanted, no, needed to talk to her. More than his pair bond, she'd been his best friend. The one person he could really talk to and not feel like he was being judged. But what would he tell her? *God I miss you, Angeline. Both you and Peanut. Though you'll be happy to hear I'm finally accepting what happened. That I'm ready to try and live again. See, I think I may have finally found my true mate. Messed up, right, that I'm telling you this? Only I know you're probably up there cheering me on. Except, maybe not. See, there is a little problem. She's also a vampire and most likely a merker too. Oh, and though her soul is older, it happens to be trapped in the body of a teenager.*

Yeah. That was just… messed up.

More likely the turbulent emotions he felt for the vamp were simply protectiveness. Seeing her in danger last summer, a hairsbreadth from death and still fighting… it had struck a chord in him. Here she was, proof that one could be of darkness and still fight for the light. He'd freed her, and then she'd helped him and Roland save Karissa. And then, before he could properly analyze why she had affected him so, she'd disappeared.

Until the other night. Or so he'd thought, for a brief moment. A very brief moment when he'd first seen the succubus.

But it wasn't Gabby. Couldn't be. The woman they chased *was* a succubus through and through. Not vampire, like Gabby. Yet something in the way she held herself, the angle of her head, the cock of her hip, echoed a memory from another dim street not that long ago. He hadn't been able to resist the brush of his mind on hers, thinking maybe, just maybe…but all that brief touch had shown him was darkness. Death disguised as sex: the very mark of a succubus.

That was what convinced him it couldn't be Gabby. If she was tainted with that much darkness, she wouldn't have survived Logan's calling of the light in those mines last summer.

The door banged open, and as if his thoughts drew him, Logan stepped into the room. Valin's hand clenched around the cross as he quickly shoved it into the cushions of the couch he sat on. A musty old couch that was rarely used, which meant the resultant stirring of dust made him sneeze.

Logan ground to a halt just inside the door, his gaze zeroing in sharply on where Valin sat.

"Valin," he said, his shoulders seeming to ease slightly as he realized who it was in the room with him.

"Hey, Logan." Valin tossed a leg up onto the stack of tomes in front of him. Logan's gaze flickered to them, disapproval tightening the skin around his nose, but he didn't say anything.

"Do I want to know why you're in here?" Logan asked carefully.

"Probably not. Though no worries. I will take nothing but what I brought in with myself when I leave."

Logan shrugged, moving past him into the room. "Really, not my business."

And okay, life as Valin knew it had just ended. Did Mr. Goody Two-Shoes, next in line as major-stick-in-the-mud just say something wasn't his business?

In an amazing act of personal restraint, Valin clamped back the quip that sprang to his tongue and watched as Calhoun Senior's pride and joy (okay, maybe not joy, that man didn't seem to take pleasure in anything) ruthlessly stripped daddy dearest's shields off the trunk in the back of the room. A pop of the physical lock and few seconds of rifling later and Logan had his favorite knife in hand and, after a moment to test the sharpness of his blade, was stuffing it and its holster deep into the folds of a wadded-up sheet he grabbed from the floor. Valin's eyebrows rose even farther when the Paladin then dug back into the trunk and pulled out a smaller, but no less lethal knife and hid that in the sheet too.

Well, damn. Logan was disobeying a direct order, wasn't he?

Valin blinked, wondering if when he opened his eyes again Logan wouldn't be there. Like maybe he was asleep and—

"Do you know where Alex is?" Logan asked, letting the lid drop with a loud bang.

Guess not.

Valin shrugged. "I think he's still trying to sleep off those cracked ribs somewhere."

"Good. I have something I need to take care of tonight. I'll contact you both tomorrow."

"Anything I can help with?"

Logan didn't answer, simply stared at him with those damn steely gray eyes of his that made him look eerily like his father.

"All right. Anything you want me to do while you're off doing your thing?"

"You can start by putting the cross back."

Crap. Busted. Only…Valin let his gaze drift to the bundle Logan held conspicuously against his thigh. Tit for tat, anyone? "Okay. But can I suggest using this instead of a sheet?" He grabbed up a nearby canister of worthless maps, tossing it toward the Paladin. "Would probably fit."

Logan grabbed the canister out of the air and opened it up. "Thanks," he said as he dumped out the contents and rearranged the blades inside. When he was done he looked back at Valin, indecision plainly written on his face.

Valin arched a brow in question.

"Actually, there is something you can do for me," Logan said.

"Yeah, what's that?"

"You could make yourself scarce until I next contact you."

Valin felt his mouth tugging into a grin. A favor for Logan that was bound to twist Senior's panties? Oh yeah, he could definitely do that. And while he was out, maybe he'd go and check out that area where they ran into the succubus the other night.

—∿∿—

Jessica didn't move for a good hour, leaning on her hood, staring at the deserted block of run-down buildings as she wrestled with the block of pain that kept her from her memories. So far, nothing had come of it. The afternoon had worn through, giving over to the early fall evening. The ME van left with the CSU team. All that remained was a squad car wrapping up the scene. It was time for her to go. Only she didn't know where. It was obvious Mike didn't want her help. Not now. And she was not going to go to some damn doctor. Not yet, at least. Not until she figured out what the heck was going on.

The missing time after the alley, her encounter with those freaky jerks and their fake teeth and that third man—who according to Logan wasn't even fucking there—and now this? It felt like it was beat-down-Jessica week. And, as if that weren't enough, queue Mr. Calhoun himself. He and his damn stormy gray eyes were probably the most unnerving things of her entire week. There was just something about him that made her suck in a breath and her hands break out in a warm sweat. She'd think it was her realization that he'd obviously taken to following her, which was admittedly unnerving, but it had started before then. From the moment she'd bumped into him by those vending machines, she had a strange feeling that not only had she met him before, but that somehow she knew him on a level that she damn well knew was impossible.

Logan Calhoun was not the type of man you forgot. And she had an exceptional memory. Well, most of the time.

She rolled her shoulders. Damn it. Why couldn't she remember what happened the other night?

Even that thought brought the pain with it. She pinched the bridge of her nose, trying to breathe through the spiking pressure that ran down from her frontal lobe into her brain stem. This was pointless and useless. There were no clues here beyond what they already took for the investigation. She should leave. Told herself to. But the moment she turned and put her hand on the door handle she swore, jerking it back.

Not without some answers.

With no idea as to what else she could do to find them, she began to walk down the street, heading in the direction she would've taken as she drove away. She'd walked perhaps a half block before the first signs of civilization returned—a pimped out 1980s Bentley thumping with an oversized woofer as it made its way down the cross street. Another half block and the buildings lost some of their desperate edge; broken windows were replaced by boarded-up ones, then soon after, grimy single pane glass. She even saw a couple of street kids dart furtively into one of them, their high-pitched, prepubescent voices announcing they'd made her for what she was by sounding the alarm to whatever elicit activity was going on inside.

She strode on. Up ahead a large black man in a long trench coat stood in front of a black security gate that protected the glass front door of a shop, his overdeveloped muscles straining as he tried to juggle three good-sized boxes. Jessica paused. The man dug into the unevenly faded coat, then fumbled with a large set of keys as he tried to fit it into the lock. A dozen curses later the protective barrier swung open as well as the glass door and he struggled inside with his burden. Lights flicked on. Then, a moment later, a humming neon sign announced adult toys and movies.

Jessica cocked her head, her eyes taking in the shabby storefront. It was nothing much, but it was more than any of its neighbors could lay claim to. What's more, it had one of those bulky white security cameras proudly on display in the front window.

A place like that was bound to open late and stay open late. And even if it was closed, it was likely that those security cameras stayed on.

Jessica strode toward the door, her back stiff with determination. She pulled open the black security door, the hinges squeaking, the glass door opened more easily. Other than that one squeak, there was no little bell to announce her entrance, no buzzer either, and the dim lighting and rows of narrow shelves begged to be hidden in. She might've thought the store owner was going for discreet and anonymous for his clientele. Except the front window security camera was not the only one playing watch dog.

Better and better. Unless they were fake, of course.

"Can I help you?"

She turned to see the owner coming out of a side door. Probably led to a staircase and a second-floor storage area. The man had shrugged out of his trench coat and wore black jeans to match his black leather vest, which held in his advancing waistline beneath his stained, white undershirt. Not that he was fat. Simply big, and if the scars and tats he sported were any indication, he was a fighter before he retired to the good life of pimping porn.

The man folded his arms, muscles flexing over them as he stared her down, his eyes telling her he knew exactly who, or rather what, she was. There was nothing threatening in the look, simply a man telling a potential challenger that this was his territory and he wasn't going to take shit from any outsider—whether they wore a shield or not.

"Am I that obvious?" She went for direct, quirking her lip slightly to show him that she wasn't here to make his day bad.

"Maybe not, but the bulge under your jacket is. That coupled with the excitement down the street earlier today…" He shrugged, his shoulders rolling as he strode stiffly across the room—all that muscle, and he probably had bad knees from fighting which explained the expanding girth.

Jessica waited until he'd maneuvered behind the counter by the register, figuring he'd feel better with his own shield of authority in front of him, even if it was just one of those un-sturdy glass display cases. There were all kinds of interesting things in the cabinet. Things Jessica chose not to stare at too long. Who really used that crap anyway?

"I was hoping I could take a look at your video feed from the other night." No need to explain why. If he already knew about the commotion, then he knew she was homicide and looking for any lead she could get.

He rolled one hand within the other, cracking the knuckles. For a second Jessica got a horrible feeling that maybe she'd done it again. Misjudged the situation and was quickly sinking in over her head, but then he nodded, muttering an unenthusiastic, but not exactly disagreeable, "Yeah, okay."

She resisted the urge to shift impatiently as the owner rifled through a black lock box behind the counter. There didn't appear to be much in it. Some more keys, papers, a couple dozen of those mini-VHS tapes. He pulled one of these out that said "Tuesday-B" on it but no date. Probably had just enough tapes for a week.

"Old system," she said as he popped open a cabinet and pulled out an ancient, handheld video recorder similar to the one she grew up with.

He grunted. "Not much new around here."

True. And beggars shouldn't be choosers. She'd take what she could get.

"There are two tapes for that night. But I'm guessing you want the second half of it. Midnight on?"

Her brow rose halfway to her hairline. Least it felt like it. "How do you conclude that?"

He arched his own brow in retaliation, but otherwise ignored her as he fiddled with the video recorder. It didn't take him long and then he was swiveling the view finder around to her.

"Here. This is what you're looking for, right?" He pressed play and Jessica bent closer to stare at the grainy picture on the screen. For a few more seconds there was nothing more than the deader-than-a-morgue street scene outside, but then a figure dashed by, a female, dressed to kill—a man's wallet that is, definitely not his libido. A couple seconds later two men dashed by. One a big-ass son of a bitch and then another, not as tall, but mean and lean looking, dressed in form-fitting black.

Jessica's hand absently moved toward her gun, anger punching through her even though she knew this was something in the past and she could do nothing about it. The prostitute didn't look like anything more than a kid and those men…

Another figure scooted by, keeping low and hugging the shadows while still trying to make a decent pursuit. It took a moment for it to click; the figure never turned toward the store and was visible only a couple seconds, but then it hit her. The familiar ill-fitting blazer, the cant of the shoulders as if the person held a gun out in front of them, and the hair.

No fucking way.

"Play that again."

The guy rewound, zipping past the last pursuer and all the way to the beginning, most likely assuming she was concerned with the original three persons in the video. Not that he wasn't right, but they weren't the ones putting the chill of horror in her veins. How could she have pursued a pair of possible rapists and not remembered?

Yet there she was, sneaking by the front of the shop once more. Holy crap.

"Again?" he asked when she'd slid out of sight on the video. She nodded. And this time when he played the tape she paid more attention to the other three, straining her eyes to make out more in the fuzzy picture. Damn. They were too far away to make out any real facial features, yet…

"Is this in color on a big screen?"

"Nope. Sorry."

Of course not. Not that it would've really mattered, there wasn't enough light on the street to make much difference. Still, there was something decidedly familiar about those men. Especially the second one.

Yeah, maybe because you chased them down the friggin' street, Jess?

"Can you zoom in on the men at all?"

"Yeah, but they're low-res images, so you won't get much detail." He did what she asked, and though the face was still fuzzy…what was it about the second man that made her think she knew him? As in *knew* knew him.

She closed her eyes, concentrating hard on the images, but the more she tried the more they slipped away and the more her headache grew.

Damn it. If she could just remember…

Didn't matter. She had the evidence that something else had happened that night. Something that might account for the missing gap in her memories. Or at least give her a place to start.

"Can I have this?" she asked the owner.

The tattooed goliath shrugged. "Sure. What the hell."

His agreeability surprised her somewhat, but she didn't question it. She almost grabbed the tape and bolted, but then remembering Mike's warning about illegal collection of evidence she took a deep breath and told the shopkeeper she'd be right back. It took her fewer than five minutes to dash back down the street and get her car and get back to the shop. Digging through the piles of paperwork scattered across her backseat, she finally found the form she wanted and pushed back into the shop. She was still Tattoo Guy's only customer so he didn't grumble too much as she carefully filled out the form, having him sign it before tearing off the receipt and giving it to him. Next she popped the security tape into a plastic bag along with the rest of the paperwork. Then, with a thanks and a good-bye to her agreeable host, left.

Her heart was still thudding as she closed her car

door, tucking the new evidence into the passenger seat beside her. She didn't know why she was so keyed up. Even if those two men had anything to do with the victim in the alley, with this much distance between here and there it wasn't going to be much of a lead. Still, it held some answers, though a hundred additional questions for each one it answered.

"Where else have I seen that man?" she asked softly of the small gray tape. As expected, it remained stubbornly silent.

Sighing, she put the car in gear and drove around aimlessly, zigzagging back and forth along the various cross streets, driving past a group of abandoned buildings and their struggling counterparts that refused to join them in their early graves. She must have driven for well over an hour, but never left a half-mile radius of the alley, her route decided by the piercing pain in her head that signaled forgotten familiarity.

This street. Not that one. Right there, that lone street lamp shining among its broken friends. The headache spiked. She pulled the car over, staring at the small disc of illuminated cement and pavement. Two men. Both taller than her. One practically a giant, flanking her on silent feet. The other—

Pain split across her forehead, driving a stake deep into her skull. "Goddamn it!"

She clutched her head, breath hissing between her teeth as she fought to hold the image over the pain. Smug bastard. Smug, handsome bastard. Face didn't fit his clothes though. Too refined, too…

She sucked in a breath, logic fighting against what she wanted to believe. Or rather, what she didn't want to believe. Just like the idea of vampires was impossible, so was this.

Hand shaking with a mix of anger, betrayal, and denial, Jess dug into the back pocket of her jeans, pulling out the mangled card. She had to turn on the overhead light to read the smaller script under the name, but soon enough she'd tapped in the number and was pressing the phone against her ear. It rang once, twice. Her hand shook, a shaky breath rattling in her tight chest. Jessica stared out at the dimly lit sidewalk, using the pain to steady her. Finally he answered, his voice breathless, the sound of thumping music in the background, not like a stereo, but rather a nightclub.

The Logan she knew didn't seem the type to cruise clubs. But the one in the videos? The one who had leered at her as he dusted off his...

Black skintight tee, black leather pants, black shit-kicker boots.

"Jessica? Is that you? Where are you? Are you okay?"

Her fingers tightened on phone. She dragged her gaze from the flickering streetlight, forcing her eyes ahead. "I'm here."

There was a burst of static, then silence, his voice sounding kind of echoey when he spoke again. "Where? Where is here?"

She rattled off an address, ending with a curt, "Can you be there in an hour?"

"Are you in trouble?"

She didn't answer, closing her eyes as she pulled up the grainy image of the security tape in her mind again. Superimposing it with the up close and personal look she'd gotten of the lines of his face in his bed that morning. Oh yeah. It was definitely him. And he definitely had some answers to give.

"Jessica?"

"No. I'm not in trouble." She cut the call. *But you are.*

Chapter 12

JESSICA MADE HER WAY DOWN THE ROUGH-CUT STAIRS, refusing to respond any faster to the pounding on the front door. She'd just arrived and barely finished setting things up when headlights flashed across the loft's lone window. Probably for the best, if she was alone much longer she might have time to wallow in the memories. The beach house, squeezed in between two sets of oceanfront condos on Long Beach, had been in her family for decades. At 1,500 square feet, it was still small by prime oceanfront standards, but it had served for years as a retreat for her family, a place to catch some sun, waves, and sand to escape the demands of the high-energy city. No one had been in it for a while. Technically, the place belonged to her grandmother, but since she was in a nursing home, Jessica knew it was only a matter of time before it was sold. Her parents wouldn't keep it after grandma passed; the place held too many memories they couldn't bear.

The pounding grew louder, more insistent. He was going to break the darn thing. She leapt off the last couple steps, sprinted to the door, and jerked it open. He lowered his hand, blowing out a deep breath.

"Jessica." His large hands closed over her shoulders as he took her in. Every inch of her. And though there was nothing sensual in his perusal, only concern, her body betrayed her, heat coalescing in her center. Damn it. This was beyond stupid. She was stupid. After every-thing she'd learned about him in the last twelve hours, how could it be that she was still attracted to him?

"Are you okay?" he asked.

She quirked her head, considering his high anxiety level. "I told you I was fine."

She shrugged out of his hold, retreating a good five feet, knowing the only reason she was able to do so was because he'd let her. The man was strong, and in those tight jeans and carelessly untucked button-down, sexy enough to wake a half-dead granny's lust levels from sub-zero to boiling with a touch alone. She needed seri-ous mental help to be even thinking the thoughts she was currently having about those calloused hands.

Answers. She'd asked him here for answers, not a roll on her grandmother's braided throw rug.

His jaw rolled. He started to take a step, then paused, looking at her inquisitively. "May I come in?"

"Yes," she gestured briskly into the sheet-draped great room, "of course. I actually wanted to show you something."

His expression grew wary but he came in, closing the door behind him. She turned, walking stiffly in front of him. Now that he was here she didn't want to go through with this. That little concerned routine at the door had made serious inroads in her resolve. A resolve that was weak at best. One look at him and she was ready to for-give and forget. What was it with this man that seemed to fry all her brain cells?

And no, great abs is not an answer, she told her-self firmly.

Practically stomping, she led him up into the loft,

waiting by the top of the stairs for him to step into the open area. The wood here was left bare on the wide-planked pine flooring and the rafters above, and didn't match with the shabby-chic décor of the rest of the house. Which was fine. The loft had been her and Julia's space. It was crammed with their stuff, well, mostly Julia's stuff. Used as an artist's retreat, at least three-quarters of it was stuffed full of both new and used can-vases, drying out paints, jars of turpentine, and a wobbly antique table spread with every shape and size of brush a painter could want, often in duplicate. Simply seeing them punched Jessica in the gut. All that talent. All that passion and imagination. Gone. Forever.

Damn, Julia. I miss you so much.

It was the only place in the house with a TV though, since technology had all but been outlawed here.

Jessica had already braved the loft and set up the recorder to the TV. It sat, sound off and black static roll-ing, waiting for her to hit play. Luckily the family's old hand-held video recorder still worked. That, more than anything, was why she chose the beach house. Though she was beginning to question the brilliance of invit-ing Logan out here with her. She should have come and gotten the recorder herself, then met him somewhere on neutral ground. This place was too personal, brought up too many emotions, and was obviously screwing with her head as much as his presence was.

"Wow, great space. Are these yours?" He waved his hand at the spread of half-finished canvasses.

"My sister's," she replied statically, moving quickly across the loft to the video recorder. Might as well get this over with. Besides, she needed to hear his explanation.

And if it wasn't good enough, she'd strangle him and send him out with the tide.

Jess sucked in a deep breath. What was it about this man that made her completely unreasonable? She was an intelligent woman. If she did something a bit crazy, it was because she'd thought about it and decided to do it, not because she was acting on impulse. So why was it when Logan popped into her head, it shoved everything else right out the window? Reckless, illogical…crazy.

No, really. Crazy. All she had to do was hit play on the tape to show just how crazy. How could she not remember being there? And what the heck was up with the damn headache that struck whenever she tried to piece together the image she saw on the tape and what happened that night?

And that's why she'd invited Logan here. She had to figure it out. Her sanity depended on it. Her *job* depended on it.

Logan was her answer. He'd been there. Logically, they must've interacted. Hell, he'd probably been how she'd gotten home—it would certainly explain how he knew where her apartment was. What she didn't understand was what he was doing there in the first place. Why was he dressed in those weird clothes? Why was he chasing that woman? And why would a man, so seemingly bent on ill intentions, turn around and drive her home, then tuck her safely into her own bed?

Worse, why had she let him?

She rubbed her breast bone. Damn it. She didn't want him to be a criminal. Didn't want to believe she was so weak she'd allow an unprecedented attraction get in the way of all her hard work and training. But that was exactly what she was doing, wasn't it? This meeting to figure things out was as much for his benefit as hers. The truth was she hoped he'd be able to give her a perfectly good, logical reason for all the crap that had happened.

"Jessica?"

She cleared her throat, turning to him. He was studying her warily; his shoulders tense as if ready to either spring for her or the door. Having already seen him in action, Jess didn't bother to put her hand on her gun. If he decided to attack her, she doubted she'd even get a shot off. If he ran?

He won't run. He won't attack me either. And wasn't she the Queen of Wishful Thinking?

"Do you remember when we met in the precinct?" she asked, leaning against the rickety card table holding the VHS equipment. "How I mentioned it had been a long day after a long night?"

"Yes…" he replied, the word drawn out like she was being facetious. Not quite. She didn't feel like fencing with him though, the tension and uncertainty were eating at any sort of calm or finesse, so she cut right to the chase.

"Why were you there that night?" she asked.

"I don't know what you're talking about." The way he answered was so perfectly confused, just the slightest shake of his head, a nice furrow between his eyes. He either honestly didn't know or he had some great acting classes in his education.

She rubbed her head. She had another stupid headache. For a girl not prone to such things, it was getting annoying.

"Tuesday night, or rather early Wednesday, I pursued

two men chasing a woman…" She pulled up the image in her mind again. The scared young prostitute, the giant, then…Logan. Her head snapped up, heart skipping. "Damn it, I'm so stupid. Your friend's lawyer! He was the other man and you…it was him with you in the Bronx that night, wasn't it?"

Logan jerked back, his head shaking in denial. "What would a lawyer, or I for that matter, be doing in the Bronx at night chasing a woman?"

He hesitated only a split second before reacting, but it was enough, and frankly even if there weren't that moment of hesitation, she would've known. It was such a blatant evasion that anyone, let alone a cop, could see right through it.

Acid pooled in her stomach, threatening to send its contents into upheaval. She was so seriously stupid. She'd invited him here hoping, despite all the evidence to the contrary, that he could somehow explain away all the uneasy thoughts she'd had about him. But this proved it. He couldn't. And now she didn't know if every encounter they'd had since was simply because he was a sick fuck who got his nuts off stalking—and probably eventually chasing and raping—women or if there was something even more nefarious going on.

"Did you kill that man in the Dumpster?" she asked, her stomach twisting with a sick kind of hurt. If he'd been part of their newest victim's demise then it stood to reason that he was part of a setup from the beginning. That everything that happened, the come-on in the station, "saving" her in the garage, were all been part of a strategy to get her to trust him and ultimately find out what Grim or his informant might've told her. She supposed it was better than killing her outright, but it still hurt to think she was just some mark to him.

Confusion set in on his face, his brows scrunching together. "Man in a Dumpster?"

More prevaricating. "Do your buddies with the designer canines get their kicks pretending to be vamps? Did our victim in the Dumpster decide he was sick of getting gnawed on for fun and get killed for wanting out?"

"What victim and what Dumpster?" he demanded, his voice edged with frustration.

"The informant I was supposed to be meeting." She went on to describe the murder victim—or at least, what she could of him, but all Logan did was shake his head.

"Scars on his neck?" Logan's brow furrowed, his lips thinning as if pieces of puzzles were clicking together. "Does this informant have something to do with your Rhodes case?"

She clamped her mouth shut, cursing herself for giving away that little scar detail, though really, anyone who knew the man would've seen them, they were pretty damn obvious, and there wasn't much else to describe.

"I've never met the man," he said firmly, "and I certainly didn't kill him."

She narrowed her eyes, testing the truth of the words. She believed him. The relief of that had her relaxing, her heart falling into a slow steady rhythm as the vise around it eased. Until her gaze caught the static on the screen.

"Okay…but you still haven't told me what you were doing in the Bronx that night."

His brow rose. "What makes you think I was there?"

She folded her arms around her stomach, saying with her eyes what she couldn't with her mouth: "Try again."

He threw his arms up, looking to the ceiling as if he were asking for vast amounts of patience in face of her great insanity. "According to you, I was chasing some woman."

"Weren't you?" She reached out, pressing the play button. The static turned into a fuzzy picture. She didn't have to watch it, having already memorized every detail. Instead she observed him as his eyes caught on the screen, the flare of disbelief before his mouth clamped shut, how his entire body tightened up like a coiled spring.

Can't deny it now, can you, asshole?

Her heart joined her stomach back in the squeeze box. She closed her eyes, trying to hold in the sickness with her arms wrapped around her stomach as the tape played its irrefutable proof. Damn. Damn. Damn. She didn't want him to be a bad guy. Kiss and dimples aside, there was something about him. Something that called to her, drew her in. Something that made her want to trust him. Made her *want* him. But whatever that thing was, it wasn't real. Couldn't be real.

But, God, she wanted it to be.

"Jessica, I swear to you..."

She held up a hand, stalling him. "Whatever you're about to say, don't. We both know it's going to be another twisted lie, and I can't take three in one night. Not from you."

"Three." He cleared his throat. "So you think I've lied twice tonight. What are you, a polygraph test now?"

She opened her eyes again facing him head on. "Am I wrong?"

She took a deep breath, drawing to her full height as she tried to ease the kinks in her innards. And there was that pall of silence again. She figured she should probably kick him out since really, what more was there to say? It was obvious he wasn't going to tell her the truth and it was just as obvious she couldn't trust him. In fact, as soon as she got him out the door—and locked it—she'd call Mike and tell him everything. And she did mean everything. Even if the cost was her badge.

What makes you think you're going to get this man out of here?

She started to shift toward the stairs, not quite willing to turn her back on him but intent on reminding him of the way to the door, when Logan's resolute tone brought her up short.

"I know Roland didn't kill Thomas Rhodes because I know who did. And yes, I was there in the Bronx…but Alex and I were *not* chasing a helpless woman."

She sucked in a breath. It took her a couple moments to collect her thoughts enough to form a coherent response to that. Yeah, she wanted the truth, but when the truth was that bad? What did he hope to gain by admitting it? Unless he wanted to play the repentant criminal.

"Were you, uh," she licked her lips. "Were you involved in Tom's death then?"

He looked completely taken aback, and she knew his hesitation was from honest surprise and not manipulation.

"God, no." He shook his head vigorously in denial. "Why would you even think that?"

"Because you just said that you knew who it was and whether you admit it or not I know you *were* chasing a woman," she pointed out.

His head continued to shake, slower but firmly. "She wasn't a helpless woman."

"What was she then, a hermaphrodite?"

He smiled thinly at that but immediately wiped it off by rubbing a hand down over his face. When he looked at her again his eyes were serious, and sad. The kind of sad that spoke of a hurt beyond repair. The kind she felt when she thought of her sister never being there again. She had to ruthlessly stomp on the urge to soften. She didn't get it. How could what they were discussing have anything to do with that sort of pain?

"You wouldn't believe me if I told you."

She gritted her teeth, starting away from him again but he grabbed her arm. "Jessica, wait."

Something about the tone of his voice made her hesitate.

"I swear I'm not that man. I'm not a criminal."

"So say ninety-eight percent of the felons I've put behind bars," she retorted with a jerk of her arm, but even to her ears it sounded more like a plea for him to prove that he was in the other two percent.

"Nothing, *nothing* I have done or said was meant to harm you. If anything, I've only wanted to keep you safe."

He seemed so damn sincere, but…

She tipped her head back, sucking in a breath at the deep storm residing in his eyes. It was as if she could physically feel the despair in his gaze. It plucked at something in her chest, echoing his ache. Heartache. That's what it was. Somehow, someway, despite all the red flags that should have scared her off from him, she cared. At least enough that it hurt that she was going to have to turn the tape in and thereby implicate him.

Because whether he had a perfectly good reason for being there or not, whether he was being positively truthful in his desire to keep her safe, she couldn't withhold this. Not and live with herself.

"How can lying keep me safe?" she asked, the whispered words revealing how much she wanted him to fix this. She wasn't sure it was even possible, but damn she wanted him to try. She wanted to trust him. She wanted that chance.

He smiled. The weak movement, though enough to crease his dimples, did not reach the sorrow she saw in his eyes. "Ever heard the expression that sometimes you're better off not knowing?"

"I've never put much stock in that one, sorry," she replied tartly, breaking their gaze and staring pointedly down at his hand that still held her arm.

He released his grip and rubbed his temples, as if the entire conversation were giving him a headache. Well didn't that make two of them?

"I can't tell you, Jessica. Even if I wanted to." He dropped his hand helplessly. "You're just going to have to trust me."

"Trust." She laughed with the irony that he'd dare say that after all his quasi lies. "You have to earn trust."

One perfect eyebrow rose, his look one of incredulity. "Right. I've certainly given you no reason to trust me. Not when I found out you were the detective in charge and tried to walk away from you in the precinct. Not when I saved you from those men in the garage. Not when I brought you home to care for you. And certainly not when you were in my bed, your legs wrapped around me, your body pleading with me to take you and I didn't because you were not aware, were vulnerable though, God, I fucking wanted you. Correct that. Want you."

He wanted her. A hot little thrill slid down her body with the admission ending in a clenching need deep in her belly. It took all her self-control to ignore that need and focus on the conversation and one of the very, very important facts he'd left out.

"You wouldn't have been there to save me if you hadn't been stalking me."

His jaw firmed, the muscle rolling. "Not stalking."

"No? What then? Because in my world people don't follow other people around like that. Not if they don't want to be handed a restraining order."

"Bodyguards do."

She shook her head. "What? So now you've appointed yourself my bodyguard? What makes you think I need protecting?"

"Don't you?"

She planted a hand on her hip, making sure the movement pulled her jacket back enough to remind him of her gun. "No."

The word hung in the air, the stubborn tension in his jaw telling her he didn't agree with her. She expected him to say something, try to drive his point home, so it shouldn't have been a surprise when he countered with his own question, yet it took her aback anyhow.

"What were you doing in that area that first night, Jessica?" he asked, the import obviously on the fact that she'd been in a dangerous part of town and that he, at least, believed she was foolish to be there.

"You mean the street I was on when I saw you chasing some helpless woman?" she asked, her hackles rising.

He gave a self-defeating chuckle. "Not helpless. I guarantee you that."

"But you were there."

"As were you." He waited a beat, his head cocking to the side. "Why?"

"For my job. I'm a cop, remember? And contrary to popular police dramas, it's not all glamour and glory."

"But you went alone. Without backup. You telling me that's normal?"

She opened her mouth, then closed it. Really what was there to say? He was right, and though she could have come up with some sort of BS, it didn't matter. She'd already explained too much of herself and her actions. What she needed to do was kick him out so she could drive back to the station and file the evidence.

He began pacing; bringing attention to how tall and muscular he was as he ate up what little room there was under the slanted ceilings of the loft. His movements, the energy that seemed to radiate off him as he propelled himself across the space then back again, were both absorbing and fascinating. And again her opportunity to steer the conversation was foiled.

"Damn it, Jessica. Places like that are not safe. Not even when the sun is out. If you don't want me following you around ready to jump to your aid, then, for the love of all things holy, don't put yourself into such dangerous situations!"

"Now you sound like Mike." She folded her arms across her chest.

"Maybe you should listen to him." He stopped his pacing. His eyes narrowing on her. "Who is this Mike anyway?"

She blinked at him, choosing to let him stew instead of answering. He sounded jealous and darn it, she had to admit she was a little thrilled by that fact, even as she berated herself for feeling that way. How could he be the bad guy? Even though he wasn't being a hundred percent truthful, he wasn't exactly a proficient liar. She could tell where he was hedging the facts. She believed that he wasn't involved in either Rhodes's or her informant's death. She wanted to believe that his actions regarding the prostitute could be explained. She wanted to trust him. Really, really wanted to.

And why couldn't he be the good guy? Alex was a lawyer; he had to have shown his ID at the police station. What were the chances that he and Logan had been out in that part of town for the same reason she was? Did that woman they were chasing know something that Alex needed for one of his cases? Is that why they were there? For answers? Was Logan prevaricating because of some damn nondisclosure clause he'd signed with the stupid lawyer? If that were true, it shed a whole new light on this entire situation. One she might even be able to live with.

Hope riding high in her chest, she opened her mouth to ask, but Logan beat her to it.

"Why were you there, Jessica? Trying to get killed?"

She sucked in a breath, shaking her head at the absurdity of his accusation. "I wasn't trying to get killed."

"You weren't? Could have fooled me."

"Of course not!"

"Damn it, Jessica. I can't understand you. You won't tell me why you were there. You won't let me help you."

"I don't want your help."

"What do you want then? To die? What happened to you that you're so obsessed with avenging others' deaths that you don't even care about your own life?"

"I do care about my own life."

"Prove it."

She laughed. "How? Should I dance a jig? Maybe grab a bottle of wine and whoop it up on the beach?" She shook her head. "Staying focused and doing my job doesn't mean that I don't have a life or that I don't care about staying alive to live it."

He was silent for a long time. She could feel the burn of his stare upon her, licking at every inch of exposed skin. She hoped to hell he couldn't see through her. His words had hit a hell of a lot closer to home than she'd thought possible. How could this man have read her better than people who who'd known her her whole life? Her own partner thought her reckless, but this man—in less than two days of knowing her—had already figured out that it had nothing to do with reck-lessness but rather sheer determination. She'd solve the case. Put every one of the bastards in jail. Even if it was the last thing she did.

She figured there was no more to say on the topic. He'd made his point; she'd basically told him to shove it and mind his own business, so when he spoke, the whispered words like a caress across her senses, it made her blink in surprise. "How about you just kiss me."

She had to shake her head to clear the cobwebs that must be covering her ears. "Excuse me? What did you just say?"

"I said, kiss me."

"Kiss you."

He nodded. "Yes. We both know you want to. That I want you to."

"So kissing you would prove what exactly?"

"Not much. But it *is* what you want. Isn't it?"

"And you think I'm too busy being a cop to take what I want in life? Is that it?"

He didn't reply. Didn't need to. He was bullying her. He figured that such a challenge would get him what he wanted. That she'd back down and in so doing prove his point. She could tell by his body language—arms folded across his chest, brow cocked in smug challenge—that he didn't think she would do it.

Well joke was on him. Because, damn it, he was right. She *did* put her job before all else. Gave too damn much of her life to a cause she could never possibly win. Until tonight. Tonight she'd invited him out here. And no matter how many times she told herself she'd done so for answers, the truth was much simpler than that. She wanted him. End of story. And whether she trusted him didn't matter in the end. She'd been compromised at the first kiss. Mike was going to be pissed. There was a good chance internal affairs would be involved. At the very least she would find herself in the shrink's office, removed from duty for who knew how long. At the worst…

He won't ever want to see me again. And why should he? Why would Logan ever trust her if he compromised his values and told her his secrets only to have her turn on him by submitting the tapes anyway? All of a sudden Jessica was glad she hadn't gotten the chance to ask for sure if he was working for Alexander. It made the culpability for what she was about to do just a little less.

Because she was going to do it. She was going to kiss him, taste him, one last time before the end.

She raised her chin, taking a step forward. If possible his brow rose even higher, only this time in obvious surprise. His arms dropped to his sides, his weight shifting back on his heels.

"I'm sorry. That was…" His gaze dragged down over her, hunger in his eyes. But then he shook his head. "You don't have to, Jessica. I was just trying to…"

"Push me into a corner?" she asked, laying a hand on his chest.

"Not exactly, I was just…" His heart beat hard and heavy under her hand, his throat bobbing as he swallowed. "Damn."

And wasn't that empowering? Who knew the simple threat of a kiss, a kiss he'd asked for, could do what she'd wanted to do five minutes before: put him on guard.

Relishing her power, she dragged her finger down his sternum, thrilling at each rise and dip of his washboard abs, and when her hand got to the rim of his jeans, the tips of her fingers hitched themselves into the fabric, causing him to suck in his breath, she smiled in triumph.

Oh yeah. She was going to do it. Take. Exactly. What. She. Wanted.

"Damn it, Jessica. Don't do that."

"Why not? Isn't this what you asked for?" She slid her fingers farther into his jeans and yanked him closer. He cursed, but she noted he didn't pull back. Or remove her hand. Or try to hide how much he wanted it, too. Damn the man had a nice package. Large enough to make her fingers itch with the desire to check it out sans jeans, make sure it was real.

"I said kiss me, not toy with me."

"Why not? Obviously I like toying with you. And this is all about taking what I want, isn't it?" she asked, her voice nothing but a low purr that surprised even her. She'd had lovers, not many, but for the most part those encounters were experimentation more than anything else, an attempt to see if she could let go enough to enjoy the moment and take what her body craved. Passion. And the results of those experiments had taught her one thing: Her only passion was for justice. But her body throbbed with alarming need. Logic, right and wrong, fled her mind. She wanted him, and set out to prove it by rubbing her body up and down his.

He growled. At the same time, his hands came down on her shoulders, his grip almost bruising as he seemed to war with himself over whether to pull her in or push her away. For a moment she thought perhaps he decided on the latter, just the slightest pressure on her collarbone. Something snapped inside her, something that had her own body tensing, her fingers digging like claws into the denim fabric.

No. She hadn't gotten her kiss yet. Not that it would be enough. A simple kiss to prove him wrong was no longer an option. Not when her body practically wept at the thought of not tasting him again.

She lunged, her other hand snaking around his neck, practically pulling herself up his body so she could reach her destination. She needn't have been so scared. His hands left her shoulders, but only so they could lock on her hips, his head dipping as he ground his pelvis against her. So real, and oh God that felt so good.

Their mouths came together like two greedy animals,

ready to devour each other. It probably should've been scary or somewhat disconcerting to have gone from zero to tongue down each other's throats in two seconds flat, but it wasn't. It was sublime.

"Aw, crap. Too good." He muttered this between his attempts to swallow her whole. And she had to agree, even as she cursed herself for meeting him lip for lip, tongue for tongue, teeth for teeth. She hadn't trusted her memories of that first kiss back in his brownstone. Hadn't believed it could have been so mind-blowing, so oh-please-please-fuck-me-now good. She'd been wrong.

Hell, was that her moaning like some porno slut? Was that her hand clenching his ass? Her other tearing at the bottom of his undershirt, trying to release it from his jeans?

Something hit the back of her thighs. She realized belatedly that while she'd pulled him closer with her hand on his ass, he'd done his best to oblige, only he was so much bigger and stronger and she'd inadvertently given ground and now here they were, her ass pressed up against the antique table, her left leg lifting—without permission, darn it—to wrap around said luscious ass. He made another sound like a growl, lowering her down with one hand as his other swept behind her, dozens of paint brushes clattering on the floor. Then he was over her, his weight heavy against her pelvis, and holy heck yes those were his hands kneading at her breasts through her shirt, making them throb and ache. Only now that they were there, she didn't just want his hands *over* her shirt she wanted them under.

"Logan, wait. Let me…" She pushed his hands away,

ignoring the low growl he gave her as she did. Then, without even a thought to the implication of getting naked with him, she started pulling at the buckles on her holster. And since what she was doing obviously seemed like a good idea to him too he started doing the same, with the buttons of his shirt that is, only his buttons were easier than her stiff buckles as he just had to yank it off along with his undershirt so, considerate man that he was, he started helping her.

It didn't take them long. Seconds maybe for him to jerk her up enough off the table to free her shoulders so he could void her properly of her blazer and shoulder harness, another two to yank her tank over her head and for his mouth to come down over her breast, but way too damn long as far as she was concerned. She needed him.

He was so fucked.

Giving in to the temptation of her lips had been a fatal mistake, but the small bit of logic screaming at him that this was a stupid, stupid idea was no more than a bucket of water against the raging inferno of a forest wildfire.

He couldn't stop. But damn, he should at least find them a bed. Certainly something better than the paint-splattered floor or some unstable table. But the thought of lifting his mouth from her breast, even if it would only be for the short period of time it would take to get down the stairs and down that short hall he'd seen, to a bedroom seemed like too much. Too much time. Too much effort.

He needed to save his energy for this. Because damn if she wasn't going to consume him.

"Jessica, wait. Let me…" He tried to shift her away from the table. If they were going to do it here, he was going to be on the bottom.

He would not have her lovely ass covered in splinters.

"No. No waiting," she insisted, taking the opportunity to stand up and rapidly strip off her jeans and boots. She must have thought the process took too long because she was swearing vividly the whole time, practically ripping the laces to get her boots off, but he didn't think so. God, she was gorgeous—the spill of dark curls over her shoulders, her long torso, the tapered waist…that ass—and his. All his. He could look at her forever and not get enough, but she obviously had other ideas. Her second boot barely hit the floor and she was up, kicking her ankles free of her jeans as her fingers eagerly sought the waist of his. The button had already popped so it didn't take much for the zipper to give, and then, oh hell, her slim hand was wrapping around his cock, tugging it free from his jeans, her other hand pushing down the offending material.

"Just a second. I need to…" He tried to step back further, but her slender hands were amazingly strong and amazingly sweet on his cock and he ended up tripping in the tangle of his jeans. It was either fall backward or forward and since forward put him closer to his ultimate goal…

They bumped back into the table, only this time he helped her—okay pushed her—all the way back onto it. Her eyes widened—probably thought he was some lust-crazed monster, and wasn't that damn close to the truth. But first.

He grabbed her wrist. "Let go."

Her answer to that was a glare, and a tightening of her grip, which felt way too good. He couldn't do this much longer, not without losing all control, but before he did he had to do one thing.

"Please," he managed to articulate from behind his gritted teeth.

Hesitantly, almost reluctantly she let him go. But not before she dragged a finger across the tip of his cock, swiping up the bead of moisture that eagerly waited there, and bringing it to her lips to suck up.

He cursed, his head—both of them—practically popping off from the eroticism of it. She had no idea what she was doing to him. None. He may not know every hidden secret of her soul but he knew one thing…his Jessica, tough as she was, wasn't cruel. And what she just did was beyond so.

He tore his gaze away from her swollen lips, trying not to think of where that drop of moisture had gone and yes, where his dick now badly wanted to follow—inside the slick heat of her mouth.

Only thing better would be the slick heat of her sex.

Pulling at his rumpled jeans he worked to free his wallet from the back pocket. Even though it had been a non-issue since for pretty much forever, he always carried a condom for that just-in-case scenario. And yeah, there was a part of him that wanted to screw the condom. The thought of getting Jessica, his woman, pregnant, her belly plump and round with his child, brought a choke-hold to his throat and had him hesitating. But no, that would not be fair to her. Besides, what if the child didn't inherit his genetics for power? Then two people he loved beyond life would die on him.

As if that would really matter. Your mate is as human as they come so you're already fucked, dickwad.

But even that gut-twisting thought didn't stop him from rolling on the rubber, cursing the whole time he did because, yeah, he shouldn't do this. He knew what the consequences would be beyond the obvious losing his sanity to the mind-blowing sex he knew they would have…but she didn't.

Right now she could walk away and suffer nothing more than some momentary, soul-deep what-ifs. But even then she'd be okay. She'd move on. She'd find another man. She'd marry him and have kids and have a completely fulfilling whole other life without him in it. And damn but didn't that make him angry just thinking about it. But the point was whether it was too late for him or not, it wasn't for her, and if he were any sort of decent man at all he'd stop, pull up his pants, and walk out the door.

"Jess, I can't—"

"Logan, so help me if you don't get inside of me right now…" she didn't finish the threat, but lifted herself enough to fuse her mouth back to his. And goddamn, it was too late. Because, yup, that was his cock that he was guiding toward the slick, sweet folds of her sex and yup that was his tongue playing tonsil hockey with hers as she grabbed onto his ass, pulling him closer, urging him on. The call to claim her burning like a hungry fire.

And then he was there. His cock tucked tight into the gripping entrance of her vagina. And she was right there with him because her gasp, the sweet sound that meant she was too breathless to actually say how fucking amazing it felt, mirrored exactly what he would've said if he weren't similarly struck dumb by this most exceptional, soul-consuming experience. And as he pressed deeper into her tight, hot center, her nails biting into his hips as she tried to wiggle down further onto him, his lingering concerns disappeared in white-hot, blazing pleasure because, fuck it, there was nothing else for him. Nothing to look forward to when his time with her ended because he was there. He was in Heaven.

Chapter 13

THIS ISN'T REAL.

It was Jessica's first thought as she woke, face tucked into the crook made by Logan's arm, neck, and chest, one of her legs draped casually over his hip. Sure her body felt whole—though admittedly sore—but her mind was definitely slipping. She knew when it had started to go. Something had happened with that first kiss. A wall blocking some well-guarded emotion crumbled, exposing a selfish sliver. She let that sliver taint her, allowing emotion to overwhelm her, and to overlook her misgivings. Allowing her to dismiss what her own eyes told her as she watched the grainy video. She'd brushed her concerns away, making excuses for taking what she wanted and initiating the second kiss. And then she fought tooth and nail against logic and doubt as the passion she'd unleashed had erupted into hours and hours of lovemaking.

Lovemaking. She didn't do love. If one loved they could hurt and right now she was in for a world of it. She'd thought when it was over, when the passion subsided and she'd taken her fill, she could turn from Logan. Tuck in the shreds of her self-respect, gather her emotions and walk away. But she could deny it no longer. She was truly, irrevocably compromised and there was nothing she could do about it.

The barriers between her and her memories had

fallen. She remembered. Maybe not everything, but enough to know that the man she'd made love to, who'd pleaded with her for his trust, had already broken hers. Somehow, someway, he'd stolen her memories. And though her head screamed at the wrongness of it all and her heart howled in agony, there was a sick part of her that just didn't give a fuck.

"Mine," she whispered, fingers digging into the hard muscles of his chest.

Logan murmured a "hmmm," his arms closing tighter around her, pulling her closer. Tears slipped from the corner of her eyes as she realized what she said and was smacked upside the head with the insanity of it all. She knew she had to pull away. In her mind she pulled away, slipped out of the bed, grabbed up her clothes and evidence and snuck from the house, but the part of her that wanted to believe in Logan, in *them*, stayed.

She could not set the wheels in motion that would turn this man in. The man she'd made love to, the one curled around her with such tenderness, was not a criminal. True there was no explaining some of the things she thought she saw him do, just as there was no explanation for the serious case of brain-fog or the warped sense of knowing she'd experienced since Logan entered her life.

There were also no such things as vampires and demons. People couldn't wipe out other people's memories. And words such as kismet and soul mates were the types of things you found in one of her sister's cheesy romance novels, not real life.

Nope, the only explanation for the warped reality that she thought she remembered was either *a*, she had finally gone completely off her rocker, or *b*, it was all a dream.

She liked that idea best. The dream one, that is. Though it made her sad to realize that no matter what, if the messed-up nightmares she had weren't real, then the mind-blowing sex couldn't be real either, nor could this totally awesome post-coital cuddling.

One more time. If it's not real, then what does it matter if you indulge one last time before you wake?

Freed by this thought, Jessica boldly slipped her hand between them. Logan stirred again, making one of those half-growl warning noises as she shifted, but the moment her hand closed over him it turned into another sort of growl. She decided she liked that sound. It was empowering. More empowering was how it only took a couple of pumps for him to harden, and less than a dozen more to have his shaft slickened with liquid coaxed from the slit on its tip. Prime male. Luscious male. *Her* male.

"You're a tease," he told her, his voice all gravely and rumbly and far from his typical fluid baritone. She liked that too. What she didn't like, however, was how he tried to shift to pull her under him.

Nuh-uh. It was her imagination. Her dream lover. Therefore she could dictate the conditions.

"No. I want to be on top," she told him firmly, squeezing down on his cock to emphasize the fact that she was in the lead.

He sucked in a breath, his eyes opening, their depths all dark and stormy as he seemed to search her out, as if trying to determine her real intentions. She tilted her head questioningly, not sure what her dream self was supposed to reassure him of, but then he smiled, dimples flashing as he rolled onto his back.

"Then lead on," he said, linking his hands on the pillow under his head. "Just be gentle, I'm fragile you know."

She laughed at that. Fragile her ass. Though he *was* superb, all spread out like that, every rippling muscle, every inch of his maleness exposed and begging for her touch.

Oh, where to start.

Top to bottom? Best for last? Didn't matter, both halves were sublime.

With one last lingering twirl around the top of his cock, she dragged her hand up his body, tracing the hills and valleys of his delectable abs, curving around the underside of his pectorals. It thrilled her that as she did, his muscles tensed, showing her that he was not unaffected by her explorations. And if something as simple as her fingers tracing his torso could make him tense with anticipation, what would...

She bent down, lowered her mouth to his chest and then firmly stroked her tongue across his nipple. The small bud dimpled from her attention, his chest rising against her lips as he sucked in and held his breath. She did it again only this time she followed the lick with a gentle scrape of her top teeth.

"Fuck that's good, Jessica."

Maybe, but she was aiming for better than good. She wanted him so wild he couldn't remember how to form coherent words.

Abandoning the nipple, she slid the rest of the way up his chest. She'd meant to start there, after all, but had been distracted by that succulent stretch of man between cock and mouth. She found his mouth and was pleased she'd taken the time to explore. Gone was the smug smile he'd given her as he'd laced his hands behind his head. Yes, his arms were still raised, but he'd had to go one step further, his hands wrapped in tight fists around the bars of the wrought-iron headboard, his eyes closed tight, and his mouth pulled into a firm line. Fighting for control. Her touch made him lose control.

Oh yeah, what a most excellent dream.

Straddling him, knees on either side of his hips, hands beside his torso, she flipped her head forward and then swayed, letting the tangled mass of curls that she normally hated drag across his torso, teasing the edges of his neck then down to his abs.

"What do you want me to do first, Logan? Kiss you?"

He swallowed, his tension easing somewhat. "That would be nice."

"Where? On your lips?" she flicked her head forward, her hair lashing against his chin. "Or lower?" she asked, dragging her hair lower and lower as she started to ease down his body.

"Don't." The bed jerked, hands grabbing onto her upper arms to stop her. She tipped her head back up, staring into his stormy eyes. They were darker than she'd ever seen them, only she swore there were the smallest splotches of gleaming silver shining through.

"Logan?"

"Don't kiss me there," he explained, easing his grip somewhat. "I couldn't take your lips on me there. Not without risk of losing my mind."

"And would that be so bad?" She ran her tongue

across her lips, ending the erotic action with a slide of her bottom lip through her teeth.

He growled, his eyes flashing, doing what she could have sworn was that glowing silvery thing again. Before she could take a good look he sat up, forcing her to do the same. She opened her mouth to remind him she was leading this time, but all that came out was a yelp as he grabbed her hips and then flopped back down, pulling her up over him so she had to grasp the headboard for support.

So much for being in control.

Any objections she might've made were obliterated the moment his mouth touched her. And not to her lips—which, granted would've been impossible in this position—but *there*.

And oh God it was magnificent. And intimate. With any other man she would've been embarrassed by the vulnerability of the position. To expose that part of herself to possession, to allow herself to be seen, tasted and touched was a major thing for her. She'd always felt too awkward to let herself go to this sort of primal lovemaking, but with him? It felt right. It felt natural. It felt so…effing…good.

"Logan. God. Please…"

She'd meant it as a plea, an oh-please-stop-so-I-can-catch-my-breath, but he gave a growl followed by the shock of thick digits plunging into her weeping core. She cried out, her body clenching around the invading fingers, but all that did was make things hotter, rake her nerves a bit more, send her dangerously close to the brink.

She shook her head, trying to hold off, trying to draw

it out, make it last. An orgasm might wake her and damn it she didn't want to wake.

"Come for me, sweetheart. I want to taste your need."

His raspy voice, speaking of his own desire, coupled with another deep plunge of his fingers had her arching, clawing at the headboard. His tongue stroked across the swollen little bud of her pleasure, trying to tease her over the edge. She shook, but held on.

Another few seconds. Another few moments before I have to wake.

And then he nipped her. Not hard. Barely a scrape of teeth before he suckled her deep into his mouth, but it was enough. Nerves shattered. She screamed, hot juices slicked her channel.

"Fuck, that's it." Logan slid his fingers from her, his tongue stroking across her with such erotic languor that she shattered again, lights exploding behind her eyes. She couldn't move. Couldn't see. Her only senses were the clench of her center timed to the beat of her pounding heart.

Don't wake up. Don't wake up. This is too good to wake from.

The bed shifted. Mournfully she realized that Logan's mouth was gone and furthermore he'd left too, scooting out from under her. She didn't have more than a sliver of brainpower left to figure out where he went or what he was doing, but before she could recover, she felt the heat of him leaning over her from behind. All of him. Including his oversized and overly eager friend tapping the cheeks of her ass.

Would he take her like this?

The thought was both scary and exhilarating and sent

another bout of post-orgasmic shudders through her body. Lights were still exploding in the back of her eyes when he touched her face, twisting it to the side and kissing her so soundly she had to work double time to catch her breath again.

"You still want to be on top?" he asked, his eyes hot on hers as he laid a trail of kisses across her cheek toward her earlobe. As if she would actually be able to answer that.

She must have managed some sort of noise because he chuckled, his fingers helping pry her own from the headboard. With him steadying her, he got her turned around, then pulled her down on top of him. She probably would've flopped over—okay, most definitely would have—but he held her with one broad hand firmly on her hip, the other sliding up her front, cupping the underside of her right breast.

"Come on, sweetheart. Show me what you can do."

And that sounded distinctly like a challenge.

Tipping her chin up, she reached between them. Her orgasm ensured that she was ready for him, and when she touched his cock, finding it already sheathed in a condom, there was no reason to wait.

She thrust down, taking him all the way to the hilt. Neurons she thought were too fried to react zapped as her body stretched to accommodate him, the first tingles of the promised explosion racing through her.

Wow, this wouldn't take long. Not long at all. And judging by how hard he felt inside her and how tightly his jaw clenched, he was already fighting not to come.

Bottom lip tucked between her teeth, and what she

was sure was a smile in her eyes, she gazed down at him and began moving. She'd show him what she had. And she'd take all he had to give her at the same time.

She started to move. Up, down; hips rotating, inner muscles clenching.

"God, Jessica. You're killing me."

She was killing herself too, each movement like fire through her body, the burn in her lungs as she swallowed great gulps of air.

So much for control; it was all she could do not to melt upon him. So she moved, letting her body lead her. There was no predetermined pace to draw this out. Only the beat of heavy breathing. Only the slap of bodies as she drove herself down on him.

Only this.

Only him.

This wasn't pleasuring. It was succumbing. And as another orgasm burst through her, pulling him along, all she could think was that she hoped she wouldn't be the only one to surrender to the fall.

―⁓―

Jessica lay with her head nestled against Logan's chest, listening to the rapid whoosh of his heart. Her own thundered to match. Neither spoke. Hard to do so when they both still gasped for air. Which was good.

Jessica didn't want to speak.

So she closed her eyes, nuzzling in further as she tried to ignore the clamminess of their sweat-slicked skin. But she couldn't do it. Couldn't ignore the truth plastered all over her.

People didn't sweat in dreams. And women who had dedicated their lives to justice did not throw it out of the window for a roll in the hay.

Reality really, really sucked.

Sighing, she opened her eyes, pushing up on her elbows. "You're still here."

He smiled, pressing his hips up against her, his hard shaft stretching the desperately achy tissue of her vagina, eliciting an unconscious moan of pleasure. Tenderness aside, that felt good. Damn good.

"In more ways than one," he said, grabbing her hips and popping her off him as he rolled for the edge of the bed, his bicep straining as he reached down for the box on the floor.

She moaned again. This time in defeat. She'd never heard of a man who could recover as quickly as he did. She'd think maybe he wasn't coming but the evidence of that was there in the number of foil wrappers littering the bedspread. And yeah, maybe those wrappers should have had her questioning her original dream theory before, but, really, how many men took such care and accountability to be 100 percent responsible for keeping them safe?

It was he who pulled the condom out of his jeans and slipped that first rubber on when she'd been too lost in lust to care. And he who stopped their second round of post-sex sex asking if she had anything as he was out. She had, down in her glove compartment, thank God, and they actually made it to the bed that time since they were up anyway. But later on she didn't and it was again he who took responsibility, kissing her lovingly as she drifted off into sex-numbed sleep, saying he'd be right back. And then it was he who woke her later, fully sheathed and with an entire box of Trojans ready and waiting in the wings.

But that wasn't what had her moaning. What had her moaning was the fact that she knew now she was crazy. Crazy enough that the thought of coming apart in his arms again took over all others.

And that kind of thinking was just no longer acceptable. Crazy or not, she couldn't allow it to happen—again—because despite the impossibly awesome sex, with an impossibly perfect lover, she could no longer deny it: This was not a dream.

Which meant neither were the nightmares.

She wanted to throw up.

"Wait." She grabbed at the twisted sheets. Jerking them twice before managing to get them untangled enough from their various limbs. But finally she managed, drawing the sheet like a shield around her. "We can't do this."

He sat back up, the box of condoms already open in his hands. She watched the disappointment slide over his face, maybe even a bit of hurt, before he hid it, his eyes settling into that steely gray color she was learning to hate.

"Okay." He meticulously put the tab back in the slot of the box and then leaned over to set it back on the floor beside the bed. "Did I tucker you out?" he asked, trying, and failing at a smile.

"No, I mean yes, but that's not it."

"Oh?"

She took her time to gather her thoughts. It would take too long to collect her dignity—that was already lost. What the hell had she done? How could she have let this happen?

She lifted her chin, firming her resolve. "I remember now," she told him.

She sucked in a breath at the punch of fear that hit her gut, but almost as quickly as the strange sensation occurred, it passed, leaving her to think she must have imagined it. She must have been internalizing what she thought Logan felt, though she couldn't have figured that out by his face. He was as stoic as ever, a state confirmed by how unconcerned he seemed to be as he asked his next question.

"Remember what?"

"Everything. I remember everything."

Chapter 14

BY APPOINTMENT ONLY.

Mike stared at the elegant script scrawled under the nameplate for Alexander Hastings, Esq., and rolled his shoulders. Mr. Hastings must not have very many appointments because he was never there. Mike should know since he'd stopped by five times now in fewer than two days. Daytime, nighttime, early morning...didn't matter. Not once had there been any sign of life on the other side of that door. Nor was there any sort of message on the answering machine beyond the standard leave a message—which, thus far, had received no response. Not a very good way to run a business.

He didn't get it. Mr. Hastings' credentials had checked out and though he didn't take on many cases there were a few on record. By all appearances, he seemed legit.

Frustrated, Mike exited the building, got in his beat-up Corolla, and drove to the station. He was so damn tired. A fact he blamed on his errant partner. He should have known better than to leave her to her own devices, but he'd been pissed and needed the space. He wasn't sure what pissed him off more: that she went out without him and got injured or that her little adventure had been somewhat fruitful. He'd found witnesses who said a certain red Mustang had been sitting in that spot for ages, but by the time he got the warrant and went inside the garage, there was no Mustang. Just an empty spot and a wet oil drip. Mike ordered the scene processed anyway, despite the fact that he didn't expect anything to come of it. Definitely frustrating. Though not nearly as frustrating as the disappearing act his partner had done.

Mike had tried to call Jessica and tell her the good news/bad news but she wasn't answering her damn phone. Nor had she called. He'd headed back to the station with the hope that her cell phone was dead and she'd headed in or had at least checked in and left a message for him there, but she hadn't. He then tried her home again, even stayed well into the night, making phone calls and promising all kinds of favors to get first priority on their crime scene samples, which sucked seeing how it made almost forty-eight hours with practically no sleep. His frustration over the case had kept him up the first night, and his new worry over Jessica kept him up a good portion of the second, eventually driving him back to the station a good three hours before he was officially on the clock.

Oh the joys of being a cop.

He pushed through the back doors of the station, and was blasted with the stale heat of sweaty cop, burnt coffee, and desperation. The thermostat was broken again. Oh yeah.

He removed his jacket, rolled up his sleeves, and headed back through the narrow walkway to his desk. A mountain of sticky notes and jagged-edged notebook paper stared back at him: the research he'd done between all those phone calls last night. He'd meant to file them, but practically fell asleep on them instead, so he just shoved them into a pile on his way out.

Grunting, he slid into the seat, waited for the antiquated chunk of machinery that masqueraded as a computer to boot up, then started transferring the various notes into something resembling a cohesive report. He knew Jessica's focus had shifted after seeing Tom's car in the garage, but he couldn't help but feel their original suspect was still the best. Something about Roland set his teeth on edge, as did the man's lawyer. That niggling feeling is what sent him digging up what he could on Alexander Hastings. Mike honestly hadn't thought to check out the friend, Mr. Calhoun, having not had any interaction with him until a comment from Jessica tweaked his interest. According to Jess, Mr. Calhoun was related to their suspect by marriage. Only, from what Mike had dug up, Ms. Donovan didn't have any siblings. Though wasn't she a person of interest herself?

On paper, Karissa Donovan looked like a victim of life: orphaned at a young age, taken in by her grandparents, one of whom had passed while she was still quite young. She adjusted well enough, going to college, working at the phone company, until one day almost two months ago when she up and disappeared. It was a week before a missing persons report was filed—by the employer—and her home was searched, revealing a scene that indicated horrific violence. Miss Donovan popped up a few weeks later. Telling the police she'd come home one night and been attacked. She managed to get away, but ran. According to the lead detective's notes, her grief had seemed genuine with regard to her grandfather's disappearance, and the fact he was presumed dead. So the case was still open with little to go on and a staggeringly small pool of suspects. Which, gee, sounded familiar, didn't it?

More ironic? Ms. Donovan met her husband during the panicked flight, and, more interestingly, they weren't actually married in the legal sense but through some obscure religious ceremony. Unusual and suspicious. And the biggest common thread? Their suspect. A suspect Jessica no longer liked for the crime.

Mike tapped the desk with his knuckles, shaking his head. Compared to his supposed sister and best friend, Logan Calhoun was downright boring. An expert on antiquities—namely religious artifacts—his background was almost as obscure, yet just as squeaky clean as his lawyer pal's. Mike didn't trust squeaky clean. Especially not on men who looked like they could kick the collective asses of the NYPD.

With a curse, Mike saved the file and started the computer on its molasses-paced shutdown routine. He left the thing chugging ominously and stalked over to Damon's desk, ignoring the itchy tingle at the back of the neck. What Jessica saw in the guy, Mike would never understand. Mike didn't like the man. Didn't like how he did his job. Didn't like how he slinked around the edges of a room listening in on others' conversations or how he plastered on that cocky grin and sweet talked his way around to get whatever he wanted. Most of all, Mike didn't like how the man shuttered up when Mike was around, making excuses almost immediately that would take him anywhere else.

Probably realizes there's something off about me,

*too. Probably feels threatened by it, even if he's not sure
what that something is.*

Didn't matter. Damon wasn't the first to feel that
way. Hell, his parents kicked him out with nothing but
what he could carry in his backpack. No biggie. He'd
managed to repress the *something* that was within him
all on his own. Had made a life for himself despite it,
though, damn, sometimes that life was lonely.

Especially when the one person in the station who
he even halfway considered a friend was trying to get
herself killed.

"You see Jess recently?" Mike demanded as he
ground to a halt before Damon's desk.

The other detective didn't look up, though his pen
hesitated on the report he was filling out. "Nope. Not
since Wednesday."

Wednesday morning was when she missed her meet
and greet, and the presumed time their latest stiff had
died. Mike stifled another wave of frustration. He still
couldn't believe she went into that part of town, at that
hour, for something that involved *their* case and didn't
call him. When he was assigned to work with her, he
was warned that she had a string of less than admirable
partners, which might impede her desire to work with
another one. She also had a reputation for being head-
strong and an equally big one for worming her way into
and out of some really shit-fan-level situations. But to
cut him out of their case?

Maybe he was wrong. Maybe Jessica, having been
forced to partner with him for over a month, had begun
to sense that there was something not right about him.
Maybe she was cutting him off not because she was a

damn stubborn fool, but because she didn't want to be in his presence.

Well, that was fine. But like it or not he *was* her partner and he'd be damned if he allowed her to run off alone and get herself killed.

Damon shifted back in his chair and folded his hands behind his head, the movement easygoing in contrast to the tension around his jaw. "What's up? Why you asking?"

Mike ignored that. "What time did you see her that day?"

There was a flicker of something in the man's dark—and frankly creepy—eyes, but then he shrugged. "Morning. After my shift. We were supposed to go to breakfast but she'd had a late night and wasn't up for it."

A late night, huh? More like she'd spent *all* night waiting for a dead guy. Mike debated saying anything. Taking out the fact that Damon had always rubbed him wrong, he was a cop. Anyone else probably wouldn't hesitate to enlist Damon's help on something like this, but Mike did. He'd seen him in action once and something in those dark, normally fathomless eyes, had sparked…like he enjoyed the violence. Then again, who was Mike to talk? He climbed the ranks working undercover in narcotics. One had to be an adrenaline junkie to make it there.

Or have a death wish.

"Why? What did Jess do now?"

Mike's jaw hardened, not liking the implication that his partner had a penchant for trouble. Sure, he'd thought it himself, but he was her partner, not her supposed boyfriend. Whatever. What Damon thought wasn't Mike's problem, it was Jessica's if she actually wanted to get serious with this guy.

"Sorry, that came across wrong, didn't it?" Damon flashed him a repentant grin. "She's an excellent detective. Just sometimes too absorbed in getting her man. Of course, that's the jealous boyfriend in me talking."

Mike grunted and decided to give the guy a break. Jessica wouldn't be easy to date. Idly, he wondered if Damon had even seen Jessica since her misadventure last night. Probably not. Not if he was sitting there joking about her getting into trouble.

The grin slid from Damon's face, his brow furrowing as he sat up straighter in his chair. "Why all the questions about Jess? What's going on, Mike?"

Mike sighed, settling into the seat across from him. "I'm worried about her, Damon. I think you're right, she's gotten into something and this time she might just be in over her head."

Jessica remembered everything.

Logan scrubbed his face with his hands, knowing the time to stall was long past. It was his own damn fault he was in this situation. He knew what had done it, of course, what it was that finally broke down the last of the memory shield he'd put on her. Unlike a pair bond that needed ceremonies and rituals to form a connection, those who were mate bonded could hide nothing from one another—their emotions, their thoughts echoing through the bond, becoming stronger and more pronounced the longer they were together. And though he'd yet to actually perform the bonding ceremony that would bind their souls together for eternity, there was no denying they were meant to be.

He shouldn't have touched her. One kiss and everything was fucked.

Not that he could have resisted. When she'd spoken of that Mike guy his entire body had tightened, adrenaline pumping through him, overpowering him with the urge to go out and pound something—this Mike had come to mind—and then return to his woman and go all caveman on her.

He was a little bit more sophisticated than that. Not much, but a little. So though he didn't grab her by her hair and drag her back to his cave, he had to prove she was his. Hence the stupid challenge. Kiss me. As if he didn't know what that would lead to.

From the first moment he saw her he'd been acting irrational. But that hardly compared with how he felt after their night together. Because no matter how beautiful he thought she was before, having locked gazes with her as she came undone in his arms…damn, he'd never seen a sexier woman in his life. And he knew he never would again.

He couldn't, wouldn't lose her.

Which meant, duty be damned, he was going to have to tell her the truth.

But how did you tell someone something like that? Where did he start?

"Nothing to say?" she asked, as if she could read his mind and knew he was having trouble coming up with the words. And though he sincerely doubted the reading his mind bit, he wouldn't be surprised if she could sense his frustration. She may be human but he was a full Paladin. It would figure that his emotions were pressing at her from across their bond—even if it wasn't completely formed yet.

Or maybe she was just astute. Probably had to be, being a cop.

"It's kind of a hard thing to explain."

She folded her arms across her chest, her eyebrows rising. "How about you start with the woman. You know, the one that you *weren't* chasing."

"I never said I wasn't chasing her."

"You said—"

"That I wasn't chasing a helpless woman. Emphasis on the word helpless."

Her eyes narrowed, but she nodded her head. "Go on."

"Actually she wasn't exactly a woman either. Female certainly. And one of his. Other than that I'm not sure what she was. Part succubus certainly but there must have been something else there for her to be so strong."

"Succubus? One of his?" She shook her head. "What are you talking about?"

He took a deep breath, silently cursing his inarticulate tongue. He obviously wasn't going to be able to do this with any finesse so…*Band-Aid method*. "I'm talking about demons. And Lucifer. Though you probably know him better as the devil."

She blinked her eyes, her mouth opening and closing a couple times before she swallowed, hard. "Demons."

"Among other things."

"Wow. Okay then. Thanks for that because…" she coughed, "uh, that explains everything."

Her gaze traveled frantically around the room, landing on the clock. "Oh gee, look at the time. I'm going to be late…again." She smiled at him, all big and bright and fake. "I have your number though, so I'll give you a call later, 'kay?"

Logan frowned at her. He wasn't a fool, and that was the most tired line in the history of the world.

Her smile slipped a bit. She pulled the sheet tighter, shifting on the bed so her foot was planted on the mattress, ready to make a break for it, or just as likely, try and kick him in the head. He laid a hand on her knee, causing her to jump a bit and suck in her breath. But at least she didn't go for the knock out.

"Five minutes. That's all I ask."

He could feel the tension in her leg muscles as she studied him, her gaze traveling over his face and settling on his eyes. Something she saw there must have reassured her because she eased back down to a more comfortable position on the bed.

"Okay. Five minutes starting now."

"Good." He took a deep breath. "You see…"

He trailed off, because the truth was, she couldn't see, and that was part of the problem. She was human and had no ability to sense the otherworldly creatures around her. And he knew, just knew, that no matter what he said it wasn't going to matter because no sane person, even having had some of those creatures reveal themselves, was going to believe him. They'd pass it off as a dream, or a hallucination, or even their own insanity, but there was something about the human psyche that would not allow them to believe. And with Jessica's cynical view of God and divine judgment? Yeah, he was so screwed.

She stared at him expectantly. The clock ticking its

irreversible countdown across the room. And he was at a loss of words.

Something hard and horrible tasting rose in his throat. It took him a moment to understand what it was: despair. Because even if he could convince her—which was looking doubtful—it didn't matter whether she believed. Belief, acceptance. What did either of those things really fucking matter? He'd have what? Twenty? Forty? If he was damn lucky maybe sixty years with her?

She was human. Sooner or later she was going to die.

But I have her now. I have her this moment. And damn if I'm not going to fight for another.

As he grasped on to the thought he closed his eyes, drawing to him the memories of their night together. The average female in this country had eighty years or more. That meant that if he could keep her safe, fifty-four of hers could be with him. Piddling really, but calculated out that meant he could have her for 19,710 days which equaled 473,040 hours or, still further, 28,382,400 moments. And that number didn't seem nearly so bad.

"I know it's hard to believe," he began. "But there are demons. Just as there is a devil."

He opened his eyes, knowing his eyes shone, and that if she looked, she would note that his skin glowed as well. She didn't gasp or scream or say anything, but she sat before him, her eyes wide and round, the sheet clenched tightly in her hands, one hand raised slightly over the other. Yup, that was his little warrior, confronted with a possible threat, she brought out the fists.

"The good news is there is also a God and even though He can't help directly for fear of freeing Lucifer from his banishment, He cares enough to have sent His angels to help."

Logan lifted his hand, curling his fingers through the air as if circling a ball. Pulling the light, he formed a globe of light in that space of air. The gesture wasn't needed, of course, but he wanted to emphasize the fact that he did it so that later, when she began to doubt what she'd seen, she'd have no choice but to admit that he was the cause of it.

This time she did gasp, her chest rising and falling in time to the pulsing flutter at the base of her throat. He hated that he was the cause of her anxiety but could see no other way.

She had to believe. She had to understand. Because no matter what she might wish or what his father would claim was his duty, Logan would not block her memories again.

Not when it meant abandoning her. Not when it meant cutting himself completely from her life.

"How did you…What is it?" Her voice was trembling, but there was a quality of awe to it that gave him some hope. If she could open her mind to what most humans would consider to be impossible, then they had a chance.

"Touch it. It won't hurt you."

She reached out tentatively, like a child trying to touch a bubble. When her fingertips met the light it fluxed, shining brighter. She jerked her hand back, and rubbed her fingers.

He frowned. "It shouldn't have hurt."

She shook her head. "It didn't. Not really. It tingles though. Kind of felt like an electrical zap." She frowned. "Actually, it kind of felt like when you first touched me."

He extinguished the light. "When I'm charged with His power I probably emit some of the properties of His light."

"His light. As in God's?"

He nodded.

"Sorry. Not buying it."

"Why not?"

"Because buddy, after the things we did?" She laughed, though it wasn't a good kind of laugh, more the world's-messed kind. "Let's just say I know for a fact that you're no angel."

He frowned. "I never claimed to be."

"But you just said He," she glanced upward, shifting slightly, "that, um, God sent his angels down to help us."

"That's the short of it. The long of it was he asked for volunteers. It was a great thing to ask because it would mean certain sacrifices, and not just because the angels would have to leave His heavenly realm."

"Uh-huh," she muttered, her skepticism obvious. But then she pursed her lips, her face skewed into a considering look. "What sort of sacrifices?"

"A true angel cannot yield a weapon. To take up arms against another, a man must have the capacity to feel such human emotions as love and anger. Otherwise, the act of violence is being done in cold blood, and to let that sort of unemotional violence loose on the world would be too dangerous."

She pounced on that like a scientist would in the ring with a monotheistic philosopher. "Why?

Wouldn't it be akin to a soldier being given an order from his commander?"

"Yes and no." He gnawed on the inside of his lip, trying to think of a way to answer that correctly. "Yes if the commander were always present, always assessing the situation and always giving orders."

"And God's not?"

"He can't be. His presence is not allowed here on earth. Not without risking Lucifer breaking free from his prison."

She folded her arms across her chest. "So instead he asked for volunteers to come down for him."

He nodded.

"And you? You were one of them?"

He heard the doubt in her voice, understood it. He also knew he had to give her all the facts or those seeds of doubt would grow bigger and there would be no hope of her believing any of what he said. "I am a descendent of one of them. Originally there were only twelve warriors. Twelve Paladin as he called them."

"So, what? These Paladin got it on with a bunch of human women and made little baby Paladin?"

"Not exactly," he hedged. He'd have to explain how unusual their bond was to her later, but right now he wanted to focus his efforts on getting her to believe in the possibility of the Paladin's existence. "After the first twelve came down and the other angels saw the good they could do, there were more who volunteered. Of those there were some female Paladin and they mated."

"Were? Why do you talk as if there aren't anymore?"

"There is only one female Paladin. And she cannot bear children."

"Why?"

He shook his head. "That's not important. What you need to understand is that the Paladin, my brothers, fight as His warriors. And that we don't engage in violence heedlessly, but only to protect His children from evil they cannot see."

"Like the woman from the alley?"

He nodded. "And the demon from the garage."

She shuddered at the reminder, one arm wrapping around the other as she fingered the punctures on it. He wanted to reach over and pull her to him, but was afraid she would not accept his comfort.

"Jessica, I promised you that all I did was for your safety. I did not lie." Her brow rose into her hair with that. He quirked his lip. "Okay, I did evade your questions, but I would argue they were not outright lies."

She glared at him.

"My point is that I have only wanted to protect you."

"Why?" She lifted her chin, drawing attention to a slight dimple in its center which he hadn't noticed before. Funny, considering how much time he'd spent worshipping her body last night.

"Why do you care?" she continued. "If you're some sort of heavenly warrior why do you give a rat's ass about one stupid human?"

"I'd care about any human. But I care most about you."

"You're not making any sense."

"No, I suppose it doesn't, to you." He tugged at his bottom lip as his mind churned for a way to explain well enough that she could understand, but wouldn't be too much information too soon. He dared not speak of things such as mate-bonds and destiny to her yet.

"I care about humans because it's my duty. You are His children and I'm sworn to protect you. I enjoy humans. They are refreshing in a way that you could never fully understand, since you are one."

Her lips pursed, her tongue running across her top teeth as if she was considering biting it to keep from retorting.

He reviewed his words and cringed. "I'm sorry. That came out wrong."

"Very high and mighty," she agreed.

He blew out a frustrated breath. "It's a hard thing to explain. I guess what I want you to understand is that, though I do care, there hasn't been anyone I cared enough about to sleep with since my mother's death."

Her eyes softened, her head tipping to the side. "I'm sorry. And really, given your grief it's understandable that you weren't up for that sort of intimacy."

He shook his head. "Tell that to my brother, Bennett. He thinks almost a hundred years of celibacy is a bit much."

"A hundred?" her face closed up, her tone revealing her disbelief. "You're a hundred years old?"

Cursing his loose tongue—she wasn't ready for that—he reached out to ease her with his touch. She shrank back, her body coiling up until she hit the headboard and couldn't go any further.

"Don't touch me."

Fisting his hand, he forced it back into his lap. The rejection tore through him more completely than any blade ever could.

"Can I ask why that upsets you so much?" He tried to keep his voice soft and gentle when all he really wanted to do was grab her up and shake her as he berated her for not believing in him. In them.

She shook her head, the gesture implying that he was dense for not getting it. "Because one, um, I just slept with a really, really old man. And okay, yeah, you are a really hot old man, but damn it, this is like one of Julia's stupid vampire novels where the hero, who's never fallen in love in all the years of his existence," she tagged on, lowering her voice, "falls for the weak, vulnerable human heroine and then yada, yada, yada, something happens and she has to be turned. Only you're not a vampire, you're some sort of freaky angel spawn, which, unless you're somehow hiding one impressive set of canines, or filed them down or something, means that you're not inclined to such evil aspirations as stealing the heroine's, aka my, soul—which, don't get me wrong, I'm kind of happy about, but really, when you stop and think about it, I'm not, because *you're a hundred freaking years old*, if not more, which means that *you're going to live longer than me,* and I'm sorry, but I can't just buy that. But even if I did, I couldn't live like that."

She finally ended her tirade, her chest heaving up and down, her hair loose and frazzled around her face. And God forgive him, even as hope crumbled around him, all he wanted to do was yank that sheet from her, flip her onto her back, and plow into her again. But then the very last thing she said fully penetrated.

He narrowed his eyes. "Live like what?"

She threw her arm up in the air. "Always wondering how old was too old. Waiting for the time when you would get sick of me and my wrinkles and trade me in."

"You think I would leave you because you aged?" The insanity of that statement had him half laughing— sick of her wrinkles, he'd worship every one of them if he could keep her safe and alive that long—but the pure fire in the glare she gave sobered him quickly.

Oh but wasn't this ironic: They had the same fear, but for two obviously different reasons.

"I would never, *could* never get sick of you," he said solemnly as he carefully stood up, forcing himself to step away from the bed. "But I will go. Let you think about this."

Five minutes were more than up and she needed time. Not that he'd go far, but a few hours for her to think and for him to regroup and hopefully come up with a better plan for getting her to give them a chance than the major clusterfuck that just went down.

She nodded emphatically. "I think that's a very, very good idea."

Jaw tight, he nodded and started gathering up his clothes from the room. He pulled on his jeans and boots, tugged on his shirt. His phone was missing. Probably fell out up in the loft. He stepped out into the chilly air of the rest of the cabin. He wasn't all that surprised when he heard a shuffle behind him, the sound of drawers slamming. He *was* surprised when he made it up to the loft and began the task of searching for the little black device among the jumble of clutter to hear her light foot-falls barely squeaking the treads of the ancient stairs.

Probably making sure I actually leave.

When the sound of her advancement ended on the last step he didn't turn to her or acknowledge her pres- ence in any way, figuring she'd speak if she wanted to.

Besides, there wasn't much he could say that wouldn't
come across as either desperate or crazy…or both. He'd
told her the truth and she couldn't accept it. Couldn't
accept him.

*Maybe it's for the best. You wanted her to be able to
walk away? Well looks like she's going to.*

The question was to whom would she run? That
Mike guy?

Hot anger pulled at the back of his neck, jealousy
of the faceless man. He tried to tamp it down by taking
deep breaths, but the image that kept playing in his mind
was of Jessica, her eyes glazed with pleasure as some
other man came between her knees.

Damn it. Damn it. Damn it.

Fisting his hands to keep from smashing something,
he forced himself to fix his gaze on the artwork that was
spread around the loft.

As he studied the paintings, the beauty of each one,
he felt the anger receding. What rose instead was curiosity. There wasn't any real rhyme or reason to the paintings. Still lifes, portraits, even a splash of modern in the
mix. It didn't matter what the subject was, everything
her sister had painted celebrated life.

He would have smiled but for one small fact: They
all sat in the loft collecting dust. He'd seen the beautiful
artwork at Jessica's apartment. None of them had the
same style as these.

Why? Why didn't she display any of her sister's
paintings?

"Can I ask you something?"

"What?" She crossed her arms as she fortified herself
for war.

"Why don't you like these?" He gestured around the loft.

"My sister's paintings?" She shook her head. "I do like them."

"Really?" He shifted into her space, holding her with his gaze when he thought she might run. "If you like them, then why aren't they on display? Why don't you have a single one on the walls here or in your apartment?"

She sucked in a breath, her back going ramrod straight. "I don't see how that is any of your business."

He shook his head, taking in again the waste he saw around him. He didn't understand it. If he had a sibling with a talent like this, he'd beg to have them on display. "Do you and your sister get along?"

"We were best friends."

Logan drew his attention away from a particularly poignant portrait of a child offering up a flower. Jessica's voice was wistfully sad, but her eyes burned with an unholy anger. "Were?"

"She was murdered. Six years ago. Frat party. She got in the wrong car and ended up in some ditch. She died there, hours later. Result of a violent gang rape and subsequent beating."

Oh, God. That explained her passion for justice. Explained, too, why she abstained from life for her job. He was almost afraid to ask but needed to know. "Did they catch the guys who did it?"

Her mouth curled into a twisted smile, hatred burning in her eyes. "Yes. Twenty to life. And if they ever get out, you can be sure they won't live long enough to enjoy their freedom."

The blood chilled in his veins, constricting around his

heart. This was what was going to kill her. Not old age. Not his enemies targeting her as collateral damage. But the hatred she held so close to her heart.

She took a deep breath; let it out as she stretched her neck. "Sorry. I don't mean that, not really. Just, being here among her paintings, it hits closer to home." She gave him a slim smile, rather fake he thought. "I guess that's why I don't display any of them. Remembering her, to see them day in and day out, it would drive me crazy."

He could understand that. He had no idea how the fuck he was going to go on when she died. "Is your sister why you became a cop?"

Her eyes drifted past him to the dusty painting that still sat on the easel. A beach scene, the outline of a single feather drifting on the surf. Even unfinished it was beautiful and revelatory and lonely.

"Yeah, it is." She lifted haunted eyes. "We were twins. She was the passionate one, I'm more methodical— tenacious as my mother called it. They had all sorts of hopes for me. Law school. Med school. Didn't matter as long as it eventually ended up with a whole bunch of letters after my name. But all Julia dreamed about was painting." Her mouth quirked at the corner. "So I disappointed my parents and went to business school. I was going to make her a huge success."

"I'm sure with your help she would have been."

Jessica nodded, her knuckles cracking as she fisted and released her hand. "Instead, she died. And now I hunt down bastards who destroy other people's dreams."

And she did so under the mask of a badge and cold, hard laws. It reminded him a lot of his father. His father had learned to hide his emotions better, though not his prejudices. It scared the shit out of Logan. He'd watched the order fall further and further into ruin; adhering to traditions that no longer made sense or, quite simply, didn't work. Their enemies were winning, and his father wouldn't bend enough to change strategy. And now, on the crux of change, his father refused to take any help that wasn't "pure." His father saw the world in black and white and considered his own daughter and her mate to be just short of the enemy. They were vampires and vampires killed Logan's mother. Oh, Logan knew his father's prejudice and Jessica's obsession were not quite the same, but they both held roots in hatred, and hatred was never the path to His realm.

"I don't suppose I need to tell you that holding onto hatred isn't healthy. That it can eat away at your humanity."

She just glared at him.

"Jessica, I understand. When my mother died, I was devastated. It took me a long time and a lot of focus on other things to keep that anger from consuming me."

"Yeah? And how long was that exactly, Logan? Because frankly I don't think I have a hundred or more years."

"Damn it, Jessica. You can't hold this so close to your heart. You can't let anger drive the course of your life."

She arched her brow. "You want to bet?"

He cursed, running his hands through his hair. "Jessica—"

"I thought you were leaving," she interrupted, then emphasized her point by stepping into the loft and grabbing his phone from under an easel. "Here."

He refused the phone, folding his arms across his chest. Two could play at being obstinate. And there was no way he was leaving. It was bad enough that her association with him made her a target, but now that he understood what the true consequences could be? If his enemies sensed this stain of hatred on her heart, they would realize she was an easy mark. They wouldn't just want to kill her, they'd want her soul. Which meant she'd be more lost to him than if she actually died.

He would not let that happen.

Her eyes hardened, her nose flaring. "Take it."

"No."

"If you think I'm going to discuss this further, you're wrong. And if you think I'm going to allow you to lecture me on subjects you know nothing about, then you're doubly wrong."

"Nothing?" he asked softly, allowing his own grief to swallow most of his voice. The strike, though not intentional, hit home. She sucked in a breath, her gaze skittering away.

When she remained silent, he figured it was the only apology he would get. Didn't matter. What mattered was that she seemed to accept that he did understand her grief. If she'd allow him to tell her of his hatred, too, then maybe there was a chance.

He opened his mouth, ready to tell her about the day when over a dozen female Paladin were slaughtered, but was interrupted by the vibration of his phone in her outstretched hand.

"Crap." What timing. And awkward considering she still held it due to his stubborn power play. He could just ignore it, but very few people had his number. And every one of them were important—well, except perhaps his father. He'd blocked the man from his mind the moment he left his presence yesterday, unwilling to answer any more questions about his sister or the human whose memories he'd had to shield.

Jessica arched her brow, lifting the phone higher. He gave her a chagrined look as he took the phone from her, grunting as he recognized Roland's number.

"I'm sorry. I have to take this."

She nodded, turning her back on him as she wandered around the loft.

"This better be good," he said, letting his annoyance show in his voice.

"Karissa just got an interesting reach-out-and-touch-someone from your dad."

Logan's hand tightened around the phone. He hoped the call was about his father trying to mend fences with his estranged daughter, but having just come face to face with the reminder of what obsessive hatred could do, he somehow doubted it. "What did he want?"

"He wanted to know where Karissa and I are."

"Did you tell him?" Logan shifted his grip on the phone, his eyes going to Jessica. She was pretending not to pay any attention, her back toward him as she made busy work of picking up the scattered paint brushes. She was "holding her mad in" as his sister would say. Mad at him, mad at the world. He didn't blame her for either, and though the first stung at his heart it was the second that made him afraid. She had to let her anger go. Even if he could keep her out of direct danger, to hold that sort of burning hatred so close would be akin to having a terminal disease. Only in her case, it would not endanger her body but her soul.

"Not at first, but then he explained the reason," Roland said, answering Logan's question.

That brought his attention back. There were few things that Logan could think of that would cause Roland to tell his father their location. Not after the way he'd treated his daughter. "You going to enlighten me?"

"There was a notable wrinkle in the shielding around Haven. Your father concluded that something unpure had somehow managed to slip through."

"And he thought it might be you and Karissa." Asshole. Logan rubbed his forehead. His father's stubborn refusal to accept that both Roland and Karissa were as much His warriors as any of the other Paladin was getting old. Though damn it was not the time for him to go toe-to-toe with his father.

"Aren't you even going to ask me what it was that breached the shields?"

Logan stiffened at the same time his heart sped in his chest, the beginnings of adrenaline surging through his system.

"I assumed it was a glitch." Or even a misread by his father.

"Nope."

"What was it then?" He looked back at Jessica. She'd stopped playing at mad and was watching him with concern in her eyes, having obviously picked up on his growing tension.

"Get out your knife, Brother. Haven is under attack."

Chapter 15

JESSICA'S HANDS GRIPPED THE WHEEL, THE WINDSHIELD wipers slapping furiously at the streaming rain. She strained her eyes as she kept her focus firmly fixed on the road and the bumper-to-bumper traffic ahead of her. Looking in the review mirror wasn't going to show much of anything beyond the bus that kissed her bumper since she hit the RFK bridge. There was no silver Audi back there. Logan was already gone when she'd left the beach house. Something about a breach of Haven's walls. She hadn't asked what or where Haven was but she gathered enough from what he said to know it had something to do with the Paladin warriors he claimed to be part of. Some sort of safe zone from their enemies.

Forcing her attention on the erratic driving of the cab ahead of her, she ruthlessly ignored the choking hold that bore down on her chest since leaving the beach house. Logan had actually tried to command her to stay put, and then, when she'd responded with an *oh-really?* look, he'd practically begged. Saying that he needed to know she was safe. That he wasn't going to be able to keep his head in the game if he wasn't sure.

No, not a game. A battle. Good versus evil. Angel warrior against Lucifer's evil hordes.

It would be laughable except that she couldn't because, damn it, she was actually worried about him. And she shouldn't be, because yeah, she'd been coming around to believing him back at the beach house when he produced that freaky ball of light, but the farther away she got from what must have been some sort of tricky illusion, the more she realized that he was positively certifiable.

Angels didn't walk on the earth. People didn't live to be over a hundred. The knife tucked away in an old filing tube on her passenger seat had *not* been forged by a simple twist of *His* will. And the memories she had of that creature in the garage? Well okay, she didn't have a great explanation for that. Though obviously it was what Logan wanted her to be thinking about. Namely in terms of how helpless she was against it. Which was why, after having strapped on his own badass knife, Logan gave her the knife currently riding shotgun in her car. As long as her forearm and etched with symbols along the entire length of the curved blade, it was a wicked-looking thing that, yeah, did look really, really fricking old.

Probably stolen from someone's private collection. And even if it wasn't, the damn thing should be in a museum. Though she wasn't going to worry about that right now. She had other things to do today.

Edgy and on her last nerve, she made the series of turns that took her to Bruckner Boulevard and pulled into the lot behind the station. Normally she had to park in the way back, but Luck smiled on her and she managed to score a spot near the door when someone else pulled out.

She turned off the engine, fiddling with the keys in her hand before finally stuffing them into her pocket. Stalling wasn't going to help. Other than maybe chipping away at her resolve. She did take the time to stuff the tube under the seat, then, shoulders straight, exited her car and marched into the station.

Despite the traffic that had slowed her, it was still early and she caught the third shift desk clerk passing off the unfinished business to the day shifter. She waved to them both, and proceeded through to the back of the station house. Rancid coffee, sweaty men, tapping keys, and curses: This was the place where the real work got done.

The busy hustle and intense focus of a roomful of blues inventing new insults for their computers allowed her to pass through the room without anything more than an absentminded "hey Jess." Mike wasn't at his desk, though she figured he'd be in any minute. Her boots scraping impatiently on the gritty floor, she began to shuffle through the Post-it notes and loose papers on his desk. At first they were nothing more than a jumble of words, but then a name, Logan, jumped out at her.

She shifted through the notes again, quickly scanned each one. They weren't organized, more a puzzle for her already overtaxed brain, but it wasn't hard to see that Mike had done background checks. Fairly in-depth ones, too. There was actually an amazing amount of notes on Karissa Donovan, enough to raise Jess's eyebrows and then lower them when she saw a pair of circled words *No Siblings*. What the heck? Though, Logan did say she was a half-sister, maybe she was the illegitimate kind. Lips pursed, she shuffled through the rest. More on Karissa, Roland, Alexander Hastings, Alex, A.H. Mike had gotten tired of writing his name at the top of each note. Though despite the amount of paper, Mr. Hastings was what he appeared to be, nothing more. Jessica was left with three Post-its. All with L.C. on the top. Logan's job—expert on religious artifacts. Figured. Relatives—no known living relatives. She frowned. Police record—none. She gnawed on her lip, flipped through the papers again to see if she missed something. Nothing.

She plopped back in her chair, blowing a loose clump of hair out of her eyes. She probably looked a fright. Two days without a shower. A night of bed aerobics. The whole lot of crying she did in the driveway at the beach house before she put the car in gear. Oh yeah, she could probably scare the sobriety back into any one of the drunk and disorderlies sleeping off their hangovers in the holding cells.

She grabbed a tissue, wiping at her face. Who knew what the concealer had melted into after all she put it through? Peachy-beige streaks came off on the white fiber. She grimaced, grabbed another one, and wiped some more.

"Hopeless."

She tossed the tissues at the basket by the desk and missed. She grabbed them from the floor and went to stuff it in by hand, and stopped mid-motion. Inside rested a crumpled-up printout of a news article. The title was unreadable but part of the grainy picture was exposed and damn if it didn't look like...

She grabbed the crumpled paper out, hands shaking as she flattened it on the desk. It was an old article from 1938 about an opening of The Cloisters, a branch of the Metropolitan Museum of Art located in Fort Tryon Park.

Not what she expected to find in Mike's trash.

Except…her gaze went back to the picture. Four men stood before the almost completed structure. The architect, Charles Collen, donors John D. Rockefeller Jr., and George Grey Barnard, and his collection curator, Logan Calhoun. The last man was a dead ringer for her Logan. Only it couldn't be. That would make him…

"At least a hundred years old," she whispered.

"Well, well. Look what the cat dragged in."

Jessica jumped, her hands rumpling the already crumpled paper. She quickly shoved it into her jeans pocket, her mind spinning gears rapidly as she tried to fit in the newest wrench. Grandfather perhaps? But those eyes…

Mike grumbled something as he moved around his desk, set down his coffee cup, and sat. The wooden chair creaked as he leaned back in the seat, rocking it. He looked haggard. His eyes shadowed by dark circles, his usual meticulously trimmed whiskers grown out to the point where it was hard to discern the artful goatee.

"You okay?" she asked.

"Oh yeah. Sure. Though I suppose I should be asking you that." He snapped his fingers. "Oh wait, I did, about a dozen times. Seven of them on your cell and another five on your home phone. You. Never. Called. Back."

She blinked, unclipping her cell phone and flipping it open. Dead.

"Shit. I'm sorry, Mike."

"You're sorry." The chair squeaked again, note papers crunching as he leaned forward on the desk, lowering his voice. "Tell me exactly what you're sorry for, Jess? Lying to your partner? Putting yourself in needless danger? Breaking and entering into private parking garages—again without backup—or the worst in my book, not answering your damn phone for the last fifteen hours and making me sick with worry?"

She shook her head. There was nothing she could say to make it better. Instead, she reached into her blazer pocket and pulled out the evidence bag, setting it and its contents on the desk.

"What's that?"

"Evidence. A security tape from an adult store about a block from the alley."

His eyes lit briefly, then narrowed on the small gray tape. "Is a block close enough that we can draw a pool of suspects from its contents?"

She hesitated. In some of the busier places in the city the DA would laugh if they admitted a security tape from over a block away as evidence, but in that deserted area? "Maybe. There isn't a lot of traffic in that area. Regardless, there is something else interesting on it."

He picked up the evidence bag, taking out the receipt. He scanned it over, his eyes flicking twice to the date and time stamp.

"Yesterday at 6:15. About a half hour before I made my first call to you." He nodded, as if contemplating this. Slowly, methodically, he put the receipt back in the bag and then took out the tape. "So. You just decided to go on an unplanned vacation with possible evidence in your car?"

She remained silent, Fifth Amendment and all that. Mike sighed and stood up, jerking his head for her to follow. They made their way down to a room filled with electronic equipment. It took some digging, but he found something that would play the old style VHS and did some magic with some cables to get it set up to play on the TV. Mike folded his arms, his face unreadable as he watched her follow the two men chasing the hooker down the street. She half wondered if he'd recognize her, the video quality was that bad and the angle terrible, but her uncertainty evaporated the moment he opened his mouth.

"Jesus Christ, Jess. What the hell is this?"

She took a deep breath, forcing the words out. "That's me taking myself off the case."

Mike's gaze swiveled around to her, his eyes blinking in disbelief, but then he scoffed. "Because you went after some thugs without backup? No, that's not it. From what the Sarge says, you do that all the time. So why are you taking yourself off this case?"

She folded her arms. Mike didn't recognize the other two men, and she was unwilling to go into the sordid details of why that one little security tape was irrefutable proof of how much she was compromised. No, not unwilling. Unable. Just the thought of opening her mouth and implicating Logan in what appeared to be a criminal activity made her feel like she'd been grabbed by a mean grizzly, shaken, tossed around, then sat upon. She ached. Whole body, right down to that annoying organ behind her rib cage.

Mike shook his head, then focused back on the TV as he replayed the tape. He watched the woman, the two men—rewound. His eyes narrowed as the two men crossed the screen again, then straightened abruptly, hitting the pause. "Holy Christ. That's the damn lawyer, isn't it? I knew there was something about that guy."

She folded her arms across her aching ribs. "Could

be he was trying to track down some information for a client?"

Yeah, that's right, Jess. If you state it in question form you're not lying. Right...

"In that getup?" Mike asked.

"What do you wear when you go undercover?"

Mike looked at her sharply. Goddamn it. Totally. Compromised. Why was she going out of her way to defend them? Whether their presence there was truly as altruistic as Logan claimed or not was no longer her call. Off. The. Case. With good reason, too.

Her hand slipped into her jeans pocket, fingering the crumpled article. A hundred years old. If not older. Damn. Damn. Damn.

"You're really taking yourself off the case?"

She nodded. "I have lots of time built up. I'll, uh, tell the Sergeant that there was a personal issue I had to deal with."

And wasn't that actually the truth? How fucking honorable of her.

"I really wish you wouldn't."

She arched her brow. "Weren't you the one who told me to get my shit together?"

"Yeah, but I'm not sure this is the way."

She sighed. "Mike—"

He cut her off. "Before you decide, I got something to show you."

"You mean all the notes on your desk?"

He tipped his head.

She shrugged. "I snooped. Even pulled this from the trash." She pulled out the crumpled article, handing it to him.

"Oh, that." He shook his head. "That came up in my search. Obviously it's a different Calhoun. Maybe a relative or something."

Maybe. But that sick twist in her gut was telling her no. The article was over three quarters of a century ago and he didn't look a day older than he did now. In another seventy-five years she'd be dead. Would he still look the same?

What the hell? She was thinking like she believed him. Which she didn't. If she believed Logan's devil and hell on earth stories, then she was going to have to believe in Logan's bullshit about being an earthbound angel. And she couldn't buy that because, see, if there were angels, well then why the fuck hadn't they saved Julia?

Goddamn you, Logan. Where were you six years ago when I needed you to save someone? Julia would have been the perfect damsel for his honorable white knight routine. Would have lapped up all that angel and demon crap too. Probably would have even found the idea of immortal angel-spawn falling in love with her mortal self tragically romantic.

Love Logan. She swallowed. Most. Definitely. Tragic.

"Oh, good. I found you, Mike," a voice said from the door, drawing her focus back to the room.

Oh crap. Jessica tried to ease back further behind Mike. No go. Mike leaned forward, flicking off the TV, and giving the man at the door a clear view of her.

"Jessica?"

She lifted her gaze, past the leather jacket slung over the man's shoulder, past the stubble of five-o'clock—or eight a.m. in this case—shadow on his jaw and found herself pinned by Damon's dark gaze.

And damn it to Hell. How could she have forgotten about Damon? Yeah, true, she'd planned on telling him that it wasn't working out between them, but technically she supposed they were still dating. And what had she done but have a one nighter with another man? The fact that she desperately wished it could be more than one night had no bearing here. She couldn't allow it to.

"Oh, uh, hi." She was at a loss for what else to say. This was decidedly awkward. Thankfully, she didn't have to come up with anything more articulate because Mike took over.

"Damon, I thought you would have left by now."

"I had a few things to wrap up before my night off." His lip skewed up at the side. "Well, hopefully my night off. We'll see if I make it through the next forty-eight without a call in."

Jessica nodded, not knowing what else to say in response. Damon went on.

"It's good to see you, Jess. Mike filled me in. Said you had some trouble." His gaze landed on her cheek. She'd almost forgotten about the abrasion. "Looks like he was right."

"Yeah, it's noth—"

"Nothing," Mike spoke over her, shaking his head. "I can't tell you how sick of that I am."

She lifted her chin. Maybe she couldn't fix everything she fucked up over the last few days, but she could own up to that. "You're right. It's not nothing. I shouldn't have gone out alone. I was tired and distracted and paid the price when a couple of thugs jumped me."

Mike folded his arms. "So, just to confirm…not evening commuters?"

She grimaced, making busy by putting the tape back in the bag for Mike. The silence stretched, but when she finally turned back around she saw that the men weren't looking at her but each other. Measuring each other up? Or passing secret messages?

Reluctant allies seemed the best way to describe the two. Brothers in blue, but far from friends in any other setting. If they were having silent conversations now, then Mike must have been seriously worried about her.

Woo hoo! Way to go, Jess. Best partner. Ever. She wished there was a brick wall nearby...so she could smack her head against it.

A moment later they broke eye contact. Mike cleared his throat as he turned back to her. "Did you get the impression they might've been waiting for you, or perhaps even following you?"

"I'm not sure. Why?"

"Tom's Mustang was gone." She opened her mouth to tell him she'd seen it but he held up his hand. "It was there, I don't doubt you on that. Numerous tenants saw it in that garage and there was fresh oil on the ground."

"You think they followed me from Tom's car, then took the opportunity to attack when I was alone?"

"I don't know. You tell me."

She drummed her fingers against her thigh, remembering how she'd been paranoid that she was being followed. She'd convinced herself that it was Logan she sensed, but was it?

Damon stepped closer, his dark eyes hooded with worry. "Did you notice anything unusual about them, babe? Any distinctive features? Something that we can tell the rest of the guys to look for?"

She looked from Damon to Mike. She felt positively stupid for saying this, especially with Damon here, but… "Their teeth. I think they may have undergone some of that cosmetic dentistry that Melissa was talking about."

"You're shitting me," Mike said.

"Cosmetic dentistry?" Damon asked over him.

Mike made a motion with his hand. Two fingers extended like fangs.

Damon folded his arms, lips pulled tight.

"Melissa says there is a subculture of Goth types who like to play at vampirism," Jessica explained.

"And they attacked you? Two of them?"

She started to shrug it off, but Mike pointed his finger at her, waving it. "Don't you dare say it was nothing."

She closed her mouth.

Another significant look passed between the men.

"What?" she snapped.

Mike jerked back around, his face almost apologetic as he spoke. "That time-off thing might not be a bad idea."

She wanted to say she wasn't some fragile wallflower. That she could handle a couple of assholes in a garage. But she couldn't exactly say that truthfully now could she? And besides, wasn't the entire point of this visit to drop off the evidence and *remove herself from the case*?

She cleared her throat, pointedly not looking at Damon. God, what must he be thinking? *That you're insane? That you're chicken? Ding, ding, right on both accounts.* Though not for the reasons he must think.

"I think you're right." She glanced at the clock. "Either of you know if Sergeant Banks is in?"

"In a meeting with the captain," Damon offered.

She grumbled. Of course. "Guess I'll tag him later then."

"I'll give him the heads up," Mike said. "Tell him you'll be calling."

She nodded, started to step toward the door, but Damon shifted into her way.

"Can I see you home?"

Her first instinct was to refuse. She had so much to think about and didn't want to have to deal with the problem of Damon, but Mike was watching her, even gave her a slight nod of his head in encouragement. Damn, if she didn't, then Mike was going to insist on doing so. Hmm, the partner she'd fucked over or the guy she hadn't fucked but had cheated on?

Might as well get the dumping over with.

With a quick nod for Damon, she slipped from the room. Then, after stopping by her desk to collect a couple things, she let Damon escort her out of the building.

"Don't leave the lot. I have to get my car from the back," he said when they'd reached her beat-up Chevy.

She mumbled an okay, then sat tapping the steering wheel impatiently as he jogged off to get his car. She really, really wasn't looking forward to the upcoming conversation, but it was the right thing to do. Well, the right thing barring traveling back in time and breaking up with him correctly three mornings ago.

A minute later Damon drove up, stopping just down the row from her. She backed out of the spot and turned out of the lot. They drove slowly through the city, killing another forty-five minutes, the morning traffic having gone from snail pace to clogged-toilet speed. Damon followed her patiently. Never close enough to take off paint but never far enough to let the eager cabby between her and his Viper. It was black, of course. Everything about Damon was black, from his almost ebony eyes to his leather coat to his car. She even had an image of his apartment though she'd never actually been in it. It would be a loft studio filled with black, modern furniture and minimal decorations. Idly she found herself wondering whether he came from some sort of money because that car was definitely not purchased on a cop's salary. All of a sudden, Jess realized that she really knew nothing about the man she'd been dating. Far less than he knew of her, at least. Hell, she even told him about Julia. She never told her coworkers about Julia. Not even Mike.

She bit her lip. Definitely odd. She was not a bare your heart kind of girl, but as she thought back and analyzed their interactions, she began to realize just how unusually chatty she'd been.

Not anymore. Moment they got to her apartment she was going to thank him, break up with him, then send him on his way. Cold-hearted? Maybe. But safer—given that she didn't want to talk about what had happened over the last couple days—and frankly all she could manage at this point in time.

They reached her apartment. Damon followed her into the lot that conveniently butted up to the back of her building and stole the first spot available. She barely had time to retrieve the tube from under the seat before he opened her door for her.

"You don't have to see me up. Besides, probably better to not keep your car there long, seeing how you don't have a permit," she added as she stepped out, secretly glad for the excuse to get the whole dumping thing over with quickly.

"I'd feel better seeing you to the door," he replied, his eyes scanning the dim parking lot. Mildly alarmed, she followed his example and saw…nothing.

Paranoid.

"Nothing's going to happen to me."

"Humor me," he said, his tone leaving no room for argument. She was about to anyway when he turned his gaze back on her, the power of all that intense focus like a stiff wind snuffing her will to fight.

"Fine. Yeah, that would be nice," she said, and as they walked together toward the building, she realized it was true. The night was so dark, no moon and half the safety lights were out. Damon was strong and competent and she couldn't help but feel safe around him. It wasn't until they were inside the straining elevator, the flickering florescent light threatening to send her into an unprecedented fit of epilepsy, that the sense of ill-ease wore off. What was she doing? Letting him come up to her place was only going to confuse things. What was it her mother said: "If you don't want to see him again, then break the date at the door. Don't let him inside the building."

"Bit late, Mom," she muttered under her breath.

"What's that?" he asked just as the elevator jerked to a stop.

"Nothing." She led him down the hall in awkward silence, the only break the sounds of their own footfalls. She may have wanted to end it outside, but she didn't need to share her personal life with her neighbors.

She entered her apartment, setting the tube on the console table while Damon stepped in and closed the door. And since he was already inside, she also took the time to remove her jacket and holster too. It wasn't until she hung them both in the closet that she turned to Damon, a half-assed apology/letdown on her tongue, only he beat her to it.

"So, who's the lucky guy?"

Her head snapped back, a weird mix of horror and embarrassment rushing through her veins. How did he know? Was it written all over her or something? "Excuse me?"

He smiled, kind of sad like, reminding her of the last time he stood in her apartment foyer. "The guy you're ditching me for."

She looked down at the tube on her console, remembering, again, Logan's insistence that she keep it with her. That he needed to know she was safe. It would have been a good memory but for the bowl that sat next to the tube. The one her keys had been in, even though she'd never put them there. *Don't think about that*.

"There is no guy. Not anymore," she said, her voice sounding horse and hollow, as if the life were being sucked right out of her.

"No?" Damon's fingers brushed her cheek, pushing her hair behind her ear. "But you want there to be, don't you?"

When she didn't bother to deny it, he let his hand drop, a short, self-deprecating chuckle rumbling in his chest. "I guess we have that in common at least."

She raised her head, gave him a questioning look.

"You know," the side of his mouth quirked up, "wanting someone who doesn't want us back."

"Damon…" She trailed off, because really, what could she say? I do want you? Untrue. And to tell him that wanting Logan and Logan wanting her in return was not the problem would almost be cruel. Unless of course she went on to explain the whole sordid tale. In which case he'd probably pity her for being positively nuts for a guy who was either a criminal or so far off his rocker he might as well be in a straightjacket.

She didn't want pity.

"Jessica?"

She took a deep breath, carefully hanging her keys on the hook rather than the bowl. "Let's just say there are a million reasons why it didn't work out."

"You want to talk about it?"

No, she really didn't, only the longer he stared at her, the more she found she actually wanted to. Alarm spiked, but just as quickly faded. She weaved on her feet, her muscles going lax. The only thing holding her up was Damon's steady black gaze. Damn, he had the most gorgeous, kind eyes. And he listened so well. What would it hurt? She was so tired. So sick of holding it all in, going through life alone.

"Don't you want to talk about it, Jess?" he asked again, his voice hardly more than a soft whisper. She found herself nodding. Yeah, she did. She really did.

"You remember the day you first asked me to coffee?" she asked. He'd come to her desk and told her that people had to stop stealing his cases. The case he referred to was the Thomas Rhodes case, and the day was when they got a positive ID on a John Doe, removing it from organized crime, and tying it to Mike's attempted rape case. She inherited the case *and* Mike, but not Damon. Despite his joking, his position on a new prostitution ring task force kept him busy enough.

"Will never forget it," he said, his voice low, silken.

The heat in his tone was enough to make her suck in a breath, but nothing more. In fact, what it did was drive home everything that had been missing in their relationship and everything she found last night with Logan. Craziness aside, the moment Logan and she came together, their eyes locking as their bodies shuddered from the exquisite pleasure of taking and being taken, she'd felt something for the first time. She felt perfect, right, complete.

And then I woke up.

"Jessica?"

She blinked, looking back at Damon. His brow furrowed, his eyes filled with concern. She found herself desperately wanting to ease his worries.

She took a deep breath, blowing it out. "Sorry. I just feel so stupid about this whole thing." And so tired. She could hardly stand on her feet, let alone concentrate. Damon was looking at her expectantly though, so they must have been talking about something important. "What were we talking about?"

"You were about to tell me how our first date had anything to do with some other guy. Which, I must say, is already a real ego buster so please go gentle here, okay?"

She chuckled, grateful for his teasing. What guy would joke at their own expense to make a girl feel better? "Someday you're going to make some woman a great boyfriend."

"But not you?"

She shook her head, somewhat sadly. It was so weird. Damon was nice. And yeah, hot. She should want him. But there was something about him, something she was thinking of in the car coming over here…something to do with Julia and—

"All right then. Let's get back to the asshole currently breaking your heart. I'll make him see reason if you want." He winked, punching the palm of his own hand with the other. The action snapped her out of her thoughts and she straightened, shaking her head.

Logan, they were talking about Logan.

"Actually I'm the one breaking it off."

His brow winged up. "And this has something to do with our first date?"

She nodded.

Damon plopped down on the nearby couch, gesturing for her to sit also. "I have a feeling this could take a while."

"Not that long," she said but found herself sliding down onto the opposite end. Her legs rejoiced over the reprieve. She was thoroughly exhausted, both physically and emotionally. In fact, if she sat here long she'd simply slip down the rest of the way onto the cushy suede and start snoring.

"You look beat."

"I am," she replied, failing the fight to keep her eyes open.

"Long night, babe?" His voice rumbled deep in his chest.

Her eyes snapped back open, but he was smiling at her, his dark eyes twinkling.

She sat up straighter, shaking her finger at him. "You're bad."

"I know." He said this with all seriousness. It was enough to have her frowning, but when he didn't expound, just gestured for her to go on, she shrugged letting the comment slide.

"So, I'm assuming you remember the case that you dumped on me," she said.

He nodded. "I may not have ended up working it, but you and Mike have told me enough here and there that I know the basics."

"You're aware that our witness identified our suspect, but we had to release him?"

He nodded again, more warily.

She took a deep breath. "Let's just say that I did something stupid and allowed my emotions to sway me."

He held up his hand, his eyes narrowed on her in disbelief. "Wait, wait, wait. You're saying that this guy you're dumping me for is involved in the case?"

"I'm not dumping you because of him."

He gave her a disbelieving look.

"Okay, maybe he was the catalyst but I'm not dumping you for him. The truth is, I was trying to come up with the nerve to do that before this all happened."

"Oh yeah, and that is *so* good for the ego."

She cringed, guilt assailing her. Why had she said that? Why was she being so cruel? "I'm sorry."

"No," he shook his head. "It's all right. What is not all right is that you're personally involved with someone in a police matter."

"I know." And she should have told Mike. There must have been some reason she hadn't…She rubbed her temples, trying to figure it out but her head felt so thick, muddled.

"Wait, it's not the va—" Damon cleared his throat. "The suspect?"

"Not him," she scoffed at herself. "Just his best friend."

Damon sat up straighter, his head turned just slightly as if trying to piece something out. "His friend. Does this friend have a name?"

"I'm not so sure it's a good idea to tell you that." She didn't like the look in his eyes. They'd changed, no longer dark and inviting but dark and, well, foreboding, and in this light almost a freaky, ebony color.

What was it about the men in her life and their changing eye color?

He shook his head, as if shaking off some gloomy thought. "You're right. It doesn't matter anyway." He shifted, fidgeting. "But wow. That is definitely a conflict of interest."

"Hence the vacation," she said, sinking her chin into her hands. They sat for another few moments of silence, her head bobbing, though she couldn't sleep, not with him restlessly shifting on the couch.

She forced herself to sit up, open her eyes. "Do you want some coffee or something?"

"No. Actually I should go. There's something I've been putting off but need to take care of," he added, standing up.

"Oh. Okay." She stood as well, having to hold the arm of the couch to steady herself. The room was spinning, though at least she didn't feel as exhausted as a moment before. She'd practically fallen asleep with him sitting there! She frowned, not remembering asking him to come in and sit down…What were they talking about?

"You weren't planning on going anywhere, were you?" he asked as he headed toward the door.

"No," she replied, following him down the short

hall. Her legs were steadier. Must have been a bout of exhaustion. All those hours of *not* sleeping catching up with her. Crap, she hoped she hadn't actually dozed off on Damon.

"Good. And you have both mine and Mike's numbers on speed dial, right? And you won't answer the door for anyone."

"Not without my gun."

He pinned her with his dark gaze. She met him glare for glare. He leaned in and Jessica felt herself shrinking back. *He's going to kiss me.* But all he did was tip up her chin.

"Not even with your gun," he said sternly. "Crushed heart or not, I'm kind of fond of you." He let go, slipping on his coat on the way to the door. "Be sure to lock up after I leave."

"I will."

With one last penetrating glare he left. She closed and locked the door behind him, knowing he would most likely stand there on the other side until he heard the bolt turn. Then again, maybe he wouldn't. He'd certainly seemed antsy to leave.

And distracted. Definitely distracted.

That was okay, she was distracted too. Her mind kept on turning back to what she was going to do next. Turning in that tape may have ended her involvement in the case but it didn't solve her real problem. Logan knew where she lived. When he was done with, well, whatever it was he was actually doing, he would go to the beach house and then, not finding her, it wouldn't take him long to guess she'd come here. The question was, when he did, would she let him in?

Unable to answer that, she moved over to the refrigerator, filling a glass with some ice water. It wasn't until she'd plunked herself onto the couch that she noticed her message light blinking at her.

Groaning, she dragged her butt back up and shuffled over to the breakfast counter. The first message was a hang-up, and then Damon's voice crackled through the speaker, the connection poor as he was obviously deep in the concrete bowls of the station, his voice lowered as he first checked to see if she had any free time coming up, then asked what she'd done to put Mike in such a pisser of a mood.

She grimaced a bit at that, then moaned out loud when the next message turned out to be from Mike. As well as the next and the next. That's right, he said he'd called multiple times. She rolled her neck, listening to the brief messages—*call me; call me now; damn it, Jessica, call me will you?*—and then added them to her list of deleted, simultaneously grabbing up her cup. The next message started. Her hand paused midway to her mouth as a raspy male voice, fuzzed by an even raspier connection, greeted her by name.

She recognized that voice. It belonged to a man who supposedly didn't exist.

She set the glass back on the counter; her hand trembling as she carefully pressed 2 to save the message and then replayed it one more time just to be sure. Only she really didn't need to. She'd never forget that voice. Never.

"What the hell is going on?"

Chapter 16

DAMON STALKED DOWN THE SIDEWALK TOWARD THE subway, having left his car back at Jessica's apartment. It wasn't like he was going to need it where he was going. Just as the goody-two-shoes Paladin had their Haven, the dark brotherhood had their own little hellhole. Literally. Tucked into a condemned portion of the NYC subway system, the little gathering place conceived by the axis of evil—Lucifer, Ganelon, and the former, as in dead, master-vamp Christos—was both in this world and not. And since none of the three had access to His realms, they'd used the next best thing for their little slice of alternate reality: the big ol' H-E-double-hockey-sticks.

Damon shook his head. Since when did he go around thinking in soccer mom lingo?

When Damon took on the task of becoming a human cop, his assignment was threefold: Find susceptible souls ripe for the picking—easy when working with criminals; use his position to clog up the human's own quest for justice—which was good for Lucifer's business; and keep his nose to the ground for any leads on the Paladin and fuck up their plans as best as possible— always a pleasure.

Things had been going fine and dandy. His position on the force solid—the gullible schmucks he worked with were blind as bats—the only clog in the wheels was the occasional sensitive human—like that cop he had to kill a couple months back. Damon frowned. The uneasy feeling rolling down his shoulders whenever he thought of that stupid cop was not good for his welfare. You didn't live long as one of Ganelon's minions if you had a conscience, so this little prick at his was not exactly welcome. Especially considering how poor his batting average had been of late.

Thomas Rhodes. The case from Hell. Literally.

It had looked like a perfect opportunity for Damon. A three-fer. A soul ripe for the picking. Check. A lead on one of the Paladin. Check. And now for the triple: use Rhodes to fuck said Paladin over and screw with humanity. Win. Win. Win.

Except then Christos, the vampires' former leader, fucked up the capture of the fallen Paladin, Roland, creating a pile of shit to clean up. A misread prophecy, a hundred of their army eradicated, Christos dead— though the debate was still out on whether this was a bad thing—and then to top that all off, Thomas Rhodes's body had resurfaced. Frankly nobody but the vampires gave a rip about that—it was they who'd suffer if word of their existence got out, wary prey being difficult prey. But where others saw nothing but another failure on Christos's part, Damon saw opportunity. Roland, though fallen, still had ties to the Paladin. Enough so over a dozen of the goody-goods came out to slaughter vampires, demons, and merker alike when Roland's mate was threatened. And yeah, the vampires were hit the hardest, but that didn't change the fact that every branch of Hell's army suffered losses. And losses didn't please Lucifer. Not one bit. And when Lucifer wasn't happy? Ganelon wasn't either. And that? Well, that was actually an opportunity.

Damon figured if he could get Roland back in the NYPD's spotlight, then it was only a matter of time until at least one of his buddies came running to the rescue. And Damon had vowed to be around to claim that prize when they did. Paladin prizes made both Lucifer and Ganelon happy. And the one who brought them that prize? The reward would be more than his half-demon heart could imagine…and frankly he could imagine a lot.

Except, of course, there was going to be no reward. All Damon's tweaking and manipulations hadn't worked. Or rather, he fucking missed the opportunity.

Damn Jessica. She'd just had to keep pushing. Like a dog with a bone, she wouldn't let it go. One little *t* uncrossed and she went in sniffing like a hound dog. The case was irrevocably fucked. Damon's opportunity missed, and if things didn't shift directions in a real hurry, then he was going to have to kill another god-damn cop…though, maybe not. It looked like the vamps were going to take care of that for him.

Unless that damn Paladin came to her rescue again.

Fuck. He was so screwed. Why hadn't he picked up on the Paladin sniffing around Jessica earlier?

Maybe because you've been too busy chasing tail?

Damon shook his head. He knew the real problem. And it wasn't Jessica's stubborn refusal to give in to his seductions, though she was distracting in a sexy, kick-ass sort of way. His heart just wasn't in it anymore. He could hardly remember the last time he'd gotten enjoyment out of fucking with a human's head. It was as if by immersing himself so thoroughly within the cops' world, their humanity and values rubbed off on him. Things like loyalty and honor, friendship and respect, right and wrong.

Which was suicidal. He didn't believe in any of that crap, except the loyalty. And his loyalty was to Ganelon. Not weak-minded humans. And not the angel-spawn bastards who hyperventilated every single time one of those humans lost their souls to the landlord downstairs.

Taking the stairs instead of the clogged escalator, Damon jogged down into the bowels of the New York City subway system. A quick pat at his jacket pocket had him swearing. Left his badge in the glove compartment of his car. And since he was currently broke...

No matter. A quick pull of power and he vaulted over the barriers, the guard smiling and waving as Damon passed by. He arrived at the platform just in time and jumped on the 4. A bit of boring stop-and-go later, and he hopped onto the D. All the way to the end at Norwood. Bingo.

There was the typical flush of people getting off, but no one was very interested in anyone else's business unless it obstructed their own. Still, he waited a few seconds for things to clear out, then with a quick glance over his shoulder, jumped down on the tracks.

It wasn't far. In fact, the opening to the old, unstable tunnel was well within view of the platform. But people saw what they wanted to see and he suspected very few of them knew about this old section of subway anyway. It was never completed, probably something to do with the huge sinkhole less than a half mile into it. It was actually lucky they put the tunnel structure in before the sinkhole occurred. Otherwise, he bet there would be a missing building instead of an unusable piece of track.

Damon slowed to a stop before the illusion of rough cement, bracing himself for the unwelcome sensation of walking through molten lead. Damon had never figured out if Lucifer actually managed to trap a soul into the shield or if it simply took on its own evil intent from its master. Whatever the case, he guessed he was still bad enough because it let him through.

Ignoring the bickering gerbil talk of a couple imps and the snapping jaws of the hounds of Hell chained in an enclave near the door, he strode down the tunnel, the heat of Hell wafting up at him from the glowing sinkhole that marked its end. He didn't make it that far, fifty feet in he took a sharp right, sucking in deep breaths of the fresher air that was only slightly tainted with sulfur. His lips curled in disgust at the scents of despair, stale blood, and black hatred, but when he realized what he was doing he grimaced and schooled his face into impassivity.

He entered a chamber that had been carved out of the end of the tunnel, his only greeting a keening cry that went beyond human and signified unfathomable agony. Someone must have angered dear ol' dad because he was tearing off their hide—literally. Damon didn't know what the idiot had done but was sincerely glad it wasn't him on that table because he'd be damned surprised if even a merker could heal from such abuse and not look a monster.

No one else was in the chamber but Ganelon and his victim, everyone presumably having had the brains to go somewhere else. Gluttons for punishment or not, no one wanted to be the focus of the betrayer's finely honed motivational techniques. Damon would have fled, too, if not for one thing: He was out of time.

Or rather Jessica was. Damn her. He didn't want to have to kill her, but she was leaving him with no choice. A Paladin. Jessica was getting it on with a Paladin. How fucked up was that, dumping *him*, an incubus, for one of those goody-two-shoes freaks? If he had more time he might've risen to the challenge and stolen her back, but since Damon had recently been reproached for "a seemingly long stretch of unproductiveness," he'd better make sure Ganelon heard of the new development from him and not someone else if he wanted to stay off that table.

He stopped just inside the door, breathing through his teeth as he waited for Ganelon to either notice him or finish. It didn't take long for either. Ganelon completed his last filet of skin and stepped back, cocking his head as he eyed his handiwork critically.

"What do you think?" Ganelon asked as he dragged the tip of the knife back and forth across his pants.

"I think he'd be remiss to cross you again."

"On that I think we can all agree, can't we Haron?"

The creature made a noise. Not a merker, a demon, Damon decided, though one of the parents had to have been one of the humanoid species. Had its mother been a succubus also? No, the shoulders were wrong and even like this, Damon thought he might've felt some sort of kinship for the thing—beyond pity that is.

Pity? Man I'm getting soft.

He dragged his attention back, his gut curling as he noticed Ganelon staring at him unhappily. More alarming, Ganelon had cleaned his knife but had yet to put it away.

Damon cast a nervous glance over his shoulder, wondering if perhaps the disapproval was for someone else who'd entered behind him. Nope, no one.

"What is it? Does my jacket offend you or something?"

"It is rather off-putting. *Fake* leather?"

Damon shrugged. "It fools most humans. Besides, I got sick of paying exorbitant amounts of money to replace the ones Lucifer's fire demons singe."

Ganelon murmured something that sounded like a "Hhmm" and picked up a sharpening stone.

"What?" Damon asked, lifting his hands helplessly.

"Aren't you forgetting something?" Ganelon said, nodding toward the floor. Despite the heat, a coldness seeped into Damon's veins. He was favored. Not having to prostrate himself to Ganelon, except when they were around others, was something he'd started to take for granted. The fact that he was expected to do so now when the only one present was a half-dead demon did not bode well for his future.

Holding his breath, Damon slowly lowered his head, dropping to first one knee and then the other. Only when he was fully prostrate on the floor and hadn't been cuffed with a bolt of power did he breathe again.

"Ah. Very good, Damon. You were always one of my favorites." Damon sucked in his breath again as he felt the tip of the knife slide under his chin and lift, tipping his gaze upward. "Now, how do you greet me?"

"I am here to serve you, master."

"Yes, very good. Very good. Now." Ganelon flicked the knife around in his hand, and jabbed the blade toward

Damon's shoulder. Damon repressed a sharp expletive as the blade bit through his jacket and poked into the flesh beneath. "Let's have a talk about your fashion sense...among other things of course. You did want to talk about something, didn't you my son?"

Closing his eyes Damon let his head drop back down. His father already knew. And now Damon would pay for his incompetence.

The question was how much.

Jessica paced the limited confines of her apartment, which certainly was not enough to work off the excess energy she had. Every few steps, her gaze would dart one way or the other. One time to the clock. Once to the charging cell phone on the counter. And lastly to the knife she'd pulled out from the tube and lain out on her coffee table. The knife he gave her for protection. Because he couldn't be here to do the bodyguard duty himself.

"He will be. He'll call back and then he'll come here and tell me what the fuck is really going on." Her gaze drifted over to her home phone and the blinking light on the base unit that said she had one saved message.

She was sure the voice on the machine was the man she thought she saw in the garage, the un-Samaritan. Only it couldn't be. Men did not turn into demons. Only...

What was it Sherlock said? "When you have eliminated the impossible, whatever remains, however improbable, must be the truth?"

Well she wasn't sure anything she was thinking right now was possible, but she was hard pressed to explain away the things she'd seen with anything but paranormal answers. Her logic had been shot down, and she had nothing to go on but gut, and obviously, her gut was having a serious case of the flu. She was going to be sick.

The message on her machine echoed in her mind again: *"Tell your boyfriend that my boss said we'd see him here real soon."*

Where was here? Who, or rather what, was the man and what did his boss have to do with anything? And did he mean Damon or did he assume Logan was her boyfriend? She had no answers to any of those, or the million other questions she'd come up with since then. She tried calling the number back but had gotten an out-of-service message. Dead end.

Maybe she should call Mike and ask him to see if he could trace the number, but what if everything Logan said was true? It was tempting to believe. Logan had managed to touch her in a way that no one else ever had. Being with him, though crazy, was the most free-ing thing she'd done in what seemed like forever. And it wasn't that she condoned the practice of one-night stands. She didn't. But if there was one thing her belated breaking with Damon made Jess realize, it was that her night with Logan wasn't one. She cared about him. And though the cop Jessica knew it was the dumbest thing she had ever done, the little bit of the old Jessica that came to life in Logan's arms was telling her to trust him. Though, if she did, where did it leave her? In a fucked-up world with vampires and demons, that's where. And how the hell did you combat something like that? Not with a badge, that's for sure. And without her badge, then what the fuck was her purpose?

Jess wrapped her arms around her rib cage, trying to hold back the sensation of her world exploding. *Stop it, Jessica. There has to be a logical explanation for all this.*

The phone rang. Thinking it was Logan, she practically jumped across the room, lunging for her cell and yanking it from the charging chord.

"Hello?"

"Jessica!"

Not Logan, but she was pretty sure she recognized that voice over the static. "Grim?"

"Oh thank fu...essica! ...need your ..elp."

"What's wrong, Grim? Where are you?"

"...chasing me...iding in...arehouse on...stre..."

"What street?" More static. "Damn it. I can't hear you. Say the street again, Grim!"

"Manid...eet...Jess ...urry, please..." the phone broke up into more static, then the gut-wrenching silence of a dropped call.

Jessica hurriedly slipped on her holster and jacket and grabbed up her keys and partially charged cell phone, pressing through her contact list for Mike. But as she flung open the door, Jessica learned one undeniable truth, even if it wasn't the one she searched for: Logan wasn't the delusional one, she was. Because the thing staring down at her from the other side of the door was most certainly not human.

Logan stared at the five intruders standing on the dais of Haven's main hall. Five *human* men. No, not exactly human, just mostly so. And certainly not the breach by the horde of merkers that he expected after Roland's call, though something *was* different about them. Something that screwed with not only his Paladin mojo but with every magical thing in the room. Including the relic that kept Haven bridged between the realms.

Maybe not our enemies, but for what they've done they might as well be. The moment the group entered the hall and their magic-negating effects came in close proximity to the cross embedded in the altar, Haven fell fully into the human world, the only protection a flimsy chain-link fence, and a hope and prayer that their real enemies wouldn't stumble upon their location before the threat could be removed.

"The one in the middle. She's the null," Alex said under his breath from where he stood on Logan's left side.

"She?" Valin, flanking Logan's other side, asked, cocking his head.

Logan also took another look, his eyes narrowing on the tall individual heading up the group. Okay, so one wasn't a man. That was a woman under all that Kevlar and face paint. Hips didn't lie and that Amazon had them. She also had shit-kicker boots, more ammo than Rambo, and spiky red hair.

Valin leaned in front of Logan toward Alex. "So which ancestor liked to dip his wick in the vat of human genes?"

Alex glared at him, clearly not amused.

Knowing the best policy with Valin was to ignore his tainted humor, Logan took half a dozen steps forward to close some of the distance with their trespassers. He tried to look nonthreatening—meaning he didn't draw the knife he'd strapped on to his thigh—but they tensed, some of the men stepping to the fore, forming a tight circle around Amazon, who reacted with a "hey" and an elbow to the ribs of her nearest companion. The man grimaced, but didn't move. Not that he had to for her to see. She was taller than him. In fact, Logan noted, she was taller than everyone in the room save himself and Alex.

"Idiots," she said, rolling her eyes.

It was clear that Amazon thought she could take care of herself. She was probably right. Besides the arsenal she wore, she had an aura of competence about her that suggested she was comfortable with or without them. More importantly, though, was *what* she was, and Alex hit that right on the head. Amazon was a nullifier. No magic would work when she was near. Which explained how her little group got into Haven in the first place. What it didn't explain was whether they realized when they entered that they were putting the entire order in danger. Given the fact they hadn't used any of the weapons they carried, he was inclined to think not.

The back doors to the hall burst open and Bennett and his team of three swept in, Logan's father and two other council members marching in behind them. It didn't escape Logan's notice that both his father and the other council members were winded. Logan figured they must have run from the far side of the underground facility when the null's squelching power had Logan blipping off the projective thought radar. Judging by the taken aback look on the council members' faces, and fact that Bennett and his team were all holding their knives, they'd believed Logan dead or at best incapacitated.

Understandable. Innocent in intent or not, the inter-lopers' presence *was* alarming. When Logan arrived, Haven was a mass of confusion. It was an attack, but it wasn't. Past the first breach there wasn't any out-right aggression, just the occasional blur of movement that hinted at an uninvited presence within Haven's previously impregnable walls. The entire hall was in lockdown mode. Draw back, protect the relics, send out sweep teams led by Paladin with strong projective thought to try and track the intruders down. Logan's team had simply been the lucky ones who stumbled across them, ironically on their way to protect the holy objects housed in this very hall.

Probably a good thing it was his team. There were a number of Paladin who wouldn't have hesitated to attack first, ask later, when they saw the five humans lounging in the council's chairs upon the dais.

Good thing they'd since stood up. Logan didn't want to think of the apoplexy his father and the other council members would have if they'd seen them sitting in those chairs. As it was his father was already issuing orders, his hand cutting toward the intruders with the command to neutralize them. Which was not good. His brothers would try to neutralize the intruders using their gifts. And when that failed?

Guns and ammo verses knives? Logan could hazard a guess at how that might turn out.

"Do you realize where you are?" Logan raised his voice over the commotion, holding his hand up toward his brothers, asking them to wait. There was an uneasy shuffle but their grip eased somewhat on their blades, their curiosity enough to stay their attack for the moment.

They were probably as curious as he. The others were now close enough it should be obvious that someone in the room was a null, and that it was her power that allowed the group to find and enter Haven. Logan had no doubt where, or rather from whom, the interlopers' powers came. Those "disappointing" half-Paladin offspring weren't so disappointing after all, the recessed genes finally having worked their way to the forefront. What astounded Logan was how far removed these mixed breeds were from their original Paladin ancestors, and yet how strong their powers were—or at least Amazon's, since it was hard to tell what the others were with her around. But the real question was whether they had simply stumbled upon Haven and decided to take a peek? Or had they purposely sought the order out?

Amazon's brow furrowed her head tipped slightly, as if asking her companions for advice. One of the guys leaned in from the side. "I think he wants to know what we're doing here."

"Ah," she nodded, but didn't answer.

"Well?" Logan's father voice demanded, his impatience obvious.

Amazon glared at Logan's father. Her eyes narrowed with something akin to disgust in them. "None of your beeswax, grandpa."

Logan had never seen his father sputter before. He figured all hell was about to break loose unless he jumped in and stopped it, because as annoying as Amazon was turning out to be, and as alarming as it was for the little band of misfits to have breached Haven's walls, they were, after all, family. Too bad his father didn't see it that way.

Not relishing the thought of going toe-to-toe with his father in front of his brothers, Logan hesitated. Surprisingly it was Valin who stepped forward, his hands held up in a placating manner.

"Actually, it kind of is. You did breach our walls and disarm us of our gifts in our own sacred hall." He flashed Amazon a smile that said that was some cool shit you pulled, but you can understand our position here.

She pursed her lips, but nodded. "Guess I'd be pissed too if someone crashed my pad."

"Exactly. Especially if you thought your pad was well hidden, right? That we, in fact, were hidden."

Amazon sighed, hand planting on her cocked hip. The choke on Logan's gift eased. Around the room there was a collective expulsion of breath, indicating his brothers, too, were released from her null effects. More relieving was she'd somehow reined in her gift enough for the relic to resume working; the almost painful sting of recognition from the cross signifying that Haven had slipped back into that space between realms once more, pulling him and the others in the hall with it.

"We knew you were around. Generational stories passed down. Sightings." She quoted this with her fingers. "And the fact that someone was hunting and killing off the demons and vampires. You know, things like that."

"So this is just a little hello, how are you, cousin?" Valin asked.

"No."

"No?"

She shrugged. "I'm supposed to deliver a message. From Red."

Valin's eyes narrowed. "Red?"

"Who the hell is Red?" Logan's father exclaimed, his gaze narrowing suspiciously on Alex.

Alex firmly shook his head, though his brow furrowed, his own gaze catching Logan's and Valin's as he mouthed, "The succubus?"

"Can't be," Logan muttered in reply, breaking their conspicuous gaze. He sincerely hoped Alex was wrong, just as he sincerely hoped his father hadn't noticed that little exchange. Though based on both Valin's thoughtful expression and his father's glowering one he was probably wrong.

"Who is Red?" Logan's father asked again, his voice dangerously low and the words evenly enough spaced for an imbecile to understand.

Amazon's mouth thinned, a tight white line in the black paint. Yup, that was a zip, click, and lock if Logan ever saw one. Thankfully they didn't have to convince her to dig the key out of the trash before his father blew a gasket, because one of her male companions stepped forward.

"We don't know her real name, but she's been invaluable. Things have been kinda tense lately, you know with the bump in the night creatures and all. She knows a lot of shit and has been helping us with our defenses."

"Wait, you said things have been tense lately. Have you been having a lot of run-ins with the creatures?" Logan used their word choice, not knowing if their creature-of-the-night sensei had gotten around to giving them the complete rundown on all things evil.

"Yeah, you always had to be careful, but the last few months? Things have been intense."

Logan's father pushed forward. "Did it ever occur to you that maybe this 'Red' was setting you up? That she's been helping you because she wanted you to do exactly what you've done?" He shook his head, glaring at Amazon. "Stumbling in here, your power unchecked. Do you have any idea the ramifications of your actions? You'd better hope this *mentor* of yours is as benevolent as you say because if not, then you've just painted a nice big 'X' on our door and given our enemies the key inside!"

"They weren't very good defenses if all it took was me to get inside," Amazon snapped.

His father's face went frighteningly stony. "Bennett, take our new guest down into the sublevels under the grounds. That should be far enough for her little talent to not create any more mayhem."

"You think I'm going to kowtow to your orders, grandpa?" Amazon sneered.

His father rounded back on her, his voice menacing as he waved his finger at her. "You *will* comply. You and your little "gift" is nothing more than a bomb waiting to go off in our faces. Bad enough your little band of mutts found your way in here, but I will not allow you to leave again to present yourself to our enemies to be used as a Trojan horse!"

Amazon growled, trying to push past the ring of men surrounding her.

"Enough!" Logan cut both of them off before they could exchange more insults—or worse. He had a headache brewing. Logan suspected his father's obvious dislike of this band of "mixed" bloods was based on a blown-up case of extreme paranoia. And though he could honestly understand his father's fear, the way to gain this little group's cooperation wasn't by insulting them.

Calm, civilized discussion. Where they had it didn't matter, as long as they talked.

"Bennett, why don't you contact Warren and have him take his team for a sweep of the surrounding area to make sure our guests weren't followed. Then we can adjourn to someplace where we can discuss our options."

Amazon shook her head, glaring at his father. "Me and my 'mutt' friends aren't going anywhere but out of here." She looked back at Logan. "Though you're welcome to join us; Red's message was for you, after all."

"Me," Logan said, his brow rising.

"Yeah you, Pretty Boy."

Pretty Boy. Logan was about to ask how in the hell she'd come by that nickname, when it hit him. Pain: A soul-scorching, fiery stab of agony collapsing him to his knees. At first he couldn't pinpoint its source.

But then he did. And the bottom of his world fell out from under him.

"Jessica!"

Chapter 17

His father was staring at him.

While Bennett and Alex took him down to the ground, covering him as if he were a fallen warrior, and everyone else scrambled around, weapons raised and ready as they tried to figure out where the attack came from, his father stood perfectly still staring at him through narrowed eyes.

I called her name. He must realize.

Logan sucked in deep breaths. The pain was easing now. Enough for him to understand the ramifications of what just happened. He'd all but told his father he was mated, and since the only women of note in his life right now were his sister and the human he'd recently wiped the memories of, it wouldn't take a genius to figure out to whom.

And he won't lift a finger to help her. Help me. Not when my bond mate is an undesirable human.

"What is it, Logan? What happened? Where are you hurt?" Bennett asked as he shifted back, his brow crunching up with confusion as he looked Logan over. Of course, there was no wound on him. Nothing visible at least.

But there would be on Jessica. The pain, though it had hit him throughout his body had originated from a physical wound. He wasn't sure how he knew that but he did. Just as he knew she was still hurting, though no longer in immediate danger.

He struggled to stand up, but got nowhere against Bennett's and Alex's strong arms.

"Let me up," he growled.

"Not until you tell us what happened, because I'm telling you now there ain't nothing here that should have caused you to scream like a girl," Valin said after resolidifying behind Bennett's shoulder.

Logan's gaze tracked to his father, who was still immune to the commotion around him. He was blatantly ignoring the other councilmen's questioning as well as the rest of Bennett's team as they finished their own sweep of the hall and confirmed Valin's pronouncement that the room was clear.

"My bond mate needs me."

Bennett jerked back as if struck. "Bloody hell, Logan. Since when have you been hiding that you're mated? And why?"

"She's human. Fully human," he added lest they think perhaps he'd found another half-breed like his sister somewhere—or a mixed blood such as the cluster of humans currently standing on the dais, weapons raised and ready.

The solemn looks on his friends' faces told him they got it. Having a human bond mate, one with no Paladin blood, was akin to being cursed. At least it had been for Ganelon.

It was Valin who broke the silence, shaking his head. "Shit. You really don't know how to do anything in half measures do you?" He glanced over at Logan's father, rubbing his hands together and grinning. "Well, I've always wanted to see how much it would really take to get your dad to blow his gasket."

"What are you going to do?" Alex asked.

"That's not for you to worry about," Valin replied. "Just get ready to bolt out of here, 'kay? And Bennett, use that pretty little machine of yours to get Logan to his mate, pronto."

"Will do," Bennett replied, nodding solemnly.

Tense and ready for action, Logan waited impatiently for Valin to do whatever he was going to do. Even though it was only a minute or two since he'd been hit with Jessica's pain, the aching pull pulsing through their tentative bond was enough to spin him into crazy if they didn't get moving.

Thankfully, it didn't take long for Valin to get a move on. He shifted into his ghost form, the black smudge of particles racing across the room toward Logan's father. A second later, Calhoun Senior was engulfed in a cloud of darkness, his curses the only thing that penetrated outside it.

Logan stumbled up, relying on Alex and Bennett to steady him for the few steps it took to adjust to the aching pain and get his feet under himself fully. Behind him, he heard his father yelling, ordering the rest of his brethren to stop him.

No way in hell.

Logan pushed himself faster, taking advantage of his brothers' confusion to reach the door before they could cut him off. They hadn't cleared the anteroom when behind them Logan could feel a pull of power and then, wham, the lights in the room dimmed, screams of confusion ringing from the hall as all within Valin's realm of influence were plunged into the chaotic darkness of the shade's twisted reality.

Shit, the crazy fuck must have done something to enhance his gift. Man that was going to cause all sorts of problems later.

He didn't spare the time or energy to worry too much about Valin's welfare, but followed Bennett as they sprinted to his Lotus. The fact that it felt like they were making a jail break didn't elude him, especially as they passed through the chain-link gate marking the cross from Haven back into the real world, and Bennett peeled rubber out onto the mostly deserted streets.

"Where to?"

"Fuck, I don't know." He'd left Jessica on the Island but was she still there? The only time he had a clear connection with her was when the pain first hit him and he'd been too shocked to try and pinpoint where.

Bennett scooped up his phone, flipped through a couple screens, then tossed the high-tech gadget back at Logan. "Type her cell number into that app. If it's on her and her security is as bogus as most commercial phones, we'll find her down to the square foot."

Logan's hand shook as he typed the number in and waited. When the little blue dot finally popped up on the map, he quickly rattled off the familiar address.

She was at her apartment. Why the hell was she at her apartment? Why hadn't she stayed at the beach house like he told her?

"I'm going to call Roland," Logan said when they began to hit more steady traffic and the rumble of the engine evened out.

"Good idea," Bennett said, without hesitation.

The drive through the city was agonizing at best. Especially since it took a couple tries to actually reach

Roland, which squashed his hopes that his friend, being closer, could reach her quicker.

They ended up arriving at the same time, meeting in the stairwell a floor away from Jessica's. Logan pushed through the fire door first, taking off at a run down the hall.

The floor was swarming with police.

Sheer determination broke him through the first line of uniforms, momentum allowing him to get close enough to the door to get a real eyeful. Cops moved about the apartment, tagging and logging a stream of objects on the floor. Cell phone and keys were mixed in with jagged pieces from the shattered bowl from the console that were strewn across the entry-way. Further along in the walkway between the foyer and her living room lay an overturned pile of books. That's where the knife he gave her lay—and where the blood started.

Blood in the living room, blood smeared in a steady line toward the kitchen counter and beyond.

Logan would have lost it completely if not for the persistent thread of pain that he continued to feel from Jessica. Wherever she was, however badly she was hurt, she was still alive.

"Where is she?" he demanded, trying to push past the uniform at the door.

The man who Logan assumed was in charge—suit jacket, tie, and a face aged beyond his years with deep scowl groves—gestured to a barrel-chested cop and then at them. "William, secure this scene!"

"I've got them," someone else piped up.

"You sure, Mike?" Suit asked.

Guess so because a plainclothes brushed past Buffalo Bill, steam-boating toward them.

"Crap, not him again," Roland muttered.

Logan blinked, gears clinking. This was Jessica's Mike? How would Roland…Of course. Mike must be the sensitive cop that took Roland in. Ergo, Jessica's partner and the man full of all kinds of helpful advice and concern. Despite the direness of their meeting, Logan couldn't fully suppress a wave of jealousy.

So fucked.

"Gentlemen, if you would step back a bit?" the Mike character said, gesturing down the hall.

"Where's Jessica," Logan asked again, grinding the words from between his gritted teeth, though he allowed himself to be ushered. Jessica wasn't there anyway, and if cooperating would get him her location faster, then so be it.

"I don't see how that is any of your business," Mike replied.

"Is she at Lenox Hill Hospital?" Bennett asked, his British accent playing with the mix of x, h's, and l's.

Mike smiled, his eyes on Roland as he answered. "No."

Fury slammed through Logan and he grabbed the cop's shirt, ready to twist him around and smash him against a wall, any wall.

"Logan!" Alex grabbed his arm, using enough steady pressure to keep him from lifting the man.

"Tell me where the fuck she is or I swear to God I'll—"

"Logan!" Roland snapped from his other side, his hand closing around his and prying Logan's fingers loose. "We don't want to make a scene now do we?" he muttered in Logan's ear, nodding at the cop guarding the door who'd started toward them.

Yeah he wanted to make a scene. A big scene. But his friends were right. This was not the way to make friends and influence people.

Mike cocked his head, his gaze intent as he stared at them. Logan took a steadying breath, consciously reigning in both his temper and the power he felt building deep within him. Alex and Roland both said this cop was a sensitive. He didn't need to do anything to make the man more inclined to not help them.

Play nice. Fly low. This Mike may be your only ticket to finding Jessica.

"You need assistance, Detective Ward?" The door guard asked, his hand hovering over his issue.

"No. We're fine here." Detective Ward arched his eyebrow, his eyes questioning. "Aren't we gentlemen?"

Logan clenched his teeth but nodded, letting Roland and Alex push him back toward the far side of the hall. The other cop hesitated, but he eased his hand from his gun's grip, and took a couple steps back toward his post.

"I'll see what I can find," Bennett murmured and then walked off down the hall, away from the apartment, already tinkering with his phone. Good, he was on top of it too. Hopefully, Jessica was someplace that could be tracked down with Bennett's combination of electronic savvy and golden tongue.

The detective cleared his throat, straightening his shirt. "I know your friends," he said, nodding at Roland and Alexander, "but I don't think we've been properly introduced yet."

The way the plainclothes said it sounded like he

didn't care to be either—that he viewed them as suspects and not concerned civilians. Logan didn't give a damn what the man thought other than how it might matter in getting Jessica's location out of him.

"I'm sorry about…" he nodded at the cop's rumpled shirt. "I'm just worried about Jessica."

Okay, and that was a definite no-go on the man's face. *Suck it up*. Logan took another deep breath, offering his hand.

"I'm Logan Calhoun. And you must be Jessica's partner."

The cop's brow winged up, even as he pointedly ignored the hand. Oh yeah, Logan was right, though it was obvious Mike was not all that thrilled with Logan's advantage.

"Jessica's mentioned you a couple times," he gave in explanation.

"Well she didn't mention you," Mike said, his voice still laden with suspicion.

"We're new."

"Yeah, I gathered. New as in the last week new? Because Jessica has been having an awful lot of problems recently."

The accusatory tone, the slow drag of the cop's eyes as he said this made Logan's jaw tighten and his body still with an ice-cold fury. That anyone would suggest he could harm his mate…"I would give my life to keep her safe."

"Wow." Mike rocked back on his heels. "Those are pretty powerful words for being 'new.' And something I'm not inclined to believe either." He reached into his back pocket, pulling out a small notepad. "Where were you about, oh, forty minutes ago? And while you're at it you can tell me where you were Thursday evening or better yet, between midnight and 4 a.m. on Wednesday morning."

"You being a dick because of me?" Roland asked, planting himself between Logan and the cop.

"No. Not just you." Mike flipped the notebook shut, stuffing it away. His gaze landed on Logan, the sneer saying it all. Mike considered Logan lower than slime and not even worthy enough to breathe the air needed to say his partner's name. Given that Logan had failed to protect her, twice, Logan might've agreed, but in the end it didn't matter. Jessica was *his* mate.

Easy on the possessiveness there, Cal. You may be her mate, but you're not the only one who cares.

Breathing out a deep breath, Logan glanced back at the swarm of cops coming and going from her apartment. Out in force. She was theirs too. One of their own had been attacked and they were going to figure out who and why. Though that might prove difficult if Logan was right and the suspect wasn't human.

"Please, just tell me where she is," he said, forcing his tone to be calm, reasonable, even soothing. See? Even on the brink of totally losing it he could be polite.

"Why?" Mike retorted. "So you can go and fuck her life up more?"

"No, but I'm going to fuck you up if you don't tell me where she is," he snapped, anger licking the edges of his sanity.

The detective's eyes narrowed and he stepped closer, lowering his voice. "Threatening an officer of the law. Nice. And the perfect excuse for me to bring you in."

Logan clenched his teeth, running through the list of reasons why he shouldn't let loose and show Mike all the inventive ways his power could be used to send the asshole to kingdom come. There were witnesses. Exposure. Jessica wouldn't want him to kill her partner. Okay, that last one worked. Sort of.

Mike rocked back on his heels, his lips parting in a cocky, cat-got-your-tongue smirk. Logan began chanting to himself as he tried to cap his power. *I will not kill Jessica's partner. I will not kill Jessica's partner.* The smirk slid off the cop's face. He made an odd sound and scratched at the back of his neck, rolling his shoulders. Oh yeah, he was a sensitive. Logan wondered what the cop would do if Logan took the lid back off and lit up this hallway like a supernova.

"Logan, might want to check that."

Alex, always the voice of reason, even when the shit was hitting the fan. Logan didn't care. He'd had enough and was about to retry the physical method of persuasion—not killing, just a bit of maiming—but Roland cut him off again, his voice low and cajoling as he tried to strike a deal.

"Tell you what. You tell my buddy where his girl is and I'll come down to the station with you, give you the statement you wanted the other day."

"She's not *his* girl," Mike snipped back.

Roland merely raised a whatever-you-want-to-believe eyebrow at that.

Mike ran his tongue over his teeth, his gaze shifting to Alex before settling back on Roland. "You're really going to go against council's advice?"

"He's my lawyer, not my babysitter."

That got a growl from Alex, but he otherwise held his tongue.

"You'll confess everything?" Mike pressed.

"There's nothing to confess," Roland said tightly. "But I'll give you a statement."

"One that can be proved?"

"Well, that depends on how open-minded you are." Roland eased in closer, his gaze moving pointedly to the hand that still rubbed the back of Mike's neck. But you're not very open-minded, are you, Mikey?"

"Roland, stop," Alex said sharply. "He's not ready for this."

But Mike was already eyeing them again, his brow furrowed as if either trying to work out a puzzle or trying to fend off a massive headache. He opened his mouth, ready to either ask what the heck Roland was talking about, or tell them to go to Hell, but he never got the chance.

"I got it!" Bennett called, causing four heads to swivel as he hurried back down the hall to them. "St. Luke's," he announced triumphantly.

Roland turned back to Mike "Sorry. Guess our deal is off." He smiled, showing just the barest hint of fang. "But call me if you ever want to hear the truth."

Chapter 18

I AM SO FUCKED, LOGAN THOUGHT AS HE ANALYZED the silken skin beneath his hand.

Though Jessica was a tall woman, and practically took up the entire length of the hospital bed, she looked dainty compared to him. So sweet, her lips parted slightly as she breathed, her slender rib cage rising and falling just enough to remind him of her fragile humanity.

Human. Vulnerable. And his mate.

His hand tingled against the delicate skin at the base of her smooth throat. A soul-eating desire pressing at him from the inside out, urging him to begin the ceremony that would mark her as his mate. That would bond them body, heart, and soul.

Do it. Mark her. It's the best way to protect her.

But he couldn't. Every time he began to center his power. Every time he opened his mouth, ready to let free the words that would begin the formal bond between them, was the moment that fear clamped down around him, stifling his power.

They were already too close. Their night together allowed him a window into her soul. A connection that he both feared and desired from the very beginning. If he marked her, opening that connection completely, he would feel everything. He would know her inside and out. All her wants and desires. Where she was. What she was doing. How she felt at any given moment in time.

And though he'd been told by other bonded Paladin that those things, though alarmingly invasive, still brought with them a fucked-up sort of comfort, it wasn't that which stayed his hand.

She was human, vulnerable. And, if fully bonded, he'd *feel* her die.

So what are you going to do, Calhoun? Let her run around out there unprotected? Let your enemies take her for their pleasure and your pain?

No. He caressed her throat, the place where his mark should be, but never would be. He couldn't mark her. But he *would* stay close. Watch over her. Keep her safe. She'd live a long life because of it. And if he was lucky, she would allow him to be part of it. She'd allow him to love her with every bit of his being that he could give her, and still keep enough safe to stay sane when she passed.

And is anything short of everything really going to be enough?

"It has to be," he said aloud, forcing his hand to lift from her throat. His voice, or perhaps the removal of the slight pressure of his hand, changed the atmosphere of the hospital room. He watched Jessica's eyelids flutter, her breathing hitch slightly as she drew in her waking breath. She blinked up at him, opening her mouth, then smacked her dry lips.

"Here." He reached over to the side table, pouring some water from the pitcher into a cup. It was warm now but he didn't dare go out to track down the ice machine. He was lucky to be in here at all, and wasn't about to risk being kicked out.

He had to use all his charm, flashing dimples left and right, to gain access to her room. Not that anything could have barred his way. He didn't exactly want to start wiping the minds of nurses, doctors, and staff alike, but if there had been no other way to get to Jessica, he would have.

Good thing he hadn't had to. Who knows if he might have inadvertently wiped something important? Another patient's well-being was not something he wanted to gamble with, and the Big Guy probably wouldn't have been too pleased with him either.

Yeah, and He's obviously so happy with you right now. Sending you a human for a mate.

Shoving aside the irreverent thought, Logan carefully handed Jessica the half-full cup. She took it, and he watched her sip, her hand trembling enough that water dribbled down her chin. The urge to take the cup from her and help her was great but he didn't dare. Not after their last parting.

She drank every drop then handed the cup back to him. As she did her eyes narrowed on the IV stuck in her hand. The bandages were bloody, indicating they'd probably had to search for a vein.

"Wow. This is surreal."

"How so?" he asked carefully.

"You know how you're having a nightmare and you think that all you have to do is think one good thought and it will end?"

"Mine are normally the other way around. I'll be having a good dream, then one bad thought sends it to Hell," he explained at her puzzled look.

She sighed. "Mine do that a lot too, actually." She closed her eyes, then opened them again, smiling. "You really are here though, aren't you?"

"I am."

"It's just…How did you find me—I mean, how did you know?"

"I'll always find you," he replied solemnly.

He half expected her to freak at that, but she didn't, instead locked gazes with him.

Something had changed. Some sort of shift between them. Like maybe staring death in its face had made her more accepting of the crazy things he'd told her, or at least not care about them so much. He would have rejoiced but for one irrefutable fact: She was in a hospital bed because he hadn't protected her.

"Hey. Don't look so much like you're at a funeral. I'm okay."

"You consider being stabbed okay?"

Her gaze flitted guiltily to her bandaged arm. "It was just a scratch."

"That needed twenty-six stitches and a blood transfusion!" Fear clamped around his chest, squeezing the words out forcefully.

She laid her good hand on his arm. His gaze followed. His skin tingled from the simple touch, but even that pang of basic lust couldn't break him from his terror.

She could have been killed. The defense wound across her forearm could have dug a fraction of an inch deeper, hitting artery instead of just veins, or worse, she could have not gotten her arm up in time. Then she would have had a knife buried in her chest instead—no, not just any knife, the knife he fucking gave her.

The hurried presurgery scratches on her chart spiked the back of his retina again. Stab wound. Massive blood loss. At risk for cardiac arrest.

How had her attacker been able to handle the Paladin blade? None of Lucifer's creatures should have been able to touch the thing, let alone use it against one of His children. Unless…maybe it had been a human possessed? Or even simpler, a thug or druggie recruited for the vampires' cause of eliminating her?

Or maybe an ex-con bent on revenge? Ever think of that, Logan?

"Why in the hell did you open the door?" he found himself demanding, his voice rising as he went on. "Do you let just anybody in?"

"I didn't know he was there. I'd gotten a call from an informant and was on my way out. When I opened the door, whammo, there he was. Only…" she looked away from him, her bottom lip caught between her teeth.

Cold seeped all the way through him, his heart stuttering at the deep chill. "You just pulled another informant from a Dumpster less than twenty-four hours ago. You were attacked the night before. Do you think maybe someth—one has decided to target you?"

Her chin lifted. "If so, then it means I'm getting close to the truth, now doesn't it?"

"And the truth is worth this?" He gestured at the bandages, the IV plugged into her arm.

Her jaw squared off stubbornly. "Yes."

He started to swear, but stopped himself midstream. He had to tone it down unless he wanted to have the room full of hospital staff.

"I'm sorry. I didn't mean to yell. I was…" What? Angry? Not exactly.

Scared. Scared to death.

They sat in silence for a while. Jessica fiddled with

the IV tube as if it irritated her, but then she dropped it, exhaling. "Grim, my informant," she explained, "was in trouble. He begged for my help. Should I have just hung up and gone to bed?"

"I'm not saying that. Just…" he took a deep breath. "What sort of trouble?"

"I'm not sure. The connection was bad, breaking up. I got his location and that he was hiding from trouble but that was about it."

"Where?"

"Manida Street."

A lot of old, rundown warehouses there. Three blocks from where her other informant had died. "And you had to run right over there to see. Even knowing the situation could be dangerous."

She gave a slight lift and drop of her shoulders. "It was Grim. Punk or not, Grim's a good kid. I couldn't turn my back on him."

"So you decided to save him. Grab your badge, grab your gun, and off you go to save the day."

Her eyes narrowed. "I wasn't going to go alone. I had my cell and was about to call Mike but then…" Her breath hitched, air rasping through a constricted throat. A second later the machines started beeping as her heart rate spiked, the oxygen monitor screaming.

Crap, she was hyperventilating. And here he was without a paper bag.

Throwing a quick shield across the door, he grasped her good hand, laying his other palm against her cheek, placing his face right near hers as he tried to talk her down. "It's okay, Jessica. Breathe in, and out. In…"

He glanced at the door, then back at the machines.

She was breathing easier and the beeping machines quieted. He waited a couple more minutes, but when her breath remained even and there was no banging on the door, he sat back, letting his hold on the shield go.

"You okay?" he asked, pushing a tear-slicked strand of hair from her temple.

"I'm sorry. I haven't had one of those in forever."

"Forever being when Julia died?"

She clamped her lips tight, looking away, if not confirmation than a really big clue.

It didn't matter anyway. Obviously it took a pretty intense trauma to send his little warrior into a panic attack, which, ironically was too bad. He could have handled a woman prone to panic attacks. What he couldn't handle was this death wish his mate seemed to have.

"Did it ever occur to you that Grim could have set you up?"

She turned her face away, her lips pulled tight between her teeth.

"Jessica?"

She sighed, turning her head back. "Doesn't matter if he did or didn't."

"It doesn't matter?"

"No, because if I'm right, then Thomas Rhodes may have been killed by the same man the victim in the Dumpster was killed by. But without any leads I can't do anything. Whether Grim is in trouble or was baiting me doesn't matter because either way, he's involved, and if I play my cards right, I can use him to track the bastard down."

"Does finding their killer matter more than your life?" he asked tightly.

Her lips firmed, her jaw line getting the stubborn set to it that he was becoming used to seeing. "Finding the killer is the only thing that matters."

Logan hung his head. *The* killer. Not their killer or Tom's killer, but *the* killer. And by using those words she confirmed his greatest fear. The reckless passion she had for her job wasn't so much a calling as a personal quest. Whether the victim was a senator, a hobo, an innocent bystander, or a drug dealer didn't matter. What mattered was that someone had killed them. Someone had unnaturally ended their life. And Jessica was so damn good at tracking them down because to her, every killer out there became a representative of the bastards who took her sister away. And though she stopped short of all-out revenge, she was bound and determined to see them in the human's version of Hell: behind bars, rotting their lives away. The problem was that it was consuming her life.

Cancer. Her anger was a cancer eating at her from the inside out. He was beginning to fear that the only way to extract it was to eliminate the source. And he'd find a way to do it too, because protecting her in this life wasn't enough. She was his mate: mind, heart, body, *and* soul. And if this cancer threatened her soul? Then he'd do anything to remove it. Anything.

"God, Jessica. You are going to be the death of me, aren't you?"

"What did you say?"

He shook his head, standing.

"Where are you going?"

"There is something I have to do. But I'll be back before they release you." He stroked her cheek with his hand, basking in how she instinctively turned her face into it. It felt like the light of Heaven bathed over him when she whispered her next words.

"I don't want you to go."

"I won't be long. Just do me a favor."

"What's that?"

He lifted her hand with the IV, kissing the bruised skin around the bandage. "Don't go anywhere this time."

Jessica stared at anything but the door Logan left through, refusing to allow the tears she felt pooling in her eyes to fall. Her hand still tingled from the kiss he'd pressed there. A kiss that had awakened every nerve, every memory of their time together.

But it wasn't that moment that told her she was completely sunk, it was when she first woke and saw him there and her heart did a pitter-patter. She knew because the machines told her so.

Sitting there, so large and so obviously uncomfortable in the small plastic chair he looked so...human. Lines of strain she never noticed before. Not that she'd known him for long, but the time they shared had certainly been intimate enough that she would've thought to notice. Not to mention that immortal warriors weren't supposed to look so susceptible.

Oh yeah, she'd fully accepted that he was what he said he was. She'd meant to tell him. Meant to let him know she believed him now. Ask him to explain more about himself and what it meant for them. But his questions diverted her, rutting her in the cold-bone anger she always felt when she tracked a killer. She let him leave thinking the only thing that mattered in her life was the case, the chase, the capture. But that wasn't the truth. Not anymore.

She loved Logan. Sometime in the last three days, between all the craziness and the roller coaster ride of adrenaline and endorphins, she'd fallen for him. It scared the crap out of her. And yet it made her feel whole.

But what good was love when there was no solid foundation for it. She couldn't even tell him the truth.

It wasn't a man on the other side of her door, and it wasn't a knife that had cut her. It was a demon—or something that looked hellish enough to be one.

She'd never forget how that thing had smiled, saliva dripping from its razor-sharp teeth, its bottomless, black gaze inviting her into the depths of Hell. She hadn't screamed, just grabbed her gun and started unloading bullets. But the thing didn't even flinch, just stepped over the threshold and swiped the gun from her hand. She turned to run, her only thought to get to the knife Logan had given her. But then she tripped, crashed into the coffee table, and sent the knife skittering. She rolled, but the thing reached for her and she raised her arm. She'd never forget the fiery burn as it slashed through the skin, nor the triumphant gleam in its fathomless eyes as it had bent down and licked her gaping flesh.

She'd been shocked, horror rolled through her, but then her training snapped into gear. The knife was right there, inches away. She punched and grappled with the…thing…and somehow managed to get close enough to grab the knife. Unfortunately it had been with her bad arm so the strike she got in was halfhearted at best, the tip barely sinking into the thing's chest. It was a complete shock when the blade flared bright in her hand, the creature shrieking before it just…disappeared. Poof, a cloud of darkness, then nothing.

She was also shocked to find herself bleeding all over her rug. It had burned so much as his claw dug in that she was sure it cauterized as it slashed. And though she tried to make a tourniquet out of a dish towel and a spoon, it was just as obvious she didn't have the strength to do it properly.

Even as she whimpered Logan's name, she called Mike, knowing that since the attack was over, she had to get help fast, and Mike was her best bet. And as he screamed orders at the desk sergeant to get an ambulance and a police cruiser to her apartment, and then screamed orders at her as he jumped in his car to get to her, she tried to make coherent sentences in return—and watched herself bleed out.

She didn't want to die. Not now. Not ever. At least not without Logan to hold her.

She wasn't sure what happened next as everything had become a blur, but she did remember the banging on the door and her attempt to tell them it was unlocked, which might or might not have been heard since they opened it anyway and came in. After that, she just let go, and then woken up here. With Logan staring down at her.

At first she thought it was a dream, until she'd noticed those lines of strain. If she was dreaming she certainly wouldn't have made him look so dour and she certainly would've put them in a better setting than a sterile hospital room.

And his talk about her being the death of *him*? What

the heck was that all about? If anything she was going to be the one to die first. According to him, he'd already lived for over a century; reason stood he could live almost forever…and she wouldn't.

But you have him right now, Jessica.

She closed her eyes, taking a deep breath. That was the other Jessica talking. The one who'd snickered along with her sixteen-year-old twin as they picked out their favorite from *The Bachelorette's* lineup of men. The one who'd shared Julia's dream of seeing her paintings in a gallery and had gone to business school to make it happen. The one who came alive under Logan's skilled touch. But being that person was dangerous. If she let herself go, if she allowed herself to feel, she could be hurt. And he would hurt her. She was sure of it. Because former angel or not, what hot-blooded man—and damn was Logan hot—would stay with a woman when she was old and wrinkled and he was not?

"So, you're his little secret."

She looked up. A man stood in the door, the backlight shadowing his face but not his figure. Large, about Logan's height though definitely not him. She would have known if it was.

"Excuse me?" she asked, her hand slipping down over the call button. If this man so much as blinked wrong…

He took a step into the room, the dim light over her bed illuminating his chestnut-colored hair. She sucked in a breath. It was still too difficult to make out his eyes but she would have taken a bet they were cloudy-day gray.

"Logan. He's been distracted and not exactly forthcoming in his answers. I figured it was something to do with his sister but now I understand. He's been with you."

The way he said this suggested he didn't think that was a good thing. She couldn't explain why that upset her other than this man was no stranger. This man was Logan's father. The resemblance was too uncanny otherwise. And if she'd had any lingering doubts of who, or rather what, Logan was, they would be gone now because physically Logan's father didn't look much older than his son. Except for his eyes. There was more than one lifetime of grief there.

Logan's mother. He never told me how his mother died. Had she been human?

"You must be Logan's father."

"Oh, hooray. At least he didn't pick a complete dimwit."

And you must be an asshole. She refrained from saying that out loud, though she couldn't seem to resist the urge to say something. "I am not some sort of flower to be picked. If I'm with your son it's because we chose to be together."

"Really? You're telling me that you haven't been inexplicably drawn to him since the first moment you met? That you no doubt fell into his arms at the flimsiest of excuses?" He laughed. "Trust me, human. There was no choice because if there were, my son would never have chosen you."

She sucked in a breath at the tight pain in her chest. They were just words. Obviously meant to hurt. Though why a former angel would want to hurt her was beyond her. "It's no wonder Logan doesn't talk about you much. If you were my father I wouldn't talk about you either."

His mouth thinned. He tapped his leg, then sat down in the plastic chair Logan had vacated fewer than twenty minutes before. She watched as he ran his hand through his hair and sighed. Just like Logan. And damn if that didn't make her ache to have Logan near again.

Where did he go? What was so important that he had to leave her alone in her hospital bed?

"I apologize. My unkind words toward you are borne of frustration and worry. Nothing more." Logan's father lifted his head, his mouth tugging up at the corner. "I'm sure you are a fine human being."

"Thanks for the vote of confidence," she muttered.

"You really don't understand though, do you? You have no idea why I fear you being with my son."

"You already said. You think I'm a distraction. That he's shirking his duties because of me."

"That too."

She lifted and dropped her hand in frustration. "I don't see what the problem is. You're all but immortal aren't you? Ten, thirty, fifty years—if I'm lucky—and then I'll be out of his life and out of your hair."

And there went the wet eyes again. Was she doomed to live her life grasping for but never being able to hold onto the things she loved? She swallowed, thinking of every absurd thing in the world to keep the moisture where it belonged. She would not cry in front of Logan's father.

He rubbed his chin between his thumb and forefinger—judging her. "I forget how selfish you humans can be."

"Selfish?" She wiped a renegade escapee tear away. "You think the thought of leaving him doesn't kill me?"

His face clouded over, fury sparking in his gaze—still gray, Logan hadn't inherited the changeable iris color from his father it seemed. "You think this is killing you?

What do you think is going to happen when he has to watch you die just a little bit each day?" He scoffed. "A Paladin and a human? It's just not a compatible mating. Bad enough your human qualities will taint the pureness of his soul, but the effect your certain death will have on him?"

She sucked in a breath, her heart thudding beneath her breast. Angry, hurt, confused. "What are you saying?"

"I'm saying, my dear, that if your human impurities don't contaminate his soul beyond redemption, then your eventual death is sure to drive him insane. There has been only one other Paladin to ever form a full bond with a human, and he now sits by Lucifer's side."

She sucked in a breath, an icy chill settling into her already cold core. "Lucifer? As in the devil?"

He nodded and leaned forward. "Are you really so selfish as to condemn my son to eternal damnation?"

Chapter 19

"Wait, pull up that last email from the ME."

Bennett nodded, then doing some fancy dancing with his fingers across the touch screen, dragged over the correspondence and tapped it open. "You know, this would be easier with the fine detective's computer."

Logan grunted. Probably so. Bennett had been working his magic; shifting through the cloud, skirting privacy settings to dig up the information Logan had requested.

The mission started as a seed of an idea. An idea that had deep roots of evil. When Logan left her hospital room, he was determined to do whatever was necessary to save Jessica from herself. Tracking down Bennett and Alex in the waiting area was no harder than convincing Alex to stay and keep watch while Logan and Bennett went on a little excursion into the NYPD database. A shorter than average trip across town and less than five minutes after they'd entered The Bat Cave (what Bennett called the small room that actually lay outside the boundaries of Haven's protective relic and thus not in a technological no-zone), Bennett had the files on Julia's death. Logan wanted to know the names and locations of where her killers were being kept. Not sure why, unless he meant to kill them so they no longer haunted Jessica's life, but as he stared at the boys' mug shots, he realized he couldn't do it. They were bastards of the highest order, but even they deserved a chance to redeem their souls. Besides, they weren't worth the cost of his own. Especially if he hoped to one day find Jessica again in the afterlife in His realm.

Time. Time would heal all wounds. With his help, Jessica could get past her pain and anger. She had to.

The question was would there be enough time?

He currently had Bennett pulling up everything he could find on the Thomas Rhodes case. It was more than he expected and far from what he hoped. Some of it was also extremely interesting.

Mike had been researching them. Roland, Karissa, even Alexander and himself. The information he gathered was remarkable in that it wasn't all fluff, and alarming in the way the cop had spun it in his notes, but nothing Logan really cared about. The dead informant was the key. The meeting in the alley was when the enemy had set their focus on Jessica. Logan hoped that something would pop out that would put an end to this mess. The problem was there was no end. The ME's report confirmed what he feared: He'd been right on who—or rather what—Tom's killer was, and that thing wasn't someone that the NYPD could put behind bars. One, because vampires were something they didn't believe in, and two, because if the cops tried, they'd end up dead.

No solutions. The case wasn't ever going to be closed. Somehow, Logan had to convince Jessica to let the case die a natural death in the cold case file cabinet. She wasn't going to be safe from the vampires until it was there.

And you think she'll be safe then? Now that you're her mate and Ganelon knows about her?

"Damn it all to Hell."

"Hmm?" Bennett asked absently, his fingers still flying.

"Nothing. Sorry." He sighed, running his hands over his face, the too-long-without-sleep grit in his eyes stinging the inside of his lids. Damn, when was the last time he slept—really slept, and not just a few half-hour cat-naps while he and Jessica had recovered from the mind-blowing sex?

His phone vibrated. He straightened, shifting in the chair to pull it from his pocket. Not a call, but a text: *Heads up. I've been reassigned. Thus far a steady stream of her cop friends have come through and nothing but yawns between.*

He frowned, unease skating up his spine. Alexander. He started to text the Paladin back, not comfortable with Jess's only protection being her cop friends, when a sharp voice cracked through the air.

"Logan!"

Logan grit his teeth, flicking the phone shut. One guess on who yanked Alex from guard duty.

Logan turned in his chair, drawing his shoulders back as he prepared for confrontation. "Yes, father?"

"In my study, now," Calhoun Senior said, jerking his head down the hall.

Logan's jaw ticked, but he pushed back the chair and stood to follow.

"Good luck, Mate," Bennett intoned softly. Logan nodded his thanks and kept on going.

His father was already settled behind his desk when Logan reached the head council's favored chamber. His father had a smattering of rooms throughout Haven and dozens of other little sanctuaries throughout the city that no one, save his son, knew about. Frankly Logan suspected he only knew because someone should be told about them just in case something happened to Calhoun Senior. The many relics housed in Haven were not the only ones entrusted to the Paladin to guard. There were at least two that his family personally guarded. Two that his father didn't even trust to the brothers to defend.

Logan waited, arms folded behind his back. It was the only way he could fight the itching need to get out of Haven and back to Jessica. Frankly, he would have ignored the summons but he figured that unless his father had his say, he'd more than likely send one or more of his Paladin brothers after him, which, given Logan's current mood wouldn't be good for anyone.

It would be okay. Not many people had Bennett's skills in tracking information, and the hospital was populated enough that it should be safe, especially if Jessica was surrounded by a bunch of men and women with badges and guns.

"I'm sure I don't need to tell you how disappointed I am in you," his father said.

"And I'm sure I don't need to tell you that I think you're overreacting and trying to control things that you are not meant to control."

"Things have gotten completely out of hand. A null slipping in and then out of the halls of Haven. My son sleeping with some powerless girl. Paladin using their gifts against one another? The very foundation of our order is being threatened and you don't see a problem?"

"That girl is my mate."

"Have you performed the ceremony and bonded with her yet?"

Logan tensed, his jaw clenching. He hadn't. And not because there hadn't been opportunity. The first being during one of the many fabulously amazing moments during the night they'd spent together. Then he told himself that he hesitated because he wanted Jessica to understand who and what he was first, but he knew it was because there was a part of him that hoped by not doing so, he could somehow shield himself from the full effects of the mate bond. It stood to reason that if he didn't perform the ceremony to open the pathway between them, then he could somehow make it through her eventual death. Not that he'd let her die anytime soon, but she *would* die. Eventually.

"Good, not bonded then," his father said with some satisfaction.

Logan sighed. "Have you ever heard of a mate-bond, even if not formally acknowledged, disappearing?" That he asked with even a small measure of hope made him sick. But hell, he was scared. He honestly didn't think he could take it if she died. And he would not become his father, turning his emotions off, his life obsession, his duties, and nothing more.

Nor would he become another Ganelon.

It was his father's turn to sigh. "This is a mess."

"What would you have me do, father? You know as well as I that I cannot deny the call of that bond, fully formed or not."

"You could damn well try! Stop seeing her. Let her move on with her life."

"You think I could do that?"

His father pounded his desk. "I will lock you up for her lifetime if I have to!" He took a deep breath, ran his hands through his hair, shaking his head as he regained his control. "You will someday take my place on the council. Your duty is to the task He placed upon us. It is to Him and your brothers. Not this human."

Logan clenched his fists, knowing that to his father there was no other argument that mattered. "And her? What would you do with Jessica? She already knows what I am. I've already allowed the first link to form by becoming her lover."

His father waved that off. "Matters not."

"It doesn't?" he asked, taken aback by the easy dismissal.

"I can block memories too."

Logan shook his head. "You can't block that sort of bond. She'll always know she is missing something."

"I would turn her into a vegetable before I allowed some mere human to hold the balance of my son's sanity in her whimsical nature."

Logan sucked in a breath. The way his father said it seemed so callous. When had his father become so heartless?

He stepped forward, his hand raised, finger pointed. "If you touch a single pathway within her mind, I'll…"

"You'll what?"

He curled his fingers back, dropping his hand back down to his side. "Trust me, father. You don't want to know."

And then he turned his back on his father and took himself from the room, because the truth was he didn't like the answer any more than his father would.

He was already hanging by a thread. If his father did anything to Jessica, flesh and blood or not, Logan would treat him no differently than whoever stabbed her. And whoever that was would never touch a hair on her head again, because though they might not know it yet, they were already dead.

———〜〜〜———

Jessica was a popular lady. Logan and his father weren't the only visitors she had, though they were the ones who absorbed most of her thoughts and emotional agony. Not that her location was well known. The police were trying to keep her whereabouts hush, hush. At least until they had some leads on the attack. As if they'd ever get any. She figured tracking down a demon was not something they were equipped to do. Which is why, when Mike showed up somewhere in the stream of blue uniforms and well-wishers, she played the I-can't-really-remember card.

Stupid. For her at least, though hopefully it would keep Mike safe from harm. She realized she was in deep shit. She also realized that the only one who could fix it was the man she should never see again.

No. She absolutely *could* not see Logan again. What they had was already too scary in intensity. And if there was even a chance that what Logan's father had said was true? She shook her head. She would not risk Logan's sanity and she certainly would not risk the loss of his soul.

Damn, why had this happened to them? Why pair her, a simple human with belief issues, with one of His warriors? To test her faith? To test Logan's? It just didn't make sense.

"What am I supposed to do? Follow my heart and risk his soul?"

No, Jessica. This is where you're supposed to make the ultimate sacrifice and let him go.

She let her head flop against the stiff pillow. What a mess.

Someone knocked on the door. She looked over, half hoping, half dreading it would be Logan. It wasn't. Though her feelings for the man in the doorway were similarly mixed. There'd been something weird about their last interaction. He took the dumping well but something after that—

"Hey, you in here talking to yourself?"

"Hey, Damon," she said, struggling to sit up straighter in the bed. "I was just thinking about you."

"Only good things, I hope." He smiled, his black eyes twinkling mischievously.

"Right…" What had she been thinking about?

He stepped in, his gaze drawn to her bandaged right arm. He swallowed, the twinkle dimming, and she noticed that his coloring looked decidedly sick.

That's right, he'd left her to go do something. Probably blamed himself. Which he shouldn't. She still wasn't sure what the purpose of the attack was, but she was sure of one thing: If Damon had been there, he would have been an annoyance, nothing more, and would likely be in the same position she was—if not dead.

"Hey, this isn't your fault you know," she told him.

"You'll forgive me if I think it is." He pulled a hand down over his face, then approached and took her hand. "Damn, Jessica. I wish I could make this up to you."

She looked around the room, at the beeping machines, the sterile white curtain. God, she hated hospitals. At least, when she was the one in them. There was nothing to do but sit and wait and ponder your own faults and vulnerabilities. Not to mention the seriously fucked-up state of your life to have ended up there.

"Maybe you can," she murmured.

"Excuse me?"

"I need you to help me with something," she said, her voice low like a conspirator. "Something very important and very dangerous."

He played along, leaning in closer. "Does it involve breaking the law?"

"Maybe." She gnawed on her lip, looking by him to the open door. No one there. "Break me out of here. They said they'd release me in the morning but I can't… I can't…" she bit her lip, memories swamping her of another time. Another sterile concrete building. It was a morgue, but the vulnerability she felt had been the same. They'd told her she didn't have to do it, the ID had already been made, but she'd needed the closure. Julia was her twin. Twins were supposed to sense when the other was in danger. Only Jessica hadn't, not until the somber-faced officers had shown up at her door had she any inkling something was wrong. A day later, she still couldn't believe Julia was dead. Wouldn't she have felt it? Wouldn't some great gaping hole be present in her chest? So she'd insisted. She'd walked behind the grim-faced officer into the cold, sterile morgue and waited while they set things up. It wasn't until the white curtain opened that she finally felt it, that deep-seated agony that told her all she needed to know: She'd lost a part of herself.

And here she was, losing the rest.

Damon sighed. "Babe, I would if I could, but I'm not going to just kidnap you out of here."

She shook her head. "You won't have to. Just find some poor unsuspecting schmuck just off his residency that's been stuck on back-to-back shifts and get him to let me out of here."

He didn't look happy, but he eventually nodded.

He was gone what seemed like hours but he did return, a young frazzled man in a white lab coat in his wake. She could have kissed Damon, but just the thought struck her as wrong.

Logan. She wanted him to be the one rescuing her. With her whole world turned upside down and the cold sterile walls of the hospital pressing in on her, she needed his steady presence. Only he needed her to walk away.

Damn him for being the one. Damn him for being who he was and making it impossible for them to be together. And damn Him for the reminder of what loving someone could be like and then taking it all away again.

Pulling herself from her misery, she waited patiently as the doctor did a cursory exam. She must have passed because he called in a nurse and asked her to prep the discharge forms. The nurse didn't look thrilled but she nodded and went to get things moving.

It took too long, and Jessica both feared and wished for Logan to show up and stop her, but thirty minutes later Jessica was in a wheelchair sitting on the front curb as Damon brought his car around.

She waited until they were in the car and had pulled out of the lot before she spoke, her palms still sweaty from the jailbreak. She didn't want to go home. Didn't want to face the bloodstained floor. Didn't want to face the stillness of the apartment where violence had found her and have to think about why and what she was going to do about it. But what else was there to do?

Maybe your job, Jessica?

That's right. She'd never talked to the Sergeant. Never took that leave of absence, which meant she was still on the case.

"Can I borrow your phone?"

Damon searched her face, but pulled his phone from his pocket, his eyes locked back on the road as she typed in Grim's number from memory. It rang. And rang. Eventually clicking over to voice mail. "Damn."

"Not home?" he asked.

She shook her head, gnawing on her lip. The possibility that Grim was dead was very real, in which case it was all on her. If she'd stopped to call Mike before bolting out the door, then maybe they could have found him in time.

"What's wrong, Jess?" Damon asked, his voice soft and soothing.

She stretched her neck side to side, the bones popping. "Grim's not answering."

"Grim?"

"My informant. He called, said someone was after him. I was headed out to meet him when I was attacked."

Damon shook his head. "Jess, it's been hours. You should've told Mike that so he could check it out."

"I did tell Mike. He sent someone over to look and didn't find anything."

"Huh." He tapped his fingers on the steering wheel. "And now you can't get ahold of him?"

She lifted his phone. "Voice mail. So either he's not answering, can't answer, or the battery is dead."

He worked his jaw, his eyes on the light they were stuck at. "Where did you say he was?"

"Some warehouse on Manida Street."

The light turned green and he started forward. "I can go check it out if you want. After I drop you off of course."

"I'd appreciate it," she told him, though even as she said it her gut twisted with unease. Was sending Damon really that smart? Despite her recent close encounter, he was even less equipped to deal with all this than she. At least she knew what she was facing. Unless...

She frowned as she looked out the window at the dark night, her thoughts turning to the body in the Dumpster. It was the night she'd met Logan, could the man's death have been because of Logan and the creatures he fought and not because of her? It seemed too odd, too much of a coincidence. But hell, without Grim's confirmation, she didn't even know if their victim was the man she'd been supposed to meet. If Logan was there because of the whole angel warrior thing, then it stood to reason that the man was killed by one of the creatures Logan hunted. In which case it probably had nothing to do with her or her case. Just like the attack on her in the garage the next day was because she was a loose thread, not because of Tom's car.

It made sense. It fit. Tom's case and all this demon/ vampire crap were two totally separate things. Therefore it would be okay for Damon to check things out. Still, if Mike's officers hadn't found anything, what made her think Damon would?

"Maybe I should come with you. Maybe the officers Mike sent didn't find him because he didn't want to be found by them."

"So you think he'll come out if you're there?"

She twisted in her seat. The streetlights gave her enough light to get a decent look at him. Truth was he looked pretty crappy. His skin still had that glazed, sick look and his eyes were dull, as if he wasn't fully there.

"You don't look so good," she said.

He quirked a brow, giving her the once over. "Are you pot or kettle?"

She laughed, but it came out sounding hollow and fake.

"Babe, I really think it's best if I bring you home."

She heaved out a breath that made her ribs ache. The reminder should have made her inclined to agree, but instead it drove the opposite point home: She didn't want to go home. Not when it meant being alone. Not when she would have to eventually face Logan—and then find a way to break his heart so he'd go away. But she could find Grim and maybe, *hopefully*, she could find Rhodes's real killer and clear Logan's friend's name.

"I need to find out what happened to Grim. I need to be sure he's not still hiding in there waiting for me."

He hesitated, but eventually nodded. "Okay. But I'm coming into the building with you."

"Of course." This was something else she could do for Logan. Maybe they couldn't be together, but she could take greater care with her own life—which meant taking the help when offered.

Damon took the next cross street. A few more turns and they were on their way. Traffic was light, but Jessica couldn't help squirming in the seat. Not only was she nervous, but the painkillers were wearing off and her entire body ached.

Damon looked over at her, headlights flashing across his face, his hands tight around the wheel. "We're almost there."

She nodded, but the anxiety of not knowing what they'd find when they got there was gnawing at her nerves. It was only another five minutes before they reached their destination, but long enough for her to break out in a slick sweat that chilled quickly in the cool evening.

"Which building?" Damon asked. Jess scanned the street. Which building indeed. The entire area was one big warehouse after another.

"For him to get in and hide, it's probably either abandoned or has really poor security."

"I don't think anything in this part of town has very good security. And a good number are abandoned."

True. Which made her wonder just how vigorously the officers would have looked for Grim.

Damon coasted down the street. Jessica scanned the buildings for possibilities. Problem was they all seemed possible. What had made her think this was a good idea?

"Wait. What's that?" Damon pulled to a stop, his arm outstretched as he pointed to one of the boarded-up warehouses. A board had fallen down and stood on its end, tipped toward a stack of barrels. One of the barrels was moved, shimmied around the board so only a glint of the dull metal flashed in the reflection of the Viper's headlights.

"Want to check it out?" Damon asked.

The thought that this was all a waste of time crossed her mind but when she opened her mouth all that came out was an uneasy, "Sure."

Jessica popped her door, her feet barely hit the pavement before Damon was there offering a hand.

"Thanks."

"No problem." He pointed his remote toward the car, a couple soft beeps, though they seemed loud in the still night.

She scanned the building. Any moment now Grim would pop his head out a window, relief flooding his gaze. Any moment and the barrel of an automatic would appear out that window, thug on the end, and mow them down.

"You have your gun, right? Mine's probably in the evidence locker."

"Right," he replied solemnly.

Luckily they didn't need it right away. No one popped out of a window. No cover fire was laid down. The night remained silent.

Probably not the right building.

"You sure about this?" he asked.

She squared her shoulders. For Grim. For Logan and his friend. "I need to make sure." Besides, she was here. Might as well follow through. And that building was as good as any other on the block.

Damon grunted, falling in beside her as they made their way to the door. He kept up, though there was an almost reluctant hesitancy to his steps.

She bit her tongue, but when he started cracking his knuckles she spun on him. "If you don't want to do this, just tell me. I'll call Mike or something."

"No, it's cool. I just…" he rubbed a hand over his face. "I had a run-in with my dad. We don't see eye to eye on things these days."

"Oh. I'm sorry."

"Not much to talk about. He wants me to do something. I don't want to do it."

She tipped her head, frowning. "You're old enough to say no."

He let out a rueful chuckle and reached for the door. "You'd think."

She was going to ask who his dad was that he could push around his son who was a cop—the Godfather or something?—but the doorknob turned in his hand.

She shifted restlessly from foot to foot as he cautiously pushed open the door. No sounds or movement greeted them. She started to step forward but was abruptly stopped by Damon's hand on her arm.

"Wait here a sec. I'm the one with the gun, remember?" he said, flipping his jacket open to show the police issue.

"Right," she said, gesturing ahead.

She waited while he stepped over the threshold and was quickly swallowed by the dark.

"It's a hall. No lights. And no one appears to be home."

Taking that as an all clear she stepped in. She sensed more than saw him move forward and followed the soft sound of his tread. It was eerily quiet and pitch black. After the second time she stumbled, she found herself gripping tight to Damon's jacket. How in the hell did he see without a flashlight?

"This is stupid." And dangerous.

"Think if he's hiding somewhere in here he'll come if you call?"

"Maybe." Only when she opened her mouth nothing came out. Too dark. Too…something. "There's no light in here. Even if he were trying to hide he wouldn't have gone this far in."

"You're right. I just thought…"

She heard it. A low rumbling sound, kind of like a chuckle.

"Was that?"

"Yup. A laugh." The leather tugged in her grip. "This way."

They took another dozen steps, turning a corner. A large room sprouted from the hall they were in. No windows here either, but across the cement expanse was a slim beam of light. A slight crack spilling out into the vast space from an unclosed door.

Cautiously they eased across the expanse. The low murmur of a one-sided conversation drawing them closer. The inflection of the voice rose, then paused. A question. Another voice, sounding amazingly like Grim's, though scratchier, muttered something insulting under his breath. Her chest sagged a bit with relief. Thank God. If the kid was well enough to insult someone then he was okay. At least until she got ahold of him.

Why did he hide from the officers Mike sent?

They probably didn't even check this building out. Good chance the lazy bastards never left the warmth of their car.

"Police! Keep your hands where we can see them." Damon pushed open the door, gun leading the way as he stepped into the room, Jessica shifting to a better angle behind him.

The room wasn't large. An old office perhaps, though there was nothing in it other than two chairs and a heavy wooden desk. Both chairs were occupied, the one behind the desk by an astonishingly average-looking man. His hands were in sight, though he neglected to put down his gun. The good news/bad news was it wasn't pointed at them, but at Grim who sat sullenly in a second chair in the corner behind the desk, hands tied before him but otherwise healthy looking. Hopefully they could keep him that way.

"Oh, look. Our guests have arrived." The man from behind the desk pushed out of his seat, moving across the room with lethal grace, his gun remaining level with Grim's brain as the man advanced on his captive. The man was taller than he'd looked behind the massive desk and more muscular too. Brown hair, brown eyes. If he were on the force, he would be the first one recruited for an undercover assignment. Unless it was her picking the assignment, that is.

Dead eyes. They had no emotion in them.

"Say hi, Grim."

Grim grumbled something else—sounded like another insult—and received a smack on his head with the butt of the gun for his trouble. Instinctively Jess reached for her sig, but belatedly remembered she didn't have it.

The pause in her knee-jerk response had her re-evaluating the situation. And the conclusion she came up with was that something was seriously fucked up. Grim wasn't scared. Not really. And okay, Grim had a reputation for mouthing off a lot but even so, there should be something in his eyes. A little smidgen of fear at least.

"Grim, if you set me up…"

The man holding the gun to Grim's head smiled. "Oh, it is a setup. But not by whom you think."

"Oh? Care to enlighten me then?"

Grim's skin split, body growing, morphing as a creature emerged from the skin shell. Jess's heart skittered in her chest. Oh no. That was not what she thought it was. The thing stood, stretching out its wings, cloven hooves stomping the pile of dermis into the cement. It smiled at her, its jagged teeth splitting a face that nightmares were made of. She knew that face. It was the creature from the garage, only with taut, red skin, as if it had gone through a shedding and was growing a new hide.

Jessica stumbled back, but Damon was right there, catching her under her elbow. "Easy there, babe."

"Yes. Take it easy. *Babe*." The man chortled, the twisted rise of his laughter betraying his utter insanity.

Take it easy? Nope, the best idea of the night: run.

Jess took a step back, her arm screaming against Damon's tight grip.

Must be in shock. No other reason he wasn't plugging the demon with useless bullets and screaming his damn head off.

Wait, *easy there?*

A shiver ran down her back, her gaze automatically drawn to Damon. Denial whipped through her at the fixed expression on his face.

No. Not…"Damon?"

"I'm sorry, Jess," he said, lowering his gun to his side.

Chapter 20

"RETURNING TO THE SCENE OF THE CRIME?"

Logan folded his arms, planting his feet before the cop who came out the back entrance of Jessica's apartment building. He wasn't sure whether he was relieved or not that Detective Mike Ward wasn't one of the "cop friends" currently keeping Jess company, but that he was blocking the doors ticked him off.

"Yup. And I'm in a real pisser of a mood, so unless you have actual evidence to bring me in on, get out of my way." He had to get back to the hospital, but first he needed to pack Jessica's bag. She would not be coming back here. Not until he could get her place properly warded and even then…well, they'd see.

"Oh, I have evidence, all right." The cop held up a folded note card between his fingers. "Unfortunately I don't think you wrote this."

"What's that?" Logan tried to snatch the card but Mike held it away. Dick.

"It's a note. Found it stuffed into Jessica's door. Funny, it wasn't there earlier when CSU processed the scene."

"What does it say?"

"That's not as important as who it's for. Because whoever that is has gotten Jessica messed up in some serious shit."

Logan narrowed his gaze, not liking the prick cop's attitude any more now than he had earlier. "Any guesses?"

"About who's dishing out the shit? Not really." He tipped his head. "But about the intended recipient of the note? Actually, I have two possibilities. One I'd like to pin this on a lot better than the other. Seeing how I'm already planning on pounding that fucker's face in."

Logan folded his arms. "Aren't I lucky?"

Mike nodded. Oh yeah, the prick was enjoying himself. Logan had to give it to the cop, his protective instincts for his partner were commendable, and that made Logan uncomfortable. He didn't want to like Mike. Mike had tried to bar him from Jessica. Probably had a thing for her as well. If Logan wasn't so angry at being kept from his mate when she was hurt he would have almost felt sorry for the bastard.

Jessica was his and he was hers. End of story.

"What about the other guy. If the note's for him are you going to pound his face in too?"

"Not sure. First I have to find him. Funny thing, though, his car used to be parked right there," he added, indicating the empty spot near the building.

Logan's eyebrows shot up. The other man had been here earlier? "Is this guy another tenant?"

"Damon? No. He doesn't live here."

Then why the fuck was he here, asshole? "Who's Damon?"

Mike shrugged looking at him slyly. "A cop. Oh, and Jessica's boyfriend."

"Bullshit."

"At least three dates that I know of."

Logan fisted his hands, telling himself to calm down. Officer Michael Ward was baiting him. Even if Jessica had dated this Damon schmuck it didn't mean anything. Couldn't mean anything. Not when she was his mate.

"Let me see the note, please," he added, proud of how calmly that came out. Yup, the unsaid or-I'll-tear-your-throat-out was barely noticeable.

Mike clucked his tongue, looking between the note and Logan. Finally he held it out and Logan snatched it from his hand. Logan read it through once, twice, sweat breaking out on his skin.

"What did you say Damon's last name was?"

"I didn't."

Logan gave him a withering look. "Does he have almost black eyes?"

Mike's eyes narrowed. "Yeah…I don't see how that—"

"Does he make your neck itch?" Logan interrupted.

"What the hell kind of question is that?"

Logan shook his head. "Never mind."

Mike took a step closer, his head tipped in a suspicious tilt. "You think the note was for Damon?"

"No. It's for me," Logan corrected, all but choking on the words. But he could give a guess who it was from: a cop named Damon, who, oh by the way, was also one of Ganelon's merkers. It was the perfect cover. A position of power. Access to an unlimited amount of susceptible souls. And no one would suspect they had a demon spawn in their ranks. Not even Jessica—who'd dated him.

Fuuucking hell.

Mike's mouth thinned, the skin around his nose pinching. "Do you know what that gibberish means?"

"I thought that was obvious." Logan shoved the note back into Mike's chest. "It's an invitation to Hell."

All those Hollywood movies were bullshit. Tracking
someone across the city without the use of his gift was
not sly or easy—it sucked. But he didn't dare slip into
the shade. Not when one of the peeps he was following
could pop him out again with a simple flare of her power.
And given that he'd be naked if she did, not a good idea.

Damn nulls. And damn all the stupid fucking pedestrians in this city. Though it was probably because of
those pedestrians that he'd caught up with them at all.
A half block out from the hole in the chain link fence
they'd cut, they stopped to play cover-up. Ammo and
rifles went into padded duffel bags; trench coats went on
over the rest. Even with that little breather he almost lost
them, *twice*, the last just now as they hopped subway
lines at Lexington. He jumped on the E behind them just
in time to do the crunch-crunch dance with the closing
doors. Luckily the Hollywood movies were right on this
point: New Yorkers stuck on a subway train together
didn't pay attention to each other. And sure he was at
the other end of the car from his quarry, but not a one
of them looked over when he played the let-me-in game
with the door.

Man, all this BS better be worth it. He hoped Logan's
mate was all right. Logan, though a bit of a prick at times,
was okay. He was solid, with a good head on his shoulders, but not so much of an ego that he couldn't see the
shit going on past the end of his nose. And oh man was
Valin going to be in a pile of his own the next time he
went to Haven. Logan's daddy was not the forgive-and-
forget type. Maybe Valin went a bit far when he used

his gift on his Paladin brothers, but he'd wanted to have a chance to speak privately with the interesting null girl about the message she was supposed to deliver.

He rolled his shoulders, his skin itching from his neck down his back. Oh all right, he didn't give a rip about the message; it was the source he cared about.

Gabby. The succubus/mentor/whatever role she was playing that day had to be Gabby. She was alive. And Valin wanted to find out just what this group of li'l-bit-bloods knew about her — just not in front of his Paladin brothers.

Thank God he'd read Gabby's messenger right. She'd been all bravado back at Haven but under the act was a scared young woman. Calhoun Senior's threat of holding her there against her will had put the fear of God in her. So the first chance she got — *you're welcome, sweetheart* — she bolted. And Valin was ready to follow. And wasn't being trapped in a moving subway train the perfect time to have that chat?

Easing past a harried mother juggling an agitated toddler and bag of bottles and poo-catchers, Valin made his way to the other end of the car. He sidled right up beside their little group and still not a one of them noticed. Holy fucking crap, how had they survived so long?

"You know, if you had to go, you could have said good-bye first."

The null jumped, spinning toward him, as did the rest of her entourage, equal looks of shock on their faces. Points to her nearest companion who recovered quickest and tried to move in to shield her, but Valin gave him a don't-fuck-with-me glare that had him compromising with a shoulder in the way and a hand in his long trench coat on what was sure to be one of those pretty handguns they'd left stuffed in their pants.

"Crap. How'd you find us?" null girl said, signaling Trigger Happy to stand down.

"Not find. Follow. You really should pay more attention to your surroundings. It's amazing you all have lived so long."

She tipped her head, then jerked her chin toward the large African American across from her. "Keon can sense them. At least when I'm not pulling."

Pulling—that was an interesting name for her lights-out magic routine, but whatever. He wasn't here for chitchat. "Where's Gabby?"

Her brow furrowed, then lifted. "Oh, you mean Red. Sorry, can't tell you."

"Can't or won't?" he growled, his hand clenching with the urge to grab her and shake the answers out.

She shrugged. "She comes and goes as she pleases."

"Where? Comes and goes where?"

"Now, that I *won't* tell you."

"I could follow you."

"You could try." She smiled. "Won't be so easy now that we know you're here."

Valin clenched his teeth, checking it back. Info first, throttling later. "You had a message for us?"

"No, not all of you, just Logan, though I guess Red would be okay with me telling you."

And why was that, he wondered. Had Gabby talked about him? "Okay, I'm listening."

She glanced around the subway car around them.

"As if they'd care," he told her. She pulled her upper lip through her teeth, but nodded. "You're right."

Of course. He folded his arms, patiently waiting. Damn his neck hurt. Tension, no doubt, from all his fucking restraint.

"Okay, so we told you how Red has helped us out. Well she's also been giving us information." She tipped her head. "You know what she is right?"

He nodded. "Tiny li'l pint-sized vamp."

Null shot a quick look around the train, letting out a relieved breath when she confirmed no one was paying attention—duh.

"Okay," she went on, "so, you also probably know she doesn't bat for them anymore."

He nodded again. From what he got from Logan during their little partnership—and what his own instincts told him from their one memorable encounter—he doubted she ever truly had.

"I think we also told you that there's been a lot of pressure on us recently. The vamps, they've been especially bad."

"Why?"

"According to Red, they want to recruit us." She air-quoted the word recruit. "I guess their new leader is obsessed with refilling the ranks after some major loss last summer and he thinks that if he can turn some of us part-breeds who already have gifts, then his army will be stronger for it."

Valin frowned. "How does Gabby know all this?"

"She's been keeping tabs. Says now that the old Poobah is dead, stripping the thoughts right out of their minds is easy peasy for her."

Valin rolled his jaw. Why would that be? Yeah, he'd felt the taste of how powerful her mind gifts were back in the mine last summer, but from what he knew of vampires and how their mind powers worked it wasn't the same thing as what demons, merkers or Paladin did. A thrall could be done to anyone weaker than the vamp performing it, but a pathway into the mind could only be forged through blood. At least that's what he'd been taught.

Damn, he really had to find her. If for no other reason than to ask her what the fuck she thought she was doing.

"So, yeah, this new leader, besides looking for recruits, is taking the whole secrecy thing very seriously. No blatant displays of fangs, no drained bodies left out in the open. And that's where the message comes in."

"And that message would be?" he urged. Time was slipping away. Hopefully Logan would be reachable once he got out from under all this concrete, dirt, and steel because Valin had other things on his agenda than hand-delivering messages.

"Red said that the vamps want to kill Logan's girl because of some case she's working on, I guess."

"Yeah, we got that." With the whole Logan screaming like a girl thing. Damn. Too bad null girl didn't deliver her message earlier. Not that it was any skin off Valin's back, he still would have followed this group to find out about Gabby, though now that they knew he had, it *was* going to be difficult to continue to trail them. Fuck. He rubbed a hand through his hair, sighing as he looked down at the sticky floor.

"Why so bummed? I haven't told you the best part yet."

Valin tipped his head back up. "Oh?"

"Sometime yesterday new orders came down the pipeline. This one from some guy called Ganelon. Guy must have some weight, huh?"

"You could say that. What were the orders?"

"New rule is he doesn't want her dead, just captured. Guess whoever nabs her is going to get some kind of big reward, too."

Valin scowled. Why wouldn't Ganelon simply want her dead? He hated the Calhouns, more so than he hated the Paladin as a whole, something about Logan's grandfather refusing to help when Ganelon's mate was dying. Which, okay, Valin could see of Logan's father, but everything he heard of the eldest Calhoun said the guy had been a fucking saint.

Damn. Ganelon must be setting some sort of trap. And Logan's pretty detective was nothing more than bait. Valin had to warn Logan, and if he couldn't get in touch with him then Valin would have to call...crap. Senior Corncob was going to be fucking livid.

Chapter 21

JESSICA BREATHED IN AND OUT, IN AND OUT, TRYING TO focus on easing the burning sensation in her lungs and not the man standing rigidly beside her, gun no longer raised and ready but lowered to his side in defeat.

Damon. Damon set her up. Damon was in league with the man and that...thing across the room. Why? It didn't make sense. Not unless he was...Oh, no way in hell.

So this is what it feels like to have your world stand up and coldcock you in the face.

The room spun, her chest rattling as she choked out a demand. "Explain."

Damon shook his head, his features, normally so perfectly handsome, contorted. As if he were the one who had been attacked. As if he were the one staring betrayal in the face.

"Tell me it's not true, Damon. Tell me you didn't know what waited in this warehouse."

He stuffed the gun in his holster, his hands fisting as he turned to her. His face was twisted into a livid mask. She sucked in a sharp breath.

"I asked you if you were sure. I tried to get you to leave this alone. It was your choice, Jessica."

"So you knew."

He cracked his knuckles, his gaze straying to the man and demon on the other side of the room. She waited.

Though really, he'd put his gun away. What more could he say?

When he looked back at her his face was as smooth and handsome as it was any other day of the week. "I knew. I was supposed to bring you here."

The pain clamped down on her. Growing like some sort of high-speed cancer through her chest. Only thing that could have hurt worse was if it were Mike or Logan standing there saying those words.

Had to concentrate. Had to think. Work through it. Mike and Logan were going to kill her if she didn't get out of here.

"Oh, poor Detective Waters. Poor little *babe,* alone and betrayed."

Jessica jerked her attention back to the man across the room. That's right, Damon's betrayal was not her only worry right now.

"Here." The man looked down at the gun in his hand, glanced at the demon hissing and spitting behind him, shrugged. "Maybe you'll feel better with this?" He lifted the gun, making a point to flick on the safety as she watched, then tossed it toward her. She snatched it out of the air, her right arm screaming at the abrupt movement and forcing her to pass the gun into her nondominant hand.

What. The. Hell. Did he really just give her a weapon? Like maybe it was some sort of consolation prize before the creature behind him ripped her to shreds?

"Jessica." Damon's black boots shifted in front of her, his hands closing around her biceps, his voice harsh as he whispered in her ear. "Don't listen. Don't let him t—"

"Why?" she managed, forcing her head up to meet his gaze.

"Yes, Damon, tell her why you betrayed her. Moreover, tell her what you are."

Damon glanced back across the room, then again at her, his dark eyes impossibly black as he stared at her. "I'm an incubus."

Incubus? "What the hell is that?"

Damon hesitated, but then jerked, as if someone stabbed him, or electrified him, only she did nothing and the man sat back down in the chair, the demon crouched on the floor behind him.

"Go on, Damon. Tell her what an incubus is." He said Damon's name like someone might say *slave*, and Damon jerked again.

He's controlling him. Exactly like a master and slave, the man held Damon on a leash, keeping him in line and whipping him into obedience.

Not for long. Not if I kill him.

Damon was speaking again, his tone hollow as he recited a description of what he was that sounded right out of a text book. "...a demon of seduction. I can seduce with my body, my voice, my mind."

"Your mind?"

Damon jerked again, a shimmer running over the black pits of his eyes. The more she looked, the deeper that pit became, the black swallowing everything his gaze landed on.

Windows to the soul.

Jessica's body trembled, her eyes growing heavy; she swayed. Alarm spiked. Holy crap! What was he doing to her? And oh God, had he done it before?

"Jessica." Damon's hands gripped her shoulders, steadying her as his possession over her body eased. "It's not too late."

"Not too late?" Jessica jerked back out of his hold, the gun rising in her trembling hand. "For what? Not too late to trust you? Not too late to leave? Not too late to save Grim? Or are you trying to tell me *that*," she gestured at the demon perching on the husk of skin, "doesn't mean he's dead."

"Damon, Damon, Damon. No scaring off our guests." The way the man said it sounded more like he was a predator telling a young cub not to scare off dinner.

Damon lowered his hands, stepping back. His face shut down as he turned his head away from her and looked at the man across the room. His deference obvious.

His father. He said his father was making him do something he didn't want to do. Like a slave.

Her gun wavered between them. Godfather indeed. "Are you his father?"

"Oh, I like this one Damon. She'll be a real prize for the collection."

Collection. She could only imagine what that was. Her gaze shifted to the demon. It vibrated as it sat on its haunches, a rabid dog chomping at the bit. And though it was obviously eager for her blood she had a feeling it would sit like that for however long the man made it.

"So you're a demon too? Are you…the devil?" she asked Damon's father.

"Do I need to spell it out for you?" He tsked. "Really Jessica, you're smarter than that."

She was, but obviously not smart enough to have seen it before. She'd kissed Damon. Told him things she shared with no one. Trusted him to watch her back. And he was the son of evil incarnate.

Sins of the father. But did that make Damon all bad?

"Oh, she still has a sliver of hope. How quaint." The man motioned with his hand, urging Damon to him. "Come here, my son." As if on strings, Damon shuffled across the floor, his back rigid as he stood before his father. "Turn around. That's right." His voice lowered, seductive, sibilant. "Now tell her your assignment."

Damon opened his mouth, his voice mechanical as he began to recite one horrible word after another. "As you can see I look relatively normal. No glamour needed. This makes my assignment to infiltrate your world easy. Humans are both gullible and selective. They believe what they want to believe. Make a case for their personal version of right and wrong and they'll follow you anywhere. I find the susceptible souls. A victim bent on revenge. A drug addict on the verge of killing. A cop boiling with hate. I screw with them, point them on the path that will lead them into our Lord Lucifer's embrace."

"But…you're a cop." And oh what a stupid statement that was. Gullible indeed. Jessica knew that cops could go bad; but she never considered that she might be dating one who was inherently so. But there he was. And she'd trusted him. Let him sway her opinion. Let him into her life.

Damon's father chuckled. "Go on. Tell her what else you do."

Damon's mouth thinned, his jaw going stiff. His entire body jerked. Once. Twice.

"Now, now, don't be stubborn."

One last jerk. Damon fell to his knees, panting as he stared at the floor. "I seduce the young and gullible into fucking me. Or I convince the bastards of the world to do it instead."

She shook her head. Must have heard that wrong. Sounded like he said he was a rap—she cut the thought off, not willing to even give it life in her mind. "What did you say?"

"I said I fuck humanity. Literally." He raised his head, his black eyes like pits of rolling tar, mouth twisted into a sneer. "And I like it."

She took a step back. She was wrong. The man in the chair was not the most evil thing in here. All of a sudden, Jess couldn't breathe. The memory of the few kisses she and Damon shared clamped down on her lungs. Not enough air.

"You rape them?"

"No." Damon dragged himself back up, first one foot, then the other. "I seduce. Fast cars, long-stemmed roses." He jerked the collar of his jacket, straightening it. "The assholes I play, say a group of frat boys…they do the raping for me."

Hatred. Pure and unadulterated, it flowed through her. Every breath of air was thick with the evil bastard's taint as it filled Jess's lungs, making her stronger. She straightened. The room still spun but she could see Damon clearly. He looked at her, black eyes fathomless, his face chiseled in stone.

"I'm sorry," he said, his voice devoid of inflection.

"You're sorry? You're fucking sorry?" Her entire body shook with anger. "Was it you? Where you there whispering in their ears when they gang-banged her?"

No answer. All he did was stare at her with those empty, black eyes. Damn him. Probably didn't even remember who she was talking about. Not that it mattered. Somewhere, sometime, another family's Julia had been brutally raped because of Damon. She thumbed off the safety.

"Don't do it, Jess. I'm not worth it."

He was right. He wasn't, but Julia was.

For a split second she hesitated. A split second where the cop Jessica, the one who upheld the law, the one who firmly believed those who shot someone down in anything but immediate defense, deserved to be behind bars, stayed her finger. Her gun started to lower. But then the monster smiled.

Smiled as if all the deaths he brought meant nothing.

The room wavered in a red haze of anger as her finger squeezed down on the trigger. Darkness drenched her. Wrenching agony tore through her arm and resonated through her body, knocking her off balance. She scrambled back, trying to keep her footing even as her mind seemed to split.

"Fuck, Jessica," someone wheezed. "Why'd you do it? Why did you have to go and actually do it?"

Damon. She'd missed? How the hell could she have missed?

Lift it. Shoot it. You can still kill him. Go ahead. You know you want to.

She stared down at the gun in her shaking hand, watched clinically as it began to lift. It seemed detached from her. As if someone else were holding the weapon. As if something else were controlling her movement.

As if something was *in* her.

Someone laughed.

"I told you not to listen to him." A hand closed down over hers, strong and large—Damon, must have crossed the room while she stumbled around—but even then her arm continued to rise, as if her anger gave her super powers or something.

Only she wasn't angry anymore. Just drained. Tired. She just wanted to give up, sleep.

Somehow Damon managed to snatch the gun, tossing it across the room. In the time it took her to blink he grabbed her upper arms again, shaking her. "Stupid woman. Now it's your fight. I can't help you anymore."

Fight? Fight what?

The chuckle rose again. It snapped her enough from the sense of drifting that she was able to twist her head. She looked past Damon to where the man still sat in the chair, his hands clasped behind his head, watching the show.

Cocky bastard. Likes to play with his puppets. Let's kill him too.

She sucked in a breath. Did she just think that?

"What's happening to me?"

The man chuckled again, twisting just enough to drop his gaze toward the floor. She followed the movement. Saw the pile of skin. Cold washed over her. "Where's the demon?"

"Inside you," Damon said, shaking his head as a smile—no, a grimace—twisted his lips. "Welcome, babe. Welcome to my living hell."

———※———

Logan ended the call, Roland's furious voice still screaming at him as he flicked the cell phone shut and glanced down at the last lines of the note once more:

"...Follow the smell of sulfur."

The directions were simple enough, both in their instruction and in execution. The air in the city was positively choking with brimstone. And the more Logan suffered its effects, the closer he knew he was getting.

Should have stayed with her. That he hadn't was a test to how messed up he was back in that hospital room. But he'd been so worried over how Jessica was letting her sister's death ruin her life that he went running off on a wild goose chase. And now Ganelon had Jessica. And Logan's blood all but froze at the thought of what the insane bastard could be doing to her. He felt no pain, so hopefully she was all right.

He knew he was walking into a trap, one that he might not walk away from. He didn't care. As long as he could save Jessica. Death, damnation. Didn't matter what price he paid, so long as she was saved. She would live a long life. And then she'd enjoy a longer stay yet in Heaven. His reward as he burned in Hell would be to know he gave her the chance.

"Come alone." That part of the instructions was not a problem. The call he made to Roland wouldn't have any impact until later. It would take Roland a while to get across the city, and by then his plan would either have worked or not. Didn't matter, so long as his friend arrived in time to save Jessica—and look after her thereafter if need be.

Ditching Mike at Jessica's apartment was easy, too. A pull of light to blind the man, then he took to the shadows in a move that would have made Valin proud. Not because he wouldn't have minded if the cop saw for himself that his theories were all wrong, but because Logan was not going to be responsible for the man's death. Especially given that Jessica cared about the schmuck.

What had taken him longer was retrieving the relic from Haven without being seen.

But he'd succeeded and got what he was after. And because he had, the command to come alone wasn't really necessary.

None of his Paladin brothers would have understood why his plan included the relic and thus wouldn't have understood him having taken it. They would have tried to stop him.

He reached beneath his shirt, pulling the cross necklace out. It hummed in his hand, the power infused in it calling to him, begging him to use it.

It wasn't Logan Ganelon wanted. Oh, Logan was sure the sadist would enjoy bringing his old friend's descendent low, but in the end it was the relic he craved. A key, really. The way for his armies to breech Haven. To cave to Ganelon's demands would be akin to betraying his brothers.

Logan fisted his hand back around the necklace, tucked it beneath his shirt.

If what he did next was the price for Jessica's life, then so be it.

Chapter 22

HE WAS TOO LATE.

Logan stepped over the threshold, taking in the room in one quick sweep. The desk, the two empty chairs, the husk of human skin and the merker—probably this Damon Mike was going on about—standing over his woman. And Jessica, God, Jessica, writhing on the floor.

Possessed. He could smell the evil on her.

A demon. Mixing, melding, choking out the part of her that was *his* Jessica.

Over my dead body.

Logan stormed into the room, ready to take the merker by its throat and toss him through the boarded window behind the desk.

Three strides and six feet from his goal, something smashed into him from the side, sending him reeling into the wall. Logan's fingers clenched the gritty cement blocks, shaking his head.

That blow had been more than just physical. His entire body throbbed and his head felt like it had come face to face with an anvil.

Someone started to clap.

"Applaud, Damon. Applaud for our hero of the hour. And I do mean *our* hero."

Logan straightened, wiping the blood from beneath his nose, twisting his head to view the man who stepped into the room.

Ganelon. Must have been lying in wait. Not that Logan hadn't expected him to be near, but he must admit the sneakiness of the attack took him by surprise.

And why is that, Logan? He is called the betrayer. Stands to reason he has trouble with things such as fair fights and honor.

"Did you bring it?"

"I brought the cross," he replied, but made no move to hand it over. A bargaining chip was only so good as long as one still held it.

A flicker of annoyance creased the perfect skin of Ganelon's face. Yeah, for being one of the original twelve, he looked well preserved. Unremarkable, perhaps, but definitely still in his prime.

"Do you really think it wise to test me?"

"No, but I am not ignorant. Call your demon off first. And your prodigy," he added, glancing warily at the merker who rose when Ganelon arrived and stood, feet planted in a fighting stance, between him and Jessica.

"Damon will not interfere, will you my son?"

The merker, Damon, curled his lips back, his eyes locking with Logan's. Damon held the stare for a long moment, a split second of which Logan swore something shifted in the bottomless black gaze, but then the merker nodded and shifted two steps to the side.

Okay, whoa. Had the merker purposefully placed himself between Ganelon and Jessica? If so, why? Logan could almost credit the man with being an independent player in this game if not for one thing: He was a merker. They were born, bred, and raised to serve their master, Ganelon.

Don't analyze that now, first thing is seeing to Jessica's safety.

"And now the demon," he reminded Ganelon.

"Oh I think the demon is happy where it is, don't you?"

Logan couldn't help but chance a brief glance at where Jessica moaned and writhed on the floor. His distraction gave Ganelon the opening he'd been waiting for. A bolt of pure power split through the air. Logan dodged, but the hot burn of heat across his shoulder told him how close it was.

Logan immediately threw up a shield and pulled his knife. His father had once warned him that a shield would not fully stop Ganelon's power, but it would take the edge off the hits. A moment later he was glad he'd acted quickly; Ganelon slung three rapid bolts of searing power at him, each one crackling furiously against his shields.

Logan lunged forward, his blade seeming to sing as it cut through the air. The aim was true but a split second before it could connect, Ganelon threw up his hand, energy sizzling like a shield in the path of Logan's knife. Logan struck again, spinning around and lunging behind Ganelon's quick defense, but the betrayer simply slid back and to the side, following through with his own blistering burn of power across Logan's shields.

Twenty seconds later, with the raw power Logan had siphoned into his shields failing, and never even coming close to connecting with his knife, Logan had to admit that he was in some serious shit.

He had trained for this fight. Since childhood he'd known that as the last full-blooded Paladin, someday his duty might require him to face off against Ganelon. But, extended life spans aside, the truth was a Paladin was not immortal. The time away from His planes did eventually take their toll. In this, Ganelon had the advantage, his festered heart feeding off the dark planes of Hell which he now called home.

The betrayer wasn't aging. But he had the wisdom and battle sense of a seasoned Paladin warrior.

And Logan was, quite simply, outgunned.

He did have one weapon Ganelon didn't possess. One that, though it would not outright kill him with his Paladin heritage, should at least daze the bastard. Maybe then he could sink his knife into Ganelon where the heavenly forged blade could eat away at the betrayer's blackened heart.

Despite his continual concern for Jessica, Logan had no problems calling on His light this time. Fear, worry, whether he walked away from this or not, none of that mattered. Only Jessica mattered. If he was to save her, then, quite simply, he must do this.

Fueled by determination to see his bond mate safe, the power roared through his being. The room exploded, light shattering every shadow within, the blast of illumination carrying into the warehouse, finding every crevice, every crack around the boarded-up windows, and spilling into the surrounding city.

That would take care of any other lingering creatures of Hell.

His satisfaction was short lived. From across the room, Jessica screamed, her entire body arching and jerking. Logan watched in horror as the light he'd cast continued to burn through her body, the unholy glow pouring through pores and eyes alike. Before he could fully comprehend what had happened the light extinguished, leaving her pale and listless as she slumped back to the floor.

For a second no one moved, but then the merker screamed, skidding across the floor as he dove to her side.

"You stupid fuck! What the hell did you think you were doing?" he demanded, even as his fingers pressed into the hollow of her throat.

"Oh, that was brilliant!" Ganelon clapped, laughing so hard he had to pause to brush a tear away. "Destroy the demon while your mate is tied to it. This is beautiful really."

Logan shook his head. He understood what Ganelon was alluding to. But Ganelon was wrong.

Jessica was not dead. Nor was her soul lost. God would not allow it.

Logan clung to that thought as he fisted his knife, needing his faith more than ever. The Big Guy did not make fuck-ups like this. Maybe He gave Logan a human mate to test his faith. Or perhaps make him question his father's arrogant belief that only a full Paladin could fight the war. But He would not go so far as to purge her soul from existence.

And if Jessica died while bound to the demon, then that's what had happened.

Gone. All her beauty. All her passion. Gone. Forever. Never to be reached by him again.

It could not be true. Everything he did, everything he'd fought for, would be meaningless. Therefore he had to believe she was simply unconscious, withdrawn into herself as she had been after the attack in the garage.

Though, damn it would be easier to believe if she moved. Just a small bit. Easier yet if that damn merker wasn't fucking touching her.

He couldn't wait for the merker's verdict on a pulse though. Ganelon was still enjoying the moment, his maniacal laughter another needle against Logan's last nerve. With a roar, Logan lunged across the expanse, his knife arching out in a sideswiping arch.

He honestly didn't expect the knife to catch flesh, so when it did, bright blood spraying, he had to reorganize before following through.

Injured or not, Ganelon's recovery was amazing. Logan didn't even have time to blink before the blast of power hit him in the chest. It knocked him off his feet, throwing him halfway across the room, smacking into the desk as he fell.

He tried to sit up.

"Fuck!" he wheezed, his entire rib cage feeling like it was grinding into his spinal column, and that was after digging though his lungs. Worse, he couldn't see. The room spun so bad he barely caught the movement of someone leaping across the expanse. He couldn't miss the blast of power. It sizzled through the air, sucking the oxygen right out of the room.

He expected to die. Or rather, he expected the strike to completely knock him out, which, given the precarious situation he was in, was as good as dead. So when the sizzling ended and he wasn't any worse off than before?

He forced an arm up, holding his head as if steadying it would stop the spinning of his world. The slight movement had his ribs screaming and the foul taste of copper rising in his throat.

Ganelon stood a few steps away, looking down at the ground. But he wasn't looking at Logan. Logan followed his gaze, sucking in his breath when he saw the merker lying at Ganelon's feet.

The implication of what Logan's eyes told him seemed unimaginable.

The merker had taken the hit meant for him? Why? *Don't think. Move.*

Logan tried to roll over, push off the ground, but his arms collapsed underneath him, his energy having leached out with his hope.

He collapsed again, though somehow managed to scoot back, propping himself up against the heavy desk.

One chance, but only if he could get Ganelon close enough.

He watched warily as Ganelon touched his side, parting his shirt enough to get a good look at the cut. Not as deep as Logan had thought. Damn. "Now that wasn't at all smart, junior."

It was unclear to whom Ganelon was speaking exactly. The fallen merker or himself.

"Don't you want the relic?" Logan asked, spitting out a mouthful of blood that had been collecting in the back of his throat.

Ganelon shook his head and scoffed. "You think you're in a position to play your chips?"

"I'm not handing it over willingly, so if you want it you're going to have to come and get it."

"Okay," Ganelon said as he stepped over his fallen son.

Logan waited for his chance. The moment Ganelon started to bend, his arm reaching for the chain around

Logan's neck, Logan slammed his arm around, aiming his knife for the unprotected underside of Ganelon's armpit.

He never made it. As fast as he was, Ganelon was faster, his other hand snatching Logan's in mid-motion.

"Really, boy. Did you think I wasn't ready for that?" Ganelon asked, twisting Logan's arm until the bones cracked, his nerves screaming so loud he lost control of his grip, his fingers opening so the knife fell uselessly to the floor.

Ignoring the pain radiating throughout his body, Logan swung with his other arm. This at least connected, but other than eliciting a slight grunt, it had no effect.

"And still you hold out hope, even when you're as weak as a lowly human."

Knowing he'd run out of options, Logan offered his last bargaining chip.

"Take me, take the cross. But let her go."

Ganelon leaned in closer, his head cocking to the side. "You'd do that for a human? You'd give me your soul?"

"For hers? Yes."

"Hmmm." Ganelon's fingers closed around the chain. His hand felt hot against Logan's chilled skin. *From spending too much time in Hell's fires? Or because I'm bleeding out internally?*

"Now why would I make a bargain like that when I can have her soul, yours, and the relic?"

With a sharp movement Ganelon jerked on the chain, the metal biting into Logan's neck, cutting deep and jerking him forward before it broke. Face twisted in rapture, Ganelon lifted the necklace, the central gem sparkling in the dim office lighting.

Logan waited. One second. Two.

Ganelon frowned, his brow drawing down in a deep vee as he caught the cross in his other hand, twisting it this way and that so the light cut through the yellow gem. His eyes widened, his nostrils pinching. "Citrine? This isn't the key!"

"It is a key. Just not the one you wanted. And not one you can ever use. Not anymore." Though it pained him, Logan forced himself to smile, leaning forward. "You'll never be granted a way back into His holy realm."

Ganelon's face flashed from furious to cold as stone. He straightened, his fist unfurling from around the relic as he let it fall to the ground.

"So be it, but I can certainly send you there," he said as he raised his glowing hand above his head.

He's here.

Jessica had fought through the fog, clinging to the sound of Logan's voice. A light in the dark fight she warred against the demon who wanted her soul. She'd used it as her anchor.

Had to tell him. Had to warn him.

Bait. That's all she was. Her death or her damnation, didn't matter, either would be used to break him.

She could not, would not let it happen. Her hatred had let the demon in. And though hunting the evil that stole those like Julia from this world might have once seemed worth her own death, it was not worth Logan's.

It was at that point Jessica felt the demon's hold begin to slip. Realizing that Logan and her feelings for him held hope for her salvation, she'd clung to them, fighting harder. But the demon was strong, its lock on her anchored by years of guilt, then anger, and eventually cold hatred. She began to despair, thinking she'd never be free of it—that eventually it would wear her down and take over—when all of a sudden a bright light exploded around her.

His light. Jessica could feel the demon shrink from it and she cried out in welcome. Allowing it to fill her until she was lighter than air, a blissful peace settled into her that drove away the tendrils of anger, hatred, and evil.

In those moments, she knew she was in a place most humans never reached, at least not in their lifetimes. The human body was simply not made to contain such power. And though the thought that she might be dead was alarming, she wanted to stay. Except she couldn't. A voice, a sliver of memory, whatever it was, she knew she wasn't meant to be there. Not quite yet.

I have something to do first.

Jessica woke, her eyes fluttering open. The shock of reality against the blissful peace of the light had her wishing she could close her eyes again and forget whatever it was that needed doing, and she naturally sought solace in the hum of the florescent lights that bathed the overly warm room. But then other scents and sounds came to her. A foulness in the air. Death. Evil. And two men speaking in heated tones.

She came fully awake then, but instead of attempting to rise, she closed her eyes again, listening. It took her a moment to decipher Logan's voice as one of the two men speaking. His normally smooth baritone was laden with a mix of anger and something else: pain.

Jess felt the agonizing draw of his every breath as if it were her own. Practically choked on the thick warm taste of his blood as it coated his mouth. She was so distracted by Logan's agony, it took her a while to work out what the voices were saying. Their talk of keys and realms and who would gain entry.

But she finally did.

Jessica staggered up, her gaze immediately landing on Logan's prone form. Seemingly ignorant of her, the man from the desk—Damon's father—stood above him, his hand raised, and though it held no weapon she could see, she knew that whatever he meant to do next would mean the end of Logan's life.

She couldn't let that happen.

She'd thought that staying with Logan, growing old and dying as he didn't, would be the worst hell on earth. She'd been wrong. There was one thing that would be worse, and that would be living without him.

Jessica lunged.

———⁓———

Logan watched in horror as Jessica stumbled to her feet, her gaze quickly traveling from him to Ganelon, her chin taking that stubborn tilt. He knew the second before she lunged that she was going to try and stop Ganelon. And he could do nothing.

Ganelon spun, his hand taking the motion with him, the hit meant for Logan, sizzling from the tips of his fingers, arching outward. Logan couldn't move, couldn't breathe. His life was crumbling to the floor before him and he couldn't so much as lift a finger. Not that he didn't try, but the severing of their bond, even though never fully completed, was so painful it made Ganelon's wimpy attack of before feel like child's play.

The moment of immobility lasted only a second before the dreadful pain gave way to adrenaline-pumping fury.

He screamed, his hand fisting around his knife as he threw his body forward. A boot connected with his jaw, snapping his head back. He slashed out and found his arm pinned by a cloven hoof. At the same time a knee came down on his back, shoving him to the floor.

"Watch the knife, boys."

Logan twisted his head, catching sight of the two ugly mugs holding him down. Definitely merkers, though not the pretty kind you normally found aboveground.

"Do you want us to bring him?" the more human-looking of the two asked through his deformed mouth.

"No, let him go," Ganelon said, though his gaze never left Jessica. "I have a feeling he'll be joining us soon enough."

Then, followed by his offspring dragging the inert merker, Ganelon left the room, his diabolical laughter echoing throughout the cavernous warehouse.

Chapter 23

Logan sat in Jessica's loft studio, the distant sound of breaking waves drifting in through the broken pane of the patio door below. That he was the one who broke that window caused him less than some inconsequential guilt. He'd had to come here. Smell her scent. Draw in her essence that was stamped into every wall, every piece of furniture, every floorboard of the room.

See the spot where he completely gave himself over to love.

It may have started on some dirty street in the Bronx, but this is where he'd completely fallen. This loft where, for one night, he'd made her his.

He would never be graced with that passion again. Never watch her stretch like a cat beneath him. Never see her smile, her gaze teasing as she invited him to do his worst. Never moan as he made love to her again.

Jessica was gone.

It had been twenty-one days since she died. Twenty-one days since he almost died trying to pour his own life force into her body, anything to revive her. Anything to complete the bond.

Twenty-one days. Seven times the number he'd known her. Nothing compared to the lonely centuries of earthly life he had ahead of him, but an infinite amount of time as far as he was concerned.

He remembered Ganelon's parting words, knew his

father and brothers feared he'd snap one day and make them true.

Logan was pretty sure he wouldn't. He had a duty. He'd see it through.

He had nothing left but that. That and faith. Faith that, despite his moments of doubt, despite the fact he'd failed to complete the bond, failed to protect his mate, that He would be merciful. And that Jessica would be waiting for him when his time here ended.

She will be. She rejected the demon. Sacrificed herself for another. For me. Just please, let us be together. And let it be soon.

As much as he may have wanted to, he hadn't died—no thanks in part to Roland, who came charging in just minutes too late, followed almost immediately by Valin, Logan's father, and more than a dozen other Paladin brothers. Nor had he fallen into the spinning cycle of anger and hatred that the others had feared he would. He was simply numb. Nothing mattered anymore.

He spent hours in the dark of her apartment, wrapping and unwrapping one of her hair elastics around his hand. More just sitting in her bedroom, smelling the pillow that still carried her scent. He'd eventually had to leave though. The residual evidence of the violence done there driving him away. So tonight he'd come here. To the studio where he and Jessica had first made love.

He sat here now, the sharp scent of turpentine burning at the lining of his nose and eyes as memory after memory washed over him. Jessica laughing, Jessica smiling, Jessica raising her chin in that stubborn tilt. Still he couldn't cry. Which was good. Crying would mean he could feel, and without her? What was the point?

A shift in the air told him someone else had used the hole he'd punched in the patio door to enter the beach house. He didn't move, almost hoped it was a demon he could fight, though he knew it wouldn't be. Numb or not, his senses hadn't completely disappeared and he recognized his father's step and scent.

Even as light-footed as his father was, the stairs groaned beneath his feet. The creaking stopped when he reached the top and Logan could imagine him standing with a scowl on his face, his arms folded across his chest.

"You think this is the safest place to be?" his father asked, and then when he didn't answer, he added, "That cop, Ward, is still poking around, still asking questions. One of which is where you are."

"Let him ask, I don't care." Hell, Logan was inclined to go find Mike. New York didn't have a death penalty, but he thought if he told Mike how Jessica died because of him the cop might be willing to oblige.

A large hand connected with the side of his head—hard.

He blinked, twisting his head to look up at his father. "Did you just *smack* me?"

The absolute absurdity of it had him lifting a hand to check and see if his scalp was tender. It was.

His father stood with folded arms, and he also scowled, but there was something else there, a glint in his eyes that showed a whole lot more than annoyance. "Thought I might knock some sense into you."

Logan glared at him.

His father unfolded his arms, lifted his hands out to the side in an exaggerated gesture. "What, isn't that what you've been wanting? For me to act like a father rather than the head of the council?"

"Fine time for you to choose to do so." Years and years of indifference, followed by years and years more of annoyance-laced disapproval. And he chose now to act like he cared?

"What is that supposed to mean?"

Logan stood, poking his finger at his father and getting into his face. "It means, where were you when I needed you? Where were you when my mate was dying? No, scratch that, I remember now. You were the man pulling me off her."

"Logan. She was already dead." The way his father said this, choked up as if he had the right to mourn her too, was the greatest offense.

Logan fisted his hand, working hard to not let it connect. "I could have saved her."

"No, you couldn't have."

"Then you could have let me go too!" Logan spun away, spun back, spun away again. There it was out, he'd said it. Not insane, not consumed with vengeance, but God, he wished he could just curl up and die.

A hand fell on his shoulder, the grip tentative, almost shaking. "Logan, He may be a merciful God but do you really think He'd reward you for ending your life that way?"

Logan clenched his jaw.

His father sighed. Moving around Logan, he grabbed up a canvas and set it aside to free up a chair. He sat, with his elbows on his knees, chin cupped in his hands.

Logan tensed for the lecture, resisting the urge to turn

his back. Stubborn old man would just move around to the other side.

"When your mother was killed," his father began, "I didn't think I could go on, the absolute agony of losing my mate—"

"Don't!" He made a slashing motion with his hand. "Don't compare your life to mine. Don't. You had her for 500 years. I had my mate for three days. Three." He shook his head, swallowing past the wedge that seemed to be lodged in his throat. "Even then I was too stupid, too cowardly to claim her, to bond with her."

His father shifted forward on the chair, speaking earnestly. "Someday, Logan. Someday when our duty is done here and we've been called back to His side, you'll see her again."

"Will I?" God, why hadn't he claimed her? Why hadn't he bonded their souls forever? Then at least he would have hope of seeing her again when his time was done.

She'll forget me. She'll move on. Whether in another life or simply in Heaven, her soul is too strong, too endearingly stubborn not to attract the love of another.

His father shifted, his mouth opening.

"Don't say anything else," Logan cut him off.

"I wasn't going to. You're not in the right frame of mind to listen." He heaved himself up out of the chair, shaking his head. "Still, you know how to reach me if you need me. Even if it is just for sharpening your tongue."

His father left. Logan stood for a while, looking around the empty loft. Idly, he picked up a paintbrush, twisting the dried out bristles in his hand. Remembering how he scattered them on the floor in his eagerness to have her and then how carefully she picked them up the next morning and set them back in place. Ironic that those brushes would represent the same thing to him now as it must have to Jessica: A tie. A connection. A shared memory.

Damn his father. He'd been perfectly content not feeling anything, and if there was one thing his father's visit did it was crack him out of the ice-shell he'd managed to cocoon himself in.

Anger. He wasn't sure if his father wished to illicit the emotion, but that was the result, and now he stood here, staring at the empty jars, paintbrushes, and beautiful artwork and all he wanted to do was destroy them. To stab deep at the heart of something she'd loved. How dare she leave him? How dare she choose his life over her own? Didn't she understand he was nothing without her?

Of course not, asshole. You never told her.

There was another shift of air, the ocean breeze threatening to cleanse the cabin of Jessica's lingering scent. Which made him angrier. If anyone or anything was going to destroy the last pieces he had of her, it would be him.

"What do you want now?" he yelled, stomping to the edge of the loft.

Below, just inside the wide-open patio doors, stood not his father, but a woman in a flowing white gown, the highlights in her dark curling hair glimmering in the morning light.

"Jessica?" he asked, then raced down the stairs, but when he got to the bottom, only a couch length separating them, he forced himself to stop.

It couldn't be her; he watched her die. So therefore it was either some sort of sick joke or his mind was playing tricks on him.

"Your father's right, you know. He," she gestured with her head toward the ceiling, "wouldn't reward you for thinking such thoughts."

Logan rubbed his eyes. Definitely losing his mind. Or maybe suffering some guilt-ridden hallucinations; conjuring up his Jessica in order to scold himself into sensibility, because, damn it to Hell, Logan knew his father was right.

He reopened his eyes, not completely surprised to see her still there. Though this time he saw the things he should have before, the things that marked her as false.

His Jessica couldn't be more beautiful than she already was. But this one was. Her skin practically glowing, her eyes brighter, rounder, with almost an exotic tilt to them, her lips, always full and plump had more defined edges and a distinctive angel's kiss beneath her nose.

"Oh, I don't know, you're here," he said, playing along. Better to let his mind work this through. Then maybe he could brood in peace.

She smiled, stepping further into the house. And God, what a vision she was. Though she hadn't needed improvement, so this version seemed more imposter than not.

She stopped a few short feet away, her smile dimming as her head tipped to the side. "You look like you've seen a ghost."

He shook his head. "More like an angel."

She laughed, the same husky bedroom laugh, but it was layered with rich bell-like tones to fit her angelic features.

"Not an angel. Not anymore at least." She twisted, letting the shoulders of her flowing garment drop to show him her beautifully sculpted shoulder blades. It took him a minute to really see what she was showing him; he was so entranced by the sight of her creamy skin, the memory of what it felt like to run his calloused hands over it, but then he saw them. The two silvery lines that glowed faintly below the surface, marking a newly healed wound.

She turned back, sighing, a dreamy smile crossing her face as she rolled her shoulders freely. "But I admit, they sure were cool while I had them."

An angel. A real one. And she gave them up? Gave up the blissful peace of His light to come back down here?

"Jess." He shook his head, bewildered. "You volunteered?"

"I think it was more of a divine suggestion. Think He was sick of me disobeying orders."

Logan couldn't help it; he laughed. He could just picture it. Her up in Heaven, trying to fit in with the other angels as they monitored His creations: the epitome of the eternal desk job. She would hate it. If He were present, Logan might have asked why He'd invited such headache and even given her the wings, except Logan knew: He had planned this.

God did not choose His warriors lightly, and He would not have accepted her as a Paladin unless He thought her up to the task. And what better warrior for

His children than a head-strong cop with a soul so passionate she'd made the rank of angel?

She's real.

He hadn't believed it until this moment. He must have truly thought she was a ghost. He couldn't believe she was really with him to stay.

But she is.

He itched to touch her. Hold her.

But he didn't deserve to, didn't deserve her. Not when he'd failed her so. Not when he denied what was between them, questioning His plan.

He dropped his head, looking at his feet. "I don't deserve you. If I did, I would have told you about the bonding, made you understand what it meant."

"I wouldn't have been ready to beli—"

"It doesn't matter. You needed to know. Better, I should have just done the ceremony and bonded us so that you *could* understand."

"Why didn't you?" she asked, her voice barely a whisper.

He fisted his hands. She had to know the truth. "I loved you so much, wanted you so badly, but every time I was with you all I could think was why? What had I done? What part of me must be such a failure that He would do this to me? Why give me the perfect woman, why send me my mate, when she was destined to die on me?" He lifted his head. "I didn't want you."

She sucked in a breath.

He laughed, a self-deprecating sort of sound as he ran his hands down his face. "No. That's not true. I wanted you. God, I wanted you. But I refused to let myself need you. I didn't believe in us. Didn't believe in His plan." He nodded up toward the ceiling. "And didn't want to believe in the mate-bond. So I refused it. Never allowing it to truly form even knowing that it might cause me to someday fail you, but still I kept myself apart. Holding back. And do you know why?"

"No, why?" she whispered.

"Because I thought it would be better that way. That by holding a part of myself back, we'd never be truly bonded. And if I could do that, if I could keep you and I separate, love you but not *love* you, then if, no when, I lost you…"

He couldn't go on. He had lost her. And the black hole of pain had threatened to suck him down. He'd been ready to succumb. If she hadn't come back when she did…

Another horrible thought occurred to him. What if she couldn't forgive him? What if she didn't want to?

She crossed to him, wrapping her arms around his taunt body. "You fool. You think I didn't know that? You think I don't understand?"

She pressed her head into his shoulder, her fingers playing with his shirt. "I felt that way too. I didn't want to believe you, but then when I did, I didn't want to love you because someday I was going to age, get old and die, and you? Well you were going to keep on living. Without me."

He scoffed, glancing up at the dark studio. "I can't live without you. I think we've proved that."

She slapped his arm. "You would have gone on. I know you would have. You're too strong to have given up."

Too strong to become a monster, she meant. Was he?

"Maybe." But he could have only held out so long as

he believed that someday He would release him from his duty and let him be reunited with his mate. And considering how close he'd been to finding Mike…

"No maybes." She laid a hand on his heart. "You're His warrior. Through and through. Trust me, I know."

He swallowed, closing his eyes, drawing deep breaths through his nose. She was touching him. And damn but wasn't that a tear that had just escaped from his eye?

Delicate fingers settled on his cheek, touching the wet spot, and his skin tingled, the bond he knew was there, waiting to be formed, humming in the recesses of his mind.

Mark her, claim her. But he was scared to move, afraid that no matter how real she felt, no matter how much he wanted to believe, that the moment he opened his eyes again the vision, dream, whatever the hell it is, would end.

She gave another light touch on his chin, applying slight pressure as she tipped his head toward her. "Look at me, Logan."

He couldn't resist her, so he didn't. And this time Logan opened his eyes to look beyond the inhuman beauty, beyond the full lips, the long straight nose, her eyes…so blue, bluer than before, like the Caribbean Sea. To see something else. Something about *her*.

It was an awakening. He could see her both as she was now and as she'd been before. She was still the same Jessica, but the passion he saw in her was no longer a mere reflection of what she could be; it was the true beauty and warmth of her soul. Logan might be able to call on His light, but she *was* His light.

And with that realization came understanding. Her

soul may have been made for him, but she hadn't been ready to be a Paladin mate. All that had occurred, her sister's death, even the events leading up to her own, happened so she could learn to understand and overcome her human nature. For without that knowledge she would never have been a good protector for mankind.

Or the partner he needed.

Still, it was a great sacrifice for her to make.

"Can I see them again?"

She didn't respond, just turned, letting the gauzy material slip from her shoulders to reveal her upper back.

He traced the scars, wondering at how they glowed even more beneath his touch. Eventually they'd fade, only visible in His realm, but the fact that his touch brought out the light within her was just another proof that she'd always been meant for him. Time, distance, life, or death couldn't change that.

He sighed, finally feeling. And what he felt was peace and joy and yes, damn it, a painful need.

"You know you could have waited for me. Time does not have the same meaning there."

It would have been him who suffered their time apart. Not her. And probably the easier choice. A Paladin's life was not champagne and roses. There were hardships, sacrifice. Even with his brothers, even with his bond mate by his side, he knew his time on earth would be filled with almost as much bad as good.

But someone needed to fight evil.

"I know, but I figured…"

"You figured what?" he asked, pulling her garment back over her shoulders and twisting her back around.

Her mouth parted, her eyes sparkling as if the sun

were dancing on the water. She licked her lips. "I figured you missed me."

"God, Jessica, you have no idea how much."

"Besides, this, you…" She traced her hand down his chest, causing him to moan as she ended the movement with a taunting dip into his jeans, "Well it just wasn't Heaven for me without you there."

And then she reached up, lacing her other hand behind his head and she pressed her perfectly warm, living, lips to his.

Acknowledgments

This book came from more than just my own soul-bearing pounding at the keyboard. There are all kinds of people who helped along the way from conception to completion. From my family, who put up with more frozen dinners than they ever should have had to, to the handful of new Facebook friends who came to the rescue when I needed some good, honest BETA feedback, to my wonderful editor, Leah Hultenschmidt, who kept my sights on the goal (something far better than good enough), along with the wonderful people at Sourcebooks responsible for getting this final product into the readers' hands. This book wouldn't be what it is without their help and support. All mistakes are my own; anything that shines is because of them. Thank you.

About the Author

Daphne Award–winning author Tes Hilaire started creating whole new worlds to escape upstate New York's harsh winters before finally fleeing to sultry North Carolina. Her stories are edgy, exciting, and bring a hint of dark fantasy to paranormal romance. And no one ever has to shovel snow. For more information visit www.teshilaire.com.